THE VEXED GENERATION

THE VEXED GENERATION

SCOTT MEYER

ROCKET HAT  INDUSTRIES

Published by Rocket Hat Industries

ISBN: 978-1-950056-02-6

Cover design by Eric Constantino

The following is intended to be a fun, comedic sci-fi/fantasy novel. Any similarity between the events described and how reality actually works is purely coincidental.

Magic 2.0: A Partial Explanation

One night, while exploring a server he probably shouldn't have been, Martin Banks discovered a file that proved his reality was computer generated. By manipulating the file, he found that he could perform feats that seemed like magic—things like flight, teleportation, and time travel. He knew that his newfound power could dramatically improve his life, but he'd have to be careful and avoid drawing attention to himself.

He did neither of those things. Instead, he immediately messed up very badly and attracted the attention of government agents.

Martin fled to Medieval England, a time and place where people believed in magic and wizards were revered. He reasoned that he could be the most powerful being in the world and live a life of ease and luxury if he showed some restraint and used his power wisely.

Again, he did neither of those things. Again, he immediately messed up very badly, and attracted the attention of several other people who had found the same file, developed even better powers, and migrated back in time to live as wizards long before Martin got the idea.

Among Martin's new acquaintances were Gwen, the woman he grew to love; Phillip, who became his best friend; and Brit, a woman who had tangled her own timeline so thoroughly that her past self and her future self now have to deal with each other on a daily basis, a prospect neither of them relishes. One thing all these wizards shared in common was that they wanted nothing more than to enjoy their lives and not bother anyone.

They do neither of those things. Instead, they all tend to mess up on a regular basis and attract the attention of pretty much everybody. In an effort to rectify this, Martin and Gwen have married and moved back to their original time, started a family, and now spend their days attempting to maintain the facade of a "normal" life.

1.

"This is a bad idea, Martin."

"You agreed to it, Gwen."

"That doesn't mean it isn't a bad idea," Gwen said. "I've agreed to a lot of bad ideas. Most of them came from you."

Martin held Gwen by the shoulders and looked into her eyes. "It's gonna be fine. You'll see."

"And every single time, you've said that."

Martin turned away from Gwen and went back to straightening his black bow tie in the bathroom mirror. "Look, we both agreed that if we were going to have a normal family, we have to seem open and forthcoming with our kids. We can't come off as mysterious."

"Well, after today there won't be any mysteries. They'll know everything."

"No, they won't. All the twins are gonna learn is what every kid learns on Bring Your Children to Work Day. That the real world is much less interesting than they ever expected—even the interesting parts."

"But the interesting parts of our lives *are* interesting . . ."

"Granted, but they won't see that today."

Gwen held up a finger and cocked her head to the side.

Martin stopped talking.

They both heard a soft creaking noise, followed by a quiet giggle. Martin and Gwen stuck their heads out the door of their master bathroom and saw Mattie, their ten-year-old daughter, entering their bedroom, elbows raised and fingers splayed in a cartoonish attempt at sneaking. She saw her parents looking at her and froze. Her jet-black hair was pulled into twin braids, and she wore a knee-length, lace-fringed dress, somewhere in the middle ground between yellow and beige—an entire dress made in the color of a permanent stain. The simplicity of her hair and dowdiness of her dress stood in marked contrast to her sparkly blue sneakers and fuzzy pink socks.

Gwen said, "Mattie Banks, what have I said about eavesdropping on us?"

"You said don't do it."

"And what are you doing?"

After a long pause, Mattie said, "*It*. I'm sorry. I just came to tell you I'm ready to go."

From another room, a young boy's voice shouted, "Are not!"

Mattie shouted, "Nobody asked you, Brewster!"

Brewster ran up the hallway: a ten-year-old boy with sandy-brown hair, wearing a tweed three-piece suit and a blue tie. "Her shoes are wrong. Mom, tell her, her shoes are wrong. Dad said we have to wear our historical costumes and those aren't the right shoes."

Mattie shot a nasty look at her brother. "But Daddy, those other shoes are so *hard*. They don't feel good."

Martin said, "That's what children's shoes were like in Victorian London. Their lives back then were much worse than ours. And today, you're going to experience it for yourselves! You'll smell the air, and the people, and the horse droppings in the street! Maybe, if you're lucky, I'll arrange it so you can work a shift on an industrial loom!"

The kids looked at each other uneasily.

Gwen said, "Now go put on the right shoes, Mattie."

Mattie ran back down the hall.

"What about my tie, Mom?" Brewster asked. "Did I tie it right?"

"You did a great job, for a ten-year-old."

Brewster looked utterly unsatisfied with that answer. "Did I tie it right?"

Martin leaned out of the bathroom and looked at his son. "Yeah, that's a decent four-in-hand knot. It'll do."

"It'll do?"

"Yeah. It's fine. That's the four-in-hand's thing. It's the easiest knot that's good enough for any occasion."

Martin smiled as Brewster looked at his tie, frowned, and walked back down the hall muttering, "*Good enough.* That's no good."

Gwen was not smiling.

"Gwen, I know you're uncomfortable, but this is the right move. Look, we agreed that if we wanted to seem like a normal family, one of us had to work outside the house. I'm happy to do it, but if it's going to seem real, I can't be secretive about it, and that means eventually letting them see me at work. That means taking them to where I work, which is all I'm doing."

"It's not taking them where you work that worries me." Gwen peeked down the hall to make sure they were alone, then lowered her voice. "It's taking them to *when* you work."

"If they're going to see me do my job, they have to be there when I do it. Right now, they're old enough to tag along but young enough to keep under control. It's only going to get harder as they grow up."

"We should have done this last year," Gwen replied.

"Last year you put me off until next year, which is this year."

"Maybe we should put it off again, and you can use the time to phony up an office job."

Martin shook his head. "It wouldn't work, and it's not necessary anyway. They already know what I do, and they already think it's boring."

"They think you're a magician at a theme park."

"A historically accurate educational theme park. To a kid, that's an offensive concept, like a raisin cookie, or underwear for Christmas. And I've told you a hundred times: People think they like magic tricks until someone does one. The average person's eyes glaze over as soon as you say *pick a card or please observe this simple handkerchief.*"

"But people pay to see your act."

"They're made to pay up front. That's not by accident. And besides, even if some of the audience members do really enjoy magic, we know our children don't. Gwen, I've been pulling coins and scarves and live doves out of every orifice in those kids' heads since they've been old enough to know it was wrong. Has either of them ever seemed even the slightest bit impressed?"

Mattie ran back into the bedroom. "Okay, I put on the shoes. I'm ready to go."

Without turning to look, Gwen asked, "Did you change your socks?"

Gwen tried to hide the amusement on her face as she waited through the moment of thick silence that followed. When she and Martin did look at their daughter, they saw her crouching down, attempting to poke the exposed parts of her pink fuzzy socks into the tops of her shoes.

"Mattie," Gwen said. "Go change socks."

"But, Mom, who says they didn't have pink fuzzy socks back then? They had socks. They had the color pink. They had . . . *fuzziness.*"

"But they hadn't put it all together yet. Go."

"Do I have to? I don't wanna untie and retie the shoes again."

"I said, go."

Mattie trudged, slump-shouldered, back down the hall to her room.

"She is *just* smart enough to be dangerous," Gwen said.

Martin laughed. "Yeah, she gets that from me."

Brewster walked in, looking much the same as when he left, only with a larger, more symmetrical knot in his tie.

Gwen said, "Retied the tie, huh? What is that, a Windsor knot?"

Brewster replied, "A half Windsor."

"Oh. A *half* Windsor," Martin said.

Gwen asked, "Where are you learning all these knots?"

"There are instructions online. Didn't I do it right?"

Gwen said, "You did fine."

"*Fine?*"

"You tied it very well."

"But there's something wrong."

"No," Martin said. "Nothing's wrong. The half Windsor knot is okay."

Brewster looked down at his tie, mumbled, "*Okay,*" and walked back to his room.

Martin said, "That boy's going to give himself a nervous breakdown."

"No," Gwen said. "You're going to give him a nervous breakdown. He gets that from me. I don't like this, Martin. It's a terrible risk."

"Making what I do every day seem like a big secret would be a risk, too."

"Yeah, but is this the lesser of the two risks?"

"Maybe. Maybe not. It's definitely the more fun of the two risks."

Martin pulled on his black satin tuxedo jacket with tails.

Mattie's feet made an exaggerated clomping noise as she ran up the hall. "Mom, Dad, you know what I just figured out? Cowboy boots are from the same time as the rest of my costume, just about. They don't have laces, and they hide my pink fuzzy socks!"

Martin nodded knowingly at Gwen. "It's true. That's why Wyatt Earp wore them."

Mattie proudly pointed below the hem of her drab knee-length dress to her red-and-black vinyl cowboy boots.

Gwen stared back and said nothing.

Mattie said, "No?"

Gwen stared.

Mattie said, "No."

Gwen stared.

Mattie said, "I'll put on the shoes and socks you laid out for me," and went back to her room. As she walked away, Brewster passed her. His suit and shoes were unchanged, but the knot in his tie was as large as his fist. "I jumped up to a double Windsor knot, though it looked like it and the single Windsor might be the same thing. It's confusing. Maybe I should go try again."

"No, Brewster," Gwen said. "You look perfect."

"Perfect?"

Martin opened his mouth to speak, saw the look on Gwen's face, and said, "Perfect."

Gwen raised her voice to be heard a few rooms away. "And Mattie will look perfect, too, once she has the right shoes and socks on."

Mattie shouted. "Just a minute! I'm tying them. It takes for eeeeever."

Martin said, "We'd better get moving. It's Bring Your Children to Work Day, not Bring Your Children to Work *Late* Day."

Mattie came out of her room and stood in the hallway, wearing black leather shoes and drab, off-white socks.

Martin said, "Don't you both look darling."

Brewster glared at Martin. So did Mattie.

"Your mother worked hard making those historically accurate outfits. You should thank her."

The twins said, "Thanks, Mom," in a slow, unenthusiastic tone, their voices creating an unpleasant minor-key harmony.

Martin smiled and pointed at the kids. "Ah-ah-ah! Thank her in a period-accurate manner."

The kids glared at him again, then Brewster bowed, Mattie curtsied, and both said, "Thank you, Mother."

Gwen chuckled in spite of herself. "You're welcome. Now go. You all have to get on the road."

"But before we go, there's one last thing." Martin stepped toward the kids. "No child in Victorian London would go anywhere without their handkerchief!" He reached down and pulled a white hankie out of Mattie's ear.

"And you'll want to have some pocket change, just in case!" He reached out, placed his hand over Brewster's nose, then placed his other hand beneath it and caught several coins that seemed to fall from the boy's nostrils. Martin looked at the children expectantly.

They smiled uneasily.

Martin beamed at Gwen. "See! It's gonna be fine."

They went down the hall, past the kids' rooms, and down the stairs to the family room. Gwen followed, shaking her head.

Martin stepped into the middle of the family room and swept his arms out wide. "Kids, are you ready for a magic-filled journey into the past?"

The children made unconvincing but vaguely affirmative sounds. Martin smiled at Gwen, who came dangerously close to laughing.

He opened the front door for the children.

Gwen knelt down next to them. "Do you both have your emergency necklaces?"

Mattie and Brewster said "yeah," more or less in unison.

"Let me see."

They both reached into their collars and pulled out identical woven lanyards holding blue plastic triangles decorated with white stars and moons, which formed a stylized wizard hat.

Gwen nodded. "Good. Now, remember, if you're in trouble, you just break the wizard hat in half between the moon and the star, and you'll be taken somewhere safe."

Mattie asked, "How does that work?"

Gwen said, "It's very complicated."

Brewster looked at the plastic wizard hat in his hand. "Is it like a radio?"

Gwen said, "It has to do with computers. Your father and I set it up. Hopefully, you'll never have to find out how it works. Why is that?"

The kids both said, "Because we can only ever use it once."

"And they won't need it today," Martin said. "They'll be with me!"

Gwen looked both children square in the eyes and said, "Keep the necklaces handy." She hugged the twins as if she might never see them again.

She followed them out the front door, stopped on the front porch, and called after them. "Okay, be good, be safe, and do what your father tells you, except when it contradicts the first two things I said."

"Wave to your mother," Martin said, pulling his nondescript black sedan out of the driveway of their unremarkable yellow Arts and Crafts bungalow, and drove down the street, past all the other Arts and Crafts bungalows and neutral-colored sedans.

The kids both sat in the back seat, which was standard Banks family procedure. It prevented fights about who got to ride in the front at the cost of occasional complaints about having to sit together.

Martin glanced at them in the rearview mirror. Mattie sat sideways in her seat, her face pressed against the window. Brewster looked Martin square in the eyes through the mirror and asked, "What's the name of the park you work at again?"

"Dickensiana. Why?"

"My friend at school, Donald, says he never heard of it."

"Well, I feel bad for Donald then. He's missing out."

"But Donald says if there was a park like that, he'd know."

"But we're going to the park, and he doesn't know about it, so he must be mistaken, right?"

"Yeah, I guess."

"How did you and Donald end up talking about the park?"

Mattie turned and smiled at Brewster, who squeezed his mouth shut like the top of a laundry bag with the drawstring pulled tight.

"Brewster," Martin asked, "were you talking about Daddy's work at school?"

Brewster said nothing.

"It's okay, Brewster. I'm not mad. We all make mistakes. But you know you're not supposed to tell people that Daddy works at the park, or even that there is a park, right?"

"Yeah, I know."

"Why?"

"Because it ruins it if they know you're just pretending."

"That's right."

"Dad?"

"Yes, Brewster?"

"Why did they make a park about what life used to be like in England here, not England?"

"Because the English already know all about it, and Seattle has the most England-like weather of any city in the United States."

Brewster said, "Oh," but still seemed puzzled.

Mattie asked, "Is your magic show like the one the guy who did his show for our school was like?"

Martin took a moment to decipher the sentence. "I don't know. What was his show like?"

"It was kinda dumb. He did a bunch of dumb tricks with rings, and cards, and foam balls, and a lady he cut in half, but there wasn't even any blood."

Martin smiled. "No. My show isn't like that. My show's cool."

Mattie smiled. "Oh. Good."

"I do amazing tricks with big gold rings, giant cards, and rubber balls. And we make a lady float in the air, then cut her in half."

Mattie's smile faded.

"You and your friend Phillip, right?" Brewster asked.

"He's *our* friend. He likes all of us."

Mattie and Brewster both said nothing.

"Don't you two like Phillip?"

Mattie said, "He's nice. He's just . . ."

"Weird," Brewster finished her thought.

Mattie nodded. "He acts weird when he comes to the house."

"Yeah," Martin agreed. "He does, but only around you two. See, Phillip's a very nice man, but he's not comfortable around children. He likes you both very much, and wants you to like him. It makes him try too hard."

"Why doesn't he stop?" Mattie asked.

"Phillip can't help himself. It's one of the things your mother and I like most about him. If you two will just make a point of being nice to him, he'll calm down eventually, and he'll start acting like himself."

"And then we'll like him?"

"I think so, but if you don't, at least it'll be the real him you don't like."

"How'd you start doing magic together?"

Martin thought for a moment before he spoke. "He taught me, actually. I was interested in magic, and taught myself a few things. Phillip knew more about it than me, so he taught me some stuff. We both sort of did magic as a hobby for a long time, but then he had kind of a bad time, hit a rough patch, as he likes to say, and he needed something to occupy himself. Right about that time, I needed a job to go to every day, and we saw a way to kill two birds with one stone. That used to be a trick we'd do in our act, by the way. Killing two birds with one stone. We didn't really kill the birds, and the stone turned into a scarf. I could do the trick for you later if you want."

Both kids said, "No thanks."

Martin turned the car into the parking lot of a large industrial park, a maze of glass people-sized doors and painted metal truck-sized doors set into otherwise featureless beige walls. He cruised down multiple streets and around multiple corners without the slightest flicker of doubt as to where he was going.

"Is this the park?" Mattie asked.

"It's the secret back entrance. It's hidden so that the guests won't see the people who work here showing up for our shifts. It would ruin the fun for them."

Martin slowed the car and turned toward one of the large roll-up doors, which opened of its own accord. The room behind the door was a vast cube of drywall, lit by fluorescent overhead lights, empty except for some dust, a few dried leaves, and bits of waste paper on the floor. On the back wall next to a lone metal door hung the only decoration: a framed poster advertising a movie called *The Prestige*.

"We're here!" Martin stepped out of the car. Mattie and Brewster followed him.

Mattie asked, "Where are all the other cars?"

"What do you mean?"

"Other people work here. Where are their cars?"

Martin walked to a lone metal door set into the back wall. "Oh, uh, this is a special entrance, just for Phillip and me. It leads right to our theater."

"Does everyone have their own entrance?" Brewster asked.

"I don't know."

"What do you mean?" Mattie asked. "How do you not know?" Both children stood still, one on either side of the car, staring at their father.

"I never asked."

Brewster squinted at Martin. "Why not?"

"Don't know," Martin said. "I didn't want to be rude, pestering my coworkers with questions."

Mattie said, "You and Mom said it's good to ask questions."

Martin muttered, "Yeah, well, we all have regrets," as he turned and pressed the power button on the side of an old smartphone stuck to the wall beside the door. The screen lit up, displaying a string of numbers. Martin swiped at the numbers until it read "16:30 4-8-1894."

Mattie asked, "What's that?"

"It's a . . . I guess you'd call it a time lock. It makes sure that this door is only opened at the right time—now—and by the right person—me."

"And Phillip."

"What?"

Mattie repeated, "And Phillip. He comes in here, too, right?"

"Oh, uh, yeah."

Brewster asked, "Where's his car?"

"He rides a bicycle to work."

The twins looked around, confused expressions on their faces, searching for a bicycle and finding none.

Martin said, "Get over here. It's time to go."

The kids made their way to the door, the looks on their faces making it clear they were forming even more questions in their minds. Martin stuck a key in the door, twisted the handle, and swung the door open wide.

The children's faces went blank, all questions erased by what they saw.

2.

Martin ushered Brewster and Mattie through the door, from the grim, musty, dimly lit garage into the charming, musty, dimly lit dressing room. Buzzing fluorescent light gave way to flickering oil lamps. The cold of the unheated garage in Seattle became the mild chill of a room in London inadequately heated by a single coal stove in the corner.

The dressing room was long and narrow, stretching the entire width of the stage. One wall held a long row of mirrors, small tables, and chairs. The other wall supported a jumble of old, dust-covered, half-broken props, all hanging from hooks or sitting on shelves.

Brewster and Mattie looked around, absorbing every detail of the cluttered, dingy dressing room. As Martin closed the door behind them, all visual reminder of the modern world disappeared, immersing the kids in the past. Of course, they thought it was just trickery—some elaborate art direction. Martin couldn't help wondering how they'd react if they knew the truth: that the trick was that it wasn't a trick.

Mattie said, "This place is filthy."

"Yes," Martin said. "That's authentic Victorian filth!"

Brewster ran a finger along a shelf, grimaced at the smudge left on his finger, attempted to wipe it off on the wall, and shuddered when the wall made his finger even dirtier. "I heard when you're someplace really filthy like this, you shouldn't rub your eyes or put anything in your mouth. You might get a disease."

Martin said, "If you do, I assure you, it'll be an authentic Victorian disease. Which, now that I think about it, would be really bad. Here, take some hand sanitizer."

Martin squeezed some clear gel out of a plastic bottle into his kids' hands. They continued exploring as they rubbed their hands together like flies standing on a cow patty—which was appropriate.

Phillip stepped out from around a corner, a delighted smile on his face. "Hello! Brewster! Mathison! Welcome. It's always so good to see you both!"

He rushed forward toward the children, then thrust out his hand, offering them a hearty handshake. Mattie shook his hand first, then Brewster. Afterward, the four of them stood in silence, waiting for someone to speak.

Martin, Mattie, and Brewster all looked at Phillip, who looked back at all of them in turn. Finally, Phillip peered down at Mattie and said, "Oh, dear, you must be freezing!"

Martin saw his daughter in her period-specific dress, standing next to her brother in his little tweed suit, while he and Phillip wore full tuxedoes, and he felt like the most neglectful father on earth. "Ugh. Mattie, I'm so sorry. It didn't even occur to me that it was so cold in here."

Phillip said, "It's easy to forget. No worry. We can fix that."

He bolted across the dressing room and opened a small, unmarked door, revealing a closet, which he stepped into and closed the door behind him.

Mattie asked, "What's he doing?"

"Looking in the closet," Martin replied.

"Why'd he shut himself in?"

Martin shrugged. "Just being thorough."

The door opened, and Phillip stepped out with a period-appropriate brown wool coat, which he offered to Mattie as if it were made of spun gold. "Milady."

Mattie chuckled uncomfortably and put on the coat, which fit perfectly.

Martin asked, "What do you say, Mattie?"

"Thank you."

"You're welcome," Phillip said.

"Why did you have this?"

"What?"

"Why did you have a girl's coat?"

Phillip and Martin looked at each other for a moment, then Phillip said, "We're magicians. We make people disappear. All kinds of people. Adults, children, anyone who volunteers. Sometimes they leave stuff behind, so we chuck it in the lost and found."

Phillip smiled at Martin, who stared back for a moment, then laughed and looked down at the twins, nodding his head, encouraging them to laugh at Phillip's joke as well. They both made a valiant effort.

Martin allowed his laugh to trail off, then pointed to the far end of the room, toward a set of cages. "Why don't you two go look at the doves while Phillip and I talk grown-up business, okay?"

Martin and Phillip watched as the kids ambled off to the distant reaches of the dressing room. Once they were out of whisper range and absorbed in poking at the cooing doves, Phillip asked, "Do you really think this was a good idea, Martin?"

"Yeah. I do."

"And Gwen agrees?"

"Yeah, pretty much. I mean, she agreed to let me do it. That's close enough."

Phillip said, "It's the best you can hope for most of the time, at least."

"True. How're you doing? Anything new?"

"The annual wizards' conclave was today."

"And you're sober?"

"I jumped back in time long enough to sleep it off. I'm a bit hungover, to be honest."

"How'd it go?"

"I'm still the chairman."

"That's not a surprise. The wizards only hold the vote every year because you insist. You were running unopposed again?"

"Yeah. There were just two joke votes for Magnus."

"Which Magnus? There are two of them."

"Yeah, and the votes didn't specify. Either vote could have been for either Magnus, or maybe for both of them like they're the same person."

Martin frowned. "We should work on that."

"I don't know that it's worth the trouble. They're inseparable anyway, they're both wizards, both are named Magnus, and they both have a best friend named Magnus: each other. They even listen to the same awful death metal, usually at the same time. I guess they're pretty much a package deal."

Martin thought for a moment, then said, "Huh. That's true. *The Magnuses. The Magni. Magnus squared. Magnus.* Ha! If you try to put their names together like a celebrity couple's names, you'd just end up calling them *Magnus* anyway. Oh well. How is everybody? Anyone ask about me?"

Phillip winced. "Yeah, about that, Martin. I've got good news and bad news. The good news is that they did ask about you. Everybody's curious how things are going with you and Gwen living in the future, especially now that you have the kids."

"And what's the bad news?"

"I mentioned that you were bringing the kids to the show tonight."

"No."

"Yes." Phillip followed as Martin ran around the end of the row of makeup tables. They deftly dodged through the props cluttering the darkened wing and out onto the empty stage behind the closed theater curtain. Martin held the curtains shut with one hand while using the other to make a small peephole through which he saw the entire group of Medieval European wizards—nearly two dozen of them in all—sitting in the audience, fidgeting as one would when one wears a full Victorian suit after years of swanning around in flowing wizard robes.

Martin closed up the gap in the curtain and glared at Phillip.

"Martin, they just want to meet the kids."

"I understand that. I don't want the kids to meet them. At least not yet."

Phillip put his hand on Martin's shoulder. "I know. I tried to talk them out of it, but they wouldn't listen."

"But they just reelected you chairman."

"Yeah, well, they vote for me because I listen to them. Not the other way around."

"I told the kids I'd let them watch the show."

"*Let them.*"

"Let them, make them, whatever. The point is, if they watch it from backstage, they'll see that we're doing real magic. They have to watch from the audience, and now they'll be surrounded by those dummies."

"Hey, those dummies are your friends."

"Yeah, and I know better than anyone how dumb they can be."

"Look, Martin, you have a simple choice to make. You can either trust your fellow wizards—"

"Who we both know are completely untrustworthy."

"—or you can hop back in the car, drive them home, and tell Gwen this was a bad idea."

"Okay, your seats are right over here," Martin said, ushering Brewster and Mattie through a door into the theater's lobby. "I'm setting you up at the rear of the audience. Don't kick the seats of the people in front of you and don't talk to anybody. I'll check up on you during the intermission, and we'll head home after the show. Okay?"

Both of the children agreed, but neither was listening. Brewster walked progressively slower, distracted by the ornate theater lobby filled with Victorians—people who overdressed for every occasion save for bathing—dolled up for a night on the town. Martin managed to shove the boy along, but it was Mattie who stopped dead in her tracks when a set of double doors to the outside opened, revealing a dark street teeming with people and horse-drawn carriages.

"Are those real horses?" she asked.

"What? Where?" Martin looked out the doors as they swung shut. "Oh, uh, yeah. There are horses. That's how they traveled in Victorian London."

"Really?"

"Uh, yeah. If you're interested, I can arrange for us to follow the guy who shovels their poop when they go in the road. It's fascinating."

That broke her attention long enough for Martin to push her and Brewster away from the doors.

He'd nearly maneuvered them out of the lobby and into the theater when he had to stop to keep from running into the two wizards from Norway: a small, affable man with good hair and straight teeth named Magnus and his best friend, a doughier, greasy-haired man with a forced-looking smile, also named Magnus.

"I voted for you," the larger, less good-looking Magnus said.

The more attractive Magnus said, "Great! Thanks, Magnus! So both of the votes for *Magnus* were for me!"

"Uh, yeah, Magnus. I guess they were."

"Hey, guys," Martin said.

Both Magnuses said, "Hey."

The better-groomed Magnus smiled. "Good to see you, Martin. These must be the kids!"

The other Magnus bowed theatrically. "Zounds! What an honor it be to meet the offspring of Martin and fair Gwen!"

Martin, the twins, and the other Magnus all stood in awkward silence until he came out of his bow, because they didn't know what else to do.

"Yeah," Martin said. "Mattie, Brewster, this is Magnus, and Magnus. Uh, guys, about that. I was just thinking, maybe we could use your last names for stuff like the vote, you know, to make it clear who we're talking about. What's your last name?"

The more handsome Magnus said, "Rex."

"Magnus Rex, like a dinosaur. I like that! It's got real—" Martin made a fist and shook it in front of himself to convey the sense of strength he was unable to find a word for.

Magnus Rex said, "I know exactly what you mean, and you're right. It's a good, muscular name."

"Yes! Muscular! That's a good way to put it." Martin turned to the other Magnus. "And your last name?"

The other Magnus sneered almost imperceptibly and, in a voice devoid of enthusiasm, said, "Galka."

"Galka," Martin said, and immediately winced.

He said it a couple more times, involuntarily jutting his head forward as he pronounced the *L* and the *K* together. "Galka. Galka. Ugh, it almost triggers my gag reflex just saying it!"

Mattie and Brewster both said "Galka," and scrunched up their little faces like they'd tasted something sour.

Martin shook his head. "Well, anyway, I was sorry to hear you lost the election today. Better luck next time."

Magnus Rex brightened. "Can we count on your vote next year?"

"No," Martin said, already walking away. "But I don't plan on voting at all, so it's not like I'll be voting against you."

"That doesn't really help us," Magnus Galka said.

"But it doesn't hurt."

Martin led the kids into the theater and along the back of the last row. The house was almost packed, but there were two empty seats in the back row. Martin didn't think this was a coincidence, as the seats were next to two of his friends, Tyler and Gary, and behind two more, Roy and Jeff.

Martin stopped, gathering his thoughts and deciding what to say to his friends, and how to say it. As he stood there, he heard the wizards and the rest of the audience making pleasant pre-show conversation.

Martin stepped out into the aisle where all of the wizards would be able to see him, and he cleared his throat. "Hi, everyone."

All of the wizards twisted in their seats and cheered. Martin smiled and tried to shush them, which caused them to get louder for a second or two before they finally stopped.

"It's good to see all of you. These are my children, Brewster and Mathison. Brewster, Mattie, these gentlemen"—several wizards laughed—"are friends of mine. You're going to sit with them."

Martin looked over the wizards and saw a sea of smug, amused smiles.

"They know that this is the first time the two of you have visited this historical theme park, where we make history come alive through the use of costumes and false accents. Do you *all* understand that?"

The wizards nodded.

"Good. Now, kids, if there's a problem, I'm sure these men will help you because they know that if anything happens to upset either of you, your mother will not be happy with them."

Martin glanced up at the wizards again and saw their smiles fade at the idea of Gwen's hypothetical revenge.

He watched as the kids took their seats next to Tyler and Gary.

Gary said, "Don't worry, Martin. We'll watch them like they were our own children."

Martin winced.

Tyler shook his head and looked Martin in the eye. "No, Martin, we'll treat them like they're *your* children, and you'll rain furious vengeance on us for the rest of our days if anything happens to them."

Satisfied, Martin went backstage, where he had just enough time to put on his top hat and satin cape before the show started.

The curtains opened to Phillip, standing alone in the center of an otherwise empty stage.

"Good evening, ladies and gentlemen. As you are aware, I am the Phenomenal Phillip."

After a respectable round of applause, Phillip continued. "Thank you. Thank you. Yes, alliteration using a *PH* to create an *F* sound does have a high degree of difficulty. Thank you, one and all, for joining us this evening for a show filled with magic, mystery, and veiled insulting references to our great, sensational friends across the way."

The audience gave a small, knowing laugh.

"But before the show can truly begin, I must introduce my friend and partner." Phillip held his hand out toward the side of the stage, gripping his cape so that it hung from his arm like a curtain. "Please welcome, Mystical Martin!"

The audience's applause filled the theater for several seconds before trailing off into a confused smattering as Phillip stood still, nobody entered from the side of the stage, and absolutely nothing happened. Once the audience had lapsed into confused silence, Phillip curled his extended arm around his head, covering his face with his cape, spun in place, and threw his arms wide, revealing that he had transformed into Martin.

The audience erupted in amazed gasps and raucous applause.

Martin smiled at them as he took off his hat and dropped it brim down on the floor. The hat sat there for a moment, then a bright light, a loud *foomp*, and a cloud of smoke propelled it into the air, where it hovered as the smoke cleared, eventually revealing that the hat now sat perched on Phillip's head.

Again, thunderous applause. As the ovation faded, Martin said, "I can't wait to see our friends across the street try to copy that!" Applause gave way to laughs.

From Martin's point of view onstage, fixed in the spotlight, the world beyond the proscenium arch was a void of inky darkness surrounding the single, brilliant white light source. He held up his hand to shade his eyes, and could dimly make out Mattie and Brewster, sitting forward in their seats, watching the show with great intensity.

Phillip took the hat from his head and waved it around to blow the smoke away, then pulled a piece of brightly colored cloth from his pocket. "Excellent. For our first trick, please observe this simple handkerchief."

Martin watched as the enthusiasm drained from his children's faces, and they settled back into their seats.

After a few minutes' worth of Martin and Phillip making various handkerchiefs appear and disappear from various places, he shielded his eyes again and saw Brewster fidgeting, and Mattie looking around at the theater.

"Now," Phillip said, "for our next trick, observe these solid steel rings."

Both children sagged in their seats.

Martin and Phillip at least performed a variation on the linking rings that neither of the twins had ever seen, demonstrating that they were solid, then throwing the rings so that they collided and linked in midair. Then, a bar lowered from the catwalks above the stage. Martin threw a ring, which seemed to pass through the solid metal rod before turning solid again and hanging above the stage. Martin threw another ring, which linked with, and hung from, the first ring. He threw another, and another, and another, until the chain of thin chrome rings hung at his eye level.

Martin picked up a final, larger ring, more of a chrome hula hoop. He spun around to build up speed, and threw the hoop, Frisbee style, at the dangling chain. The hoop snagged the bottommost ring, and the whole chain moved from the force of the impact. The hoop swung offstage, then returned, with Phillip sitting in the hoop as if it were a schoolyard swing.

As Phillip swung back and forth across the stage, Martin again peered out into the audience and, instead of his kids, saw two empty chairs next to Tyler. He tried to get Tyler's attention, but Phillip's swinging back and forth drew everybody's focus.

Phillip started into their rehearsed patter, setting up the next trick, in which Martin would push Phillip so hard that he traveled offstage, the swing returning without him, only to travel off the other end of the stage and return with Phillip again.

"Say, Martin, would you please give me a push?"

Martin shielded his eyes and glared out again into the audience. He saw that the empty seats remained empty and his blood ran cold. He hesitated for a moment, then said, "No."

"Thanks, just a little—I'm sorry, what?"

"No," Martin said, his eyes darting around the audience, then to the wings on either side of the stage. "I won't give you a push. I think we should, uh, stop playing around and get serious."

Martin nearly ran offstage, leaving Phillip lazily moving back and forth on his swing made of silver rings.

Martin rushed back onstage pulling a tall, slender box, like an upturned casket on wheels. The box sat at the center of a constellation of swords, spears, pokers, lances, and a couple of crudely sharpened sticks, all mounted on powerful springs and pointed in toward the box. "I think we need to step up our game."

Phillip dragged his feet to stop swinging. "But, Martin, we don't usually pull out the Chamber of Certain Death until the end of the show."

"Yeah, well, I'm calling an audible. I think this audience deserves a hit of the good stuff."

"Okay. Well, um, fine." Phillip untangled himself from the rings. "Ladies and gentlemen, for your education, we'll now talk briefly about the Spanish Inquisition. In that dark—"

"Yeah, blah blah, blah. Let's just cut to the chase." Martin set the brakes on the Chamber of Certain Death's casters, opened the door, and nearly leaped inside. "I'm a heretic. I won't repent. You have to make an example of me. Let's go, Torquemada."

Martin closed himself into the box and immediately transported himself to the back of the theater. Standing there, in the dark, he watched as a confused-looking Phillip threw the switch that made all of the sharpened implements pierce the box—and whatever was inside.

The audience's gasp was not as loud as usual, as it was born of confusion rather than horror. The chamber's door swung open to reveal that Martin was no longer in the box.

Gary leaned in toward Tyler and asked, "How'd he do that?"

Martin muttered, "Magic," and knocked Gary and Tyler's heads together like coconuts. They both turned and looked at Martin, angry and hurt.

Martin asked, "Where are my kids?"

Tyler and Gary looked at the empty seats, frozen in horror.

Tyler said, "They were right there!"

"I know where they were," Martin said through clenched teeth. "Where *are* they?"

Gary said, "I'm sure they weren't kidnapped or anything."

Martin said, "If they were kidnapped, Gary, that'd mean their disappearance isn't *all* your fault."

"Oh. Yeah. Maybe they were kidnapped," but Martin couldn't hear, as he was already running to the lobby.

Up on stage, Phillip said, "Perhaps Martin will turn up again later. In the meantime, does anyone here have a pocket watch?"

Martin burst out of the theater into the lobby, looking frantically for his children, but he saw no sign of them. He ran toward the restrooms, hoping they'd both had to go. As he passed the entrance doors, he glanced outside and caught sight of the twins running across the street.

Martin changed direction so quickly that he slid to a stop and took three steps toward the door before actually making any progress, his feet sliding beneath him on the lobby's tile floor. He ran out to the sidewalk and shouted the kids' names, but it was no good.

People generally assume—correctly—that Victorian London was crowded and dirty and smelly, but they usually underestimate how loud it was. Between the hooves of the horses and the steel-rimmed wheels striking the cobblestones, and the shouting of the people trying to be heard over the already existing noise, the sound of a busy Victorian street was often described by observers at the time as being similar to standing at the base of a towering waterfall.

Martin called out as loudly as he could, but the cacophony drowned him out. He watched as the kids made it to the opposite sidewalk without being trampled; looked around, amazed at their surroundings; and disappeared into the building across the street, a theater bearing a marquee that read:

The Great Gilbert and the Sensational Sid:
Professional Purveyors of Authentic Amazement
"Much better than Mystical Martin and Phenomenal Phillip."
– Jacob Higgenbotham, *The Times*

Martin looked both ways several times, waiting for an opening. A dense fog limited visibility to only a half block or so in each direction. Martin considered this a lucky break, in that it helped maintain the illusion for the kids that they were in a theme park.

Traffic moved slowly but steadily, with very little space between the carriages and wagons. Martin ran across the street, dodging several horses, stepping lightly around a pile of horse droppings, and ignoring the barely audible curses the cart drivers bellowed at him as he went.

He burst into the lobby of Gilbert and Sid's theater just in time to see one of his children's tiny hands pull out of view and the barely opened doors into the theater gently close. Martin ran forward, more focused on reuniting with his children than with manners. He flung the doors open, bringing a distracting burst of light into the darkened theater and creating a loud squeak. A few feet down the aisle, Mattie and Brewster turned and froze, seeing their concerned father, cutting a dramatic figure, lit from behind in the doorway.

Many of the theater patrons also turned and looked. One of them shouted, "It's Mystical Martin!"

Every head swiveled to look at Martin. On the stage, Gilbert and Sid paused midtrick. Sid stood toward the front of the stage in his black top hat and tails with a red-lined black satin cape, and a monocle clamped into his right eye socket, toying with the curve of his waxed mustache and Van Dyke beard as he addressed the audience. Gilbert, similarly attired but with only a mustache and no monocle, sat uneasily on a swing made of a chain of trick linking rings. Even though he kept most of his weight on his feet, gingerly moving his mass back and forth to give the impression of swinging, the rings stretched and deformed under the load. They both shielded their eyes to see what was causing the commotion.

One of the spotlights swung around and focused on Martin.

Gilbert stood up. He and Sid both walked to the front of the stage.

"Ah, *quelle surprise*! What have we here?" Sid said. "One of our esteemed colleagues from across the street. Perhaps he's come to see what the state of the art in stage magic looks like, in hopes of more convincingly imitating it later."

Gilbert waved. "Hello, Martin."

Martin waved back. "Hello, Gil. Sid. Sorry to interrupt the show. I was just, uh, just coming to get my kids here."

The spotlight widened to reveal Brewster and Mattie, still standing in the middle of the aisle, mortified.

The expression of the two magicians on the stage transformed instantly from snooty and superior to warm and friendly.

"Oh," Gilbert said. "These are the kids? Good to meet you!"

Sid waved again. "Greetings, offspring of Martin! It's a pleasure to meet you both. We've both known your parents for a long time."

Gilbert nodded. "Very long."

"And it must be said that we both hold *your mother* in the absolute highest esteem."

A wave of polite laughter rippled through the audience. Gilbert said, "Just a joke, kids. Your old man's a competitor, but he's all right, and any children of his are always welcome here."

The spontaneous act of civility sent an approving murmur through the crowd.

Sid gripped his monocle to keep it from falling out as he arched an eyebrow at Martin. "That said, any observer privy to the secrets we share must wonder why one such as yourself would bring two children such as them to a place such as this."

Martin said, "I wanted to show them our act, let them see what their old man does for a living."

Gilbert nodded. "Yeah, okay, but that doesn't explain why they're in our theater."

Mattie said, "We got bored."

Martin ushered the kids out of the theater, the thunderous and prolonged laughter of the audience still audible as they stepped out onto the sidewalk. They crossed the street in silence, as talking would have been impossible in the constant drone of traffic anyway.

As they reentered Martin and Phillip's theater lobby, Brewster said, "We're sorry, Dad."

"Yeah," Mattie agreed.

Martin said, "Eh, it's not your fault. Your mom was right. This was a bad idea. Let this be a lesson that we should all listen to your mom more."

"Brewster and I listened to Mom," Mattie said.

"Yeah, but that's not all of us, is it?" Martin asked. He directed the kids to a side door that led backstage, rather than back into the theater.

Mattie asked, "Aren't we going back to the show?"

"No, I'm just going to run the two of you home for the rest of the day. This, uh, *park* is really intended for adults. I'll bring you back when you're both older. Hey, what say tonight we go out for pizza?"

"Yay!" Mattie shouted.

"But don't you have to finish the show?" Brewster asked.

"Yeah, it's not a problem. Phillip will vamp, and you'd be surprised how fast I can get back."

Six Years Later

3.

The other students cleared out in the traditional tenth-grade manner: as quickly as possible. They almost fully evacuated the room before the bell had stopped ringing, leaving only Mattie Banks sitting at her desk, facing Mrs. Hackett.

Mrs. Hackett stared at Mattie, smiling.

Mattie stared back with her eyes one-third closed and her mouth forming a straight line.

Mrs. Hackett said, "Mathison, I think you know why you're staying late."

"Because you asked me to."

"No, Mathison, because I *told* you to."

"I asked you to call me Mattie, or Miss Banks."

"I told you to stay late, Mathison, because of your *performance* on the weekly quiz. Why did you answer every question with the phrase *I don't know*?"

Mattie shrugged. "I didn't know."

"Then why not at least guess?"

"Do you want your students to hide it from you when we're having difficulty? Wouldn't that make it harder for you to teach us?"

"Mathison, I think you pretended not to know any of the answers because you thought I intended to read all of your answers out to the whole class."

"And you did, just like you've done every Friday for the last three weeks."

"Yes. There's nothing wrong with your grasp of the calendar. Mathison, I use a student's paper to give the class the answers every week. Why shouldn't I use yours?"

"Again."

"What?"

"Why shouldn't you use mine *again*. You already used mine a bunch of times, like twice a month, at least, and then for the last three weeks straight. I think the other students should get a chance, so I asked you to stop. You're supposed to be teaching the class about history, not about me."

"Asked? As I remember, you *told* me not to."

"No, I asked."

"You didn't say *please*."

"Really? That's the problem? You've been picking on me for the last three weeks because when I asked you to stop, I didn't ask nicely?"

"When you demanded that I stop, you made it so that I had to continue, Mathison. I won't be controlled by my students."

"But if you have to do the opposite of what I ask, then I'm still controlling you. You've gotta admit, I have a point there."

"No, you don't."

Mattie laughed. "You just did the opposite of what I said. That's funny."

"No, it isn't."

Mattie laughed again, harder. "Look, I wasn't trying to control you. I asked you not to do something."

"And when I didn't comply, you deliberately got an F on your quiz. What do you think that proves?"

"You're my teacher. I'm not learning. What does that prove?"

"You're only hurting yourself."

"What else can I do? Give you what you want?"

"Yes! I am your teacher. You should give me what I want."

"You don't give me what I want."

"Again, I'm the teacher. You're the student. It's not my job to give you what you want. It's my job to give you what you earn. If you work hard to give me what I want all year, at the end of the year, I'll probably give you what you want."

"I spend all year knuckling under to please you, and you might make it worthwhile? What kind of deal is that?"

"That's the deal we all get. That's how life works. Mathison, you need to learn your place."

"Oh, so that's what you're teaching me. *My place.* I thought you taught history, but you're instructing me in the importance of conformity and accepting authority. What an interesting thing to find out by failing a quiz about Nazi Germany."

Mrs. Hackett squinted at Mattie. "The fact that you know how ironic that is just proves you've learned more from class this week then you're letting on."

Brewster and a petite blonde girl stood in the hallway. Brewster leaned against the doorjamb, peering into the gymnasium at the girls' volleyball practice. Even though there were multiple games in progress, he only looked at one girl with long black hair and a laser-like focus on the game.

The blonde girl standing next to Brewster said, "I really enjoyed the monologue you did in drama class."

Brewster said, "Thanks," without turning to look at her.

"The way you mimed opening the door when you walked on stage, it was almost as if I could see the door."

"Thanks, Abby. I, uh, I practiced a lot."

"How?"

"Uh, by opening doors."

Abby looked at Brewster, then into the gym, then back to Brewster. "You like volleyball?"

"Yeah."

"Do you play?"

"No."

She looked into the gym again. "I'm going to walk home now, I guess."

Brewster said, "Cool. See you tomorrow."

Abby said, "Yeah, see you," and walked away.

In the gymnasium, the coach blew a whistle, and all the games broke up. As the girls walked to the bleachers, Brewster shouted, "That was some great work, Lorraine! Really well . . . volleyed!"

The girl with the long black hair shouted "Thanks," without turning to see who had addressed her.

Brewster's phone vibrated in his pocket. He pulled it out and looked at his texts. He had one new message from Mattie, which read: "You're an idiot."

He quickly tapped out: "Where are you?"

Mattie said, "Right behind you, idiot."

Brewster turned around and saw his twin sister standing a few feet behind him, putting her phone in her pocket.

"How long have you been there?"

Mattie shook her head, walked forward, put her arm around Brewster's shoulder, and shoved him away from the gym door and down the hall. "Too long. We're going home."

Brewster walked of his own accord, allowing Mattie to stop shoving him, but he glared at her as he relented. "I was watching volleyball practice."

"Oh, I know. Why don't you just ask Lorraine out?"

"Do you think she'd say yes?"

"No. She doesn't like you in that way. I'm not sure she likes you in *any* way."

"Well, she hasn't really given me a chance."

"You should go ahead and ask. Then she'll say no, and you can move on."

"Move on to who?"

"How about Abby?"

"Hmm, yeah. I mean, she's cute, but I don't think I like her in that way."

"Have you given her a chance?"

Brewster said nothing.

Mattie shook her head. "You're an idiot."

Both Brewster and Mattie heard the sound of heavy footsteps approaching quickly. They looked to see Dolan, a guy they'd both loathed since kindergarten, running down the hall toward them hauling a musical instrument case the size of a piece of carry-on luggage, but with no wheels. He held the case out forward as if it were precious to him, or useful as a battering ram.

Mattie and Brewster followed the other students' lead and stepped aside so Dolan could pass unimpeded. As he ran by, he turned his head and looked at the twins. "What," he panted, slowing his pace. "You dorks aren't wearing your special outfits today?"

Dolan believed that insults counted as jokes, and that any emotional reaction was as good as a laugh, two mistaken impressions that fed each other and resulted in his current radiantly toxic personality.

Mattie asked, "What are you talking about, Dolan?"

Dolan smiled sickeningly. "After how you two were dressed yesterday, I figured you'd be all pimped out today, too. Did you lose your nerve, or just come to your senses?"

Brewster looked at Dolan as if he'd lost his mind. "We don't have any idea what you're talking about."

Dolan laughed once, mostly through his nose. "Sure you don't."

Mattie said, "Go play your bassoon, Dolan."

Brewster and several other students laughed.

Dolan thrust the oversized instrument case toward Mattie. "Don't bag on the bassoon just 'cause it's got a funny name. It's a serious instrument!"

Brewster said, "It's a giant clarinet you play through a straw."

Dolan started stumbling away again. "Whatever. I gotta go. Late for practice."

"All it's good for is making honking noises," Mattie shouted after him. "You're playing a huge goose call, Dolan."

Brewster looked at his sister. "You're in a fine mood."

Mattie grunted.

"Another run-in with Hackett?"

Again, Mattie grunted.

"What happened?"

"She held me after class."

"Why?"

"I got an F on the weekly quiz."

"An F?"

"An F."

"How many questions did you get wrong?"

"All of them."

Brewster let out a long, impressed whistle. "And you call me an idiot."

"Nothing says we can't both be idiots."

The twins walked home in sullen silence, Brewster because he suspected his sister had been right when she called him an idiot, and Mattie because she suspected she'd been wrong when she played dumb on her quiz.

They entered the house through the front door to find Martin sitting in his recliner, reading. They exchanged warm but perfunctory greetings with him as they walked through on their way to the kitchen. Gwen sat in the dining room, large pieces of fabric spread out all over the table, hand stitching two of the pieces with a magnifying visor lowered over her eyes. Without looking up from her sewing, she said, "Hi, kids. How was school?"

Mattie and Brewster said, "Fine," accidentally speaking in unison.

Gwen's head snapped up as if someone had poured ice water down her back. "What's wrong?"

The twins said, "Nothing," again, speaking in unison.

Gwen put down her sewing. "Seriously. What's wrong?"

Mattie said, "We already told you, nothing's wrong!"

"I don't believe you."

"Me neither." Martin had gotten up from his chair and stood behind the twins. "There's always something wrong. It's when neither of you is willing to complain to us about it that we know there's real trouble."

Brewster and Mattie looked at each other, then Mattie blurted, "Brewster's into a girl at school who isn't interested in him."

Gwen said, "Oh, honey. I'm sorry to hear that. It's just part of life, though."

Martin shrugged. "Are you sure she's not interested? Some girls do play hard to get."

Gwen tried to hide a small smirk.

"Maybe," Brewster said.

Mattie said, "No. She's not interested at all."

Gwen said, "Well, sorry to say it, but a woman can always tell. If Mattie says she isn't interested, I believe her."

"What?!" Brewster sputtered.

Martin clapped his hand on his son's shoulder. "Yeah, I wouldn't argue with the ladies on this. Better to just cut your losses and look for someone new. And you should thank your sister. You feel bad right now, but she probably saved you a lot of time and heartache."

Mattie smiled beatifically at Brewster.

Brewster said, "Mattie got an F on a quiz today. She got every question wrong."

"Mattie," Gwen said, "how did that happen? Did you study the wrong chapter or something? Do you need a tutor?"

"No, Mom. Relax. It's nothing like that. I flunked the test deliberately."

Martin and Gwen stared at their daughter, agape, for several seconds. Then Gwen said, "She gets this from you."

Martin said, "Oh, totally. You should talk to her about it."

"Agreed," Gwen said.

"Mom, Dad, it's not a big deal. The teacher's a jerk."

"So you're scuttling your own GPA?" Gwen asked.

Martin sat down at the table, shaking his head. "Maybe if you do badly enough, you'll get summer school, and she could be your teacher for another three months. That'll show her."

"You guys aren't listening to me," Mattie said.

From the living room, Phillip said, "She's right. You should give her a chance to fully explain herself."

Brewster and Mattie turned. Martin and Gwen stood up and craned their necks to see around their children. All of them saw Phillip, standing in the middle of the living room, wearing a sky-blue robe and matching pointed hat, and holding a staff made of gnarled wood with a vial of acrid-looking red fluid lashed to its top.

Mattie looked at the front door, then squinted at Phillip. "Were you here the whole time?"

"No. I just got here."

"From where?" Brewster asked. "And why are you wearing a bathrobe?"

"And a dunce cap?" Mattie added.

Phillip said. "Good lord, kids, you're bigger every time I see you! Look, sorry, but I don't have time to explain. I need to talk to your parents alone. It's very important grown-up business."

Mattie and Brewster looked at Phillip, confused. Then they looked at each other. They turned around and looked at Gwen and Martin, hoping to be reassured by their parents' steady nerves and command of the situation.

Martin and Gwen looked deeply unsettled.

Martin said, "Kids, uh, why don't you go to your rooms or the rec room, you know, *away*, and do . . ." As he trailed off, he looked at Gwen.

"Something," Gwen said. "Go to the rec room and do something. We need to talk with Phillip."

Brewster and Mattie trudged down the stairs to the partially finished basement the family referred to as the rec room.

As the door swung closed behind them, they heard Martin ask, "Okay, what's the deal?! You know better than to just appear in our home dressed like that!"

The door clicked shut, closing out most of the sound.

The rec room held Martin's surprisingly robust home theater setup, which Gwen only tolerated because of the heavily insulated door and soundproofing in the walls. None of the higher frequencies could get through, but the low tones carried. Mattie stayed on the top step with her ear pressed to the door, but didn't hear any better than Brewster, who was hovering two steps down. That didn't stop him from forcing his head around her to press his ear to the door as well.

They heard Phillip say, "I know, I'm sorry, there's no time!" and their father replying, "But the kids, Phillip. They saw—"

They didn't hear the next word, because Gwen pulled the door open quickly, causing them both to fall on the floor at the top of the stairs. They gazed up at the faces of their angry parents, and Phillip, looking panic-stricken and dressed in his bizarre costume.

The three adults watched as Mattie and Brewster walked all the way down the stairs. Gwen said, "Soundproofing or not, I'll hear if you try to come up the stairs. Just stay down there while we talk."

The twins stood at the foot of the stairs. The rec room looked the same as it always did. Fabric swatches and model kit parts covered the pool table. The big, comfy sectional, covered with big, comfy pillows and blankets, sat empty in front of the darkened projection screen. Completed model spaceships hung from the ceiling, old movie posters hung on the walls, and on either side of the screen, next to large speakers, full-sized replicas of Darth Vader and Kylo Ren stood guard over a low cabinet holding several gaming systems in varying degrees of obsolescence and a DVR full of movies and TV shows. There was much for the kids to occupy themselves with in this room. The twins ignored all of it, instead straining to hear the conversation half a house away.

They couldn't make out any words, just who was talking and general attitudes.

Gwen sounded irritated.

Phillip sounded apologetic.

Martin sounded curious.

Phillip said several things, in an increasingly fast and agitated voice, gaining volume as he spoke. Martin interrupted, but Phillip talked over him. Gwen also attempted to cut in. They talked over each other until Martin shouted, "You bring this to where our children live?!"

The three of them fell silent for a few seconds, long enough for Brewster and Mattie to look at each other, then Gwen and Martin shouted in obvious alarm, followed by anger. The shouting stopped abruptly, midword, falling to total silence.

The twins stood still, listening for nearly thirty seconds. Mattie took the first step up the stairs, but stood there, not moving, waiting for their mother to open the door and tell her to step back down. When that didn't happen, she took the next step and again waited. After three halting steps she crept the rest of the way up the stairs, Brewster following behind her. She turned the knob and they both pushed the door open.

The living room looked exactly as it had when they left it. Nothing was out of place. Their parents both looked angry. The only differences were that Phillip was no longer there, and their parents were not moving.

4.

Brewster and Mattie crept across the living room toward their motionless parents.

Mattie said, "Mom? Dad?"

Brewster stepped out from behind his sister and approached Martin and Gwen, head cocked to the side.

Martin stood, feet spread, knees bent, mouth wide open, as if he'd been photographed shouting at someone. Both of his hands reached forward as if gesturing toward something in the dining room. Beside him, Gwen's lips curled upward into a snarl. She stood sideways, pointing toward the same general area as Martin. Neither of them moved so much as an eyelid as their children approached.

Brewster said, "This isn't funny, Dad. Mom. Come on."

Mattie shouted, "Phillip? You still here, Phillip?"

Brewster waved his hands in front of Gwen's face, looking for any motion. Seeing none, he snapped his fingers twice, right next to her left ear.

Mattie walked quickly into the kitchen, then ran upstairs while Brewster waved and poked at their parents. Mattie ran back down the stairs and panted, "He's not here. I even looked under the beds." She ran to the back door and rattled it.

"What the hell, man! Mattie, they're frozen," Brewster said. "Completely still!"

Mattie ran past on her way to the front door. "No way. They're messing with us."

"I touched dad's eyeball, and he didn't flinch! Here, look." He pressed the tip of his index finger to Martin's left eyeball repeatedly, as if pressing a button in the back of a limousine to see what it did. Martin didn't move. "See? Nothing!"

Mattie turned the front doorknob and rattled the door in its frame. "Phillip's gone, and both of the doors are locked, I mean, like, with the deadbolts. Unless he has a key, he didn't go out through the doors."

"Are you sure?"

"Check for yourself."

Mattie snapped her fingers at Gwen and poked Martin in the eye while Brewster ran around the house, checking both doors and looking in all of the closets and under all of the beds, each essentially checking the other's work.

Brewster returned, panting. "Nothing. I checked all the places I'd hide. Phillip's not here. What are you doing?"

Mattie stood beside and slightly behind Martin, her face scrunched in concentration as she knocked with great force and precision on the inside of her father's left elbow. "I'm punching him in the funny bone. Still nothing."

"Have you tried Mom?"

"What? No! I wouldn't do this to Mom. Did you touch her eyeball?"

"God, no!" Brewster looked at their parents. "What is this? I've never heard of anything like it!"

"Coma?"

"Nah, they'd have fallen down."

"Seizure?"

"They'd be moving. I think that's kinda the whole deal with seizures."

"Locked-in syndrome? Stroke? Sleep paralysis?"

Brewster shook his head. "No, all of those would make them either move or fall down."

"Then it must be something Phillip did to them. That doesn't make much sense either, though. Why would Phillip hurt Mom and Dad? He's supposed to be their friend."

"Can you think of a situation where any of this would make sense? We don't even understand what he did. I've never heard of anything that'll just turn people into statues like this. Mattie, what are we gonna do?"

Mattie walked over beside her brother. "Mom always said if we're in really bad trouble, we should break our necklaces."

"Yeah, if *we're* in trouble. We aren't. Our parents are. Mom never really told us what would actually happen if we broke the necklaces, did she?"

Mattie pulled out her phone. "Only that she'd punish us if we broke them without good reason, and she always looked at me when she said it. Maybe we should just call Aunt Brit. Or the police. We could call the police."

Brewster thought for a moment, staring at their parents. "What would we tell them? *Dad's best friend appeared out of nowhere, dressed like Dumbledore, froze them while we were in another room, and disappeared?* That's not a great story. And even if they don't arrest us, they'll take us into custody, which from what I've seen on TV looks pretty much like being arrested, except instead of being put in a cell, you just hang around with a cop all day."

"Yeah. Okay," Mattie said. "We call Aunt Brit. We don't want to involve the police. You agree?"

"Yeah."

Both Mattie and Brewster jumped when the doorbell rang. They clutched at each other, looked at their frozen parents, then each other, then the door.

The doorbell rang again.

Mattie carefully tiptoed toward the door while Brewster started drawing the curtains on any window that might provide a view of Gwen and Martin.

As Mattie peered through the peephole, the doorbell rang a third time.

Brewster whispered to Mattie, "Who is it?"

Mattie whispered back, "I think it's the police!"

A stern male voice on the far side of the door said, "We can hear you talking. We know you're home."

Mattie shouted, "Who is it?"

A second man said, "Federal agents. Please open the door."

Mattie and Brewster opened the door just enough for both of them to look out through the gap, Mattie stooping a bit, and Brewster up on the tips of his toes to look over her head.

Three men were on the doorstep. Two stood in front, wearing dark colored suits and striped ties. One was husky but solid, and smiled kindly at the kids. The other was thinner and more weathered. He appeared unhappy, but not at the kids so much as the world the kids were a part of. Behind them, an older man in a black turtleneck and khaki pants stood, looking concerned.

The friendlier of the two men in front said, "Hello. My name is Murphy; this is my partner, Miller. We're federal agents."

The two men in suits produced badges and ID cards and held them up close to the barely open door. The twins looked at the identification with the serious air of two people who were just realizing that they wouldn't know a fake ID or a counterfeit badge if they saw one.

The cheerful agent jerked a thumb back at the man in the turtleneck. "This gentleman is James Sadler, our civilian consultant."

Sadler smiled. "You two can call me Jimmy."

The twins peered at him, saying nothing.

Jimmy glanced down at his pockets, as if mentally inventorying their contents, then held up his hands, at a loss. "I don't have anything I can show you that'll prove I'm a civilian."

Mattie said, "I'm sorry. Our parents aren't available right now."

"That's fine. We aren't here for them. I take it you're Mathison Banks and Brewster Banks?"

Brewster and Mattie looked at each other, then, in unison, said, "Yeah."

Agent Murphy said, "Good. We're here for you."

"You want to talk to us?" Brewster asked.

Agent Miller chuckled under his breath. Mr. Sadler glared at him.

Agent Murphy smiled, "Yes, we'll talk, but our orders are to take the two of you into protective custody, so you'll be hanging around with us for the rest of the day."

Mattie and Brewster sat beside each other in the back seat of a massive silver SUV. Brewster sat by the door, behind the driver's seat. Mattie perched on the slight hump in the middle. Sadler, the civilian consultant, sat behind the front passenger seat, looking over at the children, trying a little too hard to seem friendly and harmless.

Agent Murphy, who was riding shotgun, was turned sideways, smiling back at the twins. Agent Miller drove, reducing his presence to a back of a head covered with pewter-gray hair, and a pair of steely eyes that glanced at the kids in the rearview mirror at regular intervals.

Agent Murphy asked, "You kids comfortable?"

Both Brewster and Mattie nodded yes.

"Good. It's a big back seat. This truck had plenty of room for passengers. I'll say that for it."

Miller grunted. "Too much room. It's like driving a small building."

Sadler smiled. "You'll have to excuse Agent Miller. We have a very nice car of our own, but we had to leave it behind and fly here to get to you in time."

"In time for what?" Mattie asked.

"We don't know. We were ordered to pick you up at a specific place and time, and to keep you safe and comfortable while we bring you in."

"Who ordered you to do that?" Brewster asked.

"The director of our task force. Our boss."

"Why?"

"We can't say."

"Why not?"

"Because she didn't."

"Did you ask?"

Miller and Murphy both laughed.

Sadler said, "No, we didn't. We trust our boss. We trust her to have a good reason, and we trust her to take it badly if we respond to one of her orders by asking *why*."

Agent Miller muttered, "It's a shame we can't trust her to give us a reasonable amount of notice."

Agent Murphy said, "We made it there in time. In fact, we were a little early, so we had enough notice, Miller."

Sadler continued, "Anyway, we upgraded from the base rental car, because why wouldn't we, and our only two choices were this and a Mustang convertible that would have been completely unsuitable."

"Too small?" Brewster asked.

"No. If we had to arrest someone, the ragtop would've made it easy to escape. Oh, hey, that reminds me, the agents here know your father. Isn't that right, guys?"

Murphy frowned at Sadler. Miller made a noise that was a weird mix of a groan and a growl.

Sadler laughed. "They never met your mother, though. I know both of your parents. We go way back. Wonderful people."

Mattie said, "They never mentioned you."

"Yeah, I'm not surprised. It's all pretty complicated."

Brewster and Mattie glanced at each other, each trying not to let on how scared they were in an effort to comfort their sibling, and in the process, freaking each other out even more.

Mattie asked, "Shouldn't you have gotten our parents' permission before you took us prisoner?"

"You're not a prisoner, Ms. Banks," Sadler said. "You're just in protective custody. And we were instructed that we had all the legal authorization we needed. Besides, you told us your parents weren't available, and you came with us willingly. You didn't put up any argument at all."

Miller shook his head. "Although, you might've invited us into the house, instead of making us stand on the stoop while you got your toothbrushes. It was like we had delivered a pizza and you were scrounging for tip money."

Mattie said, "Well, give me my phone back. I want to make a call. You know, just to let people know where we are."

"I'm afraid I can't do that. I have to hold on to your phones, and nobody makes any calls, not even us. Our orders are to bring you straight to the director, and to go radio silent until we do, for security reasons."

Brewster asked, "Don't we have a legal right to a phone call?"

Sadler smiled. "That's for people who've been arrested, Brewster. You aren't under arrest. You're in protective custody."

"So we can leave?" Mattie asked.

"No. It's not safe."

"And we can't call anyone," Brewster said.

Sadler said, "You can call anybody you want, as many times as you want, when we get to HQ. Until then, for safety's sake, we have to keep a low profile, and that means no calls."

Brewster and Mattie looked at each other, again, trying to disguise their concern.

"But hey," Sadler continued, "in the meantime, you're going to get to ride in a private jet! Won't that be fun?"

The twins looked at each other. Mattie smiled and Brewster dropped all pretense at not being alarmed.

Mattie reached into her collar, pulling out her wizard hat necklace, while staring at Brewster and nodding.

Brewster said, "Mattie—"

Before he could talk her out of it, Mattie snapped the wizard hat in half, right between the star and the moon, as their mother had instructed them many times. As the plastic triangle broke, Mattie vanished.

In the five seconds of chaos that followed, Brewster shouted most of the curse words he knew, Agent Miller taught him several more, Agent Murphy drew his pistol and frantically searched the area around the still-moving car for possible attackers, and Sadler lunged to grab Brewster.

"Don't worry," Sadler shouted. "We've got you. You're not going anywhere!"

Brewster pulled out his necklace, snapped it in half, and disappeared.

5.

Mattie and Brewster appeared at the same time, in the living room of their home, in a seated position next to each other, three feet off the ground. They fell instantly, hit the floor hard, and lay there, writhing in pain, struggling to regain their breath.

"What the hell?" Mattie croaked.

Brewster coughed and rolled over on his side. "Are we back home?"

"I dunno how, but yeah."

Everything looked exactly as it had when they'd left, complete with their frozen parents standing in the middle of the room.

The twins struggled up onto their hands and knees.

"What'd you do that for?" Brewster asked.

Mattie scuttled, like an injured crab, across the room to the window. "Mom said to use it if we were in bad trouble. Three men we didn't know were about to put us on a plane, which sounds like pretty bad trouble to me. Aw, man, they still have our phones!"

"That's what you're worried about?!"

"It's one of the things I'm worried about!" Mattie shoved the drapes aside, looked out the window, then drew back as if the curtain burned her hand.

"What?" Brewster asked.

Mattie said nothing, instead pushing the curtain aside much more slowly, and by a smaller amount this time, to peer cautiously out the window again. Brewster joined her at the window. The agents' rented SUV was parked on the street, exactly where it had been before. Murphy, Miller, and Sadler stood around the car, but they didn't approach the house. Instead, they watched as Mattie and Brewster reluctantly climbed into the back seat.

The twins watched themselves hand over their phones, then get into the SUV, followed by the two federal agents and the civilian consultant.

"Look," Brewster said. "There are our phones. Maybe you could go ask for them back."

"Shut up."

As the other *them* drove away, Brewster and Mattie stepped back from the window and sat down on the couch, looking at their frozen parents.

After some silent contemplation, Brewster said, "The necklaces took us someplace safe. Mom said that if we were in trouble, breaking the necklaces would help make us safe. We broke them, and we ended up back at home, in the moment right after we'd left."

"Yeah. The question is how did that happen and how did she know it'd happen?" Mattie looked down at the pendant hanging around her neck, then hastily grabbed it and held it up for a closer look. "And how did this happen?"

The wizard hat pendant she held in her hand was unbroken. Brewster checked his own and found it unbroken as well.

"This can't be real."

"It is," Mattie said.

"But it can't be."

"But it is. The proof's right in front of us. What'll it take to convince you? Would you like to poke Dad in the eye a few more times?"

"But it doesn't make any sense."

"I'm not saying it does."

"Yeah. I know. You're right. I just don't understand any of this."

"Neither do I, Brewster. I mean, what is it we're even dealing with? Is it magic? Is it science? Is it a little of both?"

"Arthur C. Clarke said that any truly advanced technology would look like magic."

Mattie turned and stared at her brother, mulling over his words. "You know what, Brewster? That was no help at all."

"Sorry."

"You just told me that one thing it might be is indistinguishable from another thing it might be."

"I know. I said I'm sorry."

Mattie shook her head. "No, I'm sorry. We're both upset, and I'm taking it out on you. Maybe we should call Aunt Brit like we were gonna do before the cops showed up. She might be able to explain all of this."

Brewster thought for several seconds before answering. "Hmm. We've known Aunt Brit our whole lives, right?"

"Yeah."

"So, either she doesn't know about any of this stuff, and she'll think we're crazy, or she does know, she's been hiding it from us since we were babies, and we can't trust her to tell us the whole truth now. Either way, we're dragging her into our problems, including the federal agents who want to take us into custody."

"I see what you mean. If she's part of the problem, we don't want her involved. If she isn't, we don't want to involve her." Mattie stood up. "Looks like we have to go find some answers."

"Do you think it's wise to leave the house?"

"Do you think it's wise to stay here?"

"Good point." Brewster stood up, then turned to look at Gwen and Martin. "We can't just leave them here like this though, can we? What if someone breaks in?"

"No. You're right. What should we do with them? We can't help them. Maybe we should at least hide them."

After an amount of conversation that Brewster thought was too little and Mattie thought was too much, they carefully turned Gwen around and tilted her back. Brewster held her up off the floor by her shoulders while Mattie lifted her ankles. Gwen remained perfectly rigid as her children carried her down the stairs into the rec room.

The kids tried to do the same with Martin, but he weighed considerably more than Gwen. Mattie, walking backward while gripping her father's ankles like a wheelbarrow, managed to walk down the first few stairs without incident, but Brewster made the mistake of gripping Martin's shoulders underhand. As Martin's body tilted downward, his shoulders rotated slightly, loosening Brewster's grip and decreasing his leverage until Martin slipped out of Brewster's hands.

Martin's upper body fell. His shoulders slammed down on the edge of the top step. His joints remained as stiff as if he were carved from wood. The impact went through his body and into Mattie's hands. His weight shifted from hanging straight down in his children's hands to wanting to slide down the stairs. The combination of the jolt, the weight shift, and the surprise of seeing her brother drop their father caused Mattie also to let go.

Mattie saw Martin sliding down the stairs toward her. She braced herself in hopes of blocking his descent, but he already had some momentum. He ran into her and never even slowed down. Instead, he swept Mattie's feet out from under her, causing her to fall on top of him. Mattie gripped her father's shirt and held on like she was on a sled as they barreled down the stairs and onto the landing below.

Brewster watched the entire disaster unfold from above, powerless to stop it. As Martin slid to a stop, Mattie let go and rolled onto the floor, eyes shut tight, teeth gritted, but making no sound.

"You okay?" Brewster shouted.

Mattie rolled from side to side, her face contorted, but still silent. Brewster ran down the stairs, nearly falling himself as he rushed to his sister's side.

"Mattie! Mattie! What's wrong? Where does it hurt?" He knelt down over his sister, studying her face for any clue of what was wrong. It quickly became obvious that she couldn't breathe because she was laughing too hard.

When they'd both stopped laughing, they got to work. After a few minutes of intense effort, two mannequins were naked, and their parents, still stuck in the same poses, were disguised as Darth Vader and Kylo Ren.

Mattie said, "I don't know how Mom would like wearing the Kylo Ren costume."

"So, what do you think we should do now?"

Mattie looked around. "We have to get out of here. The agents could be back any second."

"Why would they come back here? Is that the logical thing to do after the two kids you took into custody disappear into thin air?"

"Is there a logical thing to do after something impossible happens? No, so there's no telling what they'll do, which means they might come back here. We have to go."

"How, Mattie? How are we gonna go? We won't get far on foot. We need to think."

"No, Brewster, we need to do something."

"Thinking *is* doing something."

"Not the way you do it." Mattie started up the stairs. "We'll take one of the cars. Where are Dad's keys?"

"Wait, no, Mattie, that's a terrible idea."

"No, it isn't."

"Yes, it is. I don't have a license, just a learner's permit."

"You're not driving."

"You don't have your license either."

"So? I'm just as qualified as you are."

"No, Mattie, come on now. Who says you get to drive?"

"Brewster, just a few seconds ago you said that taking a car was a terrible idea. Are you really going to argue with me over which one of us gets to drive?"

"Hey, I never noticed that the speed limit drops to thirty-five here," Mattie said.

Brewster said, "Keep your eyes on the road."

"I am. The sign's right next to the road."

"But it's not in the road, is it? Keep your eyes on the road."

"Fine, whatever. Worrywart."

"You're mocking me for not wanting to die in a car accident."

"I'm mocking you for being a worrywart."

"I'm not a worrywart."

"Brewster, you're panicking, and you're just a passenger. I'm the one driving without a license. Do I look concerned?"

"No! You don't! And you should! You really should! That's why I'm panicking!"

"Whatever. Just keep a look out for our turn, would you?"

"Sure. I'm risking my life to go someplace; I might as well make sure we get there. Hey, are we sure the car has enough charge? Did you even look?"

"Yes! It was, like, the first thing I checked, okay?" Mattie looked at the gauge. "The car has a full charge. Dad must've just topped it off."

Brewster scanned the road ahead, brow furrowed, then he cocked his head to one side and asked, "Mattie, have you ever seen Dad charge the car? I can't remember ever seeing Dad charge up the car."

Mattie thought for several seconds. "No. I don't remember ever seeing him charge the car. Or Mom. Any car, now that I think about it. I've never noticed either of them charging or putting gas in any car. That's weird, right?"

"Yeah. That's weird. Hey, I think that's where we're going."

Mattie steered the car into an unmarked entrance of a nondescript office park. "Do you remember which office it was?"

Brewster shook his head. "We came here once when we were ten. I'm surprised we're in the right part of town."

They drove slowly through the industrial park, reading the signs on the glass doors. Some were painted on in simple sans-serif lettering. Some were colorful paper signs, made up entirely of fonts that came for free on any Windows PC and were taped to the inside of the glass. A few were spelled out in the kind of reflective letter stickers one might use to put registration numbers on a fishing boat. All of the signs were small and hard to read from a moving car.

The large rollaway doors held no-parking signs, but no other markings, aside from dents, scrapes, and streaks of tire rubber.

"I think this is the wrong place," Brewster said. "I'm sure of it, in fact."

"Why?"

"Because we're looking for the back entrance to a theme park."

"The hidden back entrance."

"Yeah, but we just went through an intersection. I could see out in all four directions, and I didn't see any park. I didn't see a fence, a wall, the back of a big building. Nothing. Just more roads and more of these office buildings."

"I dunno, Brew. I think this is where Dad took us."

"I thought so, too, but I don't see how it can be."

"Maybe the park's underground or something. How should I know?"

"Maybe we should ask directions."

Mattie snorted. "Yeah. Great idea. *Pardon me, my good man. We're just two teenagers out for an unlicensed drive, which is certainly not weird. Can you please direct us to the secret entrance to the historical theme park that the employees aren't allowed to talk about?*" She drummed her fingers on the steering wheel. "Hey, Brewster, has anybody other than Mom and Dad ever mentioned the park to you?"

"No, but you just said why. They're not allowed to."

"The employees aren't allowed to, but nobody's ever mentioned it to me. Other kids. Adults. Our history teachers. You'd think someone would have said something about it. There'd at least be commercials for it somewhere."

"What are you saying, that there's no park? Mattie, we've been there."

"I'm just saying it's crazy that we've never heard of it other than from Mom and Dad."

"Yeah, that is weird, but it's only, like, the fifth weirdest thing about today."

"So far."

"I don't see how things could get any weirder at this point."

One of the large metal loading doors started to roll open as they approached. They drove past and Mattie glanced inside, idly curious as to what kind of business occupied the space. She stomped on the brake pedal. The car lurched to a stop with a chirp from the tires.

Brewster said, "What is your problem?"

Mattie said, "That's it."

"What's what?"

"There, that's the rear entrance."

"It can't be. We're in the middle of the office complex, physically it isn't . . ." Brewster trailed off as he looked into the open loading door. He and Mattie gaped at the empty interior, holding nothing but a framed poster for *The Prestige*, a metal door, and a smartphone taped to the wall.

"This is the place," Mattie said.

"I agree, but it can't be," Brewster said, as Mattie pulled the car into the building. The door closed behind them, and the lights came on.

"I agree, but it is."

They got out of the car and walked to the metal door. Mattie touched the screen of the smartphone. It lit up, displaying "23:26 4-6-1896."

Mattie said, "It's a time and a date."

Brewster shook his head. "That can't be right. Maybe it's a combination, disguised as a time and a date. But wait, no. This can't be the rear entrance to a theater, let alone a theme park. We've seen all four sides of this building, driven almost a full lap."

Mattie said, "Let's see if you're right."

She tried to turn the handle, but it wouldn't move. "Keys."

Brewster said, "Keys."

Mattie pulled her father's hefty key ring out of her pocket and set about methodically trying every key.

Brewster asked, "Man, what's Dad got all those keys for?"

"I know, right? And some of them are really weird. This one's glowing, this one's made of glass. Here's an iron one like from a cartoon dungeon."

After trying almost every key, one finally fit. With noticeable pride, she said, "Okay. That's the one. Now, let's see if you're right."

"Just open it."

She turned the handle and pulled the door open.

6.

Mattie stepped through the door first, Brewster following close behind. Their footsteps made a hollow sound as the twins stepped from the concrete floor of the storage space to the worn wooden floor of the backstage dressing room. Brewster stopped the door before it swung all the way closed. He and Mattie looked at the door, then at each other. Brewster grabbed a flimsy metal stand meant to hold an overturned top hat and wedged it in the doorframe to hold the door open. Mattie nodded her approval.

As with most things one recalls from childhood, the dressing room felt instantly familiar, yet completely different from how they remembered it. The smell of dust, wood polish, and the dove cages cut more sharply into their nasal passages. The clutter of old props and costumes felt more chaotic and oppressive. And, of course, everything seemed much smaller than it had when they'd last been there.

Brewster said, "We haven't stepped down at all, so we're not underground. We're still in the building."

Mattie nodded. "Looks like it."

The twins stalked quietly around the room, examining everything they saw in greater detail than they usually would, though neither of them could have told you what they were looking for, nor why they felt the need to be so quiet.

Mattie looked at the large, round light bulbs surrounding the makeup mirrors, with their visible glowing filaments. "Ugh, Edison bulbs. So ten years ago. They're so old, they've become outdated twice."

"So, what do we do now?" Brewster asked.

"We keep looking around. Hopefully, we'll get an idea."

"That's your best plan?"

"Your best plan was to ask me what to do."

"I never said I had a better idea, just that yours wasn't good."

They slowly worked their way down the length of the dressing room and rounded the corner into the area beside the stage. The curtains hung open, allowing the twins to see the empty theater. They stepped onto the stage, looking out into the cavernous space.

Brewster said, "This room is too big to fit in this building."

"Some buildings look bigger on the inside. Or maybe it's one of those things where the whole floor slants down without you knowing."

"That doesn't seem likely."

"No, it doesn't." Mattie shouted, "Phillip?"

"What are you doing?"

Mattie shrugged. "We're looking for answers, right? Unless he left a written explanation lying around, we're going to have to talk to Phillip, and we can't do that without letting him know we're here, so I figured I'd cut to the chase and shout for him."

"But he froze Mom and Dad! Just calling out to him like this seems risky."

"Calling out to him is risky. Not calling out to him is risky. Rushing around is risky. Wasting time debating it is risky. Doing anything is risky, and so is doing nothing. Playing it safe isn't going to help Mom and Dad. So what do you want more—to be safe, or to get our parents back?"

Brewster gritted his teeth at his sister, then shouted, "Phillip? You here, Phillip?"

Both kids shouted Phillip's name several times before deciding that he wasn't there. They walked down toward the seats, up the aisles, and into the darkened lobby.

"The place is empty," Brewster said.

"Yeah. I guess there are no shows tonight. Maybe we should go out into the park. Maybe we can find an employee who can tell us where Phillip might be."

They tried the front doors and found them locked, with no obvious way to unlock them. Mattie scouted around until she found an exit door. She unlocked it, and she and Brewster stepped out of the theater into an alleyway.

"It's dark out here," Mattie said. "And cold."

Brewster said, "We can't be outside. It was a lot brighter when we drove up a couple of minutes ago. We must be inside a building."

"Okay," Mattie said. "It's dark *in* here. And cold."

"And dirty."

A large pile of trash cluttered the alley: a great heap of rotting food, splintered wood, and hopelessly soiled fabric scraps. Unidentifiable fluids oozed from the pile and soaked into the gaps between the paving bricks. Putrid odors filled the twins' nostrils.

Mattie stepped back, away from the garbage. Brewster moved closer to her.

"No plastic bags," he said. "No straws, no drink cups. I guess if everything in the park's historically accurate, the trash would be, too."

Mattie said, "Come on, we gotta go."

Brewster shook his head. "Still, you'd think one of the guests would toss out a gum wrapper or something. They could have deliberately put this trash here to make the street feel more real. I don't think they'd do that."

"Brewster—"

"Why any theme park would include something like that, even if it's historically accurate—"

Mattie said, "We aren't in a theme park."

Brewster turned to face the same direction as his sister, out of the alley, toward the street. The road stretched off until it seemed to vanish in the distance. The whole way down, horse-drawn carriages clattered, driven by men in hats. On either side of the road, brick-and-timber buildings crowded each other, filling the space with barely enough room left over for people to walk. The view looked much the same in the other direction, except that the road came to a fork, splitting off two ways and winding out of sight.

The theater across the street disgorged a full house of patrons. Their clothing, facial hair, and what accents Mattie and Brewster could hear over the racket of hooves and wheels on the cobblestones all impeccably matched the surroundings.

Above them, occasional clouds blocked the view of the stars—not twinkling LEDs or glitter embedded in a painted ceiling. The stars were as they always appeared when viewed on a cold, mostly clear night, hours after sundown.

Without a word, Mattie and Brewster looked at each other, then went back in through the exit door to the lobby of the theater.

"What the hell is this?" Mattie asked.

"I don't know. This can't be real."

"We're in London! In the past!"

"Looks like it, Mattie, but that can't be right."

"Our parents are statues. Phillip disappeared. We somehow . . . I don't know, *transported* from a moving car back to our house in time to see ourselves leave, and now we are in friggin' Victorian London. Either everything we've ever been taught was wrong, or I've lost my mind and am imagining this."

"You haven't lost your mind."

"That's reassuring."

"I see all of this, too, so maybe I've lost my mind, and you're part of my hallucination."

"Brewster, we can argue about which one of us is crazy later. We need to find out what's going on here."

"Well, how do we do that? Your plan to confront Phillip doesn't seem to have worked out."

"Phillip's not the only person around here who knows Dad."

Mattie stormed back out to the alley, Brewster following behind. They crossed the street, dodging the carriages and wagons, trying not to step in any horse droppings as they made their way to the theater that bore the marquee advertising "The Great Gilbert and the Sensational Sid." Once they'd reached the opposite sidewalk, they made their way inside, pushing past the last few patrons trickling out onto the street.

Mattie squeezed past a man in a black wool suit and bowler hat, and a woman in a gown that cinched tight around her neck and flared wide at her ankles.

The twins drew their fair share of attention, more for barging through traffic than for their anachronistic clothing, but nobody tried to stop them or give them a hard time. Despite the different culture and historical period, London was still a city, and in many ways, all cities are the same. There is never a shortage of people dressed oddly. Indeed, openly gawking or acting uncomfortable is the greater infraction, as intolerance of other people's habits or tastes is a larger threat to the peace in an urban area than someone's outfit not looking *quite right*.

"I'm not sure about this," Brewster said. "These guys knew Dad, but they didn't seem to like him that much."

Mattie shrugged. "Yeah, but they didn't seem to like Phillip much either, so if they aren't willing to help Dad, maybe they'll be willing to squeal on Phillip."

"Mattie, I don't think that logic works."

"My logic has worked well enough to get us this far."

"Is that a good thing?"

The twins blended in with the hubbub, but only for a moment or two. As the final stragglers left, it became obvious that soon Mattie and Brewster would be the only ones remaining in the lobby aside from the ushers, who would definitely tell them to leave.

The kids bolted into the theater proper before anyone could even try to stop them.

A couple of ushers in red velvet uniforms walked up and down the rows of seats. The closed curtains blocked any view of the stage.

"The show's over," Mattie said. "Where would the magicians be?"

Brewster shrugged. "Backstage, in their dressing room, I guess."

One of the ushers said, "Oi, you two. Show's over. Time to go."

Mattie said, "Yeah, we know. We're just looking for something."

"What?"

"This," Mattie replied, and sprinted down the aisle toward a door set into the wall next to the stage. Brewster followed her, and the ushers chased them. Mattie cranked on the knob, yanked the door open, and lurched inside. Brewster followed, and the two of them pulled the door closed, bracing themselves against the doorjamb, holding the door shut against the usher's attempts to open it, Mattie by pulling on the doorknob, and Brewster by pulling on Mattie's wrists.

"That's not really helping," Mattie grunted.

Brewster let go. Immediately, the door started to pull open.

"It was helping," Mattie yelped. "It was helping!"

Brewster grabbed her wrists and pulled. The door rattled, occasionally opening by a half inch or so only to slam back as the twins tried harder to keep the ushers at bay. Beyond the door, the ushers shouted threats in increasingly harsher terms.

"What now?" Brewster asked.

"We keep them out there while we stay in here," Mattie said.

"And after that?"

Mattie attempted to sound relaxed. "Try to focus on the now. Live in the moment. You'll be happier."

"Not for long."

"See, that's what I'm talking about."

Without warning, the door stopped rattling. All conversation on the other side of the door ceased. Mattie and Brewster kept pulling. Brewster looked at Mattie, confused by their pursuers' apparent disappearance.

"It's a trick," Mattie said.

The doorknob detached from the door. The twins staggered backward several steps to keep their balance. The door fell away like a large domino, making a deep *whump* as it hit the floor. Brewster let go, leaving Mattie with the doorknob in her hand.

Instead of the theater, the space beyond the doorjamb was a vast, black emptiness.

A booming male voice said, "Correct! It is a trick! A rather excellent trick. We're so very gratified that you've noticed."

The wall around the doorframe also fell away from the twins, as did the brick walls on either side of them. They spun around to face whoever was addressing them, just in time to see the last remaining wall of the backstage area fall away and all of the furnishings, props, and rigging collapse into dust, which disappeared as if drifting on a breeze, leaving the two of them standing in a black void.

Mattie shouted, "Where are you?"

The voice said, "Oh dear. Our intruders can't see."

A second man's voice said, "Yeah, well, of course, they can't. It's bloody dark in here, isn't it?"

"Happily, we can remedy that."

With a sound like fingers snapping, only amplified hundreds of times, the world seemed flooded with brilliant white light. A glossy white floor and a matte white ceiling extended far into the distance, where they terminated not in walls, but with what looked like thin support posts. Very far away, Brewster and Mattie saw the slightest hint of people, many people, standing side by side in regularly spaced pairs, surrounding them. The twins shielded their eyes, a futile exercise, as there was no one visible light source. Still, they peered into the distance, trying to get a better idea of who the people all around them might be.

"It looks as if they still can't see," the first voice said. "Perhaps we should bring things in closer."

"Yeah," the second voice agreed. "And if that doesn't work, get them some bifocals or something."

The support posts seemed to slide toward them without any sound or visible tracks. As they did, the distant people also appeared to approach, gliding forward faster than the posts without moving their legs or feet. It became clear that what appeared to be posts were in fact frames around large mirrors, and the people surrounding Mattie and Brewster were simply their own reflections. Some of the mirrors spun as they approached, turning to tuck in behind faster-moving mirrors, and causing all of the reflections to move to one side or the other, offering the twins a kaleidoscopic view of themselves, from every angle, standing together, looking frightened and confused.

The mirrors stopped after closing to a three-meter radius around the kids. Mattie and Brewster turned in opposite directions, looking for a way out, but found only their reflections. Mattie gritted her teeth and threw the doorknob as hard as she could at one of the mirrors, aiming at her own image as a guide. The knob and its reflection whizzed toward each other in a blur of motion. When they met, instead of an impact and the sound of shattering glass, the knobs seemed to pass through each other. Mattie had only a fraction of a second to recognize that the doorknob she'd thrown at her reflection was quickly approaching her real body. She turned to the left, shielded her head with her arms, and pulled her right leg up just in time for the knob to hit her hard on the side of her thigh with a dull thud.

Mattie cried out, "Ow! What the hell, man?!"

The first male voice said, "Your accents and vocabulary mark you as Americans. Your clothing suggests that you're visiting here from more than just a different country and continent. What do you want?"

Brewster said, "We'd be happy to tell you, but first, we wanna know who's asking."

The mirrors began to spin, causing the twins' reflections to slide in and out of view. After a few spins the mirrors slowed, but the reflections had changed. Now, instead of Mattie and Brewster looking alarmed and more than a little sick, two men appeared in the mirrors, both wearing black tuxedos, top hats, silk capes, and white gloves, with which they held black walking sticks with white tips. One had a well-oiled handlebar mustache; the other sported a mustache, a Van Dyke, and a monocle. The twins recognized the reflections surrounding them as the Great Gilbert and the Sensational Sid.

The reflection of the magician with the monocle said, "I am the renowned prestidigitator referred to in hushed, reverent tones as *Sid*. The well-dressed, yet delightfully plainspoken chap to my left is my associate and good friend Gilbert, but I suspect you knew that, as it is our theater in which you are trespassing. Now, who, exactly are you?"

"I'm Mattie. This is my brother, Brewster."

Brewster added, "Our parents are Martin and Gwen Banks. We met you once, about six years ago."

The magicians' stern expressions melted away to astonishment. They both approached the kids. As they moved, so did their reflections, but as Sid and Gilbert stepped out of the mirror in front of the twins, their reflections disappeared from all of the others, replaced by a reflection of all four of the people in the room, standing together.

"You've gotten so big!" Gilbert said, delighted.

"Yes," Sid said. "You're practically grownups! To us, it was only a couple of years ago that you interrupted our show."

"Sorry about that," Brewster said.

Gilbert said, "Don't be. As I remember, the audience ate it up. How old are you now, if you don't mind me asking?"

"Sixteen," Brewster said.

Sid shook his head. "Time flies when it flows asynchronously."

"It does," Gilbert agreed. "It really does. How's your mum? It's been too long since we've seen Gwen."

Mattie said, "She can't move. She's frozen, like a statue. Dad, too, and we don't know why."

"Or how it's even possible," Brewster said.

"That's why we're here," Mattie said. "We're hoping you can explain."

"Explain how your parents are frozen?" Gilbert asked.

"That, and everything else."

"Including how you just did all of these tricks with the mirrors."

Sid smiled. "If I'm understanding you properly, and I flatter myself that I am, it's your hope that we can explain not only why your parents are stuck, but how their predicament, and all of the other things you've experienced in getting here, including teleportation and time travel, is possible."

"Yes," Brewster and Mattie said, in unison.

"Well, all right then. I'm pleased to report that we can, in fact, explain, as you say, *everything else*."

Gilbert said "Yeah, but it's going to take a while."

Sid nodded. "As one might reasonably expect."

7.

Mattie and Brewster sat to Gilbert's right on a tufted velvet bench seat. They both held on for dear life and leaned as far away from him as they could, making room for his elbows as he used both hands to manhandle both a tiller and a throttle lever.

The horseless carriage's three oversized bicycle wheels fought back against Gilbert's attempts to steer, sliding down into the ruts between paving stones instead of rolling over them. The squawking leaf-spring suspension exaggerated the bumps instead of softening them, and the high position of the bench gave the twins the impression that they were perched on top of the vehicle, rather than riding in it.

"You call this thing a car?" Mattie shouted.

Gilbert didn't answer, as he was concentrating on steering the three-wheeled beast through the darkness of the gaslit London streets.

Sid shouted, "It's not just a car. It's an electric car!" He'd volunteered to give up his customary place on the bench. For his kindness, he got to ride on the back, where there was no seat. He braced his feet on the frame, straddling the single rear wheel. His fingers dug into the seat back, and his tuxedo tails flapped in the wind as he suspended his body above the spinning tire. If his right foot slipped, he would surely fall from the back of the car, landing on and, essentially, getting peeled out on by the tire as he went. It was a grim prospect, but preferable to his left foot slipping, which would have the same result, with the added problem of getting tangled in the drive belt.

"It's called the Riker Electric. Well ahead of its time, and not just because it shares its name with the first officer of the *Enterprise*."

"They had electric cars back . . . now?" Brewster asked.

"Time travel makes it hard to frame a sentence sometimes," Gilbert grunted, holding the throttle lever steady with his left hand while using his right to wrestle the tiller as the car rounded a corner, its solid rubber tires sliding on the wet stones. "You get used to it. And, yeah, they had electric cars. Of course, we modified this one. Put in a Tesla drivetrain. Can't go above ten percent throttle or else the torque'll rip the frame apart, but still, it's good to know we have the power if we need it."

A horse hitched to a hansom cab bucked and whinnied as the Riker passed. The man holding the reins shouted something, but he was already too far behind them to be audible.

Mattie asked, "How is this better than a carriage?"

"It very much is not," Sid said. "But it draws ever so much more attention, which is, to us, the most important thing. We'll explain further when we arrive home."

They creaked and clattered and squeaked their way through the darkened streets without talking, as conversation required too much effort to be worthwhile. They only broke what was passing for the silence when Gilbert pulled back on the throttle lever, slowing the Riker Electric.

"Are we there?" Brewster asked.

"Almost," Gilbert answered. "Just a block or so left to go. I have to slow down now to reduce wear on the leather brake pads."

The Riker Electric tricycle nearly coasted to a stop by the waterfront on its own. Gilbert stomped on the brake pedal at the last moment, bringing the vehicle to a halt.

They all climbed down from the contraption, and Mattie and Brewster followed the two magicians as they walked toward the docks.

Sid used a large iron key, the kind that one sees in old cartoons or movies about dungeons or pirates, and slotted it into a padlock holding a metal gate shut. Turning the key, operating the latch, and opening the gate each emitted a separate, unique, and irritating squeak.

Inside the gate, all the kids could see was a dock leading into the darkened river, a thick rope tied to a mooring cleat stretching up into the black night sky, and what appeared to be some machinery wired to a rusted old searchlight.

Brewster squinted into the darkness. "So do you two live on a houseboat, or are we going to have to row across the river?"

Gilbert opened an electrical panel and smiled at Brewster. "Neither," he said, and threw a large Dr. Frankenstein–style knife switch.

With a loud mechanical clunk and a dangerous-sounding buzz, the searchlight sprang to life. A blinding white beam of light shot straight up into the sky four hundred feet above them, where it illuminated a huge airship, painted with the message "Go See the Great Gilbert and the Sensational Sid: Professional Purveyors of Authentic Amazement: Always to a Higher Standard Than the Competition." On either side of the word *competition*, caricatures of Sid and Gilbert stood on the top hats of an annoyed-looking Martin and Phillip.

Gilbert threw a second knife switch. Up on the airship, a basket similar to one that would hang beneath a hot air balloon began to descend from the gondola.

"You live in a blimp?" Mattie asked.

"Dirigible," Sid said. "A blimp derives its shape from internal gas pressure. A dirigible, such as ours, boasts a rigid internal structure."

"But you live in it?"

Sid nodded, crisply. "Affirmative, young lady. It's good for the image, you see? We live in a technological marvel that impresses and frightens the populace. We commute to work in a technological marvel that impresses and frightens the populace. Then, at work, we perform feats that impress and frighten the populace. Maintaining our image at all times helps us stand out from the competition."

"Dad and Phillip."

"Yes."

"And do you?" Brewster asked. "Stand out from Dad, I mean."

"Bit of a sore spot, that," Gilbert said. "Your father and Phillip do get more attention at the moment, but we'll figure a way to upstage them."

"How are they getting more attention than you with your dirigible and your electric three-wheeler?"

"By never showing their faces. As far as the audience can see, your father and Phillip never leave their theater. Martin goes home to you lot, and Phillip goes to his shed without ever setting foot outside."

"They can't be bothered to provide a convincing cover story," Sid grumbled. "And because whatever they're up to takes place in secret, the public assumes that it must be something far more impressive than our dirigible, simply because they don't know what it is."

The wicker basket touched down. Sid opened a door built into the side and motioned for the kids to enter.

Brewster asked, "Is it safe?"

Sid stepped into the basket himself. "Does it seem likely that I would ride in it if it weren't?"

Mattie said, "You just rode on the back of that motorized tricycle."

Gilbert laughed. "The lady's got you there, Sid. Look, we promise, it's safe. Besides, you can't tell me you don't want to see the inside of our dirigible."

Mattie stepped into the basket. After a moment's hesitation, Brewster followed. Gilbert stepped in as well, closing the door behind them. He waved his white-tipped ebony walking stick toward the electrical box. One of the knife switches appeared to throw itself, causing the basket to rise.

"Okay, when are you going to tell us how you're doing this stuff?" Instead of seeming awestruck, or even impressed, Mattie sounded irritated.

Sid and Gilbert exchanged a concerned look, then Gilbert said, "In a bit. We'll tell you everything we can. Enough, at least, for all this stuff you've seen to make sense. First, I think you two should tell us what's been going on with your parents so we can figure out how to help. Fair enough?"

Neither Mattie nor Brewster said anything. Riding in a wicker basket as it traveled up a rope to a dirigible hundreds of feet over the ground didn't leave either of them in a chatty mood.

An aperture like the iris in an expensive camera, only much larger and made of what looked like copper, opened in the floor of the gondola above them. Warm, yellow light spilled out, drawing the attention of the twins. They stared up into the light like moths approaching a flame and remained silent as the basket rose through the opening, which closed behind them, leaving nothing but the guide rope hanging in the cold night air.

Mattie and Brewster sat in the cramped but sumptuously decorated Victorian parlor built inside the dirigible's gondola, on a small red velvet couch with gracefully turned wooden legs, holding tiny, delicate china cups full of hot chocolate as they told Sid and Gilbert their entire story. They started with Phillip's mysterious appearance in their home and ended with their arrival at Gilbert and Sid's theater. They took turns talking, and each made sure that their sibling left out no detail, no matter how weird.

Sid and Gilbert sat opposite them in armchairs that matched the couch. They listened carefully, asking the occasional question to clarify some specific detail or other, and requested that Brewster and Mattie write down the date and time when their parents got frozen, along with their street address. Once the twins had disgorged the entire tale, the magicians excused themselves, saying that they needed to discuss what they'd heard. They opened a hatch in the ceiling, climbed up a telescoping brass ladder, and closed the hatch behind them.

After several seconds of silence, Mattie said, "I guess there's a second floor."

"I guess," Brewster said.

Mattie frowned at him and clarified her point. "Clearly, it must extend up into the balloon."

"Clearly."

"Look, it's not like you've ever been up in a dirigible before."

"What? I'm agreeing with you!"

"But you're doing it in a way to make it sound like I'm stupid."

"Why would I agree with someone who I thought was stupid? That's stupid."

"So now you admit you think I'm stupid."

"Yeah, now, about this."

The twins heard the hatch above them open and instantly stopped bickering, watching in silence as Sid and Gilbert climbed down the ladder to stand before them.

Sid said, "We've thoroughly discussed the issues at hand, and we have a few specific points we'd like to address. First, we want you to know how deeply impressed we are with the both of you. You've shown great courage, adaptability, and teamwork, aside from the immature, pointless argument we heard clearly through the hatch."

Brewster said, "Thank you."

"Yes. Thanks," Mattie said. "And, he started it."

"I did not!"

Gilbert said, "You did, mate."

Sid nodded. "Indeed, but it's quite understandable. You've both been under a tremendous amount of stress. And you are, after all, siblings. We often take that sort of thing out on the people who are closest to us."

"Because they're the ones who're there."

"Quite right, Gilbert. Quite right. At any rate, we've decided to assist you in any way we can."

"You'll help us get Phillip?" Mattie asked.

"That depends," Sid said, "on what you mean by *get*. If you mean that we will help you find Phillip so that he may explain himself, then absolutely, yes, we will. If, you mean that we'll assist you in tracking him down and exacting some sort of grim retribution, then I'm afraid you'll be disappointed. We simply don't believe that Phillip would ever deliberately harm your parents."

Brewster said, "We know what we saw."

Gilbert said, "Sorry, kid, but it seems to me that you didn't see anything. What you said is that you heard some things, then found Phillip gone and your parents doing their Pompeii act."

Sid held up a finger to silence Gilbert and the twins. "We know what you two believe, and we aren't claiming that you don't have your reasons. Suffice it to say that the discrepancy between what you believe of Phillip and what we know of him is part of what, to the bottom of which, we're anxious to get. Acceptable?"

Mattie and Brewster nodded.

"Splendid. Toward that end, we are now going to explain, more or less, everything."

"Everything?" Brewster asked.

Gilbert nodded. "Yup. All of it. The time travel, the teleportation, your parents' condition, the lot. The full *welcome to the desert of the real* treatment."

The four of them remained in an awkward silence for a moment, until Mattie said, "Great! Good! We'd like that, wouldn't we, Brewster?"

"Yeah, totally. Bring it on."

Sid said, "I assure you, my young friend, *on* is exactly where we intend to bring *it.*"

"Just not here," Gilbert said. "There's something we want to show you first."

Sid led the way, climbing the ladder while the other three waited below. Mattie followed at a brisk pace until her head rose above the level of the hatch, where she froze. Sid took her by the hand and pulled her the rest of the way up, as Mattie was too stunned by what she saw to offer more than a half-hearted attempt at climbing any further herself. Brewster followed, concentrating on the ladder in his hands instead of his sister's behavior. As he reached the top, he cast his eyes around for a handhold on the floor above, saw the room the floor was part of, and his mind ground to a halt, choking on the task of processing the data coming in from his optic nerves.

As Mattie had theorized before, the ladder and hatch led from the gondola into the interior of the envelope, the cigar-shaped fabric structure that usually contained the lighter-than-air gas and held the dirigible aloft. One would normally expect to see large bladders full of gas secured to a metal framework, but there were none. Gigantic hoop-shaped trusses, like those that might support the lighting rig at a large rock concert, only turned on their sides, ran the length of the interior of the envelope, reducing in size as they formed the tapered ends. They defined the shape of the dirigible from the outside, and the boundaries of what appeared to be Gilbert and Sid's living quarters inside.

Toward the rear of the envelope they saw a charming two-story Victorian house behind a prim cluster of rosebushes and an impeccable lawn. Up at the nose, there stood a two-story stucco McMansion, painted in a manner meant to make it look like an ancient Tuscan villa, but which actually made it look like a ten-year-old Olive Garden. The swimming pool, hot tub, outdoor kitchen, bar, and what appeared to be a DJ station all had a similar, and similarly inappropriate, faux-antique finish.

Brewster said, "This can't be! It's a lighter-than-air ship. Houses are heavier than air!"

"And the swimming pool!" Mattie said. "How? How does this all stay up without any helium?"

Sid stood straight and tall, his arms spread wide, and in the high-pitched voice of a cartoon gnome, said, "What makes you think there's no helium?"

"Don't pay attention to him," Gilbert said in a perfectly normal voice. "He's just messing with you."

Sid waved the end of his walking stick in small circles in front of his throat, then in his regular voice said, "Terribly, sorry. Couldn't resist. Just a bit of dirigible humor. The air's perfectly safe in here. Nothing but oxygen and nitrogen, just like on the ground."

"Only less smelly," Gilbert added, walking to the edge of the lawn to look down at the city below.

Sid joined him. "Yes, thankfully."

Mattie and Brewster followed them, their steps growing slower and more tentative as they got closer to the edge.

The envelope itself seemed mostly transparent. The fabric that looked so solid and opaque from the outside let in a tremendous amount of light, providing a spectacular view of London by gaslight. The seams and folds of the canvas and the outlines of the advertising mural painted on the outside remained barely visible but tended to fade away as the twins instead focused on the panoramic view.

Gilbert waved his ebony walking stick. Two of the poolside chairs slid across the floor and stopped right behind Brewster and Mattie.

"Please," Gilbert said, "have a seat."

Brewster and Mattie sat down. Two more chairs slid over of their own accord, and Gilbert and Sid sat down opposite the twins.

"You see, kids," Gilbert began, "there are people in the world who can do things. Things that most people believe impossible. Things that would amaze the staunchest skeptic. Sid and I are two such people. So are your parents, and so is Phillip."

"Magic," Mattie said. "You're trying to tell us that you can do magic."

"You don't buy it? After all the stuff you've seen, everything that's happened, right up to how you got the chairs you're sitting in, and where those chairs are, are you gonna tell me magic isn't real?"

Brewster shook his head, while Mattie mumbled, "I guess not."

Sid said, "Well you should, because magic is not real. I mean, granted, we call what we do *magic* because that's the only way most people can make any sort of sense of it, including ourselves. But, in truth, what you'd think of as magic is just a lot of old superstitions. All that you've seen, the spells, the tricks, it's all just a friendly veneer placed over a more complex and disquieting reality."

"What is it?" Mattie asked. "What's going on?"

Sid said, "You, your parents, your home, your school, this planet, the solar system, the entire human race, and everything it has ever encountered is part of a computer program."

Brewster said, "I've heard that theory before."

"Sure you have," Gilbert said. "I'd bet your parents went out of their way to point it out. It'll make things easier to explain later."

"Or indeed, right now," Sid continued. "And like most people, when presented with this concept, you either disregarded it out of hand or asked yourself if it would change anything about how you go about your life."

"To which the answer is, *not one bit*," Gilbert said. "Just because you're the product of an algorithm doesn't mean you can get out of paying the rent."

"Quite. But Gilbert and I are here to tell you that it isn't just a fun idea. It's a fact. And it does affect how you will live the rest of your lives because it is what has enabled your parents' predicament, Phillip's disappearance, your day trip to the Victorian era, and your current position, four hundred feet above London in a lighter-than-air ship that is, very much, not."

Mattie studied the two men, looking for a sign that they might be joking. "You're saying we're in a computer program. How'd we get in it?"

"You were born in it," Sid said. "You're part of it. Everything you see, including each other, is a collection of potentialities, described by a set of numbers in a file. By finding and changing those numbers, or writing programs to do it for us, we can alter the world in some fairly surprising ways, as you've learned in the past few hours. We call the things we can do *magic*, as a sort of shorthand, but there's nothing magical about it. It's just coding."

Brewster squinted at the magicians. "And that's how all of this was done? Our parents, Phillip, transporting back to the house, coming back in time, this blimp?"

"Dirigible," Sid and Gilbert both said.

Sid said, "It's confusing, I know, but think about it. If you're an asset in a computer program, then everything about you is just information. Who you are, what you are, where you are, when you are—it's all just numbers, numbers that can be edited."

"How do you know this?" Mattie asked.

Gilbert smiled. "See, there's this file floating around out there. There are loads of copies, hiding away in various places on the internet where no reasonable person would ever look. We looked."

"We two met at university in late 2005 and dropped out to try our hands at a tech startup. We had an idea for a search engine that would help harness the power of serendipity."

Gilbert took over. "See, the problem with searching the internet is that the page you find's usually the one you *want*, but seldom the one you *need*. You punch in the words you think of to take you to the page you want, and it usually tells you what you kind of already knew, because that's what you searched for."

"Typically," Sid said, "one must click a few links, sometimes at random, to find the information one didn't know he or she vitally needs. We were attempting to create an engine that would bypass the pages full of things you already know and instead take you directly to the file you needed."

Brewster asked, "And your search engine took you to the file that proves the world's a program?"

"Yes," Gilbert said. "While we were running a test search for how to darn socks, so the test has to be counted as a failure. I mean, I guess you could use the file to repair the socks, but you'd have to admit that the engine's result was overkill."

Sid shrugged. "I'd classify it as a calibration error."

Mattie said, "And now you have the power to travel through time, mess with the laws of physics, and beam yourselves around like on *Star Trek*?"

Both magicians nodded. Gilbert said, "Yes."

Brewster furrowed his brow. "Who wrote the program? What does it do?"

Gilbert said, "We don't know."

"What do you mean, you don't know?"

Sid nodded. "I know that sounds odd. The first question everybody asks upon being told any of this is, *Who wrote the program and what does it do?* And the first answer they get is, *We don't know*, leading inexorably to the first argument they have about the program, which is invariably over how can we not have already ascertained those seemingly basic facts."

"If this argument is so annoying to you, then why haven't you just figured out the answers?"

Gilbert said, "It's not that easy, is it? Just because we're part of the program doesn't mean we have access to every part of it, any more than a can of cola in an airliner's beverage cart can program the autopilot. We don't have access to any of the code, just the files that define the assets. All we know about the program itself is what we can learn from the world it creates, and trying to get anything from that is like trying to figure out who wrote Microsoft Word by looking at a single printed page of someone's letter to their aunt."

Mattie said, "So you haven't figured out what the program does, or why, or for who, but you *have* figured out how to use it to give yourselves superpowers."

Gilbert shrugged. "Are you saying our priorities are out of whack?"

"No. I think that's pretty much what I'd do. So what happened? Somehow Mom and Dad found out your secret, or got caught up with you somehow, and had to be silenced?"

"What?" Sid asked. "Heavens, no! Not at all! Your parents didn't discover our secret. It's their secret, too! They found the file all on their own, both of them. They're just like us!"

"Only more so," Gilbert said. "If you think we're weird, wait until you get a load of how they live."

"We know how they live," Mattie said. "We live with them! They don't have any kind of magical powers."

Sid stared wide-eyed at Mattie. "How the devil can you say that, after everything you've witnessed today?"

Gilbert said, "Now, now, Sid. You might want to calm down a bit. These two have been through an awful lot."

"That's precisely my point! They've been through a lot today, and all of it bolsters the conclusion that what we're telling them is true."

Mattie said, "What we've seen is something weird happening *to* Mom and Dad, and a bunch of other weird stuff happening *around* them. Not them doing any of it. You're telling us that everything we know about our own parents is wrong, and we're just supposed to believe you and ignore what we've seen all our lives?"

Brewster arched an eyebrow. "Besides, you want us to take your word for it that our parents have superpowers and lied to us about it, but when we tell you that Phillip froze them, you don't wanna buy it."

Gilbert said, "Kids, it's just that we know Phillip—"

"Yeah, and we know what we saw."

Gilbert said, "You saw a closed door, while stuff happened in the next room."

Mattie said, "But we heard—"

"Mumbling," Gilbert interrupted. "Then yelling, but you couldn't make out any words."

Brewster asked, "But if you can travel in time and space like you say, you can go to the moment Phillip froze Mom and Dad. We can all go, and you'll see that he did it, and we can all find out why."

Sid nodded. "Logical, young man. Unquestionably logical. That is, in fact, the only reasonable course of action."

They all stared at each other for a long moment, until Mattie said, "Then let's go."

Gilbert said, "We can't."

"You just said you can go anywhere at any time!"

"Yeah," Gilbert said, "but we can't go there."

Sid said, "The problem is, you see, we already tried, a few minutes ago, when we left you alone down in the gondola and we came up here to talk. The very first thing we did was try to go to the event to see what happened."

"And?" Brewster asked.

"It's like I told you," Gilbert said. "We can't. Somebody set up a redirect. It's all just computer programming, and someone put some code in place to keep anyone from witnessing whatever happened. If anyone tries to go to that exact time and place, they get bounced back to where they started."

Mattie said, "That just proves that Phillip is covering his tracks."

Gilbert shook his head. "It proves nothing, it just suggests. And, anyway, we have no evidence that Phillip set the redirect—it could've been anyone. Also, there are loads of reasons, other than to cover their tracks, that someone could make a redirect like that."

Sid said, "I'm afraid, Mattie, that every word in your sentence was incorrect, save for the *that* at the beginning, which, to look on the bright side, was spot on. Just to be clear, we don't doubt any part of your story. We believe every word you've said to us is accurate. We just don't quite agree with the conclusion that Phillip has hurt your parents. Your parents are frozen, but we don't know that they're hurt. And even if they are, and even if Phillip did it, it's possible that he hurt them by accident."

"All too possible," Gilbert added. "Likely, even."

"But you'll help us?" Brewster asked.

"Of course. We want to get to the bottom of what's going on with Phillip. We think the world of your mother and wish no specific ill on your father. We'd never even think of turning away their children in a time of need."

"Besides," Gilbert said. "What's the point of living in Victorian England if you can't solve a mystery now and then?"

Mattie sprung up from her seat. "Great! Let's go."

Sid and Gilbert both put up their hands to slow her down. Gilbert said, "No, love, I'm afraid if we're going to help you, we'll have to insist on doing it our way."

"But our parents are frozen and Phillip's getting away! We don't have any time to waste."

Sid said, "We have all of the time to waste. We are time travelers. We can travel through time. We're in Victorian England at the moment. The supposed confrontation between your parents and Phillip will not even occur until more than a hundred years from now."

Brewster said, "It seems like you could use that as an excuse to put off doing anything you don't want to do."

Sid said, "Your description is needlessly insulting, dear chap. We prefer to think of it as *an opportunity* to put off doing anything we don't want to do. Or, as in this case, to delay taking action until we've had time to think things through. To plan. To prepare."

Gilbert said, "For example, it's going to take a day to train the two of you in how to use magic."

Mattie and Brewster looked at the two magicians, thinking about what Gilbert had said and trying to determine if he was serious. When neither Gilbert nor Sid started laughing or yelling *psych!*, Mattie said, "I think that's a good idea."

Brewster nodded. "Yes. I agree. But, why do you two think it's a good idea?"

Gilbert said, "Because we're going to be investigating, aren't we? And when you investigate, you learn things that other people are trying to keep you from learning. It could get gritty, if you know what I'm saying."

"Yes," Sid said. "Should something malodorous make high-velocity contact with what you Americans colloquially refer to as *the fan,* we'll be much more comfortable knowing you have the ability to defend yourselves. And the whole process will be much more convenient if you can fly and teleport yourselves to and fro, rather than depending on us for transportation, like two impeccably dressed ponies. So what say you? Will you accept our assistance, even if it means enduring the inconvenience of delaying a day or so while we bestow magical powers upon you?"

Mattie tried hard to hide her excitement which, as usual, only made it more obvious. "Yeah, I think taking a day to think about things is probably wise."

Gilbert said, "We thought you might."

9.

The twins slept fitfully that night, their rest disturbed by a mix of anxiety over their parents' condition, excitement over the amazing things they hoped to learn the next day, and discomfort from their "beds." The semi-transparent skin of the dirigible kept them warm and sheltered from the elements, but their small air mattresses did little to make the brick pavers around the magicians' swimming pool more comfortable.

Mattie awakened first, but immediately woke up Brewster with her groaning. They both sat up, twisting and stretching, and squinting in the filtered sunlight. As their eyes adjusted, they took in their surroundings, and the groaning and grumbling stopped. They kicked their way out of their sleeping bags, rolled off their inflatable mattresses, and staggered, still only partially awake, closer to the edge of the patio. There, the floor gave way to the metal supports and semi-transparent fabric of the dirigible's envelope, and the panoramic view of Dickensian London stretched out beneath them.

They stood there silently, processing what they saw and scratching various itches until a distant voice shouted, "Morning, ye wee sproggies! Welcome to the land of the wakeful!"

Brewster and Mattie turned and squinted. Gilbert stood behind the burners of the outdoor kitchen beyond the swimming pool. He wore a black silk bathrobe over what appeared to be white silk pajamas, smiling at the twins while his hands managed several griddle- and frying pan-related tasks at once.

"View's a lot different in daylight, isn't it? You can see the smoke and the filth a lot better. Come, sit down. Breakfast will be done in a bit. In the meantime, we have orange juice or tea."

Behind them, at the far end of the dirigible's envelope, Sid shambled to the second-story window of his Victorian home in a pair of baggy shorts and a stretched-out T-shirt. "My apologies, kids," he shouted, leaning out the window. "I should have warned you that Gilbert is the absolute worst sort of morning person."

"So I wake up with gusto. Arrest me!"

"You laugh, but someday, we'll get that legislation passed, and we will arrest you and the rest of you chipper morning larks. You'll be the first to have your back against the wall, my friend. I'll see to it."

Gilbert smiled at the kids as they climbed up onto barstools on the opposite side of the concrete bar top. He leaned around the kids to shout at Sid. "You'll try, but we morning people will be long gone before the rest of you have even gotten out of bed."

Mattie and Brewster poured themselves each a cup of tea. Gilbert pushed a plate piled high with bacon toward them. They descended on it with such ferocity that Gilbert jerked his hand away in fear for his fingers.

"What are you making?" Mattie asked.

"Just a quick fry up. Nothing fancy," Gilbert answered. "You two like beans on toast?"

"Don't know," Brewster said. "We haven't ever had it."

Gilbert asked, "You like beans?"

Brewster said, "Yeah."

Gilbert asked, "You like toast?"

Mattie said, "Yeah."

"Then I'm prepared to proceed." He nodded and turned back to his cooktop. "How'd you sleep?"

The kids both said, "Fine," but they said it slowly, in a tone that descended in pitch over time, and their voices harmonized to form a note in a minor key.

"Worried about your folks, were you?"

"Yeah," Brewster said.

Mattie frowned, thought for a moment, and said, "And, sleeping out under the stars was a nice idea, but sleeping on those air mattresses wasn't. They aren't the most comfortable things in the world."

"Sorry about that." Gilbert jerked a thumb over his shoulder at his house. "These may look like full-sized houses, but they need to fit inside a dirigible envelope. They're one bedroom, one bath. We never really planned to have any sleepovers up here."

Mattie said, "Yeah, we get that, but if you have magic, couldn't you have made a couple of real beds?"

Gilbert smiled at her. "Big, complicated objects are tricky. It can be done, but it takes a lot of programming. No, the best I coulda done on short notice would've been computer-generated models of beds, and they would be just as hard as the concrete. I'll look into finding some better padding for you."

Sid emerged from his Victorian at the far end of the envelope, still in his shorts and T-shirt, but having added a thick pair of woolen socks instead of slippers, his monocle hanging from a chain around his neck and, for some reason, wearing his white gloves. He carried a tiny plastic laptop computer about the size of a sheet of paper, but nearly two inches thick. Colorful stickers covered the laptop's lid. In his other hand, he carried his white-tipped ebony cane. His black silk top hat sat incongruously on his head tilted at an angle that wasn't so much *jaunty* as *haphazard*.

"Morning, all," he said, putting his computer down on the counter and pulling up a stool. "Hope my friend's nauseating cheerfulness hasn't put you off the breakfast he's making."

"I'm being hospitable. You should try it."

Sid wedged his monocle under his brow and opened the lid of his stubby plastic laptop. "Yeah, well. While you play short-order cook, I'm going to bestow our young friends with life-changing magical powers. Which do you think they'll appreciate more? Hmmm?"

Gilbert turned around with two steaming plates, each piled high with fried sausage, fried ham, fried eggs, and the beans and toast, which might have been fried as well, for all the kids knew. "Don't underestimate how magical and life-altering a good breakfast can be."

He put the plates down in front of the twins, who barely took the time to thank him before they started shoveling the food into their mouths.

Mattie said, "Hmm, thanks! This is so good!"

Gilbert smiled. "Don't mention it."

"So," Mattie continued, between mouthfuls of food. "What kind of powers are we talking about?"

"Yeah," Brewster said, covering his food-filled mouth with his hand. "I was wondering that myself."

"Indeed," Sid said, "I suspected you might. I, my young friends, intend to set you up with what our friends of the Hebrew faith have been known to call *the whole schmeer*. When we're done, you should be able to defend yourselves against pretty much anybody. To do any less would be irresponsible, given the circumstances."

Gilbert cracked two more eggs into the frying pan. "Are you sure we want to get into this so quick?"

"You make a valid point. Since we can bend time itself to our will, we can afford to take things slowly. But on the other hand, I'm sure the kids here would prefer get their parents sorted sooner rather than later." Sid turned toward the twins. "Am I right?"

Brewster and Mattie agreed as heartily as they could with mouths full of food.

"Good," Sid said. "So, we might as well get cracking."

He pointed his walking stick at Mattie. She stopped eating and stared at its slightly off-white tip.

"I should make one thing absolutely clear before we go any further. It's of the utmost importance that you both understand"—he pointed at the cane's white tip—"this isn't real ivory."

"What?" Mattie asked.

"On my wand here, the tip and the handle. We designed the canes to look like oversized magic wands. They're made of period-correct materials, so the ends are ivory, but I promise you, no elephants were harmed or even slightly inconvenienced. We replicated the ivory using a copying program."

"Oh," Mattie said. "Cool. Good to know."

Brewster stroked his chin. "Wait a minute. If you can make fake ivory that's exactly like the real thing, couldn't you sell it for a huge profit?"

Gilbert said, "Sure we could."

Mattie said, "Or why not make something even more valuable? Like gold!"

"Or diamonds," Brewster said. "They'd make even more money!"

"Or," Sid said, "we could just make some money and avoid the trouble of selling anything."

"You can just make money, like, out of nothing?" Mattie asked.

"Of course."

"Why don't you?"

"We do when we need to buy something, but really, think it through. What are we going to buy? Gold? Diamonds? Ivory?"

"You don't see a refrigerator in here, do you?" Gilbert spoke without looking up from his fry pans. "You think I rode down in the bucket to buy eggs in a time before food safety standards were invented?"

Sid took off his top hat and placed it upside down on the counter. He reached in, rummaged his hand around while peering into the hat, and pulled out a pristine white egg.

Mattie and Brewster stared at him, awestruck, their hands putting food into their mouths as if on autopilot.

He put the egg back in the hat. "You kids are going to have to learn to think bigger, or at least more creatively. It's an adjustment we all have to go through. You're simply going through it earlier than the rest of us. Just keep in mind, your lives are about to change forever."

Sid again pointed his walking stick at Mattie. With the other hand, he tapped a few keys on his keyboard. Mattie said, "I don't feel any different."

"You shouldn't. All I've done is identify your entry in the file." Sid taped a few more keys, then pointed his cane at Brewster. "And now I've identified you."

Mattie and Brewster looked at each other uneasily while they continued eating. Sid typed, slid his index finger around the minuscule trackpad, then typed some more. He clicked a few times. While he worked, the twins watched, and Gilbert put down a plate of food in front of him. Sid muttered his thanks, tapped out a few more words, then looked up, smiled, and ate a forkful of his breakfast.

Brewster asked, "Are you done?"

"You're in the system. It's a sort of programming environment Gilbert and I whipped up to help us interface with the file."

Mattie said, "I still don't feel any different."

"Good," Gilbert said. "If you did, it'd mean Sid screwed up."

"So we can do magic now?"

"Not quite yet," Sid said. "You need a few more things."

He looked into his top hat, reached in, moved his hand as if pushing things out of his way, then pulled out a black cane with an ivory handle and ivory tip, just like the ones he and Gilbert carried. He handed it to Brewster, then reached in again and pulled out another, which he handed to Mattie.

He reached in again, and after some rummaging around, brought out a black disk, which he gave a sharp tap. The center of the disk expanded instantly, forming a top hat. He pushed it down on Brewster's head like a major league ballplayer placing his used cap on a young fan's head.

He pulled a second hat from his own, popped it open, and handed it to Mattie. "Sorry, it's not terribly feminine. We'll work with your mother to come up with something better when this is all over. It's just that all of the women's costumes from the magic industry at this time tend toward the skimpy and frilly."

"And fishnetty," Gilbert added.

"Yes, quite. And that doesn't feel appropriate."

Mattie turned the top hat around in her hands. "Do we really have to wear these?"

"Absolutely. Everyone who finds the file starts out by editing it manually to change reality. But it's a fiddly, labor-intensive process, so they invariably end up writing some sort of program to edit the file for them in an automated manner. They often collaborate with other users to make their program more robust. These programs usually require a user to wear or hold certain specific items to identify themselves as a user, or to facilitate the interface. Your parents' program is built around their wizard costumes, whereas ours is predicated on the much more elegant, stylish image of the classic stage magician. Gilbert and I call it the *Programming Interface*. That's what we'll be training you to use. You don't have to carry them at all times. We'll teach you the rather snazzy spell we've devised to make your hat appear and disappear. I just pulled your hats out of my hat, but you can't pull yours out of your hat when you don't have your hat already. We make our actions confusing, but not quite that confusing."

Gilbert said, "You're lucky we're training you."

"Indeed! A magician's stage costume fairly reeks of grace and dignity. You'll see what I mean once I've conjured up your capes and white gloves."

Gilbert nodded. "It's a hell of a lot better than the crazy getup your parents were going to make you wear."

Mattie narrowed her eyes at Gilbert. "You two say you like our parents, but sometimes I'm not sure."

Sid said, "Your father's a fine gentleman, in his way. So's Phillip, though I know you're loath to hear that at the moment. And I'm certain I speak for Gilbert as well as myself when I say that neither of us could think of a single negative thing to say about your mother."

"Too right," Gilbert said.

"Admittedly, there is some friction between us and your father and Phillip, but I assure you, all of our grievances, plentiful though they may be, are purely professional in nature, and will not inhibit us from assisting you in any way we can."

"We're stage magicians," Gilbert said. "We're proud of that, and we take it seriously. If I tell an audience that I've made Sid here disappear, they can rest assured that I had to design the box I stuck him in to hide him, and that Sid is crammed into some uncomfortably small space listening for his cue to reappear. Your father and Phillip can't be bothered with all that. When your dad disappears, he just teleports backstage and eats a burrito until Phillip gives him his cue to teleport back."

Brewster said, "I don't get it. If you have all of these powers, why not use them in your act? I mean, the audience comes to see magic. You can do magic. I don't see the problem."

Sid said, "Nobody in our audience expects to see genuine feats of magic, because they're certain that magic does not exist. Patrons attend our performances hoping to be tricked through the use of cleverness and skill into thinking that they've seen magic."

Gilbert added, "If we showed them real magic, it would be like cheating."

"Besides," Sid said, "they only enjoy our illusions because they know they're just that. We entertain and amaze without shaking their dual beliefs that magic isn't real, and men in tuxedos aren't to be trusted. If we showed them real magic and they found out about it, they'd probably try to stone us to death."

Mattie said, "The more you two explain, the less I feel like I understand."

Sid laughed. "Yes. I've had the very feeling that you describe. I find it's often a sign that someone's telling me the truth."

Gilbert said, "Look at it this way. Imagine someone told you they were a master puppeteer, and that they were going to show you the world's most lifelike dog puppet. Then they show it to you, and you'd swear you were looking at a real dog. Wouldn't you be disappointed if you found out later that it was a real dog, even though a living dog is more amazing than any puppet could ever be?"

Mattie said, "Yeah, and I'd wonder where the puppeteer had put his hand."

Gilbert laughed. "Oh, I like her!"

Sid said, "Yes, you're both very lively company. You've got your father's creativity, which is another problem. He and Phillip keep *inventing* new tricks that are easy enough for them to do because they're using their magic. But then, to be competitive, Gilbert and I have to figure out a way to do them, and eventually surpass them, using good, honest trickery. It's bloody difficult."

"Yeah, but that's our own fault, isn't it? We started out the friendship on an overly confrontational note."

"Why'd you do that?" Brewster asked.

"Not did. Will. We won't meet them for the first time for a few years, from their point of view, and by then we have a real head of steam for revenge. We'll want payback for them getting a theater across the street and making our lives more difficult."

"Which, from their point of view, they hadn't done yet," Sid added.

"It won't even occur to them as a possibility until we get back at them for it. Let that be a lesson for you kids: don't take revenge, especially for things they haven't even done yet."

Brewster squinted as if he had an ice cream headache. "You're telling us not to get back at people, but you say you're going to in the future, even though you know it works out badly."

Sid said, "Yes, well, we're hardly the first people in history to be guilty of not following their own advice."

10.

Forty-five minutes later, after Sid and Gilbert ate their breakfasts, Gilbert cleaned up, and Sid tapped some more at his tiny laptop.

It was time for the lessons to begin.

The two magicians stood on the patio in front of the house, looking crisp and clean in their impeccable matching tuxedos, with top hats, silk capes, and white gloves grasping their ebony walking sticks.

Opposite them, Mattie and Brewster stood with their backs to the dirigible's envelope and the city of London beneath and beyond it. Both had on jeans and T-shirts in addition to their own top hats, silk capes, white gloves, and canes.

Gilbert asked, "How do you feel?"

Mattie said, "Like the Monopoly guy."

"Splendid," Sid said. "You'll be happy to know that beyond making one feel stylish, dignified, and commanding—"

"Like the Monopoly guy," Gilbert interrupted.

"His name was Rich Uncle Pennybags—a great man, to be sure. Aside from that, which would be quite enough, every item we've given you serves a specific purpose. For example, take your hat." Sid took off his top hat and held it out in front of him.

Brewster and Mattie watched with undivided attention.

Sid stared at them for a moment, then said, "I mean literally. Take your hat."

The twins grimaced in embarrassment as they removed their hats. Sid said, "If a normal person got hold of your hat, it would do them no good unless what they wanted was a perfectly ordinary hat. The same goes for the gloves. But, if you put on the gloves and reach into the hat . . ."

Sid looked into his hat, reached in with his free, gloved hand, then looked at Mattie and Brewster, a clear signal that they should do the same. As they did, they saw glowing green words appear deep within the recesses of their hats. The words formed a list that included *props, weapons, household*, and *other*. As they moved their fingers up and down through the words, the ones they touched got larger while the others receded. Moving their fingers to the right caused the list to disappear and the next sub-list of items to render. From the outside, these movements looked a great deal like a theatrical attempt to rummage around inside the hats.

Gilbert said, "Anything you put into the hat will disappear, either transported to a safe place—the basement of our theater, specifically—or just deleted if it's something the hat created in the first place. All the things you're seeing listed in the hats right now are things you can make, at any time, as many as you want, free of charge. Give 'er a go."

Brewster pulled a chocolate chip cookie out of his hat, which he stared at in awe for a couple of seconds, then ate.

Mattie pulled out a rabbit.

Sid and Gilbert both held their hands out in front of them as if imploring her to stop.

"Whoa, okay, careful there, Mattie," Gilbert said. "Of all the things to pick, she goes right for the rabbit."

Mattie looked at the obviously fake rabbit in her hand, hanging by the scruff of its neck, its legs kicking in a repeating pattern. "It seemed like the obvious thing to pull out of a hat."

"That's true," Sid said. "It is, and was, the obvious thing, but did you not notice that it was listed under weapons? Don't worry, and don't panic. You're not in any trouble, Mattie. You haven't done anything wrong. Just, please, put the rabbit back in the hat now."

Mattie eyed the magicians suspiciously but did as she was told, lowering the rabbit back into the hat, then pulling her empty, gloved hand back out. "Okay? I don't understand why you're both freaking out. It was just a rabbit."

Sid said, "It looked like just a rabbit because we created it to. As long as you held onto it, the little beast was perfectly harmless, but if you had let go, something we like to call *chaos*, would, in short order, have *ensued*. That rabbit is a monster, as fast as it is vicious."

Gilbert held his right hand up in front of his mouth with his palm facing forward, and his fingers curled into gnarled fangs. "With nasty, big, pointy teeth."

The twins said nothing.

Gilbert said, "Sid, when this thing is over, we've gotta talk to Martin and Gwen about showing these two some *Monty Python*."

"Agreed. In the meantime, let's move on to the canes. As you've seen this morning, the cane, or *wand* if you like, can be used as a selection device. I used mine to select the two of you for inclusion in our programming environment. They can also be used to target objects or people for various spells. Lastly, these particular canes have been modified to serve other uses. These features are technologically feasible for a cane in the current time frame. But without magic, they could never coexist in one cane, Swiss Army style, as they do here. Look at your cane's handle. You should see some markings where the handle meets the shaft."

Brewster and Mattie both examined their canes. On the ivory handles, they saw the numbers 1, 2 and 3 engraved around the handle's base. A single line was carved into the polished black shafts, directly under the number 1.

"Currently," Sid continued, "your wands are in walking-stick mode. You can use them for creating magic, or as a simple cane."

"Or you could bean a guy over the head with it," Gilbert said.

"Yes, as goes without saying. Now, if you were to twist the handle so that the line on the shaft aligns with the number 2, then pull the handle and shaft apart . . ." Sid pulled on the handle of his cane. The two pieces came apart readily, making a clear, ringing sound of metal sliding against metal and exposing a silver blade two feet long.

Sid said, "That's right, a sword cane. An elegant weapon for a more civilized age. Now you try."

Sid and Gilbert gave them a moment to enjoy swishing the blades around in the air while shouting things like *en garde* and *touché*.

"Okay," Gilbert said. "Settle down. There'll be plenty of time for all that later. Please resheathe your swords."

The twins reluctantly did as he said.

Gilbert held up his cane, gripping the handle with one hand, and using the second to lightly grasp the shaft. "If you go ahead and turn the handle to the third position, this happens."

Gilbert rotated the body of the cane until the handle clicked into place. The junction between the ivory handle and the rest of the cane gave way. The shaft fell four inches before stopping, as a short section of chrome chain connecting it to the handle pulled tight. The bulk of the cane dangled for a moment, then dropped and separated into two more sections, connected by chrome chain and ending in a few last chrome links and a ring extended from the very end.

Mattie asked, "What's that? Some kinda weird nunchucks?"

"Not quite." Gilbert grasped the steel ring at the base of the cane and threaded it over the top of the handle. The ring settled into place at the first chain segment, forming the segments of intact cane into a triangle with a base much longer than its sides. He allowed the triangle to hang free for a moment. Then Sid removed his cape and tuxedo jacket in one quick flourish and carefully hung them on the triangle.

Mattie and Brewster both groaned, then Mattie shouted, "Boo!"

"Did you just boo us?" Sid asked. "That privilege is reserved for paying audience members, not guests in our home. Besides, that coat hanger you so cavalierly dismiss is a reference to two separate Spielberg movies, if you know your film history sufficiently to comprehend it. Your father was quite impressed when we showed it to him."

Mattie asked, "Can the cane do anything else?"

"Anything else?" Gilbert asked. "You mean aside from the two useful and stylish functions we've managed to make coexist in what, by all rights, should be a simple piece of wood? No, I'm afraid that's all it does. It's not the only item in your ensemble that serves multiple functions, but I hesitate to show it to you now, for fear of boring you."

Mattie said, "I'm sorry. The sword cane is really cool, but after that, the coat hanger was a bit of a letdown."

Brewster asked, "Did you ever think about making the cane turn into a gun?"

Sid blinked at him. "A gun? A gun! Gilbert, I think I must have misheard him. Did he just suggest that we make the cane turn into a gun?"

"Yes," Gilbert said. "He did. Probably in an attempt to remind us that he's an American."

Sid shook his head. "His nationality is a likely explanation, but it's not a valid excuse. Brewster, my friend, might I enquire what people who can do magic would need with a gun? We can alter the very fabric of reality, hem time if it's too long, let space out a few inches if the midsection's too tight, and so forth. We have the power to warp an enemy's perceptions and render them utterly helpless. To finish them off by shooting them would be gauche."

Gilbert said, "Snape didn't kill Dumbledore with an Uzi. Gandalf didn't shoot Durin's Bane with a squirrel rifle. When Houdini escaped from a sealed box, he didn't blast his way out with a shotgun."

"No," Sid said. "They did not! And besides, if, for some inexplicable reason, I were inclined to bust, as they say, a cap, as bullets are sometimes called, into someone's ass, as custom dictates, I would not use something as crude as a firearm to do so. I have the option to make said cap materialize, magically, in the target ass without any entry or exit wound, creating debilitating pain, the desired deterrent effect, and a puzzle that would haunt the target and his primary-care provider for the rest of their days."

"Okay," Brewster nearly shouted. "I get it. Sorry."

Gilbert put a hand on Sid's shoulder and looked at Brewster. "It's all right. No harm done. It's just—we worked hard on all of this stuff. We're proud of it. And you two don't seem all that impressed."

Mattie said, "But we are. We're amazed at the dirigible, and we love the sword canes. The hats, capes, and gloves aren't really our style, but we get why we need them. It's just the coat hanger. Also, we grew up with Dad. References to movies that came out before we were born aren't new or exciting to us."

Sid said, "Yes, I admit, that makes sense. Sorry I got carried away there."

"I'm sorry, too," Brewster said. "So, what do you want to show us next?"

Gilbert looked at Sid expectantly.

Sid said, "I don't know. Maybe we should just leave it."

"No," Mattie said. "Please. Show us."

"Yeah," Brewster said. "We want to see it."

Gilbert smiled at Sid. "You know you're dying to."

"Okay. But I warn you, this next one's a bit whimsical."

"More whimsical than the coat hanger sword-cane?" Mattie asked. "What is it? A rubber duck that plays circus music?"

"Look, do you want to see this, or not?"

The twins nodded, as did Gilbert.

Sid reached up and grasped the sides of his top hat's brim with both hands. The top of the hat hinged open like the top of a soup can that still has one edge attached. A bent tube, like a very large articulated plastic straw with a glass lens set into the open end, raised smoothly from the hat. A flap swung down from the underside of the hat's brim, directly in front of Sid's right eye, while folds of fabric on each side swung into place, completely blocking the eye from view. Sid bent his neck so that the entire construction tilted forward, and the lens pointed at the twins. As they looked up at it, they could see a tiny image of Sid's eye, looking down at them, occasionally blinking.

The twins blinked back.

Sid said, "It's a periscope, isn't it! I know the American educational system isn't the best, but do you not know a periscope when you see one?"

Mattie said, "Obviously, we know it's a periscope. Sorry we didn't say anything. I guess I'm just trying to figure out why a magic user needs a periscope."

Brewster said, "Yeah, and even if we hadn't recognized what it was, there's no need to drag our educational system into it."

Gilbert laughed. "First rule of getting along with Americans, mate. Don't say anything bad about America. Maybe we should stop showing them the equipment for a bit and let them practice with it for a while."

Mattie raised her hand.

Gilbert said, "Yes, Mattie?"

"Does your monocle do anything cool?"

"Yes," Sid said. "It corrects for nearsightedness in one eye."

11.

They all took a ten-minute break, which Sid and Gilbert spent plotting their lesson plan for the rest of the day, and Mattie and Brewster spent pretend sword fighting with real swords, which caused them to swing the swords with much less speed and force than they would have with sticks, or with cardboard tubes. Once everyone was ready, the tutorial resumed.

"I'm going to start the next lesson with a question," Sid said. "The two of you just spent several minutes engaged in dangerous horseplay with actual weapons, and neither Gilbert nor I made any move to stop you. Care to venture a guess why?"

Mattie meekly said, "Because you're not our parents?"

"No. Gilbert and I both feel that we owe it to your parents to keep you as safe as we can. The reason we didn't mind the two of you seemingly attempting to put each other's eyes out is this." As he finished his sentence, Sid unsheathed his sword cane, swung it through the air, and thrust the tip of the blade down as hard as he could into Gilbert's right foot.

Both of the kids let out a startled yelp.

Gilbert jumped, then hopped in place, cursing and cradling his foot. "You said you were going to stab your own foot."

Sid nodded. "Yes, I did, and you believed me, so we were both in the wrong. Anyway, if you would please show our young guests the damage done, I'd be most appreciative."

Gilbert muttered several inaudible but distinctly unfriendly-sounding things under his breath as he lifted his foot, then untied and removed his shoe. He bent the shoe, showing the large hole the sword had cut. Next, he pulled off his sock, then stuck his hand in it and out through the sword damage. Last, he held his bare foot forward. Mattie and Brewster noted with awe that it didn't have a scratch on it.

"We're pretty much invincible, as far as physical violence goes," Gilbert said, as he pulled a fresh pair of shoes and socks from his hat. "We can't be bruised, cut, or burned by fire or friction. We can still feel pain, though, so you'll want to avoid rug burns, purple nurples, and noogies."

"Wedgies are still rather unpleasant as well. And, mere moments from now, you will both be capable of executing a first-rate wedgie without the unpleasantness of touching an enemy's underpants. We're going to teach you how to make objects levitate. The first thing you need in order to make something levitate is something to make levitate. Sid, if you'd do the honors."

Sid reached into his top hat, moved his hand around a bit, and pulled out a small rubber ball. "We're starting small, naturally, but the same spell will work on bigger, heavier items, or even people." He bent down and rolled the ball, which stopped a few yards in front of them.

Gilbert pointed his walking stick at the ball and said, "*Abra—*" He paused, fine-tuning his aim before he finished. "—*Cadabra!*"

He lifted the cane. The ball rose into the air, moving as if connected by an invisible steel rod to the end of his cane.

Mattie and Brewster watched attentively, applauded out of impulse, then stopped when they realized what they were doing.

Sid let out a small chuckle. "That happens quite often. Something about the wand, the hat, and the clichéd magic words just drives people to applaud out of some deeply ingrained Pavlovian instinct. You'll see."

Gilbert said, "Levitating things can be right handy, both as a way of getting work done and for defending yourself. You want to be careful though, especially if you're lifting things close to people, or if you're lifting people. It's easy to misjudge how fast things are moving, and running things into each other can be real bad news."

"And you say the word to trigger that is—*Abracadabra?*" Mattie asked.

"Yes, that's right." Gilbert sent the ball up into the metal gantry work of the dirigible, carefully maneuvering it around the supports and trusses as he spoke. "Also, you can't pick up anything too large. The weight isn't the problem. It's hard to control what part of a big complex object you're lifting it by, so things tend to crumble or bend when you try to levitate them."

Sid put a hand on Gilbert's shoulder. "You might want to pause the lesson for a moment. I'm afraid you don't have your students' undivided attention, and won't until Mattie puts Brewster down."

"Yeah," Brewster said, his voice raised in a mixture of fear and anger. "Put me down!"

Mattie closed one eye to sight along her walking stick as she smiled up at him. "I will. Eventually. If you say the magic word."

Brewster smiled viciously. Mattie's smile faded.

"No! Don't do it! I'll put you—"

Brewster aimed his cane, shouted, "*Abracadabra*," and flicked the tip of the cane into the air, causing Mattie to lift off the ground.

As she rose, she swung her walking stick wildly, trying to keep her balance. Brewster flew through the air in wild loops, his motion determined by his sister's wand. As he whipped about, his own aim became unsteady, causing Mattie to tumble even more erratically through the air, making her wand less steady and further amplifying Brewster's instability.

They tried to get the situation under control, but any attempt to adjust their own aim moved their sibling, in turn moving them and unsteadying their aim. Their position felt all the more perilous because they didn't start on the ground; they both swirled, out of control, above a platform that itself floated hundreds of feet above the city. They wobbled and swirled through the air, making the kind of involuntary noises one makes when they sense they're about to fall off a balance beam, or the car they're riding in is dangerously close to a cliff—lots of tremulous, concerned-sounding oohs and aahs, like a ghost slowly lowering itself into a bath that is three degrees too hot.

Gilbert and Sid watched, shaking their heads.

Gilbert said, "They take after their old man."

"Yes," Sid agreed. "I must admit, I'm beginning to wonder if perhaps we aren't really up to the task of training these two."

"Maybe not. But is the problem that we're bad teachers, or that they're bad learners?"

Mattie said, "Look, Brewster, put me down gently, then I promise I'll put you down gently. Okay?"

"Yeah, okay, but for this to work, I think you'll have to raise your wand as I lower mine."

"Sure. I'm starting . . . NOW!"

Mattie lifted the tip of her walking stick. At the same moment, Brewster lowered his. In a slow, almost stately pace, Brewster rose higher into the air while Mattie remained stationary.

Sid said, "I fear the answer might be *both*, old friend."

"Okay you two," Gilbert shouted. "Here's what's going to happen. When I say go, you're both going to slowly, carefully drop the tips of your wands. That'll make you both come down, but your speeds will magnify each other's, if that makes sense. So you have to do it very slowly. Understand? Good. Ready. Steady. Go!"

The twins did as they were told, and they both slowly descended. Mattie touched down first, carefully lowering her brother, who had been up much higher.

Both twins put down their walking sticks, dropped to their knees, and placed their hands on the patio, appearing to enjoy its solidity and lack of motion.

"Well then," Sid said. "Now that we have that unpleasantness behind us, I propose a brief break, after which, we'll move along to the next lesson: Flying. And, no, the irony is not lost on me."

Mattie and Brewster flew through the air with that unique mixture of excitement and fear that a young person usually experiences the first time they drive. The rigid metal structure and semi-transparent skin of the dirigible's envelope served as an ever-present reminder that they could not go too far off course. If they made a mistake, they would not fall to their deaths. The worst-case scenario was that they'd either fall twenty feet onto the lawn or the patio, or they'd fly face-first into a metal girder.

Also, the presence of their teachers and the carefully laid-out course of floating traffic cones mitigated their fear.

Mattie stood almost perfectly straight up and down, her left white-gloved hand on her hip, and her right extended to the side, grasping the handle of her cane as if using it to help support her weight. Her satin cape fluttered in the breeze behind her as she leaned imperceptibly forward and to the left to negotiate a sweeping left-hand turn, weaving slightly to stay between the two lines of cones.

"Good, Mattie!" Gilbert shouted. She glanced down and saw him, seated at the patio table, a large glass tumbler full of something with lots of ice cubes in his hand, watching the flight practice while Sid pounded on his netbook's minuscule keyboard.

Gilbert motioned toward her with his drink. "Look where you're going! Eyes always on where you're going, girl!"

Mattie looked up and corrected her trajectory, narrowly avoiding a collision with a levitating traffic cone. "Thanks! Sorry!"

"It happens," Gilbert said. "Remember, our flying system is based on a Segway. It's all leaning. It's very intuitive, but that means it's also easy to fly into things if you lose concentration."

Further back, at the rear of the envelope, Brewster wove through a set of carefully laid-out S curves, standing in the same upright posture as his sister, his cape flapping in his wake. "Hey, Gilbert, why do we fly standing up like this? Isn't it more, I dunno, normal to fly stretched out forward like Superman?"

Sid spoke without looking up from his netbook. "No, that is most assuredly not *more normal*. You're a human being flying through the air under your own power. There simply is no normal way to do that. Any posture you choose, under those circumstances, aside from swinging your limbs in a wild panic, would be abnormal. All of us who have written flight programs have been forced to come up with the system we think makes sense. Your parents opted for the Superman approach. Perhaps zooming through the sky while laid out like you're getting stretched on the rack looks natural to them, but I disagree."

Gilbert said, "That said, most magic users do fly like Superman."

"Just because most magic users are making a mistake, that doesn't mean we have to join them. And not all of the other magic users do. Some fly with their legs folded, like they're meditating. One guy goes feet-first and bent at the midsection like he's performing an abnormally long Kung Fu kick."

"Where does he live?" Mattie asked.

"Hong Kong in the seventies. There's one woman who flies around in a seated position with her hands on unseen controls, like Wonder Woman in her invisible jet."

"How many magic users are there?" Mattie asked.

"Hard to say," Gilbert said, after taking a sip of his drink. "We've never all gotten together. I think there were something like a hundred gathered for a big meeting once, but they were just representatives. I'd say there's somewhere under a thousand, all told. Some of the groups meet up regularly. Your dad's lot gets together once a year, I believe, to pick their leader. It's mostly just a party since they've only ever picked Phillip."

"Phillip?" Mattie said, disgusted. She looked at them to see if they were joking and blew right through some cones, flying off course.

Brewster scowled as he swept through the long left-hand turn. "Figures. How does he con them into that?"

"He doesn't con them into anything," Gilbert said. "From what I hear, he doesn't even want the job."

Sid said, "Phillip has, very much, had power thrust upon him. I suggest the two of you land now. I sense your concentration is slipping."

As the twins touched down, Mattie asked, "Why on earth would anybody choose Phillip to be their leader?"

"That's the thing," Gilbert said. "Phillip ain't perfect, but he's quite a bit better than you two seem to think."

Brewster said, "We'll see."

Sid shook his head. "We will, but will we accurately perceive it when we do? At this point, I suspect we could show you a picture of Phillip saving orphans from a fire, and you'd call it proof that he's a kidnapper and an arsonist."

Gilbert put a hand on Sid's shoulder. "Look, this is no good. We're working at crossed purposes. If we go on this way, we'll just spend all our time telling each other what we think probably happened instead of finding out what really did. Do any of you need to go to visit the restroom?"

"Why?' Mattie asked. "Can your powers help with that?"

"As a matter of fact, they can, but that's not why I asked. Please just answer the question. Do you need to go to the restroom?"

Both twins shook their heads. Mattie asked, "Why?"

Gilbert said, "Because we're going on a trip."

"Where?"

"To get on the same page."

"So, we're traveling to the same page?" Brewster asked.

"We're going to show you why we don't think Phillip's an enemy."

"And how are you gonna do that?" Brewster asked.

"By snooping on your parents."

"Oh. We're cool with that."

"Of course, you are," Sid said. "You're teenagers. Your thirst to know all of your parents' secrets is only topped by your disinterest in telling them any of yours."

12.

Centuries earlier (and surprisingly near the spot where Gilbert and Sid moored their dirigible), in the immense, window-lined grand gallery of a massive golden castle, Martin and Gwen celebrated their just-completed wedding vows, aided by their closest friends. All of them wore costumes themed to David Lynch's 1984 film *Dune*.

In an out-of-the-way corner of the upper gallery, well out of the wedding party's line of sight and concealed by shadows, Gilbert and Sid stood with Mattie and Brewster, watching the festivities.

"What year did you say this was, again?" Mattie asked.

"It's 1157," Gilbert replied.

Brewster asked, "And how did Mom and Dad get here?"

"They found the file."

"Separately," Sid added. "My understanding is your father found the file, made some sort of hideous mess of it, and had to go hide in Medieval England. That's where he met your mother."

"Mom's from Medieval England?" Brewster asked.

"No," Sid said. "I believe she's from the twenty teens. She was just living in Medieval England at the time. So was Phillip, come to think of it."

"That's where you all met," Brewster said.

"No," Gilbert said, "We don't visit the Dark Ages much. Not very fond of roughing it. No, we'll meet your parents a few years later on, and hundreds of years earlier, in Atlantis."

Brewster said, "I'm sorry. What? You don't really mean Atlantis? Not the ancient lost city of Atlantis?"

"Yes. When I said Atlantis, I meant Atlantis. That's why I called it Atlantis."

"It's real?"

Sid said, "That depends on what you mean by *real*, and what you mean by *Atlantis*."

"But yes," Gilbert said. "There was, at one time, a city called Atlantis. I believe your mother lived there for a while."

"That's where your parents first met us," Sid said.

"We'd met them before," Gilbert added. "But that was later on."

"You two enjoy confusing people, don't you?" Mattie asked.

Sid smiled. "Would we have become magicians if we didn't?"

"Why would a guy from the future think he could hide in the past?" Brewster asked.

"Good question. He came here, they all came here, to pose as wizards as a cover for using the file to give themselves powers."

Mattie furrowed her brow. "They hid their powers by. . . claiming to have magical powers?"

Sid said, "Exactly. If you're in the modern world and someone happens to catch you levitating in thin air, you'll end up drugged in a government lab somewhere. In the Dark Ages, if someone catches you levitating, they'll assume you know magic, and while they may desire to burn you at the stake, they'll be far too afraid of you to attempt it."

Gilbert said, "And if they do, you can levitate away without having to worry about some chav with a smartphone uploading you to YouTube and making you famous. Yeah, the only people who got burned at the stake for witchcraft were the ones who didn't have magic."

Sid nodded. "Such is the irony of life."

"And that's why you pretend to be magicians," Mattie said.

Sid's eyes went wide, and his voice raised an octave. "I beg your pardon! We may hold your parents in rather high esteem on a personal level, but what we're doing is a very different thing from what they do. They deceive people and pretend to be wizards to cover for their powers. We went to the trouble to learn stage magic and develop an act. We aren't pretending to be magicians. We genuinely *are* magicians, and we take it seriously."

Gilbert put a hand on Sid's shoulder and took over talking while his partner calmed down. "We take a different approach than your folks. Let's just leave it at that for the moment. So, kids, not everybody gets to see their parents' wedding. What do you think of their big day?"

Mattie said, "Our parents' *big day, Gilbert,* was at Blood Ridge on Glapflap's third moon, against the Gromflomites."

Gilbert and Sid both stared at Mattie.

Brewster said, "It's from a show. *Rick and Morty.* They were at a wedding and—"

Gilbert cut him off, "Yeah, we're familiar with *Rick and Morty.* Being a time traveler means infinite free time to binge-watch cartoons. It's just, hearing you say that made me realize you two don't make a lot of pop culture references."

Mattie motioned toward the wedding below. "Look down there."

Down below, Martin used his powers to make a piñata shaped like Baron Vladimir Harkonnen rise up and down as a blindfolded Gwen swiped at it with a wizard staff, and all of their friends cheered and ate pieces of a cake shaped like a sandworm.

Brewster said, "When you're raised by our dad, not constantly referring to some TV show or movie is a way to rebel."

"What a bunch of dorks," Mattie said.

"Quite," said Sid.

Brewster said, "I don't know. They aren't hurting anyone, but it's all kind of self-indulgent, isn't it?"

Mattie shrugged. "It is their wedding day."

"I understand that it's their wedding. I just didn't expect it to be a big, extravagant party like this that's just meant to impress their friends."

Mattie laughed. "You didn't expect that? Are you sure you understand what a wedding is?"

"I just didn't think they'd be so . . . frivolous."

Gilbert put a reassuring hand on Brewster's back. "Don't judge 'em too harshly. They were young."

Mattie glared down at Phillip, who stood by smiling and joking in his Mentat costume. "I'm just surprised that they invited an enemy to their wedding."

Sid said, "Just because they might be enemies now doesn't mean they always were, does it? Anyway, we promised to show you how Martin and Gwen were when they were younger. We didn't promise that you'd like them, or that what you saw would make sense."

Gilbert nodded. "You need to have a real understanding of who your parents are if you're going to have a chance at saving them."

"And some conception of who your enemy is, or at least the person you believe to be your enemy," Sid said. "Look, kids, we've known both your parents and Phillip for quite some time, and looking at this, can you see why we're both certain that Phillip wouldn't hurt your parents? Or, at least, if he did, he'd need to have a bloody good reason. He's an old, dear friend to both of them. He's your father's best man."

"Or," Mattie said, "he's just been pretending to be their friend the entire time, and he's fooled Dad into making him best man."

"Yeah," Brewster agreed. "And that makes all this even worse, doesn't it?"

Gilbert and Sid both sighed.

Sid said, "This certainly seems to have boomeranged on us."

"Yeah. Oh well. If one thing doesn't work, you try something else. C'mon kids. I've got an idea. And the best part is, you're going to get to take a break from learning about magic to help us perform an illusion."

Centuries later, and about halfway across town, Gilbert and Sid stood on the stage of their theater, resplendent in their customary tuxedoes, top hats, and capes. Sid stood straight and tall on his mark, behind the closed curtains, while Gilbert stood where the two curtains met, using his hands to simultaneously hold the curtains closed while opening a small gap to peek through. In the wings to the magicians' left, Mattie and Brewster stood, wearing black velvet robes and white porcelain masks pulled up on their heads like hats.

Sid said, "Our audience of one shall arrive at any moment. We've rehearsed. You both know what to do, and when to do it. Stay relaxed and you'll be fine. There's no need for nervousness."

Mattie said, "We aren't nervous. We're irritated."

Gilbert said, "No problem there. I've done some of my best shows while irritated."

Sid said, "And I while irritating him."

"True that."

Mattie asked, "Why didn't you tell us that we're doing this trick as a favor to Phillip to begin with? There's no way we'd have spent all afternoon practicing if we'd known that."

Sid said, "I do so love it when they answer their own questions."

Brewster scowled. "When did Phillip put you two up to this anyway? You said he hasn't been in contact in days."

Gilbert said, "He asked us to do this years ago."

"And you're only just doing it now?" Mattie asked.

Sid said, "He told us that there was no rush. He knew for a fact that we would get around to it eventually, because Martin had told him we already had."

Gilbert said, "As Brewster pointed out before, time travel makes it easy to procrastinate, which is good. You usually need the extra time just to figure out what's going on."

"Besides," Sid said, "we couldn't perform the illusion as it was described to us until we procured two assistants we could fully trust. Life's irony never ceases to amaze. We were unable to do this favor for Phillip until you two came along, and you wouldn't be here if not for your deep and abiding distrust for Phillip."

Mattie and Brewster both opened their mouths to speak but stopped short when Gilbert said, "Oop! Martin's here!"

Gilbert stepped backward to stand on his mark beside Sid, and he pointed at the twins.

Mattie gritted her teeth as she threw a large knife switch bolted to the wall. As the points made contact, the house lights went out and two spotlights blazed to life. Brewster hauled on a loop of rope stretched between two pulleys on the floor and ceiling, making the stage curtains part, revealing Gilbert and Sid in all of their glory.

Out in the seats, Martin groaned, "Oh, Lord."

Sid addressed Martin with his customary verbosity, interrupted occasionally with a few friendly syllables from Gilbert or an angry question from Martin himself. Brewster and Mattie listened intently to all of it, waiting only for their cue.

Finally, Sid waved his walking stick/magic wand in the prearranged pattern while flourishing with his free hand. Mattie threw a second knife switch that flooded the entire stage with light, and Brewster hit the play button on a large, CD-powered boombox that blasted out a recording of a small brass ensemble performing the song "The Final Countdown" by Europe. They both lowered their white porcelain masks, raised their hoods, and rushed out onto the stage, pushing a steamer trunk on casters and a wheeled frame suspending a red velvet curtain.

In the ensuing two minutes, the four of them performed a complex, carefully choreographed magic trick that involved locking Gilbert in the trunk, swapping masks, Gilbert and Sid switching places through a false back, and a lot of arm waving. At the end of the trick, Sid stood in the now open trunk with a message to Martin, from Phillip, embroidered on the back of his robe. Gilbert sat behind Martin, in a position carefully chosen to allow Gilbert to "accidentally" startle him. Brewster stood in the wings, and Mattie hid in a secret compartment beneath the stage.

She stayed crouched beneath the trapdoor, listening to her father talking with Gilbert and Sid until she was given the signal that Martin had left and it was okay to come out. The curtain made opening the trapdoor a bit of a challenge, but she managed it. She removed her mask and the robe as she stood up and stepped out of the hidden compartment beneath the stage floor.

Brewster walked out onto the stage, also shedding his mask and robe as he went.

Sid stepped out of the steamer trunk and began removing his robe with the special message embroidered on its back:

Martin—
You're embarrassing yourself. Just drop it.
—Phillip

This was the first time the twins had seen the younger version of their father up close and not wearing a Fremen stillsuit. Sid couldn't help asking, "So that was him. What did you think?"

Mattie said, "He was so young."

"And angry," Brewster added. "Really angry."

Sid said, "Indeed. I'm sure he's mellowed with age. Most men do."

"They get wiser, and stop letting things bother them?" Brewster asked.

Gilbert said, "No. Things bother them more. It's just they don't have the energy to act on it like they used to."

"Whatever. I just don't see what the point of this was. Why did you show us this? We got to see Phillip tormenting Dad. What does that prove?"

Mattie said, "It's worse. We saw you torment our dad *for* Phillip, and you got us to help."

"What?" Gilbert sputtered. "Did you not read the writing on my back? Could you not hear what Martin said? I mean, they do have a tendency to mess with each other, but at the end of the day, they are the best of friends. Even here, as you just saw, Phillip jerked Martin around and wasted his time, but he did it because Martin's making himself look foolish, and Phillip's trying to warn him off of it."

Brewster said, "Or maybe Dad's getting close to figuring out what Phillip's up to, and he's trying to throw Dad off."

Sid smiled down at Gilbert from the stage and said, "I believe the proper American vernacular for this scenario would be *strike two*."

Mattie, Brewster, Gilbert, and Sid materialized. At first, all the twins could see was that they'd appeared outside, in the dark, behind a tree. A quick look around revealed that they had also appeared in front of another tree, and beside one as well. They both spun around for a moment, taking in the forest that almost surrounded them. The trees and ground plants thinned in front of them, and in the distance a few hundred feet away, there appeared to be some buildings with a dirt road between them that stretched off into the woods. They found it hard to see, as it was dark, and there were no exterior lights aside from a couple of flaming torches. They stared at the quaint buildings and could just make out the sound of raised voices from inside them until Sid made a hissing noise to draw their attention.

Gilbert and Sid both looked up from their position, crouching behind a bush, holding on to their satin capes so they wouldn't drag in the mud.

"Get down," Gilbert said. "You don't wanna get seen."

Mattie dropped into a squat, then reached up and pulled Brewster down as well. They waddled over next to Gilbert and Sid.

"Welcome back to Medieval England," Sid said. "It's a few years before the wedding, on what is undoubtedly the single most eventful day of your father's life."

Gilbert said, "Yeah, so far, he's gone on a shopping spree, bought a new car, gotten arrested, escaped, led the police on a high-speed chase, crashed his brand new car, fled to the distant past, and now he's about to fight in a duel." He pointed toward the buildings.

Sid nodded. "And it's in times of stress, such as this very much is, that one finds out who one's true friends are."

All four of them adjusted their positions to raise their eyes and peer over the bush.

What at first glance appeared to be a few small huts clustered together in the woods, now, as their eyes adjusted to the dark, seemed to be the edge of a smallish town. Beyond them, many one- and two-story buildings, all made of drab materials, sat soaking up the light from the moon, stars, and occasional torches without reflecting much of it for anyone to see.

The sound of raised voices from inside the nearest building grew both louder and angrier, although it sounded like only one person was doing all of the talking.

Gilbert said, "Any second now, they're going to come out into the street. That's when the real fun begins."

"How do you know all of this?" Brewster asked. "Were you there?"

"Not as such," Sid said. "We weren't involved, or present as far as your father knows. But when we heard the story, we had to come back and witness the spectacle for ourselves. In fact, even as we speak, we're somewhere over there, lurking in the bushes."

Sid motioned toward an area on the far side of the path. All four of them looked in the general area he pointed and saw the crowns of two top hats sticking up from behind a shrub.

Gilbert and Sid both quickly took off their top hats.

Gilbert grinned sheepishly. "You kinda forget you're wearing them after a while."

Sid whispered, "Silence, please. It begins."

People streamed out of the nearest building, many of them holding large mugs. A few held torches. More people lit torches as they exited. Soon, the section of dirt road between the buildings was flooded with light.

Martin walked out into the middle of the road, wearing a Harry Potter–branded wizard robe meant for a much younger and smaller person. He turned to face back toward town.

Opposite him, Phillip stood, looking exactly as he did when they saw him last, right down to the sky-blue robe, pointed hat, and staff.

"He's fighting Phillip?" Mattie said. "I thought you said they're friends."

Gilbert said, "Just watch."

A hush fell over the assembled crowd. They heard Phillip say, "Whenever you're ready."

Martin lifted three feet into the air, and stayed there, suspended above the ground without any visible support. He shouted, "Behold," but his voice sounded odd, as if he were imitating a sheep, or shouting through a box fan.

"Phillip," Martin continued. "Can your powers match this?"

"Let's see." Phillip's staff emitted an eerie blue light and a deep, resonant hum. Phillip rose thirty feet into the air and hovered above the buildings, twirling his staff like a giant baton. As his twirling grew faster, the glowing staff began to resemble a glowing disk, then a glowing sphere. The light grew brighter, becoming a brilliant white that illuminated the crowd below it and the town behind him like a small sun.

In a voice both ear-splittingly loud and maddeningly casual, Phillip asked, "What do you think, Martin? How's this?"

Martin turned and tried to run but didn't think to drop back to the ground first, so he merely twisted and tumbled in midair without going anywhere. He came to a rest hanging upside down, tilted at a sharp angle, and immediately threw up.

The ball of light shrunk until it was just the pinnacle of Phillip's staff, glowing as he floated serenely above the rooftops. "Thanks for visiting us, Martin. I'm sure we'll meet again soon."

The ball of light shot from Phillip's staff and hit Martin in the gut. Suspended above the ground, Martin offered no resistance, so the force of the impact sent his limp body flying out of town and into the woods at a constant altitude of three feet.

He shot past his future children's hiding spot, into the dark forest beyond, stopping only when he hit a tree.

"Friends?" Brewster hissed. "You call that being Dad's friend?"

Gilbert shushed Brewster, and Sid grabbed Mattie's arm, holding her back from her attempt to go help their father as he hung in the air, eyes closed, mouth open, and arms and legs dangling while he drifted slowly, having rebounded off of the tree.

Mattie tried to pull herself free of Sid's grip but stopped when their mother appeared out of thin air, wearing a long brown hooded cloak and carrying two magic wands.

The kids watched in silence as Gwen grabbed Martin by the leg. She withdrew her hand instantly after making initial contact, but then she grabbed him firmly and started rotating his body into a more dignified pose, standing upright, though with his head still lolling forward and his limbs hanging limp.

She looked up at his slack face in the moonlight. She tried to close his mouth, but it fell back open as soon as she took her hand away.

Phillip appeared behind her. "What do you think?"

Gwen said. "He's trouble. He's cute, but he's trouble. Why is he vibrating?"

Phillip laughed. "I think it has something to do with how his flight macro works. It seems pretty crude. He doesn't seem to know what he's doing."

Gwen said, "Yeah, but that doesn't stop him from doing it. You should have seen him when I picked him up on the road today. He was totally confident, and completely unprepared. That's why he's trouble. I say we banish him."

"Gwen, the lad just got here. We don't even know him."

"We know that he's arrogant and foolhardy, and for someone with access to the file, that's dangerous. We have a nice equilibrium going here, and he's going to throw it out of balance."

"Maybe."

"How long had you known him before he challenged you to a duel, Phillip?"

"Less than five minutes. Okay, point taken, he's definitely going to throw things out of balance, but sometimes that's a good thing. Besides, we don't know what kind of trouble we'd be sending him back to."

"The idea that he might have caused a mess where he came from isn't a very good argument to keep him here."

"Maybe not, but it's good enough for me. I'm going to train him, get him all sussed out."

"Whatever," Gwen said. "Just try to calm him down before you bring him 'round to my place. The last thing I need is this guy slobbering all over me."

"Done. Thanks for coming out."

"Happy to. Anything for you, Phillip," Gwen said, and disappeared.

Phillip looked up at the still-unconscious Martin. "Don't worry, lad. We'll get you fixed up. I think you'll work out just fine." He gripped Martin's wrist, muttered "*Transporti hejmen*," and they both vanished.

"So," Gilbert said. "You see now why we don't think Phillip would do anything to hurt either of your parents."

Mattie said, "But he did. You literally just showed us Phillip hurting Dad."

Gilbert sputtered for a moment, his eyes wide, staring at Mattie until he finally said, "Not much. And he only did it after Martin challenged him to a duel."

Sid said, "And he was exceedingly kind to your father after the duel. Far kinder than your mother wanted to be."

"Okay, I guess," Brewster said. "At least from this last bit, it looks like Phillip is one of our parents' oldest, closest friends."

"Thank you."

"Which will make it that much worse if he's turned on them."

"We don't know that he has!"

Brewster shrugged. "I said *if*."

Gilbert said, "That is progress."

Mattie nodded. "It's possible. Phillip might not be our parents' enemy. But can you admit that he might not be their friend anymore?"

Gilbert and Sid looked at each other, each hoping the other would have an intelligent answer to the question.

After a long silence, Mattie said. "You have your opinion. We have ours. We can keep arguing about it, or we can get to work finding out which opinion is right."

Gilbert said, "The only thing worse than a stubborn teenager is one who has a valid point."

"We admitted we might be wrong," said Brewster. "That's not stubborn."

Sid said, "And now you have two valid points."

13.

They materialized on the patch of lawn in front of Sid's Victorian house and split up in sullen silence, Mattie and Brewster sulking because the magicians wouldn't accept that Phillip was the enemy, Gilbert and Sid moping because the twins wouldn't take their word for it that he wasn't.

They each used the restroom, got a drink, and reconvened at the outdoor kitchen, drawn instinctively by the smell of the grilled cheese sandwiches Gilbert was making. As they ate, Mattie stifled a small laugh.

"What?" Gilbert asked.

"Nothing."

"C'mon, what is it?"

Mattie rolled her eyes. "Oh, it's dumb, but, I was just thinking about how funny Dad looked flying through the woods unconscious. The little stream of drool trailing out of his mouth as he went is what got me."

The four of them either chuckled or let out the single sharp exhalation through their nostrils that signals that something didn't make you laugh, but that you recognize it as funny anyway.

Brewster swallowed a bite of sandwich and said, "I liked how unimpressed he looked after our magic trick. I think that's pretty much how Mattie and I always look after he shows us one of his."

Again, they shared a laugh, not entirely at Martin's expense, but not exactly to his credit either.

Gilbert said, "I was just wondering how many times your father had to watch *Dune* to plan that wedding. Recreating the Guild Navigator especially must have taken a ton of time and effort. We all want our special day to be perfect, but he went to an awful lot of trouble to decorate his wedding ceremony with a giant smoking scrotum."

They all laughed, Mattie shot water out her nose, they all laughed harder, and by the time they stopped, they had all forgotten that they were irritated with each other.

Sid tapped a few keys on his netbook as he finished his sandwich, then closed the lid and said, "Now then, my young apprentices, I do believe it's time to finish up your training."

"What do you mean, *finish up*?" Mattie asked. "We're done?"

Gilbert smiled. "You can fly, you can levitate objects, you can make things appear and disappear. We haven't figured a way to read minds yet, so there really isn't much left to teach you."

Sid said, "Quite. You'll want to learn to code so you can come up with powers of your own, but you'll have to handle that yourself."

Brewster said, "Oh, Mom and Dad have been making us take coding classes."

"There you go," Gilbert said. "Good parents, thinking ahead."

"Almost certainly Gwen's doing." Sid motioned toward his netbook. "I've accessed your hats and enabled the last few powers I'm going to give you. You're now able to teleport. You'll find it in the menu. You can choose from one of the preset places we've already programmed, or you can use MapQuest to pick a place."

Mattie scrunched her nose. "MapQuest? What is that? Some sort of ancient precursor to Google Maps?"

Gilbert said, "I prefer to think of it as a high-tech alternative to Microsoft Automap on CD-ROM."

Sid ignored the digression. "If you teleport using your hat, we have an animation programmed that makes it look like the hat sucks you in and then vanishes. Also, anyone touching you will teleport as well, which can be either rather convenient or exceedingly inconvenient, depending on the person in question. Still, we suggest avoiding teleporting in front of people if you can help it. Also, in addition to the map interface, you'll see that there's a time selector, meaning that you can teleport to any place, at any time. So, that's teleporting and time travel sorted. We won't have you try it now, as it's all very straightforward. You can play around with it later if you like. You won't be doing any of it alone anyway, as Gilbert and I are going to accompany you until the investigation is complete."

"Damn straight," Gilbert agreed. "So, that just leaves one thing to teach you. We weren't sure we were going to tell you this part. It's kind of a trade secret of ours. But we want to do right by you, and your parents, so we're gonna spill the beans. First, though, you lot need to swear, *swear*, that you won't tell anybody, not even your parents, what you're about to learn."

The twins' interest was piqued, and keeping secrets from their parents is pretty much what teenagers do. They talked over one another, rushing to swear secrecy.

Sid said, "One of the great disappointments of the magic community is that nobody has successfully developed a means of turning invisible without unpleasant side effects. Except, that is to say, for us."

Gilbert held his arms outward, drawing the twins' attention, made a showy little flourish with his fingertips, then threw some small object at the ground in front of his feet, shouting *"Ninja vanish!"*

The thrown object exploded in a blinding light, a billowing cloud of grayish-white smoke, and a low, slow, *foomp* noise. When the twins' eyes recovered from the flash, Gilbert was gone. Sid stood, smiling at Mattie and Brewster, neither of whom said a word. After several seconds of silence, Sid asked, "So, then, where did he go?"

"Uh, he didn't go anywhere, did he?" Mattie said. "You said he was going to turn invisible, so I guess he's still here."

Brewster said, "Yeah. We didn't doubt he could do it. He said he was gonna, after all. We just want to know how it's done."

Sid shook his head. "That's the damnable irony of magic. It's a lot more impressive when you don't believe in it."

Gilbert's disembodied voice said, "Yeah, I'm over here. Don't bother to look for me waving or anything. You won't see me. Look to the right of Sid, and I mean look carefully. Really study the background— you'll see an area where whatever's behind me seems a little warped. That's where I am."

"Oh," Mattie said. "Yeah, I think I see it."

Brewster squinted. "It's like the wall of your house has a dent in it."

Sid nodded. "You see, my young friends, all the other wizards have tried to make themselves invisible by changing themselves somehow. That's invariably too dangerous, too difficult, or in most cases, both. We, by contrast, realized that humans see by detecting the light bouncing off of things, so we made a spell that bends the light around the magician, leaving him or her unchanged."

Gilbert's voice said, "All of the light that gets within two feet of where I'm standing is bent around me. Since no light bounces off me, you can't see me. Unfortunately, the area directly behind me looks farther away, and the pattern on the floor gets distorted."

Mattie and Brewster both looked down and saw a spot where the brick pavers bent and warped as if filmed with a fisheye lens.

"It works best if the background is far away, the floor isn't a repeating pattern, and you don't move. If you sneak around slowly, it's not so bad, but the faster you walk, the easier you are to spot."

The distortion seemed to wobble and waver for a moment, then moved from right to left, becoming more obvious as it gained speed.

"Also" Gilbert said, "if you just stay where you were when you disappeared, you're more likely to get spotted. That's why we added the flash pot. It gives you a second once you're invisible to take a couple of giant steps away. Now, how would you two like to try it yourselves?"

Mattie and Brewster practically begged, "Please!"

Sid smiled. "Splendid. To arm the spell, while wearing your white gloves, take the thumb of your right hand and touch it to the crease of the first knuckle on each finger, starting with the pinky and working your way across."

Sid demonstrated with his own right hand. The kids followed suit.

"Now, again with the right hand, mime throwing a small object, about the size of a golf ball, at the floor in front of your feet. There won't actually be an object, of course, but the audience will believe that they see one, because that's what the human brain does. You needn't shout *ninja vanish*, by the way. Gilbert just does that because he thinks it's amusing."

"And it is," Gilbert's disembodied voice said.

"Go ahead. Remember, touch the first knuckles on all fingers, make the throw, boom, flash, then take two giant steps."

Mattie and Brewster both mimed throwing an object at the floor. Two small explosions fired, followed almost immediately by soft thudding noises and both Brewster and Mattie saying "Ow!"

Sid smiled, on the verge of laughing. "First lesson: if disappearing with someone, compare notes so you don't run into each other when you make your two giant steps. Now that you're both invisible, what's the first thing you notice?"

Mattie said, "I can't see."

"Me neither," Brewster said.

"No, you can't! All of the light's being bent around you, so none of it's reaching your eyes. You can hear everything, but you can't see, any more than you can be seen. In order to regain your vision, you'd need some way to reach out of the zone of darkness around you, collect some light, and somehow channel it back to at least one of your eyes. Some sort of periscope, perhaps, much like the one you mocked me for getting so excited about earlier!"

14.

Mattie and Brewster spent most of the afternoon and evening playing with their new powers under the guise of *practicing*. Sid took them on a field trip to the future to buy a few changes of clothes and better camping mattresses, letting Mattie transport them there and Brewster bring them back. Gilbert made a lavish dinner, which they ate by the pool, watching the sunset over London through the dirigible's semitransparent skin. Afterward, they watched a movie. They let the kids choose between *The Incredible Burt Wonderstone* and *Now You See Me*. They chose *Wonderstone*, but switched after twenty minutes and enjoyed the second movie, despite Gilbert and Sid's complaints that the depiction of magic was completely unrealistic.

The next morning, after another massive pile of delicious fried breakfast, they prepared to start their pursuit of Phillip, the truth or, preferably, both.

Gilbert and Sid put on freshly cleaned and pressed tuxedoes, along with their customary hats, capes, gloves, and canes. Mattie and Brewster were offered tuxes of their own, but declined, instead wearing their hats, capes, gloves, and canes with T-shirts and jeans.

Gilbert said, "That's gonna look weird."

Mattie shrugged. "Wearing the tuxedos at our age would look weird, too. At least this way we'll be comfortable."

Sid mumbled, "Hate to admit, she has a point."

Brewster said, "I've been thinking about this, and I say we just go back in time to before all of this started, and prevent it from happening in the first place."

Sid said, "No, I'm afraid that's not possible."

"Sure it is."

"Let me ask you this: Do you have any memory of a future version of you coming to you with any sort of warnings?"

Mattie and Brewster both said, "No."

"Then you didn't. Which means you won't."

"No. We still can," Brewster said. "If we can go anywhere at any time, we can go back to before Phillip froze our parents and stop all of this from ever happening. We're time travelers now. We need to think like time travelers."

Gilbert said, "Sid and I are time travelers, so however we think is how time travelers think. Think about it, you want to go back in time to before it happened, but we're already back in time now, over a hundred years before it happened, and it still happened, didn't it?"

"But we haven't tried yet," Brewster said.

"Yes, we have! Or, we will have by then, if we did."

Sid added, "But we almost certainly won't because we already know that it wouldn't have worked. In fact, it can't work, or else we wouldn't be here talking about trying it now. That's just logic."

"Is it? Is it really?" Mattie asked.

Gilbert shrugged. "What passes for logic these days, at least."

Sid said, "Look, I know it's terribly confusing, but do try to understand. We've come to the counterintuitively straightforward conclusion that the past is the past, and the future is the future. What has already happened has happened, even if it hasn't happened yet. Nothing we do changes anything that any of us has already experienced."

Gilbert said, "Look at it this way. To alter the future, we'd have to change the past, right? But how can anyone possibly change the past?

Whatever happened in the past already happened in the past. Doing something in the past doesn't change it. It just defines it."

Brewster asked, "But if you do something in the past, how can you ever know you didn't change it?"

"By looking at the future," Gilbert said.

"How can you say you can't change the past?" Mattie gestured all around them, calling their attention to pretty much everything in sight. "You're from the future; you've got your faces plastered on billboards all over town. You drive around in a car that shouldn't exist. You live in an airship that flies without hydrogen. You've changed everything."

Gilbert said, "To change something, it has to have been there, and been different before you came along and changed it. There's no evidence, none, that this period ever existed without us. We haven't changed the past because this is how the past is."

"Or was," Sid said.

"*And* was," Gilbert said. "We should know. We were here, and still are. And if we can't change the past, then, logically, nothing we do in it can change the future, because everything we have done, or ever will do, already hasn't. How's that make you feel?"

"Confused," Brewster said.

Mattie added, "And angry."

Gilbert nodded. "Now you're thinking like time travelers."

Brewster asked, "But how can you know you can't change the future if you don't even try?"

"Because we've all tried at one point or another," Gilbert said. "And it never works. We've all tried to prevent ourselves from doing something or to cause ourselves to do something else. Every time, we get stopped, or we screw it up, or the other us doesn't listen. Or, God help us, our attempt to prevent whatever we did turns out to be the very thing that gave us the idea to do whatever it was in the first place. It never works."

Sid said, "We concede that this all sounds like nonsense, but consider the following. In all the time people have been traveling through time, not one of us has seen any evidence of anything any of us did in the past altering the future one iota. None at all. Don't forget; we're all part of an algorithm. The computer has already done all of the math. We're just experiencing it. All we truly have is the moment we're in. Yesterday is a memory and tomorrow is a hope. All we have is now, and acting now is the only way to accomplish anything."

"But you're time travelers," Brewster said. "You can go to the past or the future."

"And when we do, from our point of view, whatever moment we travel to instantly becomes *now*."

Mattie said, "I don't buy it."

Sid said, "And you were never going to."

"Completely predictable," Gilbert agreed. "Should have written it down and sealed it in an envelope or something."

Sid looked at Mattie, amused, but with no cruelty, and said, "Okay, fine. You probably won't get it until you see it for yourselves. Go ahead. Go back to before all of this happened, over a century into the future from where and when we are now, and warn yourselves not to leave your parents alone, or whatever you think is best. We'll be waiting here."

Mattie and Brewster looked uncertainly at Gilbert and Sid, then looked at each other, then looked back to Gilbert and Sid.

Sid made a shooing motion with his hands and said, "Off you pop."

Gilbert said, "Have fun."

The day before Phillip's appearance in Mattie and Brewster's home, and the confounding events that came after, the band room at the twins' school sat empty. The sound of the marching band beginning practice out on the football field drifted in. Distance and the building's insulation filtered the higher frequencies and dulled the lower ones, making the instruments sound like a hundred kazoos attempting to play "Louie Louie."

Closed cabinets covered one entire wall of the room. One of the doors, a large one marked "Sousaphones," creaked open just a crack. After a pause, it opened further and Mattie and Brewster's heads emerged, scanning the room for potential witnesses. Convinced that the coast was clear, they stepped out of the cabinet, placing their top hats back on their heads and shaking the dust out of their silk capes.

"Okay," Mattie said. "School will let out in five minutes. Somewhere between three and eight minutes after that, we'll walk right past that door."

"And what do we do then?" Brewster asked.

Mattie shrugged. "We haven't discussed it. We could grab them—the other us—and pull them in here to talk to them. Or we could try to get their attention somehow."

Brewster furrowed his brow. "In a crowded hallway?"

"Yeah. You're right. Someone would see us. Us-us, not them-us. What if we were invisible?"

"They'd see the distortion and the periscopes."

"Yeah, and us, the other us, talking to us, this us. That'd draw attention. No good. Okay, what else? We could try to get to them on the walk home, but that's—"

They finished the sentence in unison, "just as bad."

"Broad daylight," Brewster said. "Public street."

Mattie flapped a hand as if trying to shoo the bad idea away. "Yeah, agreed. Okay, so what did we do after that? We went home, Mom and Dad were there. I went over to Audrey's to study. I had dinner there. I was with her and her family the whole night. I mean, I went to the bathroom a couple of times."

"Great. We'll teleport in there and warn you."

"No."

"What do you mean, no?"

"I don't want you breaking in on me when I'm in the bathroom."

"Fine, go alone."

"And if it doesn't work, you blame me? No thanks. Besides, Audrey kept talking to me through the door. She and Raphael are having problems."

"Again?"

"*Still.* How about you? Were you ever alone that night?"

Brewster said, "No, I studied at the table while Mom did some sewing, then we had dinner, and I did some reading on the couch while Dad watched an old movie. *Outland.*"

"What was it about?"

"Dad was watching it."

Mattie said, "Space?"

"Space. Old James Bond and *Young Frankenstein*'s monster fighting in space."

"That sounds good. How was it?"

Brewster shook his head. "It didn't distract me from my book."

"Okay, did you go to the bathroom?"

"Yes."

"Then we can—"

"No."

"Why not?"

"Same reasons you said."

"Eh, fair enough. I don't really want to see you on the toilet anyway. Hey, what if we come to ourselves after we've gone to bed?"

"I don't know, Mattie. We might think it's just a dream."

"We'll tell ourselves that it isn't."

"That's exactly what we'd say in a dream, though."

The door to the band room flew open and Dolan rushed in. He darted to the cabinets, pulling out a large brown case, which he opened on the floor. He pulled out what looked like beautifully polished sections of wooden plumbing pipe and began to fit the pieces together. His haste and concentration were such that he nearly had his bassoon assembled before he realized he wasn't alone. He muttered, "Late for practice," as a means to explain his actions as he turned to look at Mattie and Brewster, then stopped dead.

The twins stood there, quietly looking back at him.

Dolan broke into a wide, acrid smile. His voice distorted into a delighted squeal. "Nice outfits! Very fancy! Looking sharp!"

Mattie and Brewster looked down at their perfectly ordinary jeans and shirts, and how they contrasted against the gloves, capes, top hats, and walking sticks.

"You two working on a tap-dancing routine?"

Mattie said, "Go play your bassoon, Dolan!"

"This bassoon's my ticket to college. University orchestras are always desperate for a good bassoonist."

"Because nobody wants to be seen playing a bassoon."

"Yeah? Nobody wants to be seen dressing like Mr. Peanut either. Maybe you two can get a scholarship for that." Dolan snorted with laughter as he walked out of the band room, assembling the last few pieces of his instrument.

Once he'd gone, Mattie said, "The day of the attack, he mentioned—"

"Our outfits. I remember," Brewster interrupted her. "That means we were here the day before, right now, and it didn't—"

"I know what it means," Mattie said.

The school bell rang, and almost immediately the hallway outside the door filled with the sound of voices and footsteps.

Brewster asked, "You still wanna try?"

"Eh, what's the point. If we do, it didn't work. Let's go."

"Yeah," Brewster said. He placed a hand on Mattie's shoulder as she took off her hat and swiped through the interface inside its crown.

In a few seconds, they both disappeared.

Mattie and Brewster materialized on the patio to find Gilbert and Sid seated comfortably at the table with cold drinks and big smiles.

Sid asked, "Are we to surmise by your speedy return and downcast eyes that your attempt to change the past, albeit in the distant future, was not as successful as you hoped?"

Mattie said, "Nobody likes a gloater."

"And yet everybody likes to gloat. Life is full of such incongruities, don't you find?"

Gilbert said, "So now you know. We can't change what's already happened, even if it hasn't. It's a hard lesson that we all have to learn. There's no way to prevent it."

"The lack of a means to prevent it is, in fact, the nature of the problem," added Sid.

Gilbert stood up and clapped his hands together as if he relished finally getting to work. "Now that we have that out of the way, how shall we proceed? And please, try to suggest something that might work."

Brewster said, "I guess we could go to where Phillip lives and snoop around. We might find something."

"Exactly what I was thinking."

Mattie said, "Good. Where's that?"

Gilbert said, "Um, that would be Medieval England. Leadchurch. The same little town where he met your father."

"You mean the place we already were yesterday?" Brewster said.

"Yes. And stop your moaning. It's not like it's a long car ride or anything."

15.

The four of them appeared in the woods just outside of Leadchurch. They moved cautiously to the edge of town, hiding behind trees and shrubs just in case someone happened to look their way. As they walked, they plotted their route to Phillip's place. While Gilbert and Sid doubted that there was any malfeasance on Phillip's part, they had agreed that it was possible, and that it was best to catch him by surprise.

Gilbert held his arms out wide, flourished with his fingers, making sure to touch his thumb to the crease at the first knuckle of each of his fingers, then threw a nonexistent golf ball at the ground as he said, *"Ninja vanish,"* and disappeared in a puff of smoke.

Sid, Mattie, and Brewster all followed suit. Soon, there was no sign of their presence, save for some visual distortions, the remaining smoke, and the sound of coughing.

"Maybe you could make a version without the smoke bombs," Mattie said, between dry, hacking coughs. "For when nobody's going to be around."

"No," Sid said, choking back his own coughs. "It's absolutely crucial that you do things the right way, even if nobody else will ever know. You'll know, and your opinion of your work's as important as anybody else's."

Gilbert said, "At any rate, we should get a move on before some peasant sees all this smoke and comes looking for a forest fire."

After a moment, the bent upper ends of their periscopes appeared, poking out of their cloaking fields, about seven feet above the forest floor. All of the periscopes swung about and lurched back and forth as they turned to one side then the other, sweeping their glass lenses about, trying to spot each other.

Gilbert said, "Right. My periscope is the one bouncing up and down. Can you all see me?"

Brewster, Mattie, and Sid all said that they could.

"Good. I'll lead. Follow me, single file, and if someone falls behind, let us know."

The four floating periscope tips bobbed and swayed their way through the trees, across a stretch of tall grass, and into town.

"You sure you know where we're going?" Mattie whispered.

"Yeah. Been there once. Phillip invited us over for lunch. It's just around the corner here."

Brewster said, "I'm more worried about when we're going than where. Phillip can travel through time. There's no way to know at what point in his life he attacked our parents. We could be here way before, or way afterward."

"True," Sid said, "but this is an excellent place to start. When you become a time traveler, routines, patterns, and procedures become surprisingly important. Life becomes a confounding kaleidoscope of conundrums and chaos."

Gilbert said, "When we get home, you're sticking a dollar in the alliteration jar."

"Apologies, it just slipped out. Anyway, while Phillip could leave the theater every night and go literally any place and anywhere, he doesn't. Nor does Martin. They go back to the place they consider home, at a point sometime after they left, usually, about the length of time they were gone."

"Otherwise, it's easy to end up staying awake for twenty hours straight, and saying things like *I haven't slept in over a century.* It's not healthy. Messes with your sense of reality."

"Which is hard enough to keep on the straight and narrow in our case, as you can well imagine," Sid added. "So, knowing Phillip's general schedule, and how many shows he does a week, it was a matter of simple arithmetic to determine that this should be a day or two after whatever happened with him and your parents if he's kept to his pattern. If he hasn't, then maybe we can get some information."

"Or perhaps this Phillip will help us," Gilbert said.

Mattie asked, "Why would Phillip help us confront himself at some other time in his life?"

"On account of the human condition. The young tend to be disgusted at what they become, and the old have contempt for what they once were."

Mattie said, "Ugh. That's awful. That can't be true."

Gilbert laughed. "I'm going to go forward in time, to when you're in your forties, and remind you that you said that. I bet we'll share a laugh over it."

Brewster whispered, "Hey, guys, just because we're invisible, doesn't mean we're inaudible. Shouldn't we try to be quiet?"

Sid said, "Yes, we should, but it isn't essential in this case. Nobody's that close to us, and these people have been living in proximity to your parents and their friends for years now. They've grown accustomed to much stranger things than some disembodied voices. Watch this."

Sid cleared his throat, and in a loud, clear voice, said, "Pardon me, ma'am."

A peasant woman who was walking the other direction across the street stopped and looked around, searching for whoever had addressed her.

"I'm sorry to bother you and for the fact that you can't see me. I'm hoping you can direct me to the local wizard?"

The woman relaxed, and while she still kept searching around, not knowing where to address her answer, she said, "Oh, it's just a few more doors down that way on the right. Is there about to be trouble? Should I be running?"

"No, I just want to talk to him. It's about all I can do, as you can imagine, being a disembodied voice and all."

The woman nodded and walked away.

As the four floating periscopes continued down the street, Mattie grumbled, "I thought we were supposed to be sneaking. What's the point of being invisible if we go around talking to people?"

Gilbert said, "We don't want Phillip to see us coming. We don't care if a few citizens hear us coming."

"Besides," Sid said, "were it not for the invisibility spells, we would be gallivanting around in our tuxedoes, which, in this time, would draw much more attention than disembodied voices ever could. People in this time period are notorious for their irrational hostility toward the overdressed."

The four of them came to a stop in front of a two-story, thatched roof building with a sign over the door that said "Wizard," and a second sign on the door that said "Out." Through the window, they could make out shelves full of small bottles and various powders, liquids, and unidentifiable objects, but little else.

Mattie said, "The sign says he's not here."

Sid said, "Indeed it does, my young friend, but in time you'll learn that printing something on a board doesn't make it true. For example, in my experience, slower traffic seldom keeps right."

Brewster said, "The lights are out. That might suggest that he really isn't here."

"It also suggests that we're in the 1100s, and electric lights haven't been invented yet," Gilbert said. "Don't feel bad. Time travel takes a lot of getting used to, but you have to keep in mind where and when you are. Besides, it doesn't matter if he's home or not. We're going in either way. Take off your hats, kiddos. This'll be good practice for you. We're teleporting in. Ten feet forward should do it."

As the twins removed and reached into their hats, the displays built into the hats' linings lit up, allowing them to see the interfaces despite the light-warping invisibility spell surrounding them on the outside.

A few seconds later, they all stood in the front room of Phillip's shop. They removed their invisibility spells and put their hats back on.

Mattie stepped closer to the shelves lining the back wall. There, in a place of prominence, a creature that appeared to be the front half of a dead squirrel, stuffed, shaved, and sewn to the back half of a dead frog, stuffed, and with hair glued to it, lay in a large glass jar.

"What kind of person would have something like this?" she muttered, not really expecting an answer.

Sid gave her one. "A person who's attempting to convince superstitious peasants that he is a wizard. These are simply props, Mattie. Nothing more. Gilbert and I own an apparatus that looks as if it was designed solely to cut people into three equal parts and then to display the segments. Our apparatus is better designed, and far less dust covered, but the same principle applies. This way, now. If Phillip's here, he's gonna be upstairs."

Gilbert led the twins through a beaded curtain into the darkened séance room. Sid brought up the rear. They walked around a table holding a crystal ball, past velvet draperies scrawled with logos of various eighties rock bands altered slightly to look like arcane runic symbols. At the back of the room they came to a door, which led to stairs.

The four of them climbed the staircase. Gilbert looked back over his shoulder at the others. "I'm told at one time he had a lot of spells and such on this door and staircase so nobody but him could see what he had up here."

Brewster said, "That seems suspicious."

"It was," Gilbert said. "Everybody thought so, even your parents. But it turns out he wasn't up to anything bad."

"How'd they find out?" Brewster asked.

"He told them."

Mattie snorted. "Yeah, that proves it."

They stepped onto the landing and soaked in their surroundings: track lighting illuminated furniture made of white leather and chrome, and framed posters depicted women with snow-white skin and jet-black hair standing in front of pastel-colored triangles and squiggly lines. The room also contained a massive rack-mounted stereo with speakers the size of tombstones, a full-size arcade cabinet, and a white Pontiac Fiero.

"As you can see," Sid said, "Phillip chooses to live in the past, both literally and figuratively."

Mattie opened her mouth to speak, but she never got the words out. At that moment, a huge, white, furry creature with tusks on the side of its head, sharp yellow teeth, and long black claws appeared in the middle of the room. The creature roared and swiped its massive paws menacingly.

Next to the monster, a man appeared. He wore a trench coat and a fedora with a long, pointed top sewn over the crown. He had a five-o'clock shadow and iron-gray hair and wielded the bridge cue from a pool table in his hands.

On the other side of the monster, a ball of flame roared into existence, then stretched in two directions, becoming a line that bent around tight corners until it formed a pentagram of fire in midair. The light and heat from the flames flashed brighter before subsiding, fading away to reveal a thin, pale man in a black robe and hat. His right foot stuck out from the hem of the robe and appeared to consist only of bare bone stripped of flesh. Behind him another man appeared, smaller and less well-groomed, wearing a tuxedo jacket over a shirt and pants that appeared to be made of burlap. This second man held a gunny sack with a pentagram painted on its front.

The man in the trench coat said, "You're trespassing. Stop right where you are and drop those canes."

"Or what?" Sid asked. "You'll pot us like a black ball at the crucible?"

The man in the trench coat looked confused.

Sid said, "You're holding a billiards cue. It's a snooker reference. You Yanks! There are games other than Eight Ball, you know."

"And really, a Wampa?" Gilbert said to the white, furry creature. "That's the scariest thing you could think of to turn into? All it really did was slap Luke on the side of the face and scratch him with its fingernails. You might as well have shown up here as a Real Housewife of Beverly Hills."

The man in the black robe shouted, "Shut up!"

"Oh, very good," Sid said. "That's certainly in keeping with your theme. *Lo, a fearsome wizard sprang forth from a fiery pentagram, and in a voice throbbing with arcane power, bade us to shut up.*"

The wizard turned to the filthy man in the tuxedo jacket. "Hubert, hand me the Rod of Raimi!"

"What is he, your caddy?" Gilbert asked.

Mattie leaned toward Brewster and whispered, "Do they look familiar to you?"

Brewster squinted. "Yeah, maybe."

The dirty little man in the tuxedo jacket reached into his gunny sack and pulled out a bronze stick about a foot long, decorated with tiny carvings of skulls and demons. He handed it to the wizard in black, who whipped it forward at Gilbert, Sid, Mattie, and Brewster as if he were casting a rod and reel.

A bright light shone from the upper corner of the room, accompanied by a loud tearing noise. The four of them couldn't help but look at it. As their heads turned in unison, the world seemed to shift beneath their feet. Later, they theorized that the spell somehow affected their inner ears, but the result was the feeling that the entire world had suddenly, jarringly tilted twenty degrees. Then, the light went out, replaced by a torrent of viscous green-and-brown fluid that flowed down over them, covering their faces and drenching their clothing. They grabbed each other for support, but only managed to pull each other down into a slippery, writhing heap. They all wallowed for a moment, then the fluid gathered together and lifted off of them, flying back the direction it had come as if someone had simply reversed the film. Mattie, Brewster, Gilbert, and Sid all lay, bone-dry, jumbled on the floor, like the aftermath of a drunken game of Twister. Any sign of the repulsive flood that had knocked them over was gone.

Sid picked up his hat from the ground and scrambled to his feet. "Right. Enough of this foolishness!"

He bared his teeth as he reached into his hat, rummaged around a bit, then pulled out a rabbit.

Out of sheer instinct, the wizard in black and the Wampa both applauded, until the wizard in the trench coat glared at them, shaming them into silence.

Sid let go of the rabbit, which shot toward the wizards without so much as touching the ground first. It latched on to the throat of the man in the trench coat. He and the rabbit struggled briefly, then the rabbit launched itself toward the Wampa. The towering white beast swiped with its huge paw, knocking the bunny away and toward the wizard in black, who caught it just before the rabbit's teeth reached his face.

Brewster asked, "Were you at our parents' wedding?"

"Yes," Mattie shouted. "That's it! They were."

"You were dressed like a Fremen." Mattie pointed at the man in the trench coat. She moved her hand to point at the wizard in black. "And you, you were wearing a padded bodysuit and a blue Speedo. And I think we sat next to you at the theater when we went to Dad's show!"

The wizard in black looked away from the struggling rabbit in his hands and studied the twins. "Are you Brewster and Mattie? Wow! I didn't recognize you."

The wizard in the trench coat said, "You've gotten so big!"

The Wampa nodded, opened its mouth, and let out a fearsome roar. It stopped abruptly, held up a single finger, made some quiet sounds like a large dog halfheartedly barking, and transformed into a black wizard in a purple robe and hat. "I said, you're practically grown-ups. Where are your parents, and who are these guys? Are they bothering you?"

"Are we bothering them?" Gilbert asked. "You're the ones who hosed them down with gore."

Mattie said, "These are Gilbert and Sid. They're friends of Dad."

The man in the trench coat said, "Oh, yeah, of course. We've heard of you. You're the guys from across the street. I'm Roy."

The black man in the purple robe said, "I'm Tyler."

The man in black said, "I'm Gary. This is my butler, Hubert. Sorry about the Rod of Raimi. It's just that Phillip's been missing for a couple of days. We can't even find him using the file. We've got our friend Jeff working on it right now. Then you all appear at Phillip's place, and we kind of assumed the worst."

"What are you doing here?" Tyler asked.

"Looking for Phillip ourselves," Gilbert said. "The kids believe he may have attacked Martin and Gwen."

Roy said, "He didn't."

Mattie asked, "What? What do you mean, *he didn't*? How would you know?"

"If there's one thing I'm sure of, it's that Phillip would never hurt either of your parents."

"Yes," Sid said. "That's precisely what we told them."

"You don't know," Brewster said. "We were there. We know what we saw."

"And that's precisely the answer we got, as well," Sid added.

16.

They flew in a loose formation over the rooftops and out of town. Mattie, Brewster and the magicians flew standing perpendicular to the ground, hands resting on their canes, capes flapping in the wind behind them. Roy, Tyler, and Gary flew tilted far forward, Superman style. Hubert rode in a glowing bubble of energy coming from Gary's wizard staff.

Hubert looked over at Sid and examined his tuxedo. Sid noticed Hubert's attention and nodded in a friendly but noncommittal greeting.

Hubert nodded back and asked, "So, how long have you been a butler?"

They flew low over the treetops, into a clearing full of dead trees, salted earth, an above-ground swimming pool, and a brick firepit. A cliff rose on the far side of the clearing. Carved into the cliff was a giant skull, its open mouth forming a cave. The group landed just inside the entrance.

Gary welcomed everyone to his home and led them through a large set of carved, ornamental doors, then a circular chamber with a large stone altar in the middle, past a second, smaller door, and into a large, comfortable apartment. He had decorated his home with stylish, handcrafted wooden furniture that failed to go with the green shag carpeting and retro-sixties conversation pit.

Gary used a communication spell to call Jeff and invite him over. Jeff signaled his intention to accept the invitation by materializing in Gary's living room before they'd hung up the call.

Mattie and Brewster told everyone what they saw and heard the night of the attack. They described what they did after the attack, what further events transpired, and how they reacted, leading all the way to the moment they appeared, along with Gilbert and Sid, in Phillip's rec room.

The adults listened respectfully until the story reached its conclusion, then they discussed what they'd heard. In the end, the wizards quickly reached a consensus on two points.

They agreed that Martin and Gwen would be proud of the great bravery and resourcefulness that the twins had shown in dealing with a very traumatic experience.

They also agreed that now that the grown-up wizards were aware of the situation, the best course of action would be for them to take over all of the investigation and protect the twins by having them remain safe and sound in Gary's cave, "playing video games or something."

"Yeah," Gary said. "You can have a lot of fun here. I have an N64. You can play *GoldenEye!*"

Mattie said, "I'm trying very hard not to swear at you idiots right now."

Gary said, "Your mother would appreciate that. Though she probably wouldn't like you calling us idiots."

"Why not?" Roy asked. "She's called us that herself, many times."

Brewster said, "I can see why."

Roy tilted his head and smiled at the twins. "I know it's hard to understand, kids, but your parents would want us to keep you safe."

"You think we don't understand our parents caring for us? We understand that perfectly. We also understand that we care for our parents and want to help them as quickly as we can. That means having everybody who possibly can help—not leaving the two of us here alone, playing outdated video games."

"We wouldn't leave you alone," Jeff said. "We'd have someone stay here with you, to keep you safe."

Brewster said, "So that's three people out of commission, instead of out there helping."

Jeff said, "The best thing we can do to help your parents is to keep their children safe."

"Even if it's against our will?" Mattie asked.

Roy laughed. "Keeping her safe against her will. She really is her father's daughter, isn't she?"

Brewster said, "Mattie and I know our parents better than any of you. We know what happened, because we were there, and now we have powers, just like you all do. We've gotten things this far. There's nobody better to help our parents, and you want to put us on the sidelines? We've already done so much! Gilbert, Sid, tell them."

Sid said, "It is unquestionably true. The two of you have done tremendous work in assisting your parents, far more than I could have done at your age."

"Thank you."

"And though it pains me to say it, I think these chaps do have a valid point. If you wish to continue assisting your parents, your best course of action would be to stop arguing with the adults and let . . . us . . . get on with—look, please stop glaring at me like that. Back when only the four of us were on the case it made sense to keep you involved, but now we have a lot more people, and there's no need to risk you two. We're just trying to do the right thing here."

Brewster said, "But, you made us almost invincible."

Gilbert nodded. "Yeah, but *almost invincible* is another way to say *not invincible*."

Mattie asked, "If this is the way you feel about it, why'd you even bother to teach us magic in the first place?"

"So you could protect yourselves if need be," Sid said. "By that logic, do you expect us to object to a plan to protect you further?"

The wizards decided, over Mattie and Brewster's constant objections, that they would split up. Roy and Gilbert would search for Phillip at all of his known haunts, across all of the time frames he was known to frequent. Jeff would continue trying to use the file to locate Phillip, and Sid would try to identify and remove the code keeping anyone from teleporting into the kids' home at the moment that whatever happened, happened. Tyler would take the first shift *babysitting* the twins.

Mattie and Brewster objected, both to the idea that they needed to be babysat and to the use of the word *mishap* to describe what happened to their parents, but that did not prevent all of the wizards but Tyler from leaving. In fact, the protests might have accelerated the exodus.

"Okay, kids," Tyler said in a wrongheaded attempt to win them over. "The N64's all hooked up. If you need any help getting it running . . ."

His voice trailed off as Brewster stared at him, unmoving. Mattie glanced down at the console sitting on the floor in front of the massive tube TV and said, "It has two buttons. I think we can figure it out."

Hubert said, "If either of you needs anything, food, drinks, anything at all, I'll be happy to get it for you."

"Yes," Tyler said. "And I'll be happy to run any food or drinks he gets you through a spell that sterilizes it. Hubert's actually a pretty good cook, once you render his dishes biologically inert. Anyway, I know you two aren't happy about this, and I don't want to make it worse."

Tyler removed his hat, pulled out a small laptop, and sat down at the dining table. "I'll be back here getting some work done. If you need anything, just ask. Otherwise, I'll stay out of your hair."

Mattie turned on the TV, sat down cross-legged on the floor, and picked up one of the N64's controllers, puzzling for a moment over which of its three handles she should hold.

Brewster asked Tyler, "What are you working on?"

"I'm writing a novel."

"What's it about?"

"It's a really long, complex story. It'd take a while to explain."

"Oh. Okay."

"Have a seat. I think you'll find it interesting."

Brewster silently cursed himself for asking, then pulled up a chair.

Two hours later, Tyler said, "So you can see how an allegory about the Vietnam War transposed to a fantasy milieu is an idea that's just full of dramatic possibilities."

Brewster pushed his chair back from the table and stood up. "Uh, yeah, totally. I guess."

"And I think that making my protagonist one of the gnomes fighting alongside the elves who are helping them defend their home in the southern part of the forest from the gnomes in the north, who are being backed by the dwarves, is a novel touch. That way I can make the point that the whole forest war wouldn't have happened if it weren't for the pixies who invaded years before, then fled, leaving a power vacuum. . ."

Brewster backed away. "Yeah. That sounds really interesting. Especially the part with the giant dragonflies carrying elves away from the pinecone fort at the end. I'm, uh, I'm gonna see what Mattie's up to."

"You do that. I really should get to work. The sooner I get writing, the sooner I'll have a first draft for you to read."

"Great," Brewster replied, and nearly ran across the room to where his sister sat on the floor in front of the TV, playing *GoldenEye*.

Brewster sat down. "This sucks."

"Yeah," Mattie said. "I noticed. I say we get out of here."

Brewster said, "I thought about it, around the time he started explaining how the elf king's high priest represents Kissinger, whoever that is. I don't think it'd work, though. As soon as he sees us messing with our hats, he'll know something's up. He'd probably use magic to stop us before we can teleport out."

"You know, I came pretty close to taking off about a half hour ago. I had teleportation back to the dirigible all programmed and everything, but I didn't want to desert you."

"Thanks for that."

"Also, it wouldn't have worked. Gilbert and Sid could follow us super easy if we did that," Mattie said. "But what if we break our emergency pendants again?"

Tyler stopped typing and called out, "Hey, what are you two whispering about?"

"I'm just explaining the game to him. See, Brewster, you chase these rectangular guys around a maze made of nothing but right angles while you try to shoot each other with big, blocky bullets."

Tyler nodded and went back to typing.

Mattie lowered her voice. "I say we count to three and snap the pendants in half. We'll both disappear at the same time, and it should take us back home, just after the moment we left two days ago. We'll be free, and we'll have a head start."

Brewster said, "I don't know. It blows being stuck here, but they're just trying to help us."

"By keeping us from doing anything? That's not helping us. That's hindering us. It's literally the opposite, and I'm using the word *literally* correctly."

They lapsed into a sullen silence, the only sound in the house coming from the video game and Tyler's keyboard. The moment of quiet lasted for nearly a full minute, broken by Roy materializing.

Tyler and Brewster both said hello.

"Time to change shifts, Tyler." Roy walked over to the table and slumped down in one of the chairs as if teleporting had put a terrible strain on his lower back.

"One mo," Tyler muttered, quickly tapping out the end of the sentence he'd been working on. He saved his work, then looked up at Roy and smiled. "There. Done. So, yeah, the kids have been great. No problems. Very well behaved."

Brewster was the only person who saw Mattie grit her teeth.

Roy asked, "Where's Hubert?"

Tyler said, "Outside, having a dip in the pool."

Roy grimaced. "How much chlorine does Gary use to keep that water clean?"

Tyler stood up, closing his laptop. "Not enough. So, where should I go to search for Phillip?"

"I'd check with the other guys. I just got done scouring Atlantis."

Tyler winced. "Oof. He'd have to be pretty desperate to try to hide out where his ex lives."

"His exes, technically."

Tyler laughed. "Yeah. True. That doesn't make it better. Did you touch base with her—either of them?"

"No. I figured they'd either refuse to help find him or set out to destroy him. Neither of those sounded helpful."

Mattie paused the game and turned around to listen to Tyler and Roy's conversation, suddenly interested. Tyler and Roy smiled at Brewster and Mattie.

Tyler said, "Well, kids, I've got to go. Roy will be hanging out with you for a while. I'll see you later, okay?"

Mattie and Brewster both said goodbye, and Tyler disappeared.

Roy said, "So, it sounds like you two and Tyler got along well."

Brewster said, "Yeah. He's nice."

Roy squinted at Brewster. "That sentence sounded like it had a silent *but* clinging to its end."

"No! No. Tyler's cool."

Roy kept squinting. Brewster tried to keep a straight face, then squirmed for a moment before finally laughing. "Okay, okay. He really is cool, but he just kept talking about elves and dwarves, and the Vietnam War."

Roy laughed. "Ah, told you about his book, did he? Yeah. He'll talk your leg off if you let him. I can only hope his books are more entertaining than the speeches he gives about them."

"You haven't read any of them?" Mattie asked.

"No. He writes fantasy, and I don't go in for all that elf and goblin crap."

"But you're a wizard."

"Yeah, well, I don't have to read about it. I live it."

Mattie and Brewster both smiled and gave themselves room to hope that the next two hours might be less boring than the previous two had been.

Roy said, "Yeah, I don't need to hear about any gnomes or pixies. The Vietnam War though, that's an interesting topic."

Mattie's and Brewster's smiles faded.

"Yeah, for instance," Roy continued, "Kennedy got us into the war, and LBJ and Nixon both kept us in it, but did you know that all three of them agreed that going into 'Nam was a terrible mistake and that there was no way to win?"

"No," Brewster said. "I didn't."

"It's true. In fact, it could be argued that the only reason we ever got into that war was because of a miscommunication in the Kennedy White House between the president and an ambassador."

"Oh," Brewster said.

"Yeah, then neither of the next two presidents pulled out because they didn't want to be the first commander in chief to lose a war."

Brewster glanced at Mattie, who was staring at him, her eyebrows raised.

Roy said, "See, it all started when the French colonized Vietnam. This is clear back in the 1800s."

Brewster stuck his fingers down the neck of his shirt and made eye contact with Mattie. "Three. Two."

Roy asked, "Why are you counting?"

Mattie dug her pendant out of the collar of her shirt. She and Brewster said, "One," in unison, then snapped their pendants and disappeared.

Brewster and Mattie materialized, sitting on the floor of the living room of their own house back in Seattle. They scrambled to their feet and ran to the window just in time to see themselves driving away in their father's car.

Brewster said, "Okay, we're back where we started. Now what? We can't stick around here. The federal agents could be back any second. That's why we just left in such a hurry."

"Yeah, well, things are different now, aren't they?" Mattie twiddled her fingers in the specific pattern Gilbert and Sid had taught them. A black disk slid into existence twirling between her fingers and expanded into a full top hat. She held the top hat upside down and shook it once. Her black-and-white walking stick flew up out of the hat, into the air, where she caught it. She placed the hat on the back of her right hand and made it roll down her arm and across her shoulders. A silk cape appeared on her back as the hat passed. She caught the hat with her right hand and placed it on her head, smiling at Brewster.

"You forgot the gloves."

Mattie lifted her hat and grabbed the white gloves that were sitting, folded, on her head.

"My point," Mattie said, pulling on her white gloves, "is that last time the cops came, we were just normal kids. Now we have powers. We can defend ourselves."

"You just want to throw the rabbit at someone."

"Oh, like you don't! Like you aren't dying to throw the rabbit at someone!"

"Of course I want to throw the rabbit at someone, but I think it would be smarter to avoid having to."

"Well obviously, but if we have to I'm not gonna hesitate."

"So what do we do?"

Mattie said, "We go to Atlantis, and we find Phillip's ex-girlfriend. One of them anyway. From the sound of it, he has a few there. Which . . . ick. We find one of them and ask her where to find him. The way Roy was talking, she'll understand how evil he is."

"But how do we get to Atlantis?" Brewster asked.

"We'll teleport."

Brewster took a deep breath. "I'll rephrase my question. How do we go to Atlantis without knowing where or when it is?"

Mattie shrugged. "Beats me. We'll figure it out."

"That's not good enough."

"It has been so far. When this whole thing started out, we were just ordinary teenagers, Brewster. Now we're superpowered time travelers, and we got that by going with the flow. I gotta believe that if we just keep our eyes open and our wits about us, something helpful will turn up."

Brewster started to reply but stopped cold when Phillip appeared, his eyes darting around the room. When they settled on the twins, he cringed, surprised and terrified. He yelled, "Oh no!"

Mattie and Brewster both shouted, "You!"

Phillip did the world's fastest double take at the sight of a young woman Mattie's age wearing a top hat and satin cape with her T-shirt and jeans, then got over it and lunged forward, grabbing both Mattie and Brewster by their upper arms.

Brewster cried, "Let go!"

Mattie turned and bent at the waist, trying to twist free from his grip.

Phillip said, "You should have stayed in the basement!"

"You'd like that, wouldn't you? Mattie asked.

"Yes!" Phillip said, struggling to maintain his grip on the squirming teenagers. "Very much!"

Mattie shouted, "Let go of me!"

Before Phillip could respond, they all saw the hint of something: two shapes, vaguely like men, appearing in the room with them. They only had a fraction of a second to see whatever it was before Phillip, Mattie, and Brewster all teleported away.

17.

The twins appeared somewhere dark and loud.

The first impression they had was of a raging fire in the distance and a horrible cacophonous sound, like a tractor-trailer crash, or a building collapse. As their eyes adjusted and their brains made more sense of the data coming in, they quickly realized that the sound of the raging fire was actually the roar of an enthusiastic crowd, and the red light in the distance came from stage lighting. The cacophony resolved itself into energetic drumming and an overly active guitarist showing off his prowess on the pedal steel.

After a quick look around, Brewster and Mattie saw that they were standing in the aisle at the very top of the balcony of a theater, about two-thirds full of people. On the stage, the four men standing in front of a band all said "Giddyup." Then one of them sang "Oom poppa oom poppa mow mow" in an improbably deep voice.

Mattie and Brewster both asked, "Where are we?"

Phillip looked down at the stage, then back to twins as if he couldn't believe they had to ask. "An Oak Ridge Boys concert. Where are your parents?" he asked.

Brewster said, "What?"

Phillip shouted over another round of *oom poppa mow mows*, "I asked where your parents are!"

Mattie said, "We know! We heard! How can you ask us that after what you did to them?"

She began squirming, trying to wriggle free from Phillip's grip.

He clamped down tighter on her forearm. "Please, stop that! Mathison, please. Oh no—"

The vague form of two people started to appear, but Mattie, Brewster, and Phillip all vanished before the two fully materialized.

The environment around Phillip and the twins remained dark and loud, but everything else changed. Being students at an American high school, Brewster and Mattie immediately recognized that they were underneath a set of gym bleachers. They stood, surrounded by thin metal supports and struts. From above they heard the sounds of a basketball game and saw slivers of light with small glimpses of legs and backs through the gaps between the aluminum slats.

Brewster shook his head. "What is going on?"

Phillip said, "It's an emergency macro I wrote. If I identify someone as a threat, it automatically teleports me away from them to one of several places that nobody who knows me would ever think I'd go. Where are your parents? Are they okay? Will you please stop trying to get away from me?"

Mattie grabbed one of the bleachers' supporting struts and tried with all of her strength to pull herself free of Phillip. "Our parents are still frozen, thanks to you," she grunted, "but we've hidden them somewhere safe. And no, I won't stop trying to get away!"

Brewster knew a good idea when he saw one, and followed his sister's lead, grabbing a strut himself and pulling in the opposite direction from Mattie.

Phillip stood between them, holding both of their arms as best he could, grimacing and straining as if he were being pulled apart by wild stallions.

Mattie hooked her arm around the strut and used her free arm to strike Phillip about the rib cage with her cane.

"Please," he said, "Stop that! I didn't freeze your parents!"

"Then who did?" Brewster asked.

For just a moment, they saw the forms of two people begin to appear. Then Brewster, Mattie, and Phillip teleported away.

Phillip continued to pull on both of the twins as hard as he could, but Brewster and Mattie no longer had struts to pull on for leverage, so they both fell into him from opposite directions before all three spun and tumbled to the floor.

"Them," Phillip said. "They froze your parents. Must have done it after I left."

Mattie and Brewster both winced as their eyes adjusted to much brighter and more plentiful light. The hot air smelled of dust.

Brewster looked at Phillip, opening his mouth to speak, but blinked in surprise, pointed behind Phillip, and asked, "What the hell?"

"Language," Phillip said, but he also twisted around and looked. Behind a long chain of threadbare velvet ropes slung from peeling brass-plated stanchions, an ancient, open-topped Mercedes Benz sat on cracked tires. A beat-up old mannequin stood in the back seat, wearing a Nazi uniform, a toothbrush mustache hand-painted above its upper lip.

A hand-lettered sign said, "This Mercedes Benz staff car was," then, in much smaller letters, continued, "possibly," before concluding in huge, bright red letters, "used by Hitler!"

Brewster and Mattie looked around the room. Rusted farm implements, their wooden handles half rotted away, covered one entire wall, all labeled and displayed like prized artifacts. Along another wall, a hideously malformed wax dummy of a torturer wielding a metal poker, its tip painted bright red, loomed above an equally ill-proportioned wax replica of a young woman in a peasant blouse, strapped to a wooden table. A glass-topped display case dominated the center of the room, along with a garishly colored, hand-painted sign that read "What is ENIGMY?"

Phillip said, "This is a roadside tourist trap in Wyoming. Ghastly, isn't it? They have the nerve to call it a museum." He used his free right hand to lift himself to a crouch, in the process realizing that his right hand was only free because he'd let go of Mattie as they fell.

Mattie noticed as well, and immediately scrambled away from him in a sort of panicked crab walk, then sprang to her feet. Phillip lunged for her, his right arm extended to its limit, his hand grabbing at thin air. With his left he kept hold of Brewster, who hadn't managed to quite get his feet under him, and stumbled along behind Phillip in an attempt to regain his balance.

Mattie swung at Phillip's hand with her cane, walking backward, feeling her way with her left hand extended out behind her. She managed to keep Phillip just out of grabbing range, but she stumbled over velvet ropes and her cape, then ran backward into the side of the ancient Mercedes. She stepped up on the running board and clambered over the side, into the seating compartment.

Phillip said, "Look, get down from there. You'll knock Hitler over."

"You get back!" she shouted. She held up her cane like a batter waiting for a pitch. "Let go of my brother and tell us what's going on!"

"I'm happy to explain! I want to explain! But I have to hold on to you both while I do it."

Brewster finally managed to get his feet beneath him and started pulling away from Phillip as hard as he could. He grabbed at Phillip's fingers, trying to pry them off his arm. "Why? Why not just let go and tell us?"

The forms of two people began to take shape. Phillip and Brewster disappeared. Mattie remained, standing in the antique car next to the Hitler mannequin. She watched as two men appeared. Both wore wizard hats and robes decorated with bits of black fur and plates of metal armor. Their hats had curved horns sprouting from their sides, like cartoon Viking helmets.

One of the men was smaller in every dimension, but well proportioned, with a handsome face despite the fact that his eyes were about an inch too close together. His eye distance affected his nose, which affected his mouth and cheeks, and in the end, the overall impression was that of a good-looking man whose face had been sharpened. He caught a brief glimpse of the forms of Phillip and Brewster as they teleported away and shouted, "Crap! Phillip took off again!"

The second man was physically unremarkable: larger than his friend, but not by much; out of shape, but not horrendously so; and gawky, but no so gawky as for it to become interesting at all. He had keen eyes, a ruddy, flushed complexion, and an excited grin on his face. He held a smartphone only a few inches from his face as if lessening the distance between himself and the screen would get the information it displayed into his brain faster.

"Yes, but he shan't evade us for long. I swear he shan't! We willll catch him. We willll catch the hell out of him! And then . . ."

The larger man's impassioned speech lost steam when he saw his friend staring at him, unimpressed.

"Yeah, okay," the larger man said. "Just give me one sec to see where he went, and I'll plot the jump."

Mattie, still standing in the back seat of the Mercedes Benz, looked down at the men and asked, "Who're you?"

Both men jumped, then the smaller man replied, "Who're *you*?"

Mattie asked, "What do you want with Phillip?"

"What do *you* want with Phillip?"

"I won't answer any of your questions until you answer one of mine!"

The larger man said, "Okay, one thing we want to do with Phillip is tell him we captured his friend. I'm talking about you, by the way. Magnus, I suggest you just grab her."

Hearing the name Magnus jogged Mattie's memory. She had only ever met two people named Magnus, and she'd met them at the same time, long ago, when their father had taken her and Brewster to see his act. She knew instantly that it was these two men standing below her now. She remembered that the smaller, more appealing one's last name was Rex, and the other's last name was some sort of gagging sound she couldn't quite recall.

Magnus Rex shrugged. "Fine, if you say so, Magnus," and walked toward Mattie with his hands outstretched as if he intended just to reach up and grab her like a book on a shelf, exactly as his friend had suggested.

She pulled off her top hat and thrust her hand inside. "Stay back, I'm warning you!"

He furrowed his brow as if confused by her warning but kept coming. Mattie glanced into the hat as she swiped through menu options. Magnus Rex was stepping over the velvet ropes, nearly within grabbing range when, driven by adrenaline and panic, she pulled the rabbit out of the hat and threw it at him in one inelegant motion.

The rabbit homed in on Magnus Rex's throat. He fell backward, shouting in shock. He pulled the rabbit away from his exposed neck and threw it as far away from himself as he could. The rabbit rebounded off the ceiling and shot like a line drive for the throat of the other Magnus, who grabbed it by the hind leg, swung it through the air a few times to gain momentum, and flung it toward Mattie.

Mattie managed to duck in time for the rabbit to fly over her head, hitting the Hitler mannequin full force. Hitler fell backward, pivoting over the door of the car, hitting the cinder-block wall behind, and breaking apart into nothing but a collection of wooden body parts held together by an old uniform. The whole clattering jumble fell between the car and the wall, the fake rabbit still brutalizing it as they went. Mattie watched it fall, then turned to see Magnus Rex rushing toward her with murder in his eyes.

She knew she wouldn't have time to produce another rabbit. She threw her hat on and reared back with her cane, ready to swing for Magnus Rex's head if need be.

He kept coming. As she started to bring the cane around in a graceful arch, a hole seemed to open in space, just to her left. She barely had enough time to mentally register the fact that the portal was there before Phillip reached out, grabbed a handful of her shirt, and yanked her through.

Mattie stumbled, her cane still swinging as she emerged from the portal. She fell into Phillip while hitting him in the arm. They tumbled to the ground in a heap. Mattie rolled away from him and into a crouch, ready to attack the first thing that looked like trouble.

The ground felt gritty and hot beneath her fingers. Bright light reflected up at her, instinctively forcing her face into a grimacing squint. She swiveled her head to the left and the right. The ground appeared to be flat, white, and featureless almost to the horizon, where rolling brown hills waved and wobbled in the hazy distance.

Brewster ran over and helped her to her feet.

"Where are we?" she asked.

"The Bonneville Salt Flats. What happened?"

"Two guys in fur showed up and attacked me."

Phillip, still lying on the ground, reached out and grabbed them both by the ankle. "The Magnuses. Wizards from Norway."

Mattie started to pull her leg away from Phillip, but he tightened his grip. "Look, they could turn up any second, and if I'm not touching you, you'll be stuck here with them again. You want that?"

Mattie relaxed her leg, and she and Brewster offered Phillip their hands, then helped pull him to his feet.

"Thank you. Look, you say your parents are frozen. I assume you mean that they aren't moving, not literally—"

The forms of the Magnuses began to materialize, but Phillip and the twins teleported out before they fully appeared.

Brewster, Mattie, and Phillip appeared in a dimly lit room full of glass cases displaying trophies, athletic shoes, footballs, and more than one fedora, all neatly labeled with professionally engraved plastic cards. Before Brewster or Mattie had time to ask, Phillip said, "The Packers Hall of Fame in Green Bay, Wisconsin, 1997. There's a game of what you Americans insist upon calling *football* underway, so everyone who'd come here is at Lambeau Field or at home watching on TV. We won't be bothered. Anyway, your parents—they aren't covered in ice, they just can't move, yes?"

Brewster said, "Oh, God, they aren't still awake, are they? Do they know what's going on?"

Phillip said, "Well, yes and no. I don't believe they're in any pain. It's hard to explain, and we don't have time now. The Magnuses will show up any second."

Mattie asked, "How do they know where you are? Did they figure out the all the places you'd send yourself?"

"No, they knew when I broke the cycle and went back to your house to check on your parents and found you. Even if they did figure out the *wheres*, there's no way they could predict the *whens*. Besides,

I've known the Magnuses for a long time, and figuring things out isn't their style. They must be monitoring my movements somehow."

"So if you transport yourself, they know where you've gone."

"Yes, so it seems."

Brewster asked, "Is it that they know where you are, or that they know where you send yourself?"

Phillip shook his head. "What?"

Mattie pointed at her brother and snapped her fingers twice in quick succession. "Yes! That's a good point! That's a very good point! What he's asking is, are they zeroing in on your location? Or, are they seeing you teleport yourself and following you somehow, by monitoring you in your magic interface or something?"

Brewster nodded vigorously. "Because if it's the second one, then if someone *else* took you somewhere, and you weren't the one casting the spell, they might not see where you went."

Phillip's eyes bulged. "That's brilliant! But who'll we get to teleport me?"

Mattie shook her head, pulled off her top hat, and stuck her hand in. Five seconds later the Magnuses appeared, but the twins and Phillip didn't know it, because they were long gone.

18.

Mattie, Brewster, and Phillip materialized on the lawn between the two houses and next to the pool inside the envelope of Gilbert and Sid's dirigible. They stood, knees bent, ready for action, watching intently for the slightest sign of trouble. After a full sixty seconds of hypervigilance without any Magnuses to be seen, they began to relax.

Phillip spun around, looking at their surroundings. The early afternoon sun shone through the dirigible's skin. Outside, a mix of soot, steam, and various industrial gases rose from the smokestacks of Victorian London.

Phillip wandered closer to the edge and looked down at the view. "This is Gilbert and Sid's place. Why are we—of course! That's where you got the hat and learned to teleport."

Phillip turned around to face the twins. "Why did Gil—" He stopped talking abruptly when a rabbit flew at him and latched on to his throat. He fell backward over the edge and landed on the dirigible's skin. He lay there, his weight supported by a thin sheet of fabric, struggling to remove the rabbit as it furiously fought to sever his jugular vein.

Mattie said, "We should get Gilbert and Sid to teach us some more attack spells. The rabbit thing is getting kinda repetitive."

"I know where we are, but when are we here?" Brewster asked.

Mattie said, "Should be the afternoon of the last time we left here, when we went to try to find him. It's just where the hat was set to take us."

"Sounds good. We left home, spent a couple of days with Gilbert and Sid, went back to our home, met Phillip, and now we're back here, just after we left with the guys. That means we've jumped ahead a couple of days from when we left our house. That should help throw those Magnus guys off. So, what do we do now?"

"I guess we try to get the truth out of him." Mattie pointed at Phillip, still lying back on the tight fabric, suspended over a terrifying drop, struggling with the ferocious fake rabbit. "What do you say, Phillip? I'll remove the rabbit, for now, if you're willing to explain things."

"I want to explain! I'd be explaining right now if I didn't have to fight this stupid rabbit!"

"I guess we have a deal, then," Brewster said.

Mattie thrust her hand into her hat, swiped around a bit, and the rabbit vanished.

Phillip relaxed, sagging back into the fabric as if it were a hammock. He glanced back over his shoulder, saw the city hundreds of feet below, yelped in fear, rolled down off the fabric onto the more solid support of the patio, and speed-crawled several feet away from the edge.

"Okay," Mattie said. "Spill it."

Brewster said, "Yeah. What happened to Mom and Dad, and who did it?"

Phillip asked, "Do you mind if I get up off the ground first?"

"If you must," Brewster said.

Phillip rose to his feet and walked to the patio table and chairs. He sat down and motioned toward two of the other empty chairs. Mattie and Brewster sat down opposite him.

Phillip said, "Your father and I did two shows Saturday night. Good crowds. A little rowdy for the second show, but what can you do? We split up for the night, went our separate ways, as we always do. I went home."

"To Medieval England," Mattie said.

"Yes. I'd just finished my dinner when Magnus and Magnus turned up."

"Oh yeah, they're both named Magnus." Brewster said. "That's needlessly confusing."

Phillip laughed. "Spend a few years as a time traveler, and you'll find that it completely changes your standards as far as what sounds confusing and what doesn't. Anyway, they said they just wanted to talk, but they attacked me."

"Did they say why?" Mattie asked.

"They said something, but I don't know if it's the real reason. It's so stupid."

"What did they say?" Brewster asked.

Just having to repeat the conversation seemed to cause Phillip displeasure. "I don't know how much you two have learned about what we do . . . This thing of ours . . . The wizarding life. Some of us organized a few years back. Just those of us who live in Europe in the Middle Ages. We act like it's all a lot more formal than it actually is. In truth, we're a glorified social club. Anyway, I'm the chairman of the wizards. They named me chairman when we first formed, and I have been ever since. I put myself up for reelection every year. Frankly, I'd love it if someone serious would step up and take a turn, but the only one who ever runs against me is Magnus."

"Which one?" Mattie asked.

"I don't know. We've never been sure. If we ask which one's running they both say we can vote for whichever Magnus we like, and if we ask why we should, they say that we can vote for them for any reason we like. You can see why we thought they had to be joking."

"But they weren't," Mattie said.

"It seems not. See, the next vote's tomorrow. Tomorrow in Medieval England, which was of course, long ago. They came to me and said it was high time I give someone else a chance. I told them that I was perfectly happy to let someone else take over, and the whole conversation was quite companionable until it dawned on me that the someone they wanted to give a chance was one of them, and they wanted me to give them a chance by withdrawing so they could run unopposed. I told them that I wouldn't withdraw, and that if one of them wanted to be chairman, they'd have to convince the other wizards to vote for the Magnus in question over me."

"What'd they say to that?" Brewster asked.

"Magnus, the smarter one . . . well, *smarter* isn't the word. *Shrewder*, I guess you'd say. His last name's Galka, so I'll call him Magnus Galka, unpleasant as it is to make my mouth form those sounds. He laughed and said that they had another option, then he suggested to the other Magnus—the better-looking, more pleasant Magnus; his last name's Rex—that he show me what they mean. Magnus Rex pushed back a little bit. He said he didn't want to go about things that way. They argued for a second. Probably would have been a good chance to run, but it didn't occur to me to see either of those goofballs as a threat. Anyway, Magnus Rex relented and tried to hit me with some kind of spell. Luckily, we were in my home. I have emergency defensive macros set up there, just in case."

Brewster said, "Him casting a spell at you set off the macro that teleported us all those places."

"Right. Magnus Rex attacked and I found myself in the porta-potty at a folk music festival. The first thing I did was try to get help."

Mattie said, "From Mom and Dad."

"Yes. I'm so sorry. I regret involving your parents. It's just . . . they're my best friends, and when I'm in trouble, my first reflex is to check in with them. Besides, who knew the Magnuses were going to be this dangerous? I mean, they're the Magnuses. You've met them now, Mattie. Do they seem all that formidable?"

"They're both bigger than me, and they have magic powers."

Phillip nodded. "Yes, well, perhaps being just as large and as powerful as they are caused me to underestimate them. I'm clearly not as willing as they are to attack people I know well. That seems to be a disadvantage."

The twins said nothing. Phillip continued.

"Well, you were both there when I showed up. I knew I'd made a mistake the instant I materialized. I was lucky you were all arguing, and nobody saw me materialize. Something to do with your grades, Mattie? Are you having problems with one of your teachers?"

Mattie glared at Phillip but said nothing.

"Yes. Now's not the time, and I'm not the person. As you remember, I'm sure, your parents sent you out of the room so we could talk. They were rather unhappy with me for materializing in the same room as you two, in full wizard robes. They've worked hard to keep you insulated from this part of their lives, and they didn't like me risking exposure."

Brewster asked, "Why, though? Why are they keeping all this secret from us?"

"For the same reason rich kids can't get their trust fund until they're adults. They want you to grow up to be well-adjusted, and that won't happen if you can just magic your problems away. They were planning to tell you everything when you turned twenty-two."

"Not twenty-one?" Mattie asked.

"No, they figured the ability to do magic and the ability to drink legally shouldn't come at the same time. Before you get too upset with Gwen and Martin for holding out on you, I'd point out that you've been benefitting from magic your whole lives. You just didn't know it. Has either of you ever heard your parents complain about a lack of money? Losing their jobs? Has either of their cars ever needed to go into the shop? You're what now, sixteen? Has either of you ever broken a bone? Needed stitches? Had any illness worse than a cold?"

Brewster and Mattie looked at each other.

"See? Now think about how knowing you wouldn't get hurt, or that your parents could conjure up enough money to buy an entire toy store, might have changed your behavior. You can see why your parents didn't want you to know about this. So when I showed up, they were both fairly livid."

"Is this the way wizards usually raise their kids?" Mattie asked.

"There is no *usually*, in this case. Your parents are the first wizards ever to get married and have kids."

Brewster asked, "Really? Why?"

"Everyone who finds the file is some kind of computer programmer or hacker. One could argue that we're not a group that's prone to reproduction to begin with. Beyond that, the wizarding lifestyle isn't conducive to long-term relationships. When you have reason to believe you're immortal, making a commitment to be together forever becomes a lot less abstract."

"Wait," Mattie said. "What do you mean, immortal?"

Phillip laughed. "So Gilbert and Sid didn't quite tell you everything. One of the many powers we've mastered is the ability to turn off the aging process. Your parents chose to start aging again to raise you, so they didn't end up looking like twentysomethings with teenaged children. They set their aging to half speed, mind you. They're deliberately making themselves look older by brushing gray into their hair and making no effort to hide it when they're tired. If someone doesn't age, doesn't get sick, and can't be injured by physical violence or accidents, that means they're essentially immortal unless someone uses magic to do them in."

"Someone like the Magnuses," Brewster said.

Phillip nodded. "Yes, perhaps. But, to be fair, we don't know of them killing anybody yet. They've just frozen your parents for some unknown reason. Sorry I couldn't prevent that, by the way. I had enough time to just about explain what was going on, then the Magnuses appeared, my protection spell automatically transported me out, and they've been chasing me from place to place ever since. I had no idea they'd done anything to your parents. I hoped to break out of the emergency teleportation cycle by going back to your home, thinking I'd reconnect with your parents. I tried to go back to a minute or so after I left, but I couldn't. The Magnuses set up some sort of redirect to cover their tracks, I guess. So I went there a little later and was shocked to see you two, and Martin and Gwen gone. Where are they, by the way?"

Brewster and Mattie stared at Phillip for several seconds, then looked at each other. Finally, Mattie said, "We're going to need to talk about stuff before we tell you anything."

Phillip said, "I understand. I'd teleport away to give you privacy, but then the Magnuses would be able to track me."

Mattie said, "How about you just walk over there and sit at the bar?" She pointed back toward Gilbert's house, at the concrete peninsula and barstools across from the outdoor kitchen.

Phillip nodded, stood up, and went where she asked.

Mattie turned to Brewster and whispered, "Do you trust him?"

Brewster shrugged. "It's hard to. But everybody else who knows him seems to trust him."

Mattie said, "And I've dealt with the Magnuses. I sure don't trust them."

"So we agree?"

"Brewster, neither of us has really answered the question."

"If neither of us has, that means we're on the same page."

Mattie shouted toward the kitchen. "Okay, Phillip. We've decided to trust you."

Phillip turned around on his stool at the kitchen island. "Already? That was fast. I only just sat down here."

Brewster said, "Well, you can come back now."

Phillip walked back over and sat down at the patio table with the twins. They told him the entire story of everything that had happened from the moment they'd been sent out of the room by their parents up until the moment they reconnected with Phillip in their living room one minute or three days later, depending on who you asked.

"So, can you help our parents?" Brewster asked.

Phillip said, "Yes. I'll do everything I can."

Mattie stood up. "Great! Let's go unfreeze them then!"

Phillip said, "I can't."

Mattie just barely managed not to curse.

Phillip said, "Undoing someone else's macros can be very difficult. You don't just want to figure out how they're changing the code and change it back. You don't know how their macro and the macro you wrote to undo their macro will interact. You have to find their macro, analyze it carefully, and then figure out how to undo the damage as carefully as possible."

Mattie said, "It sounds to me like you know how to do it. It's just a lot of work."

"Knowing the steps to do a thing is not the same as being able to do it. It's your parents' lives we're talking about. I wouldn't want to trust the job to anyone who hasn't tried to undo someone else's magic before."

"Do you know anyone who has?"

"Yes."

"Then let's call him!" Brewster said.

Phillip stared at the twins for a long moment before saying, "It's not a *him*, and first I think we should contact the guys who are out looking for me, probably looking for all of us now. They need to know what's going on, and that you two are all right."

The twins both groaned.

"It'll just take a minute. It's the courteous thing to do, and maybe one of the guys will have a better idea."

Mattie kept herself, Brewster, and Phillip on the magicians' lawn, but teleported them all forward in time to a moment after Brewster's escape from Roy's lecture on the geopolitical forces that led to the Vietnam War. She had to guess as to the exact moment, as she hadn't been looking at a clock, and time had seemed to slow to a crawl.

Phillip held up his left hand and put in a call to Roy. An image of a cartoon skunk, and the phrase "Lockheed Skunk Works" rotated in his outstretched palm while the sound of a phone ringing repeated five times.

"You say Roy was watching you when you escaped?" Phillip asked.

The twins nodded yes.

"Then you'd think he'd be quick to answer any calls, in case it's news about you. And the others were all out looking for me?"

Again, the twins nodded.

"So the fact that the call is coming from me would make them even more likely to answer. Where was it you said Roy was watching you?"

19.

Gary's living room at Skull Gullet Cave looked much as it had when Mattie and Brewster left. Upon materializing with Phillip, the only immediate difference they could see was that Roy and Jeff were standing next to the dining table, frozen in place just like Martin and Gwen.

Phillip moaned. "Just as I feared. The Magnuses were here."

Brewster looked at Jeff, who stood motionless, his arms drawn in around his body, one leg raised defensively, teeth gritted.

"Whatever they did," Brewster said, "Jeff didn't like it."

Mattie said, "Neither did Roy." Roy's frozen body was leaning forward; his eyes were open wide, his mouth open even wider, and he had his arm out with a single extended finger. "And he pointed at them as they did it, or made an important point about it."

Phillip asked, "When you left, were Jeff and Roy the only ones here?"

Brewster said, "Jeff wasn't here when we left. It was just us, Roy, and Hubert."

Phillip muttered, "Hubert?" He looked around, sniffed, then used his hands to waft more air toward his nose. Finally, he pointed toward the hall.

Mattie didn't wait for Phillip, and crept slowly down the hall, Brewster following close behind. They passed two doors, both slightly ajar. They sniffed the air coming from each slightly open door until they reached the last one on the left. Instead of the deep inhalation she had given each other door, Mattie drew in a breath, then stopped abruptly, grimacing. Brewster, who had taken a large gulp of air through his mouth, fought a losing battle against his gag reflex.

Mattie pushed the door open just fast enough to make a small breeze blow in her and Brewster's faces, a consequence neither of them relished. They stood just outside the doorway, leaning to one side, then the other, craning their necks, trying to see as much of the room as possible before entering. A round bed covered in black satin sheets and a blanket bearing the embroidered image of a tiger sat beneath a ceiling covered with mirrors. Black lacquered closet doors and built-in drawers covered one side of the room. A raised platform similar to a stage, complete with track lights and a mirrored backdrop, sat centered on the far wall. The third wall held multiple framed paintings of attractive women in various states of undress, all rendered in garish colors on black velvet. The thick, burgundy shag carpet bore discolored tracks where Gary walked on a daily basis. Brewster tapped Mattie on the shoulder and pointed almost straight down at another discolored track, which entered the room, then took a sharp right and disappeared.

Mattie nodded. They both stepped through the door and turned to the right, where Hubert stood beside the door with his back pressed flat against the wall.

Hubert sighed and sagged visibly when he saw Mattie and Brewster. "It's you! Oh, thank the maker. I thought you were the Man-Gusses."

"Magnuses," Brewster said.

Hubert shook his head. "Whatever they're called. I was afraid you were them."

Mattie asked, "What happened?"

Hubert sat on the edge of the bed and nearly fell over backward when the mattress gave way beneath him, making a sloshing noise and sending a wave through all of the bedding.

"It was awful. After the two of you disappeared, Master Roy called Master Jeff. He came and they talked for a bit about where you might have gone and how to find you. Master Jeff received a call from a wizard I'd never met, asking to come talk. Two wizards, both named Man-gus, came over; I made one of them a sandwich. They asked Master Roy and Master Jeff to vote for them, then wanted to know why they wouldn't. They argued, then they cast some sort of spell over Master Roy and Master Jeff that made them into statues."

"Then what happened?" Mattie asked.

"They took the sandwich and left."

Mattie asked, "They took the sandwich?"

Hubert looked on the verge of tears. "Yes. I was too stunned to stop them."

Mattie and Brewster both walked over to Hubert, and each put a hand on his shoulder as he hung his head.

Without a word, Mattie and Brewster left the room, closing the door behind them. Once in the hall, Brewster reached into his hat, rummaged around, and pulled out a small squeeze bottle of hand sanitizer.

The twins walked back out into the living room, still rubbing their wet hands together. They found Phillip sitting on a dining chair, staring intently into his outstretched left hand while the motionless Jeff and Roy looked on.

Phillip glanced at the twins. "Hubert?"

Brewster said, "He's shaken up, but they didn't hurt him."

Mattie added, "On the plus side, in a few hours one of the Magnuses might have food poisoning."

"We can hope," Phillip said. "I've been trying to reach everyone. Gilbert and Sid are both okay. Gary said he couldn't talk and that he'd call back. Who knows what that's about. I can't get hold of Tyler, though. Sid said he thought Tyler was going to look for me at the tavern, so we should go there. Gilbert and Sid'll meet us. If we don't want the Magnuses to track us I'm afraid one of you'll have to drive."

Mattie took off her hat and reached in. "Same town you live in?"

"Yes. Leadchurch."

"Why do they call it that?"

"Because the town's church is covered with lead. It's their biggest landmark, as you can imagine. We can go rub up against it and get a souvenir stain, if you like. The locals think it'll ward off evil."

"I'll pass."

"Smart girl. The kids in town used to lick it. Imagine that. They'd just run up and lick the church. We put a stop to it. Incredibly unhealthy, it caused brain damage and spread germs."

Brewster said, "We're going to a tavern? You do realize we're both under twenty-one, right?"

Phillip said, "Relax. We aren't going to drink. Anyway, it'll be centuries before liquor laws are invented."

The three of them appeared in the middle of the dirt road in front of the tavern, a squat timber-and-thatch building with a sign reading "The Rotted Stump."

Mattie put her hat back on and looked at the tavern, the road, the huts across the way, and the woods beyond the edge of town. "This is where you fought Dad."

Phillip laughed. "Oh, I wouldn't say that I fought him. No, this is where I trounced your father. If I'm honest, it wasn't a fair fight, but I'm not the one who started it. How do you know about that?"

Mattie said, "We were there. Gilbert and Sid brought us. We hid in the woods. Saw the whole thing."

"Well, look, kids, I love your father, I love both of your parents, but nobody's perfect, and the first time he came here, your father made a bit of an ass of himself. Please, don't follow in his footsteps. We're just going to pop in to see if anyone knows where Tyler is, so let me do the talking and follow my lead. Okay?"

Brewster and Mattie both nodded.

Phillip led them into the tavern.

Most of the bars and taverns Brewster and Mattie had seen were in TV shows and movies, and as such were either glossy and idealized or cartoonishly dicey. Their only real-world experiences of such places consisted of walking past their entrances in shopping malls and airports. They'd never been inside one before, and as such, they didn't know what to expect. Still, they were surprised to find the tavern bright, lively, and smelling of roasted meat and spilled beer.

There were eleven or twelve people sitting around, eating, talking, and drinking in the middle of the day, enough people that it made both Mattie and Brewster uncomfortable when all conversation stopped and every head in the room turned to look at them. The world seemed to pause for a moment, then the patrons decided that Phillip and his young, oddly dressed friends weren't as interesting as what they had been discussing or drinking.

Phillip led the twins around the tables, past the seemingly unmanned bar, to the back of the room where a largish man in a leather apron whose right arm was missing from just above the elbow stood facing away from the customers, looking into an open door.

Phillip said, "Hello Pete. How are things?"

The one-armed man glanced over his shoulder, smiled, then turned back to what he was doing. "Looking up, Phillip. I hope you're well. I was just about to send someone to fetch you."

Phillip looked over Pete's shoulder into the storeroom and nodded. "I can see why."

Mattie and Brewster looked past the man in the apron. Inside the storeroom, they saw the expected barrels and crates. They also saw a very large woman moving the barrels and crates as if they weighed nothing. She placed one large crate in the center of the room, then reached to the side of the room and grasped Tyler around the waist.

Tyler stood motionless, holding his wizard staff out in front of his body, his face frozen in an expression of confusion and shock. The large woman lifted him easily. His robe hung down and flapped back and forth as she placed him on the crate, facing the door.

"Well done, Gert," Pete said. "Now adjust the lanterns to shine up at him from below."

Phillip asked, "What happened?"

"Tyler came in asking about you, actually. I told him I hadn't seen you in a while. He decided to have a quick beer before moving on. Then two wizards I've never seen before appeared."

"Horns on their hats? Lots of fur?"

"Exactly. They talked to Tyler. It all sounded friendly at first, but then they start yelling about boats."

"Might they have said *votes*, not *boats*?"

"Maybe. It all got heated, and they put a spell on Tyler that left him like this." He pointed at Tyler, standing motionless on the crate, shadows swaying wildly on his face and behind him as Gert moved the lanterns at his feet.

"Gert and I, we decided to move Tyler into the storeroom, you know, for his own safety, while he can't defend himself."

Phillip stepped into the storeroom and walked around Tyler, studying him from every angle. "And him being in a room with no windows makes it easier for you to charge people who want to come gawk at the frozen wizard."

"Yeah, well, I'm sure that since we're protecting Tyler and keeping him inside, out of the elements, he wouldn't mind earning his keep."

Phillip said, "Of course. And what happened to the other two?"

"They left. Seemed to be in a hurry to get out of here. One of 'em left that." Pete pointed. It was hard to see in the dark, but a black fur hung on the wall beside Tyler. "We'll get some light on it once Tyler's squared away. He's the main attraction, er, I mean, priority. What do you make of that fur the wizard left, Phillip? I assume it's the hide of some famed mythical beast."

"I don't know. It may be from a wolf."

"A famed, mythical wolf?"

"Perhaps, Pete. Perhaps."

"What would such a beast be called, Phillip?"

Phillip thought for a moment. "Wolfie?" He winced apologetically.

Pete stroked his chin. "We can do better. Why do people fear wolves? What are they afraid of?"

Mattie said, "That the wolves will bite them."

Pete turned and looked down at the twins.

Phillip said, "Oh, where are my manners. Pete, this is Mattie and Brewster. They're Martin and Gwen's kids."

"You don't say! Hello! Good to meet you! Your parents and I go way back. In fact, I once locked your father in this very storeroom. Perhaps I'll tell you all about it later. Maybe lock you two in there, if you play your cards wrong." He glanced down at their empty hands. "And now I'll tell you about an invention of mine I call the *two-drink minimum*."

Pete turned back to the pelt on the wall. "Hmm. People biter. Folk gnawer. Man chewer. Manchewer. That's not bad. Gert, make sure one of the lanterns is aimed up at The Mantle of Manchewer."

Gert nodded at Pete and continued moving the lanterns around.

The twins heard a faint screeching—it sounded like a distant electric guitar. Phillip stiffened, glanced at his left hand, and blurted, "Oh, I should take this call. One moment."

He held up his left hand. A KISS logo rotated in the empty space above his palm for a moment, then faded out, replaced by a miniature re-creation of Gary's head.

"Phillip! Where have you been?"

"It's a long story. Where are you?"

"I was looking for you. I'm at Martin's place in London."

Brewster asked, "Dad has a place in London?"

Phillip said, "Yeah. By your time the real estate's probably worth a mint, as if he needed money."

Gary said, "Sorry I didn't answer your call earlier. The Magnuses were here. Phil, you're never gonna guess what they wanted."

"Oh, I have an idea." Phillip put a hand on Tyler's frozen shoulder. "I'm here with Tyler. They froze—"

Phillip disappeared midword, taking Tyler with him.

Brewster and Mattie both jumped, looked around frantically, and saw the Magnuses materializing near the door.

Magnus Rex said, "I'm pretty sure I left it here."

Magnus Galka said, "I suggest you ask the innkeeper. Mayhap they have a lost and found or some . . ." Magnus Galka trailed off as he spotted Mattie. He blurted several half-strangled consonant sounds before he managed to choke out, "You!"

20.

Both Magnuses pointed at Mattie. Magnus Rex said, "You're the girl from that crappy museum!"

Mattie glanced back over her shoulder at Tyler's empty makeshift plinth and the fur hanging on display and said, "The other one, yes."

Magnus Rex asked, "Who *are* you?"

Mattie looked at Brewster, then back to the Magnuses. "The girl from that crappy museum."

Magnus Galka closed his eyes and pinched the bridge of his nose. "What's your name, and why are you following us?"

Brewster said, "We were here first."

Mattie said, "Yeah. We were at the museum first, too. If anything, you're following us!"

Magnus Rex said, "We don't even know who you are!"

"Just makes it creepier that you're following us, dude!"

"*Creepy*," Magnus Galka said. "You dare call us creepy? Let's see if you think we're creepy when we drag you out of here and whisk you both back to our hidden lair!"

Mattie said, "I'm pretty sure we will."

Brewster shook his head. "I mean, the fact that you call it your hidden *lair* . . ."

Magnus Galka waved dismissively toward the twins and looked at Magnus Rex. "This conversation is pointless. Seize them!"

Magnus Rex didn't move. "Was that a command?"

"Sorry! Sorry. Of course, you're right. I suggest you seize the girl and her boyfriend."

Mattie and Brewster both laughed, looked at each other, and made disgusted guttural sounds.

Magnus Galka nodded. "Okay, I get it. You're brother and sister. Sorry about that."

Brewster said, "You didn't know."

"Thanks. Anyway, Magnus, I suggest you seize 'em both."

Mattie said, "Still creepy."

"Yeah, fine, whatever."

Magnus Rex advanced on the twins, his hands open and outstretched, like he meant to grasp them by the throat.

Mattie and Brewster both took off their hats and spread out, giving themselves a little more room to move. Magnus Rex's attention shifted to Pete, still standing in the door to the storeroom.

"Oh, hey, barkeep," Magnus Rex said. "Has anyone turned in a fur cloak? It's black. I left it here something like fifteen minutes ago."

Magnus Galka said, "You just deal with the kids. I'll get your cloak."

Magnus Rex said, "But I'm right here. He's here. Why shouldn't I just get it?"

"Because this is how we work. You're out there, getting things done. Rolling up your sleeves. Taking action. Meanwhile, I'm in the background, dealing with the petty stuff that isn't worth your time. I'm your support."

Magnus Rex said, "Yeah, true."

"Exactly. So you chase those kids around while I talk to the bartender."

"Okay. But why don't I just freeze them?"

"Because we want to question them. They may help us unlock many mysteries, but they can't answer any questions if they're frozen."

"But we could freeze them, bring them home, then unfreeze them and ask them."

"You'll just have to grab them at home that way, instead of here. I'm trying to save you extra work. And the more you talk, the more time they have to think of a way to defend themselves."

Magnus Rex turned to look at Mattie and Brewster just in time to catch the rabbit streaking toward his face.

"Again with the rabbits?" Brewster said.

Mattie said, "It's the first thing on the list, and I know it works!"

Magnus Rex stood there, glaring at them, holding the squirming fake bunny out away from his body where it could do him no harm.

Brewster pointed at the rabbit. "You call that working?"

Mattie said, "Excuse me for trying! Maybe you should just criticize him to death!"

Magnus Galka said, "Uh-huh. Definitely brother and sister. I should have seen it before."

Magnus Rex started toward them again. Mattie let out a startled yelp and reflexively tossed another rabbit from out of her hat at him. He caught it in his left hand and kept coming toward them, now holding a wriggling fake rabbit in each hand.

Brewster and Mattie both turned to run from Magnus Rex, taking off in different directions, Brewster hugging the wall while Mattie set out across the room. Magnus Rex followed Mattie, waving the rabbits over his head. The tavern patrons whooped and shouted, some cheering, others afraid, as the twins and Magnus ran between the tables and over seats.

Brewster shouted, "Try something else!"

Mattie was already elbow deep in her hat, searching through the options. She yelled back, "You try something else! You have a hat, too!"

Brewster reached into his hat as Mattie pulled a tangled knot of thin white ropes out of her own. She glanced back and hurled them at Magnus Rex.

Magnus Rex saw the ball of ropes coming and attempted to knock it away with the rabbit in his right hand. Instead of deflecting, the rope enveloped his hand, doing nothing to restrict his movements, but affixing the thrashing false rabbit to his palm. He whipped his hand through the air as if trying to shake off something disgusting stuck to his fingers.

Mattie and Brewster didn't stop running just because Magnus Rex had stopped chasing them. Instead, they kept moving until they both stood with their backs to the wall on opposite sides of the tavern, with Magnus Rex between them in the middle of the room.

Magnus Rex gave up on shaking the rabbit loose from his hand. He growled and looked up at Mattie, standing with her feet and hands spread wide, back to the wall, ready to run in whatever direction Magnus Rex didn't. He sneered, then spun in place and lunged at Brewster directly behind him.

Brewster sprinted to his left, feeling the rope-entangled rabbit graze the back of his neck as Magnus Rex narrowly missed tackling him. Brewster glanced behind him to see Magnus Rex hit the wall, but Magnus only paused for a moment, using his arms to push away and regain the speed to keep up the chase.

Brewster pulled his hand out of his hat, grasping a fist full of colorful scarves. He threw them back over his shoulder, more to be rid of them than in any hopes of slowing Magnus Rex's pursuit. The wad of scarves flew from his hand, but a line of more scarves all knotted together into a long rope came from his hat and continued playing out as he ran, like a fishing line out of a reel.

Mattie leaped over a bench as she moved to the middle of the room, dodging around the customers fleeing for the exit and past those who kept their seats to enjoy the show. She reached into her hat, selected the next menu item after ropes and scarves, and pulled out a deck of cards. She spun midstride and threw the whole deck in one big clump as hard as she could at Magnus Rex's head. She was momentarily delighted to see the cards separate and fly at Magnus Rex like fifty-two deadly throwing stars, but that delight died when the cards all bounced off of him and tumbled to the floor. A few of the cards went under his feet, causing him to lose traction, but not so much that he fell over or even slowed down as he continued chasing Brewster.

In the corner of the room, Pete told Magnus Galka, "Now that I've lost my main attraction, I'm afraid the Mantle of Manchewer isn't for sale."

Magnus Galka replied, "He doesn't want to buy it. My friend already owns it. We're taking it. Do you know who my friend is? He's not someone to trifle with."

Brewster looked back and saw the ropes tying the squirming rabbit to Magnus Rex's right hand, the other angry rabbit he still held in his left, the long trail of scarves still spooling out in their wake, and the stray playing cards still stuck in Magnus Rex's clothing.

Brewster shouted, "This isn't working!"

Mattie said, "I agree! We don't know the magic well enough. We need something simpler."

Magnus Rex said, "You could just stop fighting back."

"Shut up," Mattie spat.

Brewster put his hat back on his head and reflexively pulled his walking stick out of his armpit, holding it in his right hand. He looked at his walking stick, and his eyes widened. He waved it in the air at his sister and shouted, "Hey! Hey!"

Mattie said, "Yes!"

Magnus Rex asked, "What?"

Mattie shouted, "He's not talking to you!"

Mattie saw the cane in her brother's hand and instantly knew what he was getting at. She put on her hat, grasped the handle of her walking stick, rotated it one click, and pulled the sword's blade clear of the cane's shaft. She smiled triumphantly as she pointed the blade at Magnus Rex. "Stop chasing my brother!"

Magnus Rex stopped and turned to face Mattie, scowling. "Or what?"

Mattie looked at the blade in her hand. "Or what? Uh, or I'll stab you." She jabbed the blade forward a couple of times to demonstrate.

Magnus Rex laughed. "Oh, will you now? Magnus, catch." He threw the still-struggling fake rabbit in his left hand to Magnus Galka, who yelped in shock, but caught it.

Magnus Rex reached back over his shoulder and closed his fist. Even though there was nothing fastened to his back, when he withdrew his hand, it held the handle of a massive double-bladed battle-axe.

Without breaking his eye contact with Mattie, he ran the axe's razor-sharp blade along the back of his right hand, cutting the rope webbing covering it as casually as if he were shaving. As the artificial rabbit squirmed free, he grabbed its hind leg, flung it violently to the ground, and cut it in two with a single axe blow, delivered with enough force to drive the blade's edge an inch into the wooden floor.

The two halves of the fake rabbit disappeared, as did the remaining tavern customers, who all scurried out the door with a smoothness and efficiency that put any fire drill to shame.

Magnus Rex pulled the axe from the floor with no noticeable effort, then tossed it from his left hand to his right, swung it through the air a few times, then choked up on the handle with both hands, holding the axe high, ready to swing. "We can throw down if that's what you two want, but those crappy sword canes of yours won't do you much good."

Mattie said, "We'll see," as she rushed forward, wielding the sword over her head as if she intended to cut Magnus Rex in half lengthwise. As she brought the blade down, Magnus Rex swung his axe blade, knocking the sword cane off course as casually as one might brush away a fly.

Mattie recovered quickly, swinging the sword at Magnus Rex's midsection with all her might, but again the axe deflected it, sending Mattie stumbling off in an unintended direction.

Mattie said, "Sword's not working!"

Magnus Rex smiled. "Told you."

Mattie swung her blade at his head, grunting, "Didn't ask you!"

Magnus Rex stopped her swing easily by raising his axe with one hand. "Maybe you should have."

Mattie shouted, "Brewster! Come on! Help me out here!"

"With what?"

"Your sword!"

"But you just said, the swords don't work!"

"Maybe two will!"

"Maybe? That's not reassuring."

Mattie lunged at Magnus Rex, attempting to stab him with the pointed tip. He stood still with his hands at his sides, allowing the sword point to hit him just above the navel. The blade bent alarmingly but didn't seem to penetrate his skin as Mattie leaned into the blow, then stopped, holding her handle with both hands, struggling to keep it from springing out of her grip and across the room.

Magnus Rex said, "I'm a wizard. I'm stab-proof. This has been a fun workout, but we should get going." He shoved Mattie aside, and the force of her sword straightening sent her spinning to the floor.

Magnus Rex turned to Brewster, smiled, and started walking forward. "Your turn."

Brewster tried to think fast but drew a blank. Every weapon they'd tried had failed, and the last suggestion he'd heard was that maybe he and Mattie working together with the swords might be slightly less useless than Mattie fighting alone had been. He tried to turn the cane handle one click, but in his panic, turned it two clicks instead. He felt the cane go limp in his hands, dividing into four segments of varying length connected by short chains.

Brewster's heart sank. He came close to cursing and saying that he couldn't believe he'd selected the coat hanger, but then he saw the look of fear on Magnus Rex's face.

"What is that?" Magnus Rex asked. "Some kinda weird nunchucks?"

Mattie said, "Uh, yeah! It is! Good thinking, Brewster. Hit him with the weird nunchucks!"

Brewster swung the collapsible coat hanger with all of his might. The short length of chain at the far end picked up an alarming amount of speed. Magnus Rex tried to block it with his axe but got hit in the hands, causing him to shriek in pain and reflexively let go of his weapon.

Brewster kept swinging, whipping Magnus Rex without mercy. Mattie sprang to her feet, rotating the handle of her own sword cane to make it a collapsible coat hanger as well, and joined in flogging the man with wild abandon until some unseen force hit them both in the side.

They staggered and swung their arms wildly but managed to keep their feet. They both looked in the direction from which the invisible shove had come and saw Magnus Galka, one hand extended toward them, the other tucked at his side with the black fur cloak that had been hanging on the wall now folded and draped over his arm. Beside him, Pete and Gert stood, frozen in place. Pete seemed stuck midword, while Gert was leaning far forward, her balled fist hanging in the air above Magnus Galka as if she intended to mash down on his head like a giant button.

Magnus Galka said, "You all right, Magnus? Good. The deed is done. I have retrieved your cloak. As for the kids here, I think you were right to begin with. I suggest you just freeze 'em. We'll figure out what to do with them when we get them home."

Magnus Rex looked at Mattie and Brewster, a big smile on his face. He took a deep breath, preparing to utter whatever spell would render the twins immobile, but stopped short when square panels of some rigid material appeared floating in space in front of him, stacked on top of each other like a tower of blocks. Similar groups of squares appeared on his sides and behind him. One solitary square materialized directly over his head.

Magnus Rex had just enough time to register that the squares existed before they flew inward, locking together, essentially cramming him into a coffin-sized rectangular stack of three square boxes, just small enough to be noticeably uncomfortable. His wincing, irate face protruded through an oval opening in the top square.

"What the hell! What is this?" Magnus Rex shouted. "What are you doing? AHHHHHH!"

The four panels forming the middle of the box all slid to the right. Magnus Rex continued to roll his eyes downward and tilted his head as far forward as he could, screaming all the while. When the middle box stopped, Magnus Rex's body appeared to be divided between three separate containers.

While Magnus Galka watched in horror as his friend was seemingly trisected alive, a dark form grew behind him, spreading like a cloud of silt in a riverbed.

The darkness resolved into a perfect rectangle stretching from his neck to his ankles. Solid black panels swung out from both sides as if anchored to the dark form by hinges, and locked into place, sealing Magnus Galka in a long, thin box with his head and feet sticking out the ends.

The box tipped, leaving him lying on his back, hovering at about chest height. Another rectangle, this one plated in shining chrome, hinged up from the lid of the box, at Magnus Galka's waist. It stopped perpendicular to his body, paused for a moment, then plunged through the box like the blade of a guillotine.

Magnus Galka yelled and kept yelling as the two halves of the box pulled apart. His feet thrashed as the boxes spun slowly in the air. He briefly stopped screaming as the rotation brought his feet and his head near each other. He paused, staring at the soles of his own shoes. He got a suspicious look on his face, watched as his feet very deliberately both swung to one side, then the other, then touched their toes together.

Magnus Galka said, "Impressive. And it doesn't actually hurt."

Magnus Rex, still cramped and contorted into three small boxes, said, "Yeah, but it's not comfortable either, and it's freaky. Like, real freaky."

Sid entered the tavern, stepping around an overturned chair. "Indubitably, my friends. That is, indeed, by design."

"Turns out that people don't like seeing themselves cut into pieces," Gilbert said, following Sid through the door. "Puts them on edge. Sorry we're late, kiddos. We don't know the town well, and materialized at the church instead of the tavern."

"Indeed. The local bishop proved most skilled in the lost art of providing clear, concise directions, but only after we had both made a mandatory donation to the church's poor box."

"He didn't seem to like it when we produced the coins from out of his nose."

Magnus Rex said, "Magnus, I can't break out of this thing. What do we do?"

Magnus Galka replied, "I suggest we teleport out."

Gilbert said, "Make sure you get all of your parts."

Both of the Magnuses blurted out a collection of discordant Scandinavian-sounding consonants and disappeared, along with the magical containers in which they'd been trapped.

Brewster asked, "Where'd they go?"

Sid shrugged. "No way to know, dear boy. But rest assured, wherever they are, they're still divided into chunks and constrained within our mystical apparati."

Gilbert smiled. "The boxes will put them back together and then disappear in about five minutes, if they haven't figured a way out on their own by then."

Mattie asked, "Could you teach us to how to do those spells? The canes didn't do much, and we've already overused the rabbits."

Gilbert shook his head. "Yeah, about that. You've had magic for, like, a day, and you've already overused the most powerful attack spell we gave you. Does giving you more weapons really sound like a good idea?"

"They were attacking us. What were we supposed to do?"

"Did you try teleporting away? No need to answer, because you're still here."

Mattie asked, "You want us to just run away?"

"Why not? It's what your enemies just did. It's what Phillip's been doing."

"It feels cowardly."

Sid shook his head. "Bravery is a fine quality, Mathison, but surviving is far finer. In my experience, most of the times someone has criticized me for being a coward, it's been a person who would have enjoyed seeing me hurt. In this case, if you'd teleported away the instant the Magnuses appeared, the only people who would have ever criticized you for it would have been them."

Mattie shook her head. "Whatever. I'm proud that Brewster and I didn't run away."

Gilbert said, "Yeah, you stood your ground, and in this case, what did it accomplish? You trashed a bar, frightened some villagers, nearly got yourselves kidnapped, and now that it's all over, we're going to leave anyway. Can you tell me one way this situation is better than it would be if you had left five minutes ago?"

Mattie looked around and thought for a second. "Now I know that there are spells that cut people to pieces."

21.

Mattie, Brewster, Gilbert, and Sid held hands, grasped the motionless wrists of Pete and Gert to form a human chain six people long, and then teleported to Gary's crowded living room. Jeff and Roy remained frozen in place, Phillip had returned with an inert Tyler, and Gary was home again.

The place was packed.

Gary stroked his chin and looked at Tyler standing in the corner while Hubert slumped nearby, concerned and exhausted.

"Yeah," Gary said. "That's better. I thought keeping Tyler in the bathroom would be funny, but seeing him in there just made things weird for me, and he didn't even know what was happening."

Phillip sat on one of the built-in couches in Gary's conversation pit, his eyes aimed straight ahead with an expression of perfect joylessness on his face. "Yeah, it sort of made you wonder who the joke was on."

Hubert said, "Indeed, Master Gary. I think you'll prefer having him out here, and I'm sure he'll prefer it, once you release him from the spell."

"Yes," Gary said. "About that. Leave him where he is, but turn him around so he's facing the wall. That should confuse him when he snaps out of it."

Hubert sighed heavily, said, "Yes, sir," and began laboriously turning Tyler to face the opposite direction.

Sid cleared his throat. "Terribly sorry to barge in like this, but I fear we have two more living statues to add to your menagerie."

Gary, Phillip, and Hubert all turned to face the newcomers. Phillip said, "Kids! I'm so glad you're okay. I'm sorry I left you with the Magnuses like that. It's just this defensive macro of mine—"

Brewster said, "We know. You couldn't help it."

Mattie asked, "When will that stop, by the way?"

"When I deactivate the macro," Phillip said.

"Is that hard?"

"No."

"Have you done it then?"

"No."

Mattie said, "You know, I had *just* about decided that you weren't the enemy."

Gilbert said, "Now, now, I understand how you feel, Mattie, but the main thing the Magnuses seem to want is to get their hands on Phillip. It's just logical that we'd keep that from happening."

Phillip said, "Exactly."

Sid said, "Quite. So you see, my wrathful young friend, in this case Phillip's cowardice works to our advantage."

Phillip's expression soured. He turned away from the others, sat back on the couch, and stared at the wall opposite him.

"Have we managed to ascertain what—besides *their hands on Phillip*—that these two hooligans actually want?" Sid asked.

Gary laughed. "Yeah, it's the dumbest thing ever. They want Phillip's job."

"*Job*," Phillip said, his voice dripping with contempt. "Being chairman isn't a job. They pay you for a job. Being chairman is a fat wad of responsibilities wrapped up in a thick sheet of blame, like some sort of wretched burrito."

Hubert, having just pulled his hands back slowly, and determining that Tyler was balanced properly, said, "Speaking of which, would anyone like something to eat? I could easily whip something up."

The room practically rang with the sound of five people saying "No, thank you."

Gary said, "The Magnuses came to me while I was out at the clearing with the old dragon pens looking for Phillip."

"Dragon pens?" Brewster asked.

Phillip said, "It's a long story."

Gary said, "Yeah. Some would say too long, too fragmented, and without clearly defined stakes. Anyway, they came to me and said that they think it's time for a change in leadership and that one of them should be chairman."

"Which one?" Gilbert asked.

"You know, I wasn't really clear on that. They said they'd been to see the rest of my friends, and then they asked if they had my vote. I have to assume that all of the guys told them no—your parents too. That must be why the Magnuses made statues out of 'em."

"How did you keep them from freezing you?" Mattie asked.

"I told them I'd be delighted to vote for a Magnus. I would be, too, as long as I knew he had no chance of winning. I didn't know they were freezing people who said no. I just agreed to it as a goof. I even agreed to nominate 'em."

"I never wanted to be chairman," Phillip said. "Everybody else just sort of decided that I was in charge and started doing what I told them. I even had them hold elections every year, to give someone else a chance at the job, but nobody serious ever ran against me."

Gary said, "Seems like the Magnuses were serious."

"I'd be happy not to be chairman anymore, but not if my successor is going to be a Magnus!"

"When are the next elections?" Sid asked.

"Tomorrow," Gary said. "During our big annual meeting at Castle Camelot."

"Camelot?" Mattie said. "Camelot's real?"

"No, but there's a castle there."

Gilbert said, "Okay then. It seems to me that we have two problems. One is that a bunch of people are frozen, and the other is that Phillip might lose his job to a Magnus. If we can solve one of the problems, it'll take care of the other."

Sid said, "Quite so. If we successfully unfreeze the Magnuses' myriad victims, they'll certainly vote against said Magni in tomorrow's election."

"So how do we do that?" Mattie asked.

Phillip said, "That's the thing. It's easy to deactivate a macro you wrote yourself, but it's harder to undo someone else's work. You don't have access to the source code, so you have to sort of pick things apart logically, figure out how the macro works, and interfere with it. It's difficult work, and our best coder is frozen." Phillip pointed at Jeff.

Gary said, "He's *our* best coder, but he's not *the* best coder."

Phillip said, "Okay, he's not the best coder in the world, but he's the best among us."

Gary shook his head. "He's the best coder in this room, but he's not the best coder we know."

Phillip shook his head. "No."

Gary said, "Oh, yes."

Gilbert slapped his palm to his head. "Of course!"

Sid looked delighted. "I feel like a fool for not thinking of it myself."

Phillip said, "We shouldn't involve her."

Sid said, "We most definitely should."

Gilbert agreed. "She'd be mad at us if we didn't."

Brewster said, "If she's so great, why haven't you already?"

Gary almost giggled with delight. "Because she's Phillip's ex, and she's mad at him."

"And there are three of her," Gilbert said.

"But only two of her will talk to me," Phillip moaned.

Five people appeared in the sky between the sparkling Mediterranean and a ceiling of blue dotted with puffy white clouds.

Brewster said, "It's very pretty."

Mattie squinted down at the sea. "Yeah. So, are we looking for an island or a boat, or what?"

Phillip said, "We materialized facing the wrong direction. Turn around."

Mattie and Brewster both twisted around to glance back over their shoulders, then froze, eyes wide, mouths agape and muttering amazed profanities.

Below them they saw a vast, perfectly round divot in the surface of the sea, as if someone had used an ice cream scoop a mile wide to remove several million gallons of seawater, and the rest of the ocean had never bothered to rush in and fill the hole.

Instead of water, sea life, or even a concrete wall—any of which would have made more sense—the inner surface of the hemispherical dent in the ocean was covered by a city, the most beautiful city the twins had ever seen. People, little more than moving black dots from this height, teemed along footpaths and pedestrian boulevards cut like terraces between the shining white buildings. The roofs all held plants and paths. Many of the buildings up around the rim of the city, where the hole in the ocean seemed shallowest, jutted up higher than the surface, looking out over the waves and towering over the city below.

"Behold," Sid said. "For there it is, Atlantis!"

"Nice, isn't it?" Gilbert added.

"Atlantis was real," Brewster gasped.

Phillip muttered, "In a sense."

Sid said, "Yes, the fantastical ancient city of Atlantis, spoken of in myth and legend is only real in the sense that there was a fantastical city, called *Atlantis*, here in ancient times, about which myths and legends will be created. In that sense, Atlantis is real, but not quite real enough to satisfy our Phillip, I'm afraid."

Phillip said, "The Atlantis we all grew up hearing about was created by mysterious, inscrutable ancients. I promise you, the woman who made Atlantis is all too scrutable."

Sid said, "She discovered the file, developed abilities as she manipulated it that the rest of us never imagined, or in many cases, can even understand. She then traveled back in time, where she found Atlantis, and herself."

"She found herself? Like an *Eat, Pray, Love* kind of thing?" Mattie asked.

"No," Sid said. "I mean that when she arrived in Atlantis, she found that she was already there. A future version of herself had gone even further back in time and founded the city, using her powers through the file to build the impossible metropolis you see before, well, beneath you. She abided there, in Atlantis, with her future self for many years, more than ample time to meet, date, and dump our friend Phillip. Then she went back in time, founded and built the city, and waited for herself to arrive."

Brewster said, "That's some story."

"And it isn't over yet!"

Gilbert said, "Yeah. The way I hear it, eventually, she leaves Atlantis, goes back to her own time, and gets some kind of a government job. There's probably a nice pension with that."

Mattie said, "That all sounds pretty mysterious and inscrutable to me."

"Indeed it is," Sid said. "I'm afraid that Phillip can't see that for himself, as he's too close to the subject. The forest is blocking his view of the trees, or words to that effect."

"That, and he's crabby about his ex-girlfriend's success," Gilbert said. "You should get used to that, Mattie, 'cause he's not the only guy who acts that way."

Phillip growled. "Whatever. Look, I let you kids come along because I thought you'd like to see Atlantis."

"And," Gilbert said, "because having other people present makes a shouting match less likely."

"I had multiple reasons, but this is going to be hard enough without a lot of smart-aleck comments or confusing chatter. When we get to her place, please let me do all the talking, okay?"

Sid laughed. "*Let you do all the talking*? Oh, Phillip, you poor chap. Having you say that to me is tantamount to attending a stunt show and having Evel Knievel *insist* that you allow him to *do all the jumping*."

Phillip squinted at Sid and Gilbert. "Remind me again why you came along?"

Gilbert said, "We're here because the kids are here. When we chose to train them, we promised that we would help them fix their parents and do everything we could to keep them both safe until that's done. We've let them out of our sight once, and it didn't work out well. We're not making that mistake again."

Sid said, "Also, we're both delighted at the prospect of watching you come to your ex-girlfriend, hat in hand. Especially seeing as she is both an old friend, and seething with residual anger at you."

Phillip stared at Sid for several seconds before finally saying, "Yeah, makes sense. Well, we might as well get this over with."

Phillip flew toward the great sunken bowl of Atlantis, stretched out forward Superman style as the Medieval English wizards always did. Brewster, Mattie, Gilbert, and Sid flew in the standard magician mode, standing up straight, hands resting on their walking sticks, and their capes flapping in the wind behind them. They flew behind Phillip for a moment, then accelerated and spread out, flanking him on both sides. Phillip looked to his left and his right, at his four companions

"I feel like the odd man out here," Phillip said. "You're all standing up while I'm lying on my belly. It's making me uncomfortable."

Sid said, "Oh, nonsense, dear fellow. Think nothing of it. If anything should make you uncomfortable, it's the fact that when we were behind you we could see right up your robe."

Phillip's eyes darted to Mattie, who was staring off into the distance, determined not to make eye contact. "I'm wearing trousers."

Mattie said, "I wouldn't know. I didn't look."

"Good."

"I made a point of not looking."

"I'd imagine."

"I didn't want to look. At all."

"I get it! I understand!"

Both Mattie and Brewster felt a surge of vertigo as they flew over the rim of the city, and the waves just a hundred feet below gave way to a steeply descending wall of buildings, plants, and people.

The group flew down through the middle of the city. Buildings towered over them. People looked out from the windows and walkways, watching them with mild curiosity as they passed. They sank to the bottom of the great bowl that formed Atlantis, toward a large circular park with paths that radiated like the spokes of a wheel from a monument at the city's exact center.

A ring of official-looking buildings sat along the outskirts of the park, with one building standing out by being the only one not drawing attention to itself. Instead of the columns, steps, decorative roof lines, and grand entrances the other buildings featured, it was constructed from plain rectangular boxes of various sizes, stacked on top of each other in a manner that was meant to look haphazard but was far too attractive to be random.

They landed in the park just in front of a large stone patio. A wall of glass doors at the patio's far side appeared to be the building's only entrance. Two tall, muscular men wearing kilts, mesh shirts, and a liberal coating of oil stood on the patio, brandishing spears and staring down at the visitors impassively.

Brewster looked at the guards and said under his breath, "Huh. That's quite an outfit."

Mattie said, "Yeah, it is," in a very different tone of voice.

Phillip approached the guards and said, "Hello."

One of the guards said, "Hello."

"We're here to see—"

"We know," the guard interrupted. "She's expecting you."

Brewster asked, "Did you tell her we were coming?"

Phillip shook his head. "You don't ever really tell Brit the Elder anything. You just remind her."

Mattie said, "Wait a second, what did you call her?"

"Brit the Elder. And I'm pretty sure you've met her. At least one of her."

Brewster and Mattie both said, "Aunt Brit?"

The wall of glass doors silently slid open. Brit the Elder stepped out onto the patio wearing a flowing floral print dress. As the door glided further to the side, a second Brit, this one in a severe black pants suit, walked out to join her. In unison, they said, "Kids!"

22.

Phillip said, "I had no idea you were the kids' godmother."

"I know," Brit the Elder said, nodding a silent *thank you* to the servant as he finished pouring glasses of bright red, ice-cold Hi-C for both Brits and all of their guests. "That was at Brit the Younger's request. She'd prefer that you know as little as possible about our business. She still feels rather raw about your falling out."

Mattie pointed at both Brits, waving her finger back and forth. "Which of you is Brit the Younger?"

Phillip said, "Neither of them."

The Brit in the dress said, "They call me Brit the Elder."

The Brit in the black suit said, "And when I come back here, which isn't very often, they call me Brit the Much Elder."

Brewster muttered, "I can see why you don't come here very often then."

"I know, right? Thank you!"

Brit the Elder said, "Neither of us *is* Brit the Younger, but we both were her, a long time ago."

"A long, *long* time ago," Brit the Much Elder added.

Brewster looked at Phillip. "And you dated all three of them?"

"No, I did not."

Brit the Elder said, "He'll tell you that he only dated Brit the Younger."

Brit the Much Elder said, "Who we were."

"They did more than date. He lived with her."

"Lived with us. We were quite happy for a while, but then he cheated on us."

Phillip glared at Brit the Much Elder. "I did not."

"Of course. Correction. He cheated on her. It depends on one's point of view. Technically, one could say he didn't cheat on either of the two of us because we'd both dumped him long before he cheated."

Phillip said, "Look. We didn't come here to talk about my past love life."

Gilbert said, "Maybe *you* didn't."

Brit the Much Elder said, "No, he's right, we have more pressing issues to discuss. But don't worry. I'll tell you all about his past love life later."

"Is that a promise?" Sid asked.

"No, it's a memory."

Phillip gritted his teeth. "Two idiots have attacked several friends of ours, including Martin and Gwen. I'm here with Martin and Gwen's children, your godchildren, looking for help. Can you please stop tormenting me and get down to business?"

"Of course," Brit the Elder said. "You were about to tell us about how the Magnuses have the asinine idea that one of them, nobody's sure which, should be the chairman instead of you. They tried to eliminate you as competition, but you managed to get away from them. In your efforts to flee, you accidentally led both Magnuses to Martin and Gwen's house, where they hit Martin and Gwen with the fast-time spell, making it appear from our point of view that they are frozen. The kids found their parents in that condition and did a fine job of following the leads they had, finding help from Gilbert and Sid, and eventually tracking you down and helping you lose the Magnuses, who had been chasing you across time and space."

"Yes," Phillip grumbled. "I was about to tell you all of that."

"And you're still free to, if you wish," Brit the Elder said.

"Wait a second," Mattie said. "You two knew about all this? You knew it was going to happen, and you didn't do anything to stop it?"

Brit the Elder said, "I wouldn't put it that way, Mattie."

"But it's true," Phillip muttered.

Brit the Much Elder said, "We didn't know it was going to happen. We knew it *had* happened. There's a big difference. And as for stopping it, it's ancient history for us. You might as well ask us why we didn't stop the Kennedy assassination."

Brewster asked, "Why didn't you stop the Kennedy assassination?"

Brit the Much Elder said, "See? It's an equally valid question."

Brewster said, "You're both time travelers. You both knew this was all going to happen, or had happened, or was happening, and you didn't do anything to stop it."

Brit the Elder said, "Brewster, dear, I don't blame you for being confused and upset."

Phillip said, "She gets that a lot."

Brit the Elder continued, "Everything you just said is technically factual, but you have it all wrong. First of all, we aren't *both* time travelers who knew this was all happening and did nothing to prevent it. As confusing as it seems, Brit the Much Elder and I are the same person. We aren't two people who did nothing to prevent all this drama. We're one person who did nothing to prevent it *twice*."

Brit the Much Elder said, "And we would have loved to prevent all of this from happening, as you said, but we couldn't."

"Why not?"

"Because we hadn't been told about it yet," Brit the Elder said.

Brewster pointed at Brit the Much Elder and stammered, "But, you . . . wait. . . you already knew."

"Yes, dear, I already knew, but I hadn't been told. We both knew before this moment that these things had happened, and were going to happen, but from your point of view, we haven't been involved until now, so we really couldn't do anything. Besides, we knew you'd successfully make it to this point without our help. You already had, so we knew you would."

Mattie turned to Phillip. "And *they* dumped *you*? Not the other way around?"

Phillip reached over and squeezed Mattie's hand. "Thank you! Oh, thank you!"

Brit the Much Elder said, "And we haven't exactly done nothing. We weren't able to do anything you'd be aware of, but we've both played our part."

"What have you done?" Mattie asked.

"I'm the Brit who lives in the same year as you when this all happens, so when you two broke your emergency pendants the first time, I'm the one who got the distress call. I knew in advance that was going to happen, so I was able to make sure that my best men were in a position to come to your house and pick you up."

Brit the Elder arched an eyebrow. "Your best men?"

Brit the Much Elder smiled. "Favorite men? Okay, most entertaining men. You should have heard their reaction when the kids got away from them."

Mattie said, "What? The federal agents? They work for you?"

"Yes, and thank you for taking them down a peg. It was priceless! Miller was apoplectic!"

Phillip said, "Miller? You sent Miller, Murphy, and Jimmy out to get them?"

Brit the Much Elder said, "Yeah, and these two escaped—disappeared on them from the back seat of a moving car."

Phillip said, "Yeah, okay. That is pretty funny."

Brit the Elder said, "I look forward to it."

Brewster asked, "Why didn't they just tell us they worked for you? You're the first person we thought to go to for help, whichever one of you it is we know. If we'd had any idea they were taking us to you, we never would have escaped."

"That's why," Brit the Much Elder said. "When this all happened, you didn't know they worked for me, and you escaped, so I had to make sure you didn't know and wanted to escape. It happened the way it happened, and it'll happen the same way next time that it did this time, because next time was last time."

Mattie stared dull-eyed at Brit the Much Elder, then turned to Brit the Elder. "Okay, that's what she did, whatever that all is. What about you? You knew this was happening. You say you've *played your part*. What was it?"

Brit the Elder smiled. "I've done the most important bit of all."

"And what is that?"

"I'll tell you in a moment, Mattie, dear. After I've started it. And that means . . ."

Brit the Much Elder stood up. "That means I must be on my way. Brit the Elder's about to call Brit the Younger, and she hasn't met me yet. At least not that she remembers."

"But you're her," Brewster said.

"Yes, I was, but she's not me. Not yet. Goodbye Brewster, Mattie, Phillip. Gilbert and Sid, good to see you again. You haven't had much to add to the conversation."

Sid said, "Frankly, this hasn't seemed like the sort of conversation to which adding more would be helpful."

Gilbert nodded. "Trained professional magicians, we are. Experts in the arts of misdirection and deception. And with all due respect, you two confuse the hell out of us."

Brit the Much Elder said, "I take that as high praise."

Sid said, "It was meant as such. We stand in awe."

"You're both sitting down."

Gilbert said, "Are we? Or is that just part of the misdirection and deception I mentioned?"

Brit the Much Elder disappeared.

Brit the Elder swiped her finger through a menu of options only she could see as they floated in the empty space in front of her. "Okay, everyone. I'm putting in a call to Brit the Younger. You should brace yourselves. She's been in a terrible mood."

"Why?" Mattie asked.

Phillip gritted his teeth.

Brit the Elder said, "There was a falling out between her and Phillip. That sent her into a bit of a tailspin. Then she immersed herself in a long-term project that isn't going well. She's trying to find the source of the program, what its purpose might be, and ultimately, who wrote it."

"How's she going to do that?" Mattie asked.

Brit the Elder said, "Unsuccessfully. She's going to spend nearly a decade trying before she fails. I know, because I was her, and that's what happened. I'll admit my memories of that time are a bit sketchy, but like I said, it was a dark time. I think I'm deliberately blocking parts of it."

Gilbert and Sid shot Phillip a look that Brit the Elder didn't catch, and the twins didn't understand.

Phillip said, "I'll fill Brewster and Mattie in later. If we have to bother Brit the Younger, I'd prefer to get it over with."

Brit the Elder repeatedly swiped her finger through and then jabbed at an empty space roughly two feet in front of her. She swiveled her chair to face the blank wall behind them, and everyone else looked up at the wall as well.

After a few seconds, an image of Brit's face filled the wall. She had bags under her eyes, and her hair was unkempt. Instead of a dress or business suit, this Brit wore a loose sweatshirt. In the background behind her, stacks of books and piles of discarded ramen bowls littered the room.

Brit the Elder said, "Hello, Brit."

Brit the Younger still said nothing, but she did take her eyes off Brit the Elder and scanned the room, her expression changing from anger to shock. "Is that Brewster and Mattie? Kids! What are you doing there? And Gilbert and Sid? Brit, what's going on?"

Phillip halfheartedly raised his hand. "Er, um, I'm here, too."

Brit the Younger remained focused on Brit the Elder. "What's going on?"

"There's been a bit of a problem, I'm afraid. With two wizards named . . ." She glanced at Phillip.

Phillip said, "Magnus."

"Magnus, and . . ."

"Also Magnus. They're both named Magnus. You know that."

"Two wizards have hit Gwen, Martin, and several other people with a version of the fast-time spell. Mattie and Brewster have managed to get some help, as you can see. Now they've come to us, hoping we can come up with a counterspell to neutralize the Magnuses' handiwork."

Brit the Younger closed her eyes to concentrate. "We'd need to either get access to the computer these *Magnuses* are using to run the spell, or we need to figure out how their spell hooks into the victims' file entries, then find a way to block that or to undo the effect. It's possible."

Brit the Elder said, "I know it is."

"But it will be a lot of work."

"I know it will."

"A lot of work for me," Brit the Younger said.

"I'm not asking you to do it," Brit the Elder said. "I know you've got your hands full with your fruitless project. I wouldn't dare drag you away from all of that pointless work."

Brit the Younger glared at Brit the Elder, but for an instant, her eyes darted to Phillip, and the anger was mixed with amusement, like one would feel when an angry child tries to storm out of the room and attempts to push open a door that needs to be pulled.

Brit the Elder continued, "I don't expect you to drop everything. I'll do it."

"When?"

"Later on."

"Later on, when I'm you."

"Yes, but honestly, Brit. You've got decades before you have to act on it. Just write about this conversation in your journal and forget about it. I'll read it later on and it'll remind me to work on the spell."

Brit the Younger's eyes flashed with a renewed fury. "You said you would stop reading my journals!"

"And I will, just not quite yet. Besides, they're my journals, too."

Brit the Younger stared at Brit the Elder, her mouth twisting into tortured shapes as she either tried to find the right words to express how she felt, or she knew exactly the right words and was trying not to say them in front of the twins. She eventually let out a breath that seemed to release much of her anger but also left her looking much smaller and more tired.

"Why don't you just make the spell?" she asked.

Brit the Elder said, "It would be too late. Mattie and Brewster need the spell now, not in a few days."

"But," Brit the Younger said, "you're a time traveler. You can make it, then go back in time and give it to them now."

Brit the Elder said, "Yes, I could do that, but what's the point? You have decades of free time before they need it, even after you give up in abject failure on your current project, which you will. To put off this favor for Mattie and Brewster until after they need it and use time travel to get it to them now would just make us look like we have poor time management skills."

Brit the Younger looked furious for a second, then her image disappeared. Brit the Elder spun her chair around to face the others. "She'll do it."

Mattie asked, "How can you be sure?"

Brit the Elder said, "Because she's already done it. Years ago, in fact. The counterspell is complete."

"You've had it this whole time?"

Brit the Elder smiled. "Yes. The counterspell has been complete and ready to go since before you were born. I spliced it into the Leadchurch shell program this morning. Phillip, all you have to do is target the person you want to unfreeze with your staff and say, *Let's kick some ice.*"

Phillip winced. "Ugh, that's a terrible joke."

Brit the Elder said, "It's a quote from a movie. A terrible movie."

"If you already have a cure for our parents, why did you make us go through all of this?" Brewster asked.

"I didn't make you go through anything," Brit the Elder said. "If you hadn't *gone through all of this*, you never would have come to me and told me you needed the counterspell, I never would have known that it was needed, and I wouldn't be in a position to help you now, when you need my help. I don't think you understand just what I've done here. You've come to me requesting a complex spell, the likes of which has never been written, and which took me weeks of effort to create. I'm delivering it to you with no delay, within ten minutes of you telling me you need it. I've had it waiting and ready to go since before you ever needed it, and you're acting like that's a bad thing. What would you have had me do?"

Mattie said, "Maybe show up as soon as our parents got frozen and fix them immediately!"

Brit the Elder shook her head. "You want me to come and fix the problem before you've even told me what the problem is? Oh, Mattie. You're just not being realistic."

Mattie and Brewster turned to the other adults in the room for help. Phillip sat with his head in his hands. Gilbert's eyes were wide and his hands covered his open mouth. Sid applauded quietly and muttered, "Masterful! Absolutely masterful!"

The guards on the patio ignored them as they walked out of Brit the Elder's house, across her patio, and down into the park beyond. They looked behind them and saw Brit the Elder standing between the still-open sliding glass doors, smiling and waving goodbye. Brewster waved back.

Mattie waved as well, but said, "She gave us exactly what we asked for, faster than we could have hoped, but I feel like she jerked us around."

Phillip said, "Yup. That's the Brit the Elder experience in a nutshell. Solutions covered with a thick coating of problem."

Sid said, "Like a thoughtful gift that comes wrapped in embossed paper far too exquisite to tear, and carefully tied with ribbons too fine to cut."

"Or," Gilbert said, "a perfectly good thought expressed in such flowery, overly fancy language as to make it either confusing or irritating to the listener."

Sid shook his head. "I haven't the foggiest notion to what you are referring."

"No surprise there."

Mattie rubbed her hands together. "Okay, we have the cure for our parents. Let's get to it."

Brewster said, "But—I don't know—shouldn't we test it or something first? What if it makes things worse?"

Phillip said, "It's wise to be concerned, but if Brit the Elder says that a macro she wrote works, I'd bet on her being right. I mean, Brit the Much Elder would know if it *was* faulty, not that she'd tell us until after it malfunctioned. We could go unfreeze the guys first, if it makes you more comfortable."

Mattie and Brewster looked at each other. Their faces each ran through several different emotions—fear, anxiousness, excitement, embarrassment—without either of them saying a word.

Brewster mumbled, "We wanna help Mom and Dad as soon as we can. But we don't want to take any stupid risks."

Mattie turned to Phillip. "Would it be terrible if I suggested that we test the spell on Dad, then unfreeze Mom second?"

When he, Gilbert, and Sid had all finished laughing, Phillip said, "It might, if I weren't absolutely certain that that's exactly what your father would tell us to do if he were here."

23.

The twins, the magicians, and Phillip all appeared in the living room.

Gilbert looked around. "So this is where you live, kids? Very nice."

Sid said, "Cozy."

"Yes, comfortable. Pleasant. I have to assume that's all your mother's doing."

"Oh, I concur. Were Martin in charge of the décor, I'd have expected movie memorabilia and model spaceships."

Phillip looked at the spot where Martin and Gwen had been standing when he'd last seen them. "So, where are your parents?"

Mattie said, "Down in the rec room."

As the five of them walked down the stairs into the finished basement, with its movie memorabilia and model spaceships, Sid said, "Ah, yes. This is more in line with my expectations. Clearly, we are now entering Martin's domain."

Brewster said, "We wanted to hide them, so we put them in the Darth Vader and Kylo Ren costumes." He pointed to the life-sized replicas of Anakin Skywalker and his grandson flanking the TV.

Mattie approached the two masked figures, her head cocked to the side. "Have they moved?"

When the twins left them there, Vader had been standing with his knees bent and both hands gesturing forward. Ren had stood sideways, pointing with one hand. Now Vader's shoulders were more hunched and his fingers had curled inward. Ren still stood sideways, but the hand was pulled in closer to the body, and the head had turned.

"Maybe," Brewster said.

"Probably," Phillip said. "Being frozen like this is terribly startling."

Mattie said, "What? They're aware of what's going on? We asked you if they were awake and you said no."

Phillip said, "No, I think I told you that they weren't in pain, then I changed the subject to get out of trying to explain. They aren't unconscious, but they don't understand what's happening. Time is passing incredibly quickly for them. The spell was originally designed as a means of forward time travel. It makes decades go by like seconds, but you stay awake through all of it. Everything happens all at once, and to anyone who sees you in the meantime, your movements are glacially slow."

Gilbert added, "The only reason you can see any movement is because they're moving so quickly, from their point of view. They're probably jumping from the shock of the spell, and any physical discomfort that might have happened to them in the meantime, like when you put the costumes on them and whatnot."

Brewster muttered, "And whatnot."

Mattie asked, "So if they've felt any pain since they got frozen, it all seemed to happen at once to them?"

"Yes," Phillip said. "And they're probably still feeling it. But that's not your fault. All you did was move and hide them. The Magnuses are to blame for all this. They're the ones who froze them."

"And . . . maybe messed with them," Mattie said. "It sounded like they might have done that." Brewster looked confused for a moment, but then he started nodding furiously. "Oh yeah. We heard that. It sounded like they beat Dad up pretty good."

"Oh, did it?" Gilbert said, almost laughing.

Sid turned and looked at the stairs. "Rather steep, that staircase. It must have been difficult, maneuvering your father down it without banging him into the doorjamb, or dropping him at all."

Phillip smiled. "Well, this is all just more reason to unfreeze them immediately. I believe we agreed to start with Martin."

Brewster said, "Well, wait a sec—"

"Okay, here we go," Phillip interrupted. He pointed his staff at the figure dressed as Darth Vader, coughed, and with an almost apologetic tone, said, "Let's kick some ice."

A ray of reddish light shot from the head of his staff, bathing Darth Vader in its glow. An otherworldly warbling sound filled the air but was immediately drowned out by a muffled shout of alarm and pain from beneath Vader's helmet. Martin jumped and cringed at the same time, appearing to crumple in on himself as he tumbled forward and rolled on the floor, curled into the fetal position, gripping his left elbow with his right hand. He ripped the Darth Vader helmet off his head and lay there, writhing in pain, his left eye pinched shut, for about two seconds before Mattie and Brewster rushed him.

Martin's pained grunts gave way to laughter as his children aggressively hugged him, told him how worried they'd been, then helped lift him to his feet.

Martin stood hunched over, his hand clamped over his left eye as if trying to keep it from falling out. "What the hell happened?"

Phillip said, "It's a long story. Why don't we unfreeze Gwen first?"

"What?" Martin said. "Gwen's frozen? What are you waiting for?"

Phillip aimed his staff at Gwen, standing immobile in the Kylo Ren costume.

Sid leaned over toward Gilbert and said, "Kylo Gwen."

Gilbert nodded. "We were all thinking it."

Phillip said, "Let's kick some ice."

As the red light shot from Phillip's staff and lit up Gwen, Martin looked at Phillip and said, "Really? You're quoting from *Batman and Robin*?"

"I don't like it any more than you do. Talk to Brit the Elder. She wrote the macro."

"You went to the Brits for help?"

"Yeah, I didn't like that either."

Gwen leaped straight up into the air, her cape fluttering around her. She whipped the Kylo mask off her head and practically threw it across the room. She quickly looked at her surroundings, then down at what she was wearing. She had only just started to seem like she knew where she was, and wouldn't try to kill anyone who got too close to her, when Brewster and Mattie abandoned their father and ran to her side.

Martin reached out and placed a hand on the wall to support himself, as he was still trying to get his wind back after the abuses he'd suffered while immobile. He tentatively opened his left eye and watched, beaming, as his children helped their mother.

Martin turned to Phillip. "You unfroze me first?"

Phillip smiled. "Yup."

Martin nodded with satisfaction and looked back to Mattie and Brewster, still hugging a giggling Gwen to within an inch of her life. "You were testing to make sure the spell worked, weren't you?"

Phillip said, "Yup."

Martin thought for a moment. "Okay. I'm cool with that. Kids, you must both be confused by everything you just saw. I guess it's time for your mother and me to explain."

Mattie said, "Don't worry about it, Dad."

"Yeah," Brewster said, "we already know."

Sid coughed. "Yes, I'm afraid in the process of helping them investigate, we had to educate your offspring in the ways of true magic."

Martin said, "Oh. Well, if you had to."

Gwen said, "I'm kinda relieved. I was worried about how we were going to tell them. It's sort of like the sex talk."

"Oh," Gilbert said. "Should we have told them about that, too?"

"Over my dead body," Gwen said.

Martin turned to Phillip. "So what happened?"

"Our side of it is a long story, and it's mostly Mattie and Brewster's to tell. You two should probably go first."

Martin shrugged. "Fair enough. There isn't much to tell. You disappeared. The Magnuses appeared. They asked where you were. We said we didn't know. We asked why they were in our home uninvited. They said they were looking for you, obviously. Galka actually said *obviously*. That didn't sit well with us."

"I'd imagine."

"Then they asked if they could count on our votes for one or both of them to be the next chairman."

"You said no?"

"While laughing. Then Magnus Galka suggested that Magnus Rex freeze us, and before we could really fight back, he did it. Weird, huh?"

Phillip said, "No, that's pretty much what we figured happened."

Martin blinked his left eye several times and continued to hold his hands around his midsection. "Anyway, it was like a really intense instant of confusing motion and blinding pain, then you all were here, and I was wearing my Darth Vader costume. It feels like they gave me a pretty good working over after they froze me."

"Yes," Mattie said, without pausing to stop hugging Gwen. "They did."

"The fiends," Brewster said.

Gwen said, "I feel fine. Seems like they left me alone."

Martin said, "That's good," shrugged, then turned and nodded to the magicians. "Gil. Sid. Good to see you. Why are you here?"

Gilbert said, "We're part of your children's long story."

"An integral part," Sid said.

"Too right," Gilbert said. "We're pretty much their Obi-Wan Kenobi and Yoda."

Gwen finally found the strength to push her kids out to arm's length to look at them. Her delight gave way to confusion. "What's with the top hats and capes? Oh . . . no. You two *taught* them magic, didn't you?"

Martin rounded on them. "What?"

Phillip said, "How about we give the kids some time to enjoy having saved their parents before we start complaining about how they did it?"

Gilbert smiled at Martin. "They did it with magic, and our help."

"Yeah, I got that. Did you show them the Spielberg coat hanger trick with your canes?"

"Yes," Gilbert said. "And they booed us."

Martin shook his head. "Kids. No appreciation for the classics."

Martin leaned back on the built-in couch in Gary's conversation pit. "One thing I don't understand—Mattie, how did you have that fight with the Magnuses without getting kicked out of the Oak Ridge Boys concert?"

Mattie, Brewster, Gilbert, and Sid all sat side by side, opposite Martin and Gwen, to facilitate the storytelling process. Mattie shook her head. "No, the fight was *after* the Oak Ridge Boys concert. By then I was standing in Hitler's car."

Martin nodded. "Ah, I see. Yeah, I was confused because you said you were standing up on the seat."

Brewster said, "You were picturing the theater seats. Hitler's car had an open top."

"Yeah," Martin said. "Hitler loved convertibles, like all dictators, and retired executives."

Gwen said, "Kids, that is a crazy story, and now that you know a little more about our background, you know what a high bar it is to have us judge something to be crazy."

Across the room, near the corner, Phillip sighed heavily and said, "Let's kick some ice." His staff bathed Tyler in a reddish glow.

Tyler leaped straight up in the air. "Hey! Whoa! What the hell?"

"The Magnuses froze you," Phillip said.

"Yeah," Tyler said. "The Magnuses froze me!"

"Because you wouldn't vote for them."

"Yeah! They asked if they could count on my vote. I said no, and they froze me."

Phillip paused and then said, "Yes. That's what happened."

Gwen said, "Gilbert. Sid. I just can't thank you enough for all the help you gave our kids. You kept them fed. You kept them safe. And when it was clear they weren't going to give up, you stuck with them to assist and guide them. You're good friends."

Sid said, "It was our pleasure."

Gilbert added, "We enjoyed every minute of it."

Martin said, "I am bummed that you taught them magic. I was looking forward to that."

Gilbert said, "We know."

Sid smiled. "That added to the pleasure."

Phillip walked across the room to the dining table, pointed his staff at Jeff, and said, "Let's kick some ice."

Jeff leaped straight up, shouting. "Whoa! What the hell? Hey!"

Phillip said, "The Magnuses froze you."

"That's right," Jeff said. "The Magnuses! They froze me!"

"Because you wouldn't vote for them."

"They said they were running against you, and they asked for my vote. Roy's, too. We said no."

Phillip said. "Yes. That's what happened."

Gwen said, "Brewster, Mattie, we didn't plan for you to have these powers yet. But now that you have them, we're not going to take them away."

Mattie said, "Good!"

"Unless you make us," Martin added. "You have to be careful when and how you use them. It's very important that you not let anybody know what you can do."

"You can't let anyone see you fly," Gwen said, "or levitate things, or teleport."

Martin said, "In fact, let's just make it a rule. No magic outside of the house."

Mattie and Brewster both let out anguished cries.

Phillip pointed his staff at Roy, moaned, and said, "Let's kick some ice."

Roy glowed red for a moment, then leaped straight up in the air. "What the hell? Whoa! Hey!"

Phillip, Gary, and Tyler said, "The Magnuses froze you."

"Yeah," Roy said. "The Magnuses froze me!"

Gary said, "The wanted you to vote for them, and you said you wouldn't."

"That's exactly what happened!"

Phillip said, "We know it is."

Jeff added, "I was there."

"Yeah," Roy said. "You were!"

Brewster said, "Mom, you can't agree with Dad about not allowing magic outside the house!"

Gwen said, "I was going to say no magic outside the house, and even inside the house, only on weekends."

"Yeah," Martin said. "Like video games."

"And we should limit how much money they can conjure for themselves. I'm thinking a hard limit of, say, two fifty a week? That's close to what they'd make at a part-time job after school, isn't it?"

Mattie and Brewster looked at their parents, their expressions a mixture of betrayal and disgust. They turned to Gilbert and Sid, looking for allies.

Sid said, "Ah, does one's heart good to see a family reunited and functioning in a healthy manner. Doesn't it, Gilbert?"

"It does, Sid. It really does."

Phillip pointed his staff at Pete, said, "Let's kick some ice," then quickly moved his staff to Gert and said it again, as if he couldn't get the syllables out of his mouth fast enough.

Both Pete and Gert leaped straight up in the air. As they landed, before either of them had a moment to say a word, Phillip said, "Two wizards named Magnus froze you. We brought you here to undo their spell. We're going to transport you both back to the tavern the instant after we left so you won't miss out on any business."

Pete said, "Well, that's all well and good, but what about the tremendous business opportunity you already denied me?"

"What opportunity?" Roy asked.

Phillip said, "When we arrived, The Magnuses had already frozen Tyler. Pete and Gert were preparing to charge people admission to come look at him and a fur cloak the Magnuses had left behind, which they were claiming was the pelt of a giant wolf."

Tyler studied Phillip's face, then turned to Pete. "You treated me like an oddity to be gawked at for money? I thought we were friends!"

"We are," Pete said. "That's why I didn't think you'd mind helping me out."

"Help you out? By being the main attraction in a two-act freak show where the opening act is a used cloak?"

Phillip said, "You and the cloak were getting equal billing, but you can discuss that later. They have to get back to the tavern." Before Pete could disagree, Phillip pointed his staff at Pete and transported him away.

Gert looked at the empty spot where Pete had been standing, then turned to Tyler and said, "I'm sorry about all of this, Tyler. Pete's been under a lot of pressure. Business at The Rotted Stump has slacked off ever since the Intact Arms opened up shop across town. It's just adding injury to insult, given what they named their tavern to begin with. Anyway, I'd have made sure that Pete didn't let the customers do anything injurious to your dignity, and that you got top billing over the cloak."

Tyler said, "Thanks, Gert."

Phillip transported Gert away.

Jeff said, "She always has been the brains of the operation."

Roy nodded. "Yeah. Pete's lucky to have her for a silent partner."

Phillip rubbed his hands together. "Okay! Now that that's all out of the way, we can move on to real business. What to do about the Magnuses."

"Yeah," Mattie said. "It's about time."

"I do have a few ideas," Brewster said.

Phillip nodded. "I'm sure you do. I have a plan, one I'm sure will work, but I can't discuss it right now because it's on a need-to-know basis. Actually, it's more secret than that. It's on a need-to-*not*-know basis. Gary, you need to not know because you're the only one here who the Magnuses expect to attend the vote tomorrow. You'll be extremely valuable as an inside man, but we can't run the risk of you tipping our hand, so you won't be privy to the whole plan. Your instructions are to act casual. Pretend that you have no idea what the Magnuses did to the rest of us, nominate one of them and vote for them, exactly as you promised. Just know that we, all of us whom the Magnuses froze, will intervene at the perfect moment."

"Yeah, that makes sense," Gary said.

"And Mattie and Brewster, you need you to not know either."

"Why not?" Mattie asked. "What will we be doing?"

24.

The mood in Martin's car as he drove the twins to school the next morning was like a jumpsuit made of fiberglass insulation: quiet and uncomfortable.

"So," Martin said, looking into the rearview mirror at his kids as they stared sullenly from the back seat. "Mattie. You drove my car, right?"

"Yeah."

"I shouldn't encourage you to break the law like that, but I'm impressed that you managed to find the rear entrance to the theater and get there without having an accident or getting pulled over by the cops."

Mattie said nothing.

"Now that you two know the truth, I can let you in on a little secret. This car is undentable. It's a trick I picked up from Phillip. It also doesn't need any gas, oil, or maintenance of any kind. And it's invisible to police radar. Pretty cool, huh? No wonder you didn't get pulled over, eh?"

The twins said nothing.

"Not that you were speeding. I'm sure you were careful." Martin said. "And it's no surprise you were able to pull that whole thing off. You're very capable. And I'm sure Brewster acting as a navigator must have helped. Right?"

Neither Mattie nor Brewster said a word.

"Yup, you two had to work together to get to the theater, just like you're working together to give me the silent treatment right now."

Mattie said, "If you want to talk, we can talk. Tell us what you and Mom and Phillip are going to do to the Magnuses."

Martin shook his head. "I can't."

Brewster said, "You can. You just choose not to."

"Yeah, well, that's adulthood in a nutshell. Not being able to do things because you decide you can't. That's going to be your harshest lesson out of this whole thing, I think. Look at all of these other schlubs driving their kids to school. Any one of them could kick their kids out of the car, go use a credit card they can't pay off to buy a console and a bunch of videogames they can't afford, then blow off work for the day to play them. And I promise you, they'd all like to. None of them will. I'd love to bring you along for what we're going to do to the Magnuses. And I have the power to! But I won't, because that would be stupid. That's adulthood. Being a grown-up is like when someone trains their dog to sit with a weenie balanced on its nose until they give the dog permission to eat it, but you're the one with the weenie on your nose *and* you're the one withholding permission from yourself to eat it. Learning not to allow yourself to do all the dumb things you'd really like to do is part of what makes you an adult. So is learning not to snicker every time your father says *weenie*."

The twins stopped snickering, laughed out loud for a second, then composed themselves.

"Being a responsible adult can be a real drag," Martin continued. "What makes it worse is that you find yourself thinking about what you would do if you were an irresponsible teenager who could get away with it. Why, if I were in your position, for example, I think I might be tempted to make nice until my father drove away, so that he could tell his friend Phillip that he dropped them off just like he was supposed to. Then, as an irresponsible teen, I'd probably find a private place, conjure up my ridiculous top hat, and look for a preset teleportation link named "meeting to mangle the Magni," or something similar, and I'd use it."

"Would you?" Brewster asked.

"Definitely, if I were an irresponsible teenager. As a responsible adult I have to tell you that it's a terrible idea, and you should one hundred percent tell Phillip that I said so. Anyway, speaking hypothetically, as an irresponsible teen, upon arriving at the castle, I suspect I'd find Gilbert and Sid there, waiting for me, as they've been cut out of Phillip's plan as well, and also will want to watch what happens. I think they'd be able to help keep me, as well as any sibling I may have brought with me, safe."

"And that's what you'd do," Mattie said.

"Oh, yes. If being an adult is not doing things you want to because you know they're bad ideas, then maybe adolescence is doing things you know are bad ideas because you want to."

Martin pulled the car up to the curb and leaned over into the front passenger seat to look out through the window as the twins stepped out onto the sidewalk.

"Have a good day," Martin said. "I expect not to see either of you until tonight, when you come home from school."

Mattie and Brewster both said, "You won't."

Martin smiled. "Good!"

They watched Martin drive away, then turned and walked toward the school.

The twins spoke to nobody, including each other, as they walked through the halls, into the band room, and to the sousaphone closet. The low-frequency portions of the morning marching band practice drifted in through the walls, assuring them that they would not be disturbed, though the fact that the band was playing "Tequila" meant that they were wrapping up. Mrs. Sanderson, the band teacher, liked to end practice with something fun and not terribly challenging.

Brewster asked, "Does it seem weird that they spend so much time trying to keep us from getting drunk, but every high school band plays that song?"

Mattie performed the graceful arm wave that made her top hat appear and roll down across her shoulders, her cape unfurl behind her, and her cane extend from her hand. She used her thumbs to extend the crown of her top hat with an audible *pop*, pulled her white gloves out, then placed the hat on her head. "Adults, man. Everything they do is weird."

Brewster followed suit, conjuring his own hat, cape, cane, and gloves. They both stepped into the sousaphone cabinet and closed the door behind them as the marching band out on the practice field shouted "Tequila!"

Hundreds of years earlier and thousands of miles away, the twins appeared in the same immense room where their parents had been married. They stood on a narrow gallery designed more for cleaning and maintenance than observation, which hung three-quarters of the way up the wall. They looked down at the people milling around the gold-on-gold inlaid floor. Along the distant wall, the golden raised dais where Martin and Gwen had taken their wedding vows now supported an empty golden throne, protected by two guards in golden armor. Raised galleries ran down both sides of the vast, rectangular room, themselves sparsely populated with people walking at the specific pace that, in any century, marked them as tourists.

A quiet, deliberate coughing noise made them both jump. The sound of two grown men laughing caused them to spin around as they tried to find the source of the noise. After several seconds of furious searching, the twins saw the telltale distortions in the background and floating periscope tips that gave away the positions of the two invisible magicians.

Gilbert's disembodied voice said, "Sorry. I really tried not to startle you."

Mattie said, "That's all right."

Sid's voice said, "I for one am delighted that he failed. All fun aside, none of us, technically speaking, are supposed to be here, so I'd appreciate it if you made yourselves harder to spot."

The twins both touched their fingers in a specific order, mimed throwing a small object straight down at the ground, and, more or less in unison said, "Ninja vanish."

They both disappeared, replaced by two hazy masses of distortion and the dull sound of bodily impacts followed by grunts of surprise and pain.

"Good work," Brewster said. "You jumped right into me."

"It's hard not to," Mattie said, "when you lunge into my way like that."

The two continued grumbling as the tips of their own hat-mounted periscopes raised up out of their distortion fields.

"These things have no peripheral vision," Mattie said.

Sid said, "Presenting a fine opportunity for you to practice caution, young Mathison, which I know is not particularly your most well-honed skill."

"Which is how we knew you would be here," Gilbert said. "We programmed this teleport location because we knew we could count on you. When foolhardiness is called for, you two don't disappoint."

Brewster said, "That's not fair. I'm cautious."

Sid said, "If your idea of caution is to stand back and wait for your sister to try things first, then yes, you're quite the cautious fellow. Oh, don't look so glum. We're just giving you a hard time."

Mattie said, "How would you know if we're looking glum? You can't see us. And also, nobody says *glum* anymore."

Brewster said, "So . . . I assume you're here as part of the plan."

Sid said, "Yes. That is what you assume."

"But you are here as part of the plan, right?" Mattie asked.

Gilbert said, "We're here as part of a plan. Our plan."

Sid added, "Which is to wait here, with you, watch the events carefully as they unfold, and attempt to discern the exact contours of Phillip's plan, which he refused to share with us."

Mattie asked, "What time is the vote?"

"Don't know," Gilbert said. "Sometime today."

"Then why don't we jump forward an hour and see if it's started yet?"

"Patience," Sid said. "I find that jumping ahead to find events scheduled to occur in the near future is like cranking up the fast forward on your VCR to its top speed."

Mattie said, "I've never used a VCR."

Brewster said, "I've never even seen a VCR. I've just heard people talk about them."

"Old people," Mattie said.

"That's fine," Sid said. "Needlessly insulting, but fine. My point is that you end up overshooting, then you have to go back. You get things ruined for you, and usually spend almost as much time dialing the timing in as you would have if you'd just waited. Only instead of a nice, relaxing wait, you have the stressful experience of trying not to overshoot your target. No, I'm sure the meeting will start quite soon. We're better off just waiting. See what I mean?"

Brewster asked, "Gilbert, you agree with this?"

"Only as much as I had to, to get him to shut up about it."

"So what do we do while we wait?" Mattie asked. "It'll be hard to play cards when we can't see each other."

Sid said, "Oh, dear girl, there's any number of games we can use to pass the time that do not require us to see each other. For example, I spy with my little eye, something that begins with *G*."

Gilbert said, "Tell me it's not gold."

"It's not. But it very well might be something golden."

"Sid, everything in this room is golden."

"Yes! And therein lies the game!"

25.

Two hours later, three periscopes floated in the still, quiet air on the catwalk high above the floor of the main hall.

Sid said, "Five."

Mattie said, "Four."

Brewster said, "Nope! You're both wrong. It was one!" His white-gloved hand extended out of the bubble of invisibility that surrounded him, holding one finger up.

Mattie asked, "How do we know you didn't change how many fingers you were holding up after we guessed?"

"If you don't trust me to be honest about how many fingers I'm holding up, then there's no point in playing this game to begin with."

Sid said, "All right, I think that's quite enough parlor games for now. They cleared out all of the sightseers ages ago. Why haven't they started their infernal meeting yet?"

"I don't know," Brewster said, his periscope tilted forward with the lens looking down toward the floor below them. "But there's someone down there now."

"Really?" Sid asked.

"Take a look."

The other two periscopes tipped over the handrail. Far below them, a solitary wizard with red-and-gold robes and black hair walked across the vast inlaid floor. He paused in front of the dais, turned to face the empty hall, and raised both arms. The deep rumble of stone sliding against stone filled the room as a long rectangle, part of the floor's pattern, raised up, stopping when it achieved table height. Smaller square tiles all around the larger rectangle rose as well, stopping below the level of the table, forming chairs, or more accurately, stools.

Mattie said, "We'd better wake up Gilbert."

"I'm already awake, but thank you for thinking of me."

"Why didn't you tell us you were awake?" Sid asked. "We'd have happily included you in the parlor games."

"That's why," Gilbert said.

Far below them, the wizard held his left hand forward. A glowing image too small for the twins to make out appeared in his hand.

"What is it?" Mattie asked.

"A globe," Gilbert said.

"How can you tell?" Brewster asked.

Sid said, "Your periscope can zoom. Slide your right hand around the edge of the brim, slowly."

After a second, Mattie said, "Ah! Thanks."

Brewster said, "We made fun of you at the time, but I have to admit, these periscope hats are pretty cool."

"I appreciate your praise, Brewster, begrudging and belated as it may be."

"You're accidentally alliterating again," Gilbert growled.

"So are you," Sid said.

Below them, the wizard in red and gold opened his mouth, and in a thick New Jersey accent said, "It is hereby announced that I, the wizard who is called Wing Po, but known within our band by my true name, Eddie, do at this moment declare the annual Convocation of Wizards officially open. All wizards of the European continent, in the medieval time period, are invited to attend to discuss the vital business of our community. BYOB."

Sid said, "Ooh, I like his style."

Suddenly, like popcorn appearing in a pan full of raw kernels and hot oil, wizards began materializing in the space around the table.

The appearances slowed, then stopped. Eddie quickly counted the wizards, stopped at nineteen, furrowed his brow, and said, "We're missing quite a few people. Phillip's one of 'em."

Magnus Rex said, "I'm sure they'll turn up sooner or later."

Eddie said, "I suppose we should get started then."

Gary, in an overly loud voice, said, "If this is everyone who's going to show up."

Everyone looked around expectantly for a moment.

Gary deflated a bit. "Which, I guess it is."

Mattie said, "No women. Huh."

Gilbert said, "My understanding is they all left. Went to Atlantis."

"Except our mom."

"Including your mom. She and your dad did a long-distance thing for a while."

Brewster asked, "Why'd the women leave?"

Sid said, "Did you notice that Mattie didn't feel it necessary to ask? There, dear fellow, is your first clue."

The wizards each selected a stool, filling less than half the length of the stone table. The two Magnuses sat side by side, looking pleased with themselves.

Each wizard removed his hat and pulled out his beverage of choice. Some produced steins, some pint glasses, some cans, and more than a few rocks glasses. All of the wizards spent a moment enjoying their drinks, then an uncomfortable silence descended as they all looked to the empty seat at the head of the table.

Eddie said, "Normally Phillip, as the chairman, runs things. You all know that. Since he's not here—"

Eddie started to rise from his seat, but Magnus Galka called out, "I move that Magnus should chair the meeting, as he got the second most votes last time we held an election."

The wizards murmured and muttered among themselves. One asked, "Is he referring to the other Magnus, or himself?"

A wizard named Carl turned to Magnus Galka and asked, "Were you referring to the other Magnus, or yourself?"

Another at the far end of the table said, "He might have been speaking of himself, but in the third person."

Another said, "No, Kirk, he wouldn't do that. He isn't a douche!"

Carl turned to Magnus Galka and asked him, "Are you a douche?"

Magnus Galka stood. "Let me clarify my earlier statement. I move that my friend, Magnus Rex, the other Magnus who is not me, should chair this meeting."

Magnus Rex stood and put his hand on Magnus Galka's shoulder. "Thank you, my friend. I am touched, and I humbly second the motion."

The wizards again collapsed into confused murmuring.

Magnus Galka said, "All in favor?"

The wizards all spoke, mostly saying either: "Eh," "Fine, whatever," or "Knock yourself out."

Up on the catwalk, Mattie asked, "When are they going to show up?"

Gilbert said, "Who knows? It has to be before the final vote though. That's just logic, isn't it?"

Magnus Rex walked to the head of the table, Magnus Galka walking along behind him. They stood there, looking down at the seated wizards, all staring up at them.

Magnus Galka said, "I suggest you call for any old business."

Magnus Rex cleared his throat and nearly shouted, "Any old business?"

Gary smiled and looked around the room expectantly, but nothing interesting happened. Quite the opposite, in fact, as Eddie read his notes for the meeting off an electronic tablet.

"The only business to carry over from the last meeting is Fred's proposal to make Ultimate Frisbee the official sport for wizards, and establish an intramural league."

"Really?" Magnus Rex said. "This is old business? Why doesn't it sound familiar?"

Magnus Galka said, "Perhaps because you weren't really paying attention at the last meeting."

"True. I do tend to focus on my drink until it's time to vote for chairman."

"Yes," Magnus Galka said, his eyes quickly darting around at the faces of the other wizards. "And that ability to eliminate the inessential and concentrate on only the truly vital issues would be useful in a chairman. As to Fred's proposal, I thought we already decided against that."

Fred said, "No, you all voted against starting a Quidditch league on account of copyright law. After you all voted that down, I suggested that we do Ultimate Frisbee instead, and Phillip promised that we'd have a debate and put it to a vote at the next session."

Gary said, "He was being sarcastic."

"Doesn't matter. He promised me a debate and a vote."

Magnus Rex said. "Fred, why do you want to start an Ultimate Frisbee league?"

Fred looked at Magnus Rex as if it were the dumbest question he'd ever heard. "Because it'd be really cool. We're wizards. We could dress it up! Make the Frisbees glow, and make the goals portals to other dimensions or something. We'd make it more . . ." Fred trailed off, looking for the right word.

Magnus Galka offered, "More ultimate?"

"Yeah!"

"Okay," Magnus Rex said. "There's the argument for an Ultimate Frisbee league. And the case against it?"

Eddie asked, "Does anyone want to play?"

For several seconds, they all sat in silence.

Eddie said, "There you go."

Fred shouted, "That's just because you're a bunch of dorks who don't like sports!"

"Yes," Eddie said. "We're dressed as wizards. We're only here because we were messing with our computers and found a file we shouldn't have. I don't think it's a surprise that many of us are, as you said, *dorks who don't like sports.*"

Magnus Rex asked, "Does that count as a debate?"

Magnus Galka said, "I think so."

Magnus Rex bellowed, "All in favor of playing Frisbee with Fred, say *aye.*"

"Aye," Fred said, alone. Then he muttered, "Jerks."

Magnus said, "All opposed?"

Everyone but Fred said, "Nay."

"Good," Magnus Rex said. "Do we vote for chairman now?"

Eddie said, "No. Now we open up the floor to any new business."

Magnus Rex shrugged. "Okay, fine. Anybody got anything?"

Up in the balcony, Brewster muttered, "Okay, here we go."

Down at the table, Gary nodded and crossed his arms, casting his eyes around the room. Again, his air of confidence faded as nobody materialized.

Fred raised his hand. "I don't know if any of you are familiar with a game called Pickleball. It's like big Ping-Pong. Or tennis, but slower."

Magnus Rex glared down at Fred, who lowered his hand and stopped talking.

Magnus Galka said, "We should move on."

Magnus Rex glanced back at him irritably. "Yeah. If there's no further new business—"

A wizard raised his hand.

Magnus Rex leaned forward, stared directly at the wizard with his hand raised, and increased the volume and stridency of his voice. "*We will* move on to the election."

"Any second now," Mattie said.

Magnus Galka turned to Eddie. "If you'd please remind everyone of the ground rules?"

Eddie said, "Well, this has never come up before, but according to the rules, if someone's not present, they cannot be nominated, as they have to accept the nomination. A vote for them doesn't count. So, if Phillip's not here before the nominations are complete, he won't be eligible."

Gary asked, "Who made up that rule?"

"Phillip," Eddie said. "But we all ratified it."

Magnus Galka said, "Right. Magnus, I suggest you open the floor for nominations."

Magnus Rex said, "Yeah, okay. If anyone has somebody they'd like to nominate, or someone they promised to nominate, now is the time."

Both Magnuses stared directly at Gary.

Through clenched teeth, Gary said, "I nominate Magnus."

A wizard raised his hand.

Magnus Galka said, "Yes, Sergio?"

"Which Magnus?"

"Well, we should ask Gary for clarification . . ." Magnus Galka's voice trailed off as he saw the look on Magnus Rex's face. He cleared his throat and said, "I think Gary meant to nominate Magnus Rex. Isn't that right, Gary?"

"I don't care. Whatever."

Magnus Galka said, "And I second it."

Magnus Rex said, "Great! Now we move on to the vote."

A wizard at the back of the table shouted, "If Phillip's not here, I nominate Eddie."

Another voice said, "Seconded."

Eddie said, "Thanks, Mitchell. Felix. That's flattering, but frankly, I don't really want to be chairman."

"So you withdraw?" Magnus Galka asked.

"No, no, I'm not saying that. If any of you really want me to be the chairman, then vote your conscience, but I have to believe there are other better options."

"Yes!" Magnus Rex said. "Now, on to—"

"In fact," Eddie said. "I'd nominate David."

Another wizard said, "Seconded!"

David said, "Thanks, but I'm not really the man for the job. I'd nominate Daniel."

Someone said, "Seconded!"

Daniel said, "No, guys, I'll do it if you really want me to, but I think it'd be better to nominate Ross."

"Seconded."

The table erupted into a shouted barrage of names, seconds, and denials of being up to the task. Magnus Rex looked angrier with each passing second, and Magnus Galka more concerned. Eddie simply stood to the side, tapping furiously at his on-screen keyboard, trying to keep track of who all had been nominated and seconded by whom, until Magnus Rex finally shouted, "Enough!"

The table fell silent.

"Eddie," Magnus Galka said. "Who has been nominated for chairman?"

Eddie held up a finger, asking for a second, as his eyes ran down the list and his lips moved, mouthing names as he read. He occasionally glanced up at the table to check the list against the people actually present. "Everyone has been nominated and seconded, except for you and Gary."

Magnus Galka said, "Yes, but I'm Magnus's best friend and closest advisor, so in a sense, a vote for Magnus is a vote for me."

Magnus Rex said, "In a sense. But really, it's a vote for me."

"Of course."

Gary said, "Fantastic! Thanks a lot, guys! You've pretty much already taken the vote and elected *anyone but me.*"

The wizard sitting next to Gary said, "I nominate Gary. It's only right."

"Thanks."

Eddie said, "Sorry, Sergio, but you already nominated someone, and you can't nominate or second two people. I'm afraid there's nobody left to nominate Gary. Sorry, Gary. Nothing personal. It's just the way the math worked out."

Gary said, "That's no surprise. Math's never really been my friend."

"So now we vote?" Magnus Rex worded it as a question, but his tone of voice made it clear he meant it as a command.

"Yeah," Eddie said, removing his wizard hat. "We'll vote via our usual procedure. Each wizard will cover his mouth and whisper *Mi voĉdonas por*, and the name of the candidate they want to be the next chairman. That'll trigger the election macro. Once everybody present has voted, the macro will tally the results, and we'll have a new chairman."

"Yes," Magnus Galka said. "It's now time for everybody to vote their conscience, and to keep any promises they may have made."

Magnus Rex stared directly at Gary. "Not *may* have made. Promises were definitely made."

Sergio turned to Gary and whispered, "I can't believe Phillip's not here."

I know, right?" Gary replied.

26.

Eddie said, "So after I count to three, we will all vote."

Gary stood up.

"Uh, I move we postpone the vote."

Eddie asked, "On what grounds?"

Gary looked around for any sign of his friends, or an excuse to delay. "I don't know. What would you suggest?"

Magnus Rex said, "No. We won't postpone. We vote now. Three. Two. One. Vote."

All of the wizards except the Magnuses and Gary put their hands over their mouths and whispered the trigger phrase. The Magnuses stared at Gary, who looked around again, sagged, nodded at the Magnuses, covered his mouth, and voted as he had promised both the Magnuses and Phillip he would. Then, and only then, did the Magnuses cover their own mouths to vote.

Behind the Magnuses, floating above the dais that held the throne, a cloud of glowing dots appeared, then contracted inwards, clumping together into letters and words. The names of every wizard present, except for Gary and one of the Magnuses, appeared with a number next to it. Most names had a one. A few had twos. One name, Magnus Rex, had a three.

Gary sagged as both Magnuses cheered and hugged.

Sergio said, "This is unbelievable."

"Completely," Gary nearly shouted. "You have no idea how unbelievable it really is, and if I told you, you wouldn't believe it, because . . . well, you get the idea."

Magnus Galka and Magnus Rex released their hug and stood laughing for several seconds until Magnus Galka said, "I suggest you address your constituents, Chairman Magnus. Here. I've prepared a speech." Magnus Galka handed a printed page of text to Magnus Rex.

Magnus Rex took the paper, turned and looked down the table lined with stunned faces, then began reading. "My fellow wizards. I thank you for the amazing honor you've bestowed on me. The idea that all of you have chosen me to be your leader, role model, and protector is truly humbling."

Gary said, "You don't sound humbled."

"I promise," Magnus Rex continued, "to do everything in my power to live up to the tremendous faith all of you have shown in me."

Sergio said, "You got three votes."

"Yeah, which is more than anyone else got," Magnus Rex shouted.

Magnus Galka cleared his throat. Magnus Rex regained his composure and continued. "I have plans, my friends. Grand plans. Overdue plans. Plans that will make life better for every wizard here."

Gary winced. "And those plans are?"

"Coming," Magnus Galka said. "The plans are coming. Just let your chairman finish his speech. Have some respect for the office."

Magnus Rex read, "It's time for us wizards to take our rightful place. To get what we are due. We are going to stand up and demand what we deserve."

Eddie said, "We're all healthy, well-fed, fabulously rich, and not one of us works for a living. Oh, and we're immortal. We're probably the most privileged people who have ever existed on the face of the earth."

"And I say it's high time we were treated as such," Magnus Galka said.

Eddie scowled. "Treated as such? If the rest of humanity understood how good we really have it, they'd rise up with torches and pitchforks. It'd be the French Revolution all over again."

"That's right," Magnus Galka said. "They resent us. They resent our power. And if they understood our power, they'd resent us even more. That's why we have to make sure that it never comes to that."

Magnus Rex elbowed Magnus Galka in the ribs; whether it was to keep him from embarrassing himself or to stop him from upstaging the newly minted chairman was unclear. Magnus Galka stopped talking and nodded apologetically to Magnus Rex, who continued reading aloud.

"We wizards have been too meek, hiding our light under humanity's bushel for too long. It's time for us to embrace our leadership role. More to the point, it's time for the nonwizards to embrace our leadership role. During my time as chairman, I will make it my primary goal to cement us wizards as the protectors and stewards of mankind."

The wizards sat in silent contemplation for several seconds before Gary said, "So you want us wizards to be the leaders of the world."

"Naturally," Magnus Rex said.

"And you are the leader of the wizards."

"You've all made me your leader."

"Uh-huh. So, what you're saying is that you want us to help you become the leader of the entire world."

Magnus Galka said, "If I may, what I believe Magnus is saying—"

"Is what you wrote down on a piece of paper for him," Gary interrupted.

"Is that we wizards are better equipped to run things than everybody else, and that he is going to help all of you attain your rightful place and hold on to it once you've got it."

"By telling us what to do."

Magnus Galka said, "He can't do the work for you."

Gary shook his head. "No, he needs us to do it for *him*. Guys, this is crazy. And stupid. It's worse than crazy and stupid. It's evil. It's evil, and crazy, *and* stupid!"

Sergio said, "You voted for it."

"You don't know that," Gary sputtered. "Besides, I gave my word. I promised more than one person. I had no choice, the way I saw it. Don't blame me for this!"

Sergio shrugged. "It's certainly not my fault. I voted for myself."

Eddie said, "Now, now, everybody. It's no use arguing over who's to blame for all of this. It's Gary. The point is, we have this mess, and we're going to have to deal with it."

"Yes," Magnus Galka said. "And with Magnus's leadership, I'm certain we'll all get through this difficult time."

Eddie locked eyes with Magnus Galka. "Yeah, about that. How exactly do you intend to make the locals see that it's in their best interest to unite under your glorious leadership?"

Magnus Galka said, "Magnus isn't a monster, Eddie. He doesn't want to go out and take control of the world by force, if that's what you're worried about. I give you my word, Magnus will negotiate control of the governments of the world through peaceful, diplomatic means, whenever possible."

"How?" Eddie asked. "Ignoring the sneaky little *whenever possible* you tacked on at the end, how do you think you're going to peacefully talk people into giving you control?"

Magnus Rex turned and looked at Magnus Galka, who opened his mouth to speak, then stopped short when he saw the look on Magnus Rex's face. Instead, he peered around Magnus Rex's shoulder at the speech he'd written, then pointed to a paragraph toward the bottom of the page. Magnus Rex nodded, looked at the paragraph, and began reading aloud.

"We need only demonstrate our power, show them how much easier their lives will be with us in control, let them enjoy the peace and security that our protection will bring, and they will gladly do whatever they can to keep us in charge. We will provide food and clean water to them at no cost, with no labor required. We will keep them safe from one another, at first by shielding them from attack by their neighbors, then, in time, by leading them, and their neighbors as well, to seek peaceful resolutions to their differences."

Magnus Galka said, "I'd suggest stopping there for now. I think that's enough. Do you see now, Eddie?"

Magnus Rex continued reading. "And in the unlikely event that some of them still voice dissent, I give you my word that our retribution, while swift and spectacular enough to act as a deterrent, will be as humane as possible."

After a moment of thick silence, Magnus Galka said, "Admittedly, in the context of this conversation, that last part didn't sound great. In my defense, I didn't think we'd . . . Magnus would get as much resistance from you as he has."

"Your defense is that you thought we'd be into it?" Gary asked.

Magnus Galka looked at Gary, then at Eddie, then at the floor while he thought for a moment before he finally said, "Yeah. I guess that is my defense. What's wrong with that? And look, yeah, I know, having to step on the occasional malcontent to keep the peace isn't a very appealing idea. Killing a cow sounds terrible, but a steak dinner sounds great. We aren't talking about widespread mayhem here, just the occasional demonstration of our power to keep dissent from spreading. Punish a few people occasionally to keep from having to punish more later on. At worst, we're talking about killing hundreds to save millions. Isn't that just the moral thing to do?"

Eddie shouted, "Not if you're the one threatening the millions in the first place! Look, I don't speak for everyone, just myself, but I won't be a party to this. I won't have anything to do with it, aside from trying my hardest to stop it."

Magnus Galka said, "We're sorry to hear that you feel that way."

Gary said, "I'm with Eddie."

Sergio said, "Uh-oh, Magnus. You've angered your base."

Gary shouted, "Shut up!"

"I will, but only after I say that I agree with you and Eddie. Magnus, I won't help you with this."

Another wizard agreed, then another, and another, until the entire table erupted in conversation about what a terrible idea it was, and how stupid Magnus Rex had been to believe Magnus Galka when he said the other wizards would go along with it.

Magnus Rex looked over the table full of wizards, clearly frustrated. He turned to Magnus Galka, who shrugged at him. Magnus Rex raised a fist in the air, inhaled deeply, and opened his mouth to shout, but went silent, as did all the other wizards, when Phillip, Martin, Gwen, Tyler, Roy, and Jeff appeared at the far end of the table.

"Now?" Gary asked. "You show up now? After the nominations? After the vote? After the Magnuses propose to set themselves up as co-dictators for life?"

"There will be only one dictator," Magnus Rex said.

"Yes," Eddie said. "Do you know who that'd be? The answer may surprise you."

Phillip said, "I told you we'd arrive at the perfect time. This is the perfect time."

"After everything happened?" Gary asked.

"Yes, because the Magnuses needed to get the job to understand what the job actually is, and why they don't want it."

"We don't?" Magnus Rex asked.

Phillip said, "No, not really. You want to be in charge. I get that. It sounds great. But what you didn't understand is that a job title doesn't make you a leader. You're only a leader if people are willing to follow you. If they aren't, the title of chairman is just a word. There was a crazy guy who called himself the Emperor of San Francisco, and a con man who called himself the Baron of Arizona. Hell, Frank Sinatra was called Chairman of the Board. Now you're Chairman of the Wizards. Can you really tell me your title is more impressive than theirs?"

Magnus Rex said, "But those people you mentioned were crazy."

Roy growled, "Frank Sinatra was not crazy."

Magnus Rex said, "Chairman of the Wizards is a real job. A real office. I was elected to it."

Phillip pointed at the wizards sitting around the table. "Yes, by a minority of the wizards, all of whom just said they aren't going to do what you told them to do. Now you see that real power doesn't come from winning elections."

"That's right," Martin said.

Phillip continued, "You may win, technically, and the job will carry certain powers and privileges, but to truly accomplish anything, you need the people to back you up. Winning a job is pointless if the people won't let you do it. You, as an elected official, work for your constituents. It's not a platitude. It's the truth. The only power you have comes from your followers choosing to follow."

Martin nodded. "Precisely."

"History's rife with examples of people who got into power without a clear mandate from the people, and spent their term mired, unable to get anything notable done."

Martin said, "I think they get it."

"Or," Phillip said, "people who have managed to gain their party's nomination for some high office, but didn't have the support of a sizeable portion—"

"Phillip, I think you're getting off track."

"I'm just saying, Martin. I'm not trying to make a point about any one politician. I'm commenting on the nature of elected offices in general."

"I think everyone understands that, Phillip."

"Do they, Martin? I hope so, because it's important to me that everyone knows I'm not picking on any one person, or party."

"I know."

"I've just been thinking about this subject a lot lately."

"Yeah, we get it."

"Because of recent—"

"Recent events," Martin interrupted. "Yeah, we all have. Let's just move on."

"You're saying that I can only get them to do what they want to do anyway?" Magnus Galka said.

"Yes."

"But as a leader, can't Magnus make his followers want to do what I think . . . he thinks . . . let me rephrase that."

"I don't think you need to," Martin said. "What you just said was plenty accurate."

"What's that supposed to mean?" Magnus Rex asked.

Magnus Galka said, "Yes! I don't have any idea what you're getting at, Martin."

"Oh come on! It's obvious that you're Wormtongueing him!"

"I don't know what you're talking about," Magnus Galka said. "And I wish you wouldn't call it that."

"Fine," Martin said. "You're Littlefingering him."

"That's not much better. What I'm saying is that as the leader, Magnus can convince everybody to do what he feels is best for all of us, yes?"

"Oh, yeah," Phillip said. "Some say that getting people to agree to the right course of action, even if it runs counter to their instincts or short-term interests, is the highest form of leadership."

Magnus Galka laughed. "Well, that's all we're talking about, Phillip! Convincing people to do what we know is best, by publicly punishing those who don't."

"No!" Phillip shouted. "No, that's not what I meant at all! A leader shows them why the desired course of action is what's best for them. A dictator tells them how it's going to be and punishes dissent."

"Okay, smart guy. Explain to me why it's best for me not to do what I want."

"Because you'll lose all of our respect."

Magnus Galka arched an eyebrow. "So, you're saying we had your respect to begin with?"

"Yes!"

The wizards behind him looked at the ceiling or the floor. A few made uncertain little humming noises.

Phillip said, "You had some of our respect. A certain number of us held you in . . . some esteem. We all agreed you had . . . qualities. The point is, however much respect we had for you before, we'll have less if you try to just ram what you want down our throats."

Magnus Rex turned to Magnus Galka. "Look, man, I didn't want to do things this way to begin with. This is your thing. You said we'd be in charge if we won. If all this is just going to be us getting insulted, I have better things to do."

Magnus Galka put a calming hand on Magnus Rex's shoulder. "I know. I know. Please be patient for just a minute more, my friend."

Magnus Rex rolled his eyes and shrugged.

Magnus Galka turned back to Phillip. "What you've been trying to tell me is that a leader would use logic and reason to explain why the path he's chosen is best, to persuade his constituents to go along."

Phillip said, "Yes."

"But a dictator would use threats to convince others not to oppose his plans."

"Exactly. I think you understand."

"I do. You've explained it to us very logically and reasonably, and we are not convinced. So, if Magnus and I were to just go ahead and start enacting our plans, what would happen?"

Phillip grimaced. Martin said, "We'll stop you."

"By force?" Magnus Galka asked.

"If necessary."

Magnus Galka nodded. "And that's a threat. So, it's not a question of who's the leader, Phillip. It's just a matter of who's going to become the dictator first."

"I don't see it that way."

"That just means I have a head start. *Rengjøring!*"

A blinding bolt of white-hot lightning blasted down from the sky, shattering the windows in its way as it shot into the main hall. The bolt hit Phillip before spreading to all of the other wizards around the table, except the two Magnuses.

Normal lightning lasts a fraction of a second, striking its target, writhing in the air for an instant, then disappearing, leaving nothing but a charred tree, a terrible smell, and a squiggly line burnt into the retinas of whoever was present to witness it. This arc persisted, twisting in space with an earsplitting buzz and delivering a constant stream of high voltage electricity into the chests of the wizards. They all remained where they'd been standing or sitting when first struck, but they were not still. They trembled violently, their muscles spasming, teeth gritting, eyes wide open.

Magnus Galka, his eyes squeezed shut, magically produced two pairs of welding goggles. He put one on and gave the other to Magnus Rex.

The Magnuses walked around the table. As they moved into the buzzing, strobing mass of writhing tendrils of electricity that encompassed and reached out from all of the wizards, the darting bolts of power seemed to warp and detour around them as if they were somehow repellent to lightning.

Magnus Galka approached Phillip, standing right in front of him.

"Electricity won't kill us wizards, but it still hurts like hell and makes the muscles clench. We learned that the hard way when Magnus Rex tried to make a lamp out of some antlers. We're going to go now. We have a whole planet full of new subjects just waiting to be informed of their place in the world. When we've done that, we'll come back, turn the lightning off, and see if you're ready to be part of the future or not."

Magnus Galka turned to Magnus Rex and shouted, "I suggest we go."

Magnus Rex said, "It's about time."

The two Magnuses flew straight through one of the floor-to-ceiling glass windows, shattering it with no concern that they might be hurt by falling glass, or anything else.

Up on the catwalk, Mattie, Brewster, Gilbert, and Sid had all averted their periscopes to keep from being blinded.

Mattie said, "We have to do something."

Sid said, "I wholeheartedly concur." He deactivated the invisibility spell. As the light-warping field dissipated, he was revealed, sitting, leaned against a handrail with his legs crossed, looking through his hat-mounted periscope.

Gilbert also became visible. Both of them, in unison, turned to the floating periscopes and blurred distortions that denoted the twins.

Mattie said, "Yeah, we know. Please don't say it."

Brewster said, "We wait here, right?"

Sid said, "Indeed. We have to tell you to stay here and stay safe. Thank you for understanding."

Sid stepped off the catwalk and began to float down toward the lightning-encrusted clump of twitching wizards.

Mattie said, "He thanked us for understanding, not for doing as he asked."

Brewster said, "He didn't ask us to stay here. He told us to."

"Which is rude. But really, he didn't even tell us to stay. He told us that he had to tell us to stay."

Brewster smiled. "So, he didn't really leave us with any clear instruction."

"No, he didn't. Quite irresponsible of him."

"Quite."

27.

Gilbert shouted, "We have to find a way to redirect this electricity."

"Agreed," Sid said. "I shall return forthwith."

Sid disappeared. Less than a second later he reappeared, standing on the ground near Phillip, wearing a wetsuit, thick rubber galoshes, and his top hat. Under one arm he held a copper cable as big around as a man's wrist. The cable snaked in front of him and attached to the bottom of a long metal rod he held in his other hand like a sword. From its connection to the metal rod, the cable stretched the full length of the great hall and disappeared out the door.

The lightning leaped from Phillip to the rod. As the bolts of electricity had been cascading out from Phillip to all the other wizards, when the lightning left Phillip, it abandoned the others as well. They all fell to the floor, moaning and writhing in pain, smoke rising from their scorched robes.

Sid, protected by his wetsuit, let go of the cable and the lightning rod, dropping the raging torrent of raw power to the floor. The electrical arc streaming down from the sky remained locked to the lightning rod.

Gilbert rushed forward and started helping the badly singed wizards back to their feet. Sid did the same.

Phillip asked, "What are you two doing here?"

"Came to watch, didn't we?" Gilbert replied.

"You couldn't possibly have dreamed that we'd allow so momentous an event to transpire without being on hand to witness said doings," Sid added.

Gwen said, "Yeah, and I'm willing to bet the kids are here, too."

"Concealed within the rafters, snug as proverbial bugs in their metaphorical rug," Sid said. "It might be an advantageous time to wave up at them, just to let them know they are not, in fact, orphans."

Martin and Gwen both waved in the direction Sid pointed.

Phillip said, "Everyone! We have to get after the Magnuses! There's no telling what those two idiots might do. Come on!" He took off, flying straight through one of the few remaining unbroken windows.

As the other wizards began lifting off the ground and following Phillip through the newly shattered window, Tyler asked, "Hey, does it look like it's getting darker out?"

Sid said, "That plays to our advantage. The sign will show up better that way."

Phillip soared above the city, followed by the rest of the wizards and the two magicians. High winds buffeted them, and a thick bank of clouds rolled in from the horizon on all sides, obscuring the sun and making the constant stream of lightning stretching from the heavens into the castle window only slightly less incongruous.

Gwen looked back over her shoulder, then turned around, flying backward to get a good look at the castle behind them.

"Sid," she said, "I assume that's your doing?"

Martin and Phillip both looked back to see a massive neon sign on the roof of the castle, made of fifty-foot letters, connected to the copper cable. The sign read, "Insufficient effort, old bean."

Beneath the large letters, smaller but still fully legible print read, "By the by, this sign is fully powered by your own lightning."

Martin said, "If you have to explain your joke like that, you probably shouldn't bother."

Sid shook his head. "I'm quite sure I don't require any presentation tips from you, Martin." He looked away from the others and adjusted his top hat, pulling it down tighter over his wetsuit cowl.

The clouds closed in, forming a hole that allowed only a single shaft of sunlight through. In the city below, people poured out of the buildings to gaze up in fascination and horror at the turbulent sky.

As the wizards and the people of London watched, the opening in the clouds divided into several distinct holes. The cloud ceiling bulged and warped until the clouds had formed into a three-dimensional image of Magnus Rex's face, smiling down at them, sunlight streaming from his eyes, mouth, and nostrils.

Beside and seemingly just behind him, the image of Magnus Galka's face also appeared.

Magnus Galka cleared his throat. The sound seemed to come from the hole in the cloud cover representing his mouth and was loud enough to be heard for miles around. He made a blowing noise, puckering his lips and constricting the sunlight from his mouth into a thin stream, then said, "Okay, I've got it working. We're live, Magnus. I'll introduce you."

Magnus Galka smiled down at the city, pausing for a moment so the people could bask in the literal light of his smile.

"Greetings friends. My name is Magnus. I come to you today with splendid news. Life-changing news. News that will ensure safety, security, and prosperity for you and everyone you love. You will remember this, the moment that I brought you this news, for the rest of your lives. I am here to tell you that for the common good, and for the good of the common, we are all going to come together, one happy family, united by our shared values, our shared sense of purpose, and guided by the compassionate judgment, optimistic vision, and firm hand of our shared ruler. Starting this very moment, you have the honor of following my friend, and our beloved leader: Magnus!"

Magnus Rex said, "Uh, hi everybody."

Magnus Galka said, "Go on, don't be shy. Address your subjects."

"You already said everything."

Below the wizards, the people lining the streets made a raucous noise, but the wind and the distance, and the great number of people yelling, muddied the sound enough to make it impossible for the wizards to make out any coherent meaning.

The image of Magnus Rex in the clouds squinted, narrowing the beams of sunlight coming from its eyes into two flat planks of yellow light. "What is that? I can't quite hear you."

The image of Magnus Galka said, "I'd suggest that it doesn't really matter all that much what the specific people on the ground right now have to say."

"Shush. I'm trying to listen to the little people. All you down there, please speak up."

The people on the ground grew louder but even more difficult to understand with the increased volume and urgency of their words.

Phillip rolled his eyes and turned to the other two dozen wizards floating in the air above the city. "I'll be right back."

Phillip flew at top speed closer to the ground, only a few feet above the heads of the crowd gathered in front of the castle gates. He hovered there for a moment, nodded, and shot back up into the sky again.

Phillip reappeared in the sky below the titanic floating faces of the Magnuses. In a voice amplified just as powerfully as the Magnuses, Phillip said, "I went down and checked. Their answer is no."

Magnus Galka nodded. "Ah. I see. I fear there's been a misunderstanding."

"Yeah," Phillip said. "I think there has."

"What Magnus said wasn't a request. It was a statement of fact. And now the people of Camelot—"

"London," Phillip said.

"It was renamed Camelot."

"Then it was renamed again, back to London."

"But most of us still call it Camelot."

"No, I don't think that's true." Phillip turned around. "Show of hands, how many of you call this city London?"

Most of the wizards raised their hands. Below, in the city's streets, not everybody raised their hands, but enough did that the height of the crowd seemed to rise by over a foot.

Phillip turned back to face the Magnuses, arms folded, and a smug smile on his face.

Magnus Rex whined, "Does it really matter?"

Magnus Galka said, "Yes, faithful friend, it does. When we make an example of a city, it's very important that people know what to call it. We don't want people saying: *Did you hear about the awful thing Magnus did to that city, you know, the one that had the castle.* It muddies the message. Bad branding."

Phillip said, "We won't let you hurt anybody."

Magnus Galka laughed. "A very wise person once said, *The question's not who's going to let me. It's who's going to stop me.*"

Phillip winced. "Isn't that Ayn Rand?"

"Yes! It is! I didn't know you were a fan."

Phillip sneered. "I'm not. First of all, if Ayn Rand had been as wise as you say, she'd have come up with a pen name where the spelling and the pronunciation matched. Secondly, I just answered the question, *Who's going to stop you? Us! We* won't let you. You should pay attention unless you think knowing what's going on around you doesn't serve your enlightened self-interest."

Magnus Galka said, "If people like you would actually read *The Fountainhead*, or preferably, *Atlas Shrugged* instead of just making fun, you might actually learn something about how the world works, but no matter. How, exactly, do you intend to stop him? Oh no, is Martin gonna turn big? Will Tyler become a clone of one of us to fight Magnus with Magnus? Will Gwen tangle us up in fabric and will Roy fly into us at high speed?"

Phillip stared at Magnus Galka's immense cloud image for a long moment before muttering, "Maybe."

"We've been watching. We've seen your moves. You will find that Magnus is prepared!"

"Which Magnus?"

"Both! Both of us! We're both prepared! Why is this so confusing?"

Phillip opened his mouth to speak, but never got the words out, as he was knocked to the side by a powerful stream of glowing blue energy that shot past him from behind and plunged into the space between the two immense Magnus heads, where it detonated in a massive explosion that blasted a hole in the cloud cover over a mile wide. The shock wave blew Phillip and the other flying wizards almost all the way to the ground. The only one unaffected was Martin, who had fired the shot in the first place.

The hole in the clouds swiftly closed, and the faces of the two Magnuses re-formed.

Magnus Galka smiled down at them. "Like I said, we studied your moves. One thing they all have in common is that they only work if you know where the person you're attacking is, which you don't, which is why you just wasted your time trying to shoot a cloud."

Gwen had clearly triggered the amplification spell herself, as her voice was easily audible across the city when she said, "Huh. You know, he has a point."

"Yes," Phillip said. "So it would seem."

"And now," Magnus Galka shouted, "you will all see what comes of resisting the will of Magnus. For lo, he shall execute the plan I devised under his supervision, and which he approved, a plan that will make Camelot—"

"London!" Phillip shouted.

"Shut up! Camelot or London! Whatever you call it, either name will be remembered for thousands of years!"

"Both names already were!"

"I told you to shut up! Camelot's remembered as a place of myth where great heroes triumphed and Helen Mirren walked around being hot. London is remembered as one of the world's great capitals where history unfolds and Helen Mirren walks around being hot. When we are finished enacting Magnus's plan, they will both be remembered for something very different."

"For being places where a guy named Magnus was hung up on Helen Mirren?"

"No!" Magnus Galka nearly screamed. "They'll be remembered for death! Unrelenting, irrevocable, and above all else, memorable death. Death that will preoccupy the thoughts and haunt the nightmares of all who hear of it! Children will cry! Parents will shudder! Teens will pretend to be unimpressed, but we'll all know it's just an act!"

Sid shook his head. "This is all getting needlessly wordy."

Gilbert said, "You're not really the best person to lodge that complaint."

Magnus Galka said, "Magnus will now unleash ten plagues upon this city, and when he has finished venting his ire, the metropolis you see now will be an uninhabitable waste."

"Oh, like in the Bible."

"That's right, we're taking our inspiration from the Bible. You approve of that, Phillip? Or do you think God's not all he's cracked up to be either?"

"No, no. It's fine, I guess. I mean, if you're going to copy your ideas from somewhere, the Bible's a pretty good choice."

"No! Not copying. *Taking inspiration.* The ten plagues of Egypt were the worst things anyone could imagine at the time. The ten plagues of Magnus are the worst things we can imagine now! There are a few classics from the old list mixed in with new—more modern, dynamic, and proactive plagues. Edgy plagues, with attitude and sass!"

"Is the first plague a torrent of poorly applied marketing buzzwords?"

"No. Shut up."

Magnus Galka shouted, "Magnus didn't want it to come to this! You've left Magnus no choice! You've refused the commands of Magnus, your rightfully elected leader, and now, instead of Magnus's benevolence, you will face his wrath!"

Magnus Rex nodded and said, "Yeah."

"Well said," Magnus Galka agreed. "Subjects, do not waste your time groveling! The time for apologies is past!"

Phillip said, "Nobody's apologizing."

"You will face the ten plagues of Magnus, starting with darkness!"

Gwen said, "That was one of the ten plagues of Egypt. You said you'd come up with your own."

"I also said we're keeping a few classics as an homage. But it was the second-to-last plague in the Bible, and we're starting with it! It's just our jumping-off point! Eh? That can't be good, can it? Ha!"

The cloud cover grew thicker, bringing the ambient light level down from the dusky gray it had been to the full pitch-black of a moonless, starless night. The only illumination came from the persistent lightning bolt streaming into the castle, and Sid's mammoth neon sign on the roof.

Magnus Galka let out an irritated grunt, and the lightning bolt disappeared. For a moment, the world went pitch-dark, until a fresh bolt of lightning shot down from the heavens, striking the neon sign, illuminating it briefly while destroying it.

Again, the world went dark and quiet, except for concerned murmuring from the people huddling in the city below.

A lone point of light appeared, a glow emanating from the head of Phillip's staff, then from the ends of the other wizards' staffs and wands. Even Gilbert's and Sid's white-tipped walking sticks began to glow.

Martin looked down. "I was about to suggest that we go down and help the citizens, but they seem to be getting along fine without us."

Below them, the wizards could see flickering points of yellow light—torches and lanterns coming out of buildings where there presumably had been cooking fires, forges, or candles. As the torches and lanterns moved out among the crowd, the city began to look much as it did on an average evening.

"Your first plague seems to have fizzled, Magnus," Phillip said. "You didn't really think it through. I mean, you are menacing the populace with a problem they already face every night."

"Yeah," Magnus Galka said, "but this night will last for weeks!"

"If your—" Phillip stopped himself and winked theatrically. "Sorry, *Magnus Rex's* reign lasts weeks. Just to be sure you know, I was winking when I said that. I don't know if you could see, what with all this dark you've made."

Magnus Galka spat, "Oh, you think you're so smart."

"Smart enough not to try to attack people with what is literally the first problem humanity ever defeated through technology. Our first invention took care of this!"

Gary said, "What, the wheel?"

"No, Gary, the wheel isn't our first invention. Think about it. We'd have to invent the chisel to make the first wheel. No, our first invention was the cooking fire."

"Not clubs?" Roy asked.

"Okay," Phillip allowed. "Maybe our first invention was the club. I give you that."

"Silence," Magnus Galka shouted. "We're gonna hit you with our second plague, and it won't be anything you can defeat with torches! Behold, the second plague of Magnus: fire!"

A hundred-foot wall of flames erupted from the forests and grasslands, surrounding the city in a perfect ring, like the burner on an immense gas stove. Waves of heat radiated inward. Everything within the circle was bathed in an ominous orange glow.

The Thames, which even in this early age flowed through the heart of the city, began to slow. Not just the speed of its flow, but the roiling motion of the surface seemed to congeal, growing more viscous. A yellow-orange light appeared deep beneath the surface—all of the water had transformed into magma.

For a moment, the buildings and people lining the riverbanks were lit eerily from beneath, as if God himself had put a flashlight under the world's chin, but the effect was shattered immediately when every wooden bridge, dock, or boat touching the river burst into flames.

The wizards shot downward toward the city, a swarm of black specks silhouetted in a sea of orange light.

Sid said, "Well, then, so much for darkness, I suppose."

Magnus Galka shouted, "We're done with darkness. You can't let yourself get hung up on your previous work."

Sid shrugged as he and Gilbert headed down to help the citizens as well.

28.

All along the path of the river, two dozen wizards flew back and forth, unleashing torrents of water from their staffs and wands. All of the structures immediately adjacent to the river were, of course, beyond help, but it didn't take long for the wizards to contain the damage, keeping the fire from spreading beyond the riverbank and into the city proper.

Instead of just relying on magic, Eddie used his organizational skills to help the people of London form a bucket brigade, so they could play a part in their own rescue.

"Good work, people," Eddie shouted. "Hey, you! No, don't fill your buckets from the river. It isn't water anymore. It's magma. No, that's not an illusion. Get water from the well. Great! Now your bucket's on fire! Put it down! No! Don't pass it!"

Just as the wizards started to feel as if they were in full command of the situation, people in some of the higher windows and balconies began pointing away from the city and shouting.

Out at the flaming perimeter, within the wall of fire, Phillip could see the shadowy forms of great moving creatures—like people, only many times larger and with much longer, thicker arms, smaller legs, and a stooped-over gait where their arms carried much of the load. They stepped out of the wall, their bodies covered with loose, slow-moving orange flames. The creatures approached the outer edge of the city from all sides.

Phillip asked, "Are those . . . chimps?"

"That's right!" Magnus Galka crowed. "Chimpanzees! Man's closest relative, and one of the most surprisingly vicious predators in the animal kingdom. They go straight for the face and the genitals! And these chimps are gigantic and made of flaming rock!"

"So, are they a separate plague then?"

"No, they're part of the fire plague. We thought it needed a little punching up."

Phillip shouted, "Eddie, you're in charge of keeping the magma from burning the city down. Take four or five guys to help you. Agreed?"

Eddie said, "Agreed," and set about picking his team.

Phillip said, "Everyone else, use Martin's giant macro to hold those things back! And you, uh, might want to protect your faces and genitals."

Martin asked, "Do you really think the word *might* belonged in that sentence?"

The wizards flew out over the city in all directions, streaking past the outer protective wall, each one bursting into hundreds of glowing objects, the shape and color of which were a matter of personal preference. Martin chose silver boxes, like extremely expensive LEGO bricks. The glowing objects swirled around the wizards before reforming into oversized versions of the wizards that flew headlong into battle while the real wizards remained protected inside. When they landed, the giant wizards formed a defensive line of glowing behemoths standing between the giant firechimps and the city's edge.

The firechimps lumbered toward the city in a contracting ring of flames. It only took a few steps before their shoulders began rubbing, so every other chimp slowed their pace, falling in behind the giant beside them. After a few more steps, they formed a two-chimps-deep ring of fire, and after a few more steps, they readjusted their pace again to form a three-deep ring.

The wizards pointed their immense glowing staffs and magic wands at the firechimps. Each unleashed an equally oversized torrent of water, driven at high enough pressure to cover the ever-shrinking gap between the two lines and hit the front row of firechimps full force. The firechimps tried to shield themselves with their arms, but the result was simply that their arms were extinguished before the rest of them. As the fire covering their bodies died away, the massive slabs of stone beneath were exposed and quickly crumbled away.

"Huh," Martin said. "Okay, that seems effective. Putting the fires out makes the chimps fall apart, I guess."

Gwen shook her head. "It doesn't make a lot of sense, but then, we're talking about giant flaming chimps. I don't think making sense was foremost in the Magnuses' minds."

In short order, the front line of firechimps was reduced to screeching armless torsos stumbling forward on flaming legs. Then they dissolved away into smoldering rubble, which the second and third rows of firechimps climbed over before breaking into a run.

The wizards continued spraying water at the advancing line, and the firechimps took substantial damage, most of them falling into rubble at the wizards' feet. The last line, however, reached the wizards unscathed and leaped over their fallen comrades to attack the wizards hand to hand.

Martin shot a focused stream of water at the approaching chimp, but it twisted in midair, pulling itself out of the path of the stream; then all Martin saw was a flaming hand coming straight for his face. He managed to jerk his glowing blue head out of the way in time to be grabbed by the shoulder. It wasn't his real shoulder, of course—it was a glowing silver simulation of his shoulder, several times larger than the real thing, and as such, he felt no pain as the flaming claws sunk in. Still, the chimp shoved him with enough force to send him back to the ground. The stream of water coming from his staff shot straight up like a fountain jet in front of a casino, looking spectacular, but serving only as a distraction. He marveled for half a second at how pretty the droplets of water were, falling in what looked like slow motion, backlit by the flames surrounding him. Then he noticed the giant flaming claw coming down quickly toward his crotch.

Martin managed to roll clear, cutting it tightly enough to feel the splash as the firechimp's weight slammed down in the mud. As Martin scrambled to his feet, he pointed his water spray at the chimp, but it turned sideways and evaded the torrent as it again dove at Martin. Soon, they were locked in a vicious embrace, grappling with one another. Martin wondered if the ground was wet enough to extinguish the firechimp. Fighting hand to hand seemed like a losing proposition. The chimp had longer arms and was stronger than he was. Also, the heat radiating from its body and its stubby little legs flailing away at Martin's crotch, as if the chimp thought his genitals were a treadmill, caused no small amount of consternation.

Martin heard someone yell his name. He turned to see a giant green representation of Gwen, standing with her feet planted wide and her immense magic wand held like a dagger in her right hand, shooting a stream of water off into the distance. The smoking ruins of a firechimp were falling in large chunks around her as another closed in. The firechimp tried to grab her by the throat, but she pivoted slightly, grabbed it by the arm, and pulled it close and held it in place so that she was looking down over the giant chimp's flaming shoulder. She turned her wand on the chimp, extinguishing its head and torso immediately. As they crumbled, the still-flaming limbs fell to the ground and went out on their own.

"Martin," she shouted. "You've gotta fight them like John Wick!"

Instead of trying to squirm out of the firechimp's grasp, Martin pulled it closer so that it couldn't get away from him. Then he bent his wrist to turn his water flow at the chimp's face, which immediately crumbled in his hand.

Martin turned to Gary and shouted, "Fight them like John Wick, pass it on!"

Gary shoved one of the chimps away and managed to wing it in the arm before it ran at him again. Gary jumped to the side as the firechimp ran past and managed to shoot it in the back, destroying it as another grabbed him around the neck from behind.

"What are you talking about?" Gary croaked.

Martin hosed the firechimp, which collapsed off Gary's back. "It's a movie. We watched it with the kids. Probably a mistake, but oh well. It just means you get them in a headlock or some other wrestling hold, then shoot them."

"But the whole point of shooting things is to kill them at a distance."

"Yeah, but if you do that, these things dodge like Neo in *The Matrix*. Huh! Keanu Reeves solved the problem Keanu Reeves caused. Everybody underestimates that guy."

In the distance, somebody shouted, "Incoming!"

Martin, Gary, and Gwen looked up to see what looked like a meteor shower, only the meteors were much too close to the ground to still be burning, and all of them were converging on the city. Many wizards pointed their staffs skyward and threw up the largest, strongest force fields they could, covering London in an invisible protective dome several layers deep. All but two of the flaming rocks hit the shield and shattered into millions of flaming bits.

The first two meteors in the pack had been close enough to end up inside the shield, and both hit the golden castle, punching holes in its gleaming golden roof, then exploding as they impacted with the intricate gold inlaid floor. The entire structure disappeared in a fireball that rose into the sky, and would have formed a classic mushroom cloud had it not hit the underside of the wizards' force field. The fireball flattened into a roof of flame covering the city, then cooled into a thick black haze of smoke and soot, contained in a perfect dome over the city. Meanwhile, on the outside of the shield, the burning remains of the meteors fell like hailstones, then bounced and rolled down the shield's outer slope, collecting in a ring of glowing hot debris around the city, well inside the still-present hundred-foot-tall wall of flames.

Phillip shouted, "The twins!"

Gwen said, "Eh, they're fine."

"What?!"

"We can't treat our kids like Ming vases, Phillip. They need to skin their knees occasionally."

"Gwen, the castle blew up around them!"

"They're invulnerable, like us. Besides, they weren't in the castle anymore."

"But that's where we left them," Phillip said.

"Which is how we know they weren't in there," Martin said. "They snuck out and are hiding somewhere by now. One of the final signs that a child has matured into an adult is that they learn the ability to *stay put*." Martin turned and shouted, "Isn't that right, kids?"

The distant, disembodied voices of the twins said, "Yeah," in unison, and without enthusiasm.

The wizards removed the shield. A thick black cloud slowly lifted into the sky.

High above them, the faces of the Magnuses looked down, sunlight from above the cloud cover streaming in through their open eyes, nostrils, and Magnus Galka's toothy grin.

"Now that the second plague of Magnus has softened you up," Magnus Galka said, "we move on to the third plague, one even more hostile to life than fire. Quake in fear, one and all, at the third plague of Magnus! The plague of extreme, bitter cold!"

A frigid wind that instantly seemed to cut through the flesh and chill the bones of everyone it hit blew straight down on the city, then rolled outward in all directions. The roofs turned white instantly. All of the buildings that were on fire blew out, leaving behind charred remains covered with a layer of glistening frost, which itself thickened and hardened into a lumpy coating of crystal-clear ice.

The wave of cold blew out past the edge of the city, instantly cooling the ring of meteor debris gathered at the former boundary of the force field. The frost expanded, beyond the zone where the wizards were still grappling with the firechimps. The spray of water coming from the wizards' staffs and wands became cascading showers of ice crystals, which would have also been effective for dousing the flames of the firechimps, had they still been burning. As the cold reached them, the firechimps extinguished and crumbled into dust, leaving most of the wizards standing alone in a fighting stance, their immense feet stuck in the frozen mud. A few had been pressing their weight down on a firechimp, and at least two had been held aloft by a chimp before the wind hit. All of these wizards fell to the frozen ground in a cloud of crumbled firechimp ash.

The hundred-foot wall of fire at the perimeter of the battleground sputtered and flickered out of existence like the flame of a birthday candle. An equally tall wall of ice grew in its place.

Martin looked up at the faces of the Magnuses etched in the clouds and asked, "Are all of your plagues going to pretty much undo the plague before it? I mean, first it was dark, then there was fire, now ice. What's next? A rain of rock salt?"

Magnus Galka said, "No, I promise, that's the last of the plagues that contrast with each other. The idea was to leave you confused and demoralized."

"Well, you failed."

"Did we? You're standing ankle-deep in mud, whining and asking questions. That seems like being confused and demoralized to me. Whether you admit I'm right or not doesn't matter. You've got seven plagues left, and from now on they stack."

"And what's this supposed to be?" Tyler shouted, hovering over the Thames, which had been a flowing river of magma, but now flowed even more slowly, and had turned a dull bluish gray.

Magnus Galka said, "I think it's obvious. During the fire plague, the river was burning hot lava. Now that we're in the ice plague it's—"

"Do not," Tyler interrupted, "say *ice-cold lava*! How many times do I have to have this conversation? I've told Gary. I've told Martin. I told Gary again. Twice. Now I'm telling you, cold lava is rock! Just rock! That's all! Hot lava is melted rock. Cold lava is solid rock. The entire crust of the world is cold lava! It doesn't freeze anything it touches, and it certainly doesn't flow like that!"

Tyler flew down, just above the surface of the river, and knocked on the crust with his staff. He examined the head of the staff and saw it was covered with fresh ice. "I mean, a river of flowing gravel pulverizing anything in its path would be one thing, but this is just dumb! It betrays a complete lack of understanding of the science behind volcanoes."

"Fine!" Magnus Galka shouted. "Okay! You don't like the ice plague, we can just move on!" His eyes lowered as if he were reading an unseen computer monitor. "And I'll tell you what, we'll give you a couple more from the Bible, just to please you purists! Here, the plants are all dead! How do you like that?"

Martin looked down at the ground, and what grass hadn't been burned, stomped into the mud, or covered with an opaque layer of frost turned brown and dropped limply to the earth. All of the trees in London dropped their foliage in one great clump, leaving behind bare trunks and branches.

Gwen said, "That is a bummer. It makes everything seem more

grim. Kinda autumnal, like I should be drinking something flavored with pumpkin spice. But there are still live plants in the world, just none in London, where, I hate to break it to you, there weren't that many live plants to begin with. And we can create all the produce the city needs with magic, so it's not a real problem."

"Yeah," Magnus Galka yelled. "Then let's try the next plague. Head lice!"

All of the wizards and the entire population of the city groaned in unison.

"Yeah!" Magnus Galka said. "That's right, you've all got head lice! You're gonna have to shave your heads, or use the tiny comb, which is a pain! And you've gotta burn all your hats! It's gonna suck! People from all the other cities will know, and talk about you behind your backs!"

Martin said, "Gwen, my head itches."

"Mine does, too, Martin. Mine does, too."

Sergio said, "Hey, Gary, we should swap hats."

"Why?" Gary asked.

"Because this is the one time in our lives we'll be able to without worrying about catching lice."

The entire populace looked up at Magnus Galka as he laughed with glee, shouting, "And your pillows! You'll have to get rid of them, too! Ha! You'll have to get used to new pillows, and you won't sleep right for days!"

29.

Beside Magnus Galka, Magnus Rex looked down at the city, his mouth a straight line, eyes half open. Phillip flew up close to the giant faces, but on Magnus Rex's opposite side, almost whispering in his ear, and completely out of Magnus Galka's field of view.

"Hey, Magnus. How are you?"

"Me? I'm great."

"You don't look it. I mean, you're gigantic, and made of clouds and light. You *look* amazing, but you don't look like you *feel* amazing."

Magnus Galka shouted, "And now that you've gotten to know your new scalp pets, we'll move on to the next plague. I've been looking forward to this one. Zombies!"

From far below them, Tyler's amplified voice said, "Oh my God! Do you have no imagination? Zombies? They've been done to death, literally, several times over. They're so tired that most people are over being over them!"

"You shouldn't let on that you're so smart, Tyler," Magnus Galka said, giggling. "The zombies will come for your brains first."

Phillip scratched his head, then saw what he was doing, and silently cursed all head lice. "Magnus, you're not happy with all of this, are you?"

Magnus Rex looked down at the city, glanced at Magnus Galka, then looked back at Phillip and shook his head.

"Yeah, I thought so. I'm betting that you like the idea of being in charge, but this isn't the way you would have chosen to go about it."

Magnus Galka bellowed, "Yes! Run! Run from the zombies, and scratch your heads while you do it, but be careful! You'll want to watch out for the next plague. I promise none of you saw this one coming! Snipers!"

In the city below, gunshots rang out.

Martin said, "That's pointless. We're bulletproof."

A shot rang out, and Martin shouted, "Ow!"

Magnus Galka laughed so hard he seemed to have trouble breathing.

Phillip said, "You know, Magnus, Martin's my best friend. And we usually want the same things, but a lot of the time, he goes off half-cocked in the wrong direction. He does things I don't think are right, but it's hard to make him stop because we're working toward the same goal. I'm betting you know how that feels."

Magnus Rex smiled.

Phillip smiled back, scratching his head.

Far below them, Martin shouted, "Your snipers are useless, you know. We aren't going to let them kill anybody. We can stop bullets."

"Yes," Magnus Galka said. "But can you stop piranhas? Yes! The next plague is an infestation of piranhas!"

"And what are they going to infest?" Tyler asked. "The river of rock?"

"It's water now," Magnus Galka blurted. "Water full of piranhas!"

"You know, piranhas don't actually eat animals down to skeletons all at once."

"Natural ones don't. But I made these piranhas, so they do!"

Tyler said, "Well, hell. Bad news everyone. In addition to the zombies and the snipers, now you can't go swimming."

Magnus Rex asked, "Phillip, what do you do when Martin gets out of hand?"

Phillip shrugged. "You have to assert yourself. Sometimes our friends need guidance. Other times they need someone to shut them down fully. It's not fun, but if you don't act, things only get worse, and really, does a friend allow a friend to make a fool of himself?"

"Yes!" Magnus Galka nearly screamed. "The river's full of piranhas! And the next plague is that the land will be covered with piranhas! Land piranhas!"

"What?" Tyler asked. "So they flop around like mudskippers?"

"No! They've got legs! An unending wave of piranhas with crab legs!"

As the people of London began seeing the onslaught of land piranhas, a wave of screams rose from the city, punctuated with intermittent sniper fire.

"Yeah," Magnus Galka said. "Tell me that's not a nightmare!"

Tyler said, "Okay, I must admit, that is a heck of a visual. I'm impressed with this one."

"Thanks, Tyler," Magnus Galka said. "That means a lot. And it's not even the best part!"

Phillip paused his scratching long enough to shake his head at Magnus Rex. "At the end of the day, it's up to you to decide how far down the wrong path you're willing to let your friend go."

Phillip and Magnus Rex looked at the city below. Most of the populace had hunkered down indoors. Only a few were left on the street, fleeing from the zombies and the land piranhas. The airspace above the city teemed with wizards, flying in every direction, many using time travel to make several passes across the city simultaneously, making twenty wizards feel like many more, putting bullet- and piranha-proof force fields around every civilian they could find. The groups huddled indoors would get one force field to cover them all. The stragglers running around outside got their own personal bubble of protection until they could join a group.

Gwen said, "I think that's everyone."

Martin said. "Yeah, I agree, but we should keep an eye out for anyone we missed. You hear that, Magnus? We've got a shield around everyone! Your zombies, your snipers, and your land piranhas can't get them."

A gunshot rang out.

Martin shouted, "Ow!"

"That's right, Martin," Magnus Galka said. "Keep your head out in the open. Maybe, if you're lucky, our snipers will shoot your lice off. If you're so certain that you've got every single person in the city protected, then you shouldn't mind if I unleash the next plague."

A dark cloud descended on the city, warping and transforming, parts of it growing darker and other parts lighter as the flapping shapes that comprised it changed direction and speed.

Magnus Galka shouted, "Brace yourselves for the sky piranhas!"

The flock descended on the city, attempting to swarm the wizards, who quickly created force fields of their own.

Tyler said, "Okay, you see, any respect I gave you for the piranhas with crab legs is shot now. Piranhas with bat wings? Way to jump the shark."

Gary said, "Shut up, Tyler. You'll give him ideas. He's not above attacking us with jumping sharks."

"You're right, Phillip," Magnus Rex said. "Magnus has made a mess of this. I need to step in."

Phillip said, "Actually, we seem to have things pretty much under control, but throwing your support behind us would probably make him see the light."

"No, Phillip." The giant image of Magnus Rex's face turned toward the rendering of Magnus Galka. "I have to take action. We've wasted enough time and effort."

Magnus Galka whipped his head around to face Magnus Rex, moving so quickly that the clouds making up his image couldn't keep up, causing his face to become a blurred smear for a second.

"What? What did you say? Phillip, what did you do?"

"I talked to your friend, helped him see the situation more clearly."

"Yes," Magnus Rex said. "That's exactly what he did, and I think it's time I took over, Magnus."

Martin and Tyler laughed. Jeff let out a long appreciative whistle. Gwen said, "Nice."

Magnus Galka's eyes darted from Magnus Rex to Phillip, to the city and the wizards below. "Look," he said, "Magnus. Don't, uh, don't do anything rash. You say Phillip talked to you. Cool."

All at once, the zombies disappeared, the gunfire stopped, and all of the varieties of piranhas faded out of existence. The ice walls that still surrounded the city and the frost on the buildings melted quickly into water. All of the people let out a simultaneous groan of relief and stopped scratching their heads.

Magnus Galka said, "Let's all talk. Okay? He can explain things to me, too."

"No," Magnus Rex said. "The time for that has passed. Talking isn't going to change anything now. You're done. I'm taking charge. I am the chairman, not you. It's time I acted like it."

Phillip looked down at the city below and said, "I think you we can remove the force fields now."

"No!" Magnus Galka shouted. "Phillip, don't! You keep those shields up! I was trying to prevent—"

Magnus Rex growled, and his face twisted in exertion. Because they were only faces etched in the clouds, the others couldn't see any of their actions below the neck, but Magnus Galka's features contorted in alarm, then appeared to be shoved before finally going slack, with his eyes closed and his mouth hanging open, letting a round shaft of sunlight through.

Magnus Rex's face turned back to face Phillip, the wizards, and the city below. "Sorry we wasted so much of everybody's time. It was all Magnus's fault. I mean, we agreed that I should be in charge, but this whole stupid plan of using the system you all put in place to take control so you'd have to admit my legitimate right to rule, that was all him.

"And his attack on this city," Magnus Rex said, his face growing larger as he spoke, dwarfing Magnus Galka's still unconscious form. "Camelot, London, whatever we were calling it. A complete disaster, wouldn't you agree, Phillip?"

"Yes?" Phillip flew backward, dropping toward the ground as Magnus Rex's mouth grew ever larger in front of him.

"Yes. Magnus thought you were going to love this. He thought that if we made the punishment spectacular enough, we could make people fear us without actually killing anyone. He thought everyone would see we were serious and get with the program. He even had me believing it. So stupid right? Phillip, I said, *right?*'"

"Yeah. Right."

"But nobody was going to see that we were serious. Because we weren't, or at least he wasn't. He wanted to be treated like a badass, but still be a nice guy. It doesn't work that way. If you want to be treated like a badass, your ass needs to be bad. If you want people to think you're a killer, you have to kill. If you want people to tell stories about how you destroyed a city and killed everyone in it, you've got to destroy the city, kill the people, and do it in a way that's interesting enough for people to want to talk about it, but simple enough for a child to understand."

All at once, as if they'd always just been waiting for their cue, every brick, every beam, every cobblestone, stick, nail, or other object made of any material harder than burlap in the entire city rose up several yards into the air. It all hung there in space for a moment, the people of London looking up at it as all the city's soft goods, all the thatching straw, fabric, paper, and rope that had been in their homes fell to the ground around them.

The floating material gathered together into clumps the size of cars, making loud cracking and crunching noises as they collided. The amorphous chunks of stone and wood spun in the air for a moment, then began slamming down in unison, like the fists of a toddler throwing a temper tantrum, beating out a steady rhythm that shook the ground and crushed whatever was beneath them.

The repeated impacts did as much damage to the pounding shapes as they did to the things being pounded. Each time the clumps rose from a strike, the individual pieces of wood, brick, and stone that made them up were smaller. Tiny pieces of rubble and dust fell, creating a thick cloud that hid the ground and anything on it from view. The pounding masses rose from the cloud like synchronized swimmers, paused a moment, then plunged downward again, mashing some of the particulate matter into the ground, but adding more to the air as they rose, damaged by their own attack. The clumps grew smaller and the pounding less severe with each beat. Soon, the thunderous shock waves diminished to a sound more like a large group of soldiers marching, and the clumps of stone shrunk to the size of softballs, then baseballs, then tennis balls, and finally marbles before they disappeared completely.

The cloud of stone dust hung in the air for a moment, and then all of the granules and particles making up the cloud fell to the ground at once, as if some unseen hand pushed them down.

When the air cleared, the wizards saw that what had been a city was now pulverized and covered with a uniform layer of finely ground stone, pressed so firmly into the ground as to, essentially, become a paved slab. The only features left on the barren plain of gray stone were thousands of people—the entire population of London. They had spent the entire onslaught cowering beneath magically generated force fields. Now they all stood, bewildered, on small islands of whatever floor or paving surface they had been standing on before the attack.

Magnus Rex looked down from the clouds. "Aw, you didn't lower the force fields? Who's keeping them up?"

The wizards, all hovering in the air above the barren, gray, plain of the former city, looked up at him and either shrugged, shook their heads, or looked around to give the impression that they were searching for whomever it was.

Magnus Rex sucked on his teeth. "I don't actually care who's making the force fields. Lower them. Now."

The wizards stopped pretending to look for the culprit, but the shields remained up.

Magnus Rex said, "I am your chairman. Now do as I say, and lower the force fields."

The wizards did nothing.

Magnus Rex said, "Phillip, tell them to lower the force fields."

Phillip laughed. "Why do you think they'd listen to me? You're the chairman."

The wizards all laughed.

Phillip laughed with them for a brief moment, then turned and said, "Okay, gang, that's enough. We don't need to rub it in."

The wizards regained their composure.

Magnus Rex, on the other hand, looked as if his gigantic cloudy head might explode.

"Phillip," he whispered, though at the level his voice was magnified, everyone could still hear him. "Surely you can see why I need these people dead. I don't want to kill them, but I've drawn a line here. They have to die to demonstrate what happens to anyone who defies me."

"But Magnus, you've already succeeded."

"Really?"

"Yes! The fact that they're all still alive, and that the wizards, your subjects, ostensibly, are laughing at you demonstrates with crystal-clear accuracy exactly what consequences await anyone who defies you."

"Look! I won that election fair and square, and I deserve just as much respect—"

"One second, please. Hold that thought. I have a call." Phillip held up his left hand and stared at it.

Magnus Rex said, "You're putting me off to answer a call?"

"No," Phillip said. "To make one. *Komuniki kun Jeff.*"

A floating image of Jeff's head appeared in Phillip's hand.

"Hey, Phillip."

"Hello, Jeff."

"Roy and I almost have a fix on where the Magnuses really are. Should only take another twenty minutes or so, we think."

"Glad to hear it. When you do come up with a location, please come back to this moment in time. Okay?"

The image of Jeff's head in Phillip's hand disappeared, and Jeff and Roy both materialized, floating in the air beside Phillip.

Jeff said, "Sure thing, Phillip."

Magnus Rex asked, "You sent them to track us down? When did you do that?"

"I didn't send them to do it. I just knew them well enough to be certain they would. As soon as the other Magnus made that comment about our weapons only working when we know where the people we want to attack actually are, it was kinda inevitable that Jeff and Roy would go try to figure out your location. So, where are the Magnuses hiding, guys?"

Jeff looked Phillip in the eye, said, "We don't know," then bugged his eyes out and looked over Phillip's left shoulder.

Phillip said, "What? You don't know? You traveled back in time to tell us that you haven't found them yet?"

"Not that we haven't found them yet. That we can't find them at all. We've looked at their place in Norway and everywhere else we can think of. We have no idea"—Jeff bugged his eyes out and glanced deliberately over Phillip's shoulder—"*where they are hiding.*"

"Well, I'm disappointed."

Jeff narrowed his eyes at Phillip. "Yeah, so am I."

Roy let out a string of painful-sounding violent coughs. When they were done, he rasped, "Gonna go get a lozenge. Be right back," and disappeared.

The instant he vanished, all of the assembled wizards heard Roy's disembodied voice ringing in their ears. "I guess I'm going to have to dust off the old battle comm macro to get our point across without Magnus hearing us. We did find the Magnuses. They're here. They're hiding in a store-bought duck blind in the middle of a field about half a mile from here, at Phillip's seven o'clock."

The wizards all turned to look over Phillip's left shoulder.

Roy shouted, "Don't look!"

The wizards all looked up at the sky or down at the ground.

Roy said, "If any of you let on that we know, they'll just take off and hide again. We all need to teleport over, right on top of them, at once. Follow my lead and be ready to attack."

Roy reappeared. He rolled a cough drop around in his mouth and said, "Much better. So, yeah, like Jeff said, we couldn't find them. Don't take it so hard, Jeff. You tried." Roy flew over to Jeff and put a hand on his shoulder.

Roy and Jeff hovered there, Roy squeezing Jeff's deltoid reassuringly, Jeff looking at Roy, deeply confused, until Jeff's eyes grew wide.

"Oh!" Jeff said. "Uh, yeah, I'm taking this real hard. I don't like failing. Thanks for comforting me Roy, but it's just not enough."

Roy raised an eyebrow at Phillip, who said, "I see! Yes, don't worry about it, Jeff. You did your best." Phillip drifted over and put a hand on Jeff's shoulder.

Phillip looked at the other wizards. "Come on everyone. Can't you see our friend is upset?"

Over the course of about fifteen seconds, all of the wizards, Gilbert and Sid included, clustered together and put a reassuring hand on Jeff, or on someone who had their hand on Jeff.

The immense face of Magnus Rex scowled down at them "You've all gone soft."

Roy said, "That's everyone, Jeff."

Jeff poked at the screen of his smartphone, and they all disappeared.

30.

They reappeared, clustered together in the sky, and started falling immediately, a flailing chain of confused, panicked wizards. A massive jolt pushed them hard to the side, as if they'd been hit by an immense, invisible Ping-Pong paddle. They crashed into a muddy field in a loose grouping, like a meteor shower, only with less fire and far more cursing.

Martin lifted his head and shoulders out of the soft, wet sod, saw that Gwen was alive, then sprang to his feet, ready to fend off any threat, a process that took longer and involved more sliding and sinking than usual, thanks to the ground conditions. The other wizards all did the same, with a similar level of success. Some whined about the difficulty. Others laughed about it, which was a healthier response, but still detracted from the image of formidability they'd been trying to project.

All of the wizards faced the duck blind, a flimsy nylon tent printed with a woodland camouflage pattern, its top made entirely out of semi-transparent mesh through which they could see Magnus Rex's hat and eyes.

They heard the sound of the zipper pull as Magnus Rex opened the blind's flap. He stepped out, looked their way, and waved.

Most of the wizards either pointed their staffs at Magnus to unleash some attack spell or ran and leaped forward to fly at their enemy. Neither of these approaches worked. The magicians trying to attack from a distance, like Phillip, looked confused as absolutely nothing happened. The ones who attempted to fly, like Martin, only dove forward and landed, sliding face first in the muddy grass as if they'd attempted to steal third base.

Magnus Rex said, "Did you think I wouldn't be prepared? I knew that once I became chairman, someone would attempt a coup. Magnus and I have been planning for years, since we lost our first election. One of the first things we did was create a macro in the shell program that hides us and sets up a nice, fat, no-magic zone."

Tyler said, "And it hides you with a Walmart duck blind?"

"Yeah," Magnus Rex said. "Why not? I mean, invisibility hasn't been cracked yet."

Sid glanced meaningfully at Gilbert. Gilbert made a point of not looking at Sid.

Tyler said, "Come on, man. You don't think you could've come up with something better than the exact piece of equipment Elmer Fudd would use?"

Magnus Rex shook his head. "This is a quality product, Tyler. It was designed by professionals. It's big enough for two grown men and a full-sized cooler, but it folds down to the size of a small hula hoop, and when you throw it on the ground, it erects itself! But you're sure you could do better. Where does your arrogance come from?"

Martin reached into his pocket and pulled out the silver box he used to hide his smartphone, but Magnus Rex was not as distracted as Martin had hoped.

"Don't bother, Martin. The macro disabled all of your smartphones. We remembered how you used yours to get to Jimmy. No, you're stuck in place where there's no magic or cell phone coverage." Magnus Rex rose into the air. "Except for this area over here where I am, right next to the blind, of course."

"Uh-huh," Phillip said. "So, how large is this area of no magic? How far out does it go?"

"Oh, it ends about two hundred yards out, just beyond the invisible force field wall you can't get through. Neat, huh? Magnus thought of everything. Oh, speaking of the other Magnus."

Magnus Rex made a sort of scoop-and-throw motion with his right hand. The limp form of Magnus Galka floated out of the duck blind and flew across the field, landing and skidding to a stop in a muddy heap at the wizards' feet. "He got us this far, and I'll always be grateful, but it's time for me to govern on my own."

Martin and Gwen knelt by Magnus Galka's side.

Gwen asked, "Are you awake?"

Martin slapped Magnus Galka once, hard, across the face.

"Ow," Magnus Galka said. "Thanks. Yeah, I'm awake!"

Martin slapped him again.

"Ow!"

Phillip said, "Martin, stop. There'll be time enough for that later. Right now, we need to see if Magnus here has come to his senses enough to help us stop Magnus over there."

"What can I do? He won't listen to me anymore."

"How about magic?" Martin asked.

"No good. The only place anyone can do magic inside the invisible wall is a twenty-foot radius around the blind."

"Even you two?"

"Yeah, he wrote the program and missed that wrinkle. I could have corrected it, but . . ."

"But," Phillip said, "you planned to kick him out and take all the power for yourself."

"It was an emergency measure. I hoped I wouldn't ever have to do that."

Gwen said, "Well, you didn't, so good for you."

Martin asked, "If we can get over there, we can do magic again?"

Magnus Galka said, "Yeah. But he can use any magic he wants to stop you."

Large rocks and small boulders, hundreds of them, rose into the air, leaving craters in the ground where they had been buried. They flew in toward the blind and began to orbit around Magnus Rex. "That's right. None of you can get anywhere near me without catching a giant rock right in the kisser, so I guess magic's off the table."

Sid raised his hand. "Pardon me, dear fellow. Just to clarify, am I to understand that your macro, as you call it, prevents the castigation . . . is that the word, Gilbert? Castigation? I'm looking for the past tense of the act of casting a spell."

Gilbert shrugged. "Wouldn't it just be *casting*?"

"No, there's got to be a term more baroque than that, but *castigation* doesn't sound right."

Gilbert said, "Castration?"

Sid said, "Never mind." He turned his attention back to Magnus Rex. "You say this amazing macro of yours makes it impossible to perform any magic based on the Leadchurch Shell Program, yes?"

"Yeah."

"Well, I'm afraid I must inform you that my compatriot and I are not tied into this archaic shell program of yours."

Gilbert made jazz hands. "We got our own thing, baby!"

He reached into his hat, pulled out a rabbit, and flung it toward Magnus Rex. The rabbit traveled straight, like a line drive sailing across the field, and clamped onto Magnus Rex's bicep.

Magnus held his arm out straight, the wriggling rabbit hanging from it like damp trousers on a clothesline. Magnus used his free arm to point at the wizards. The giant boulders broke free from their orbits and flew toward them. Sid managed to get a force field up in time for the boulders to smash themselves, one by one, onto the shield, shattering into gravel from the impact.

Gilbert pulled his hand from his hat, then flung the hat straight up into the air. It flipped several times and landed on his head, perched at the perfect angle. He pointed his white-tipped ebony walking stick at Magnus Rex, and a bolt of blue light shot from the end, striking Magnus Rex in the chest. At first, he seemed unaffected, then thick chains whipped around from behind him, wrapping him in so many loops that he resembled a chrome-plated mummy. Four rectangles of plexiglass hinged up from the ground around him, slamming together to form a box similar to a phone booth, but roughly twice as large.

As the edges of the transparent box sealed, thousands of gallons of water appeared in the air above Magnus Rex and fell, instantly filling the tank and splashing on the ground surrounding it. A square steel hatch slammed shut over the top of the tank. A large metal handwheel set into its top spun, sealing Magnus Rex in, and a velvet cover rolled down along the sides, hiding the struggling wizard from view.

Martin said, "Nice!"

Gilbert nodded. "Thanks, but I don't think it'll hold him for lo—"

The tank exploded. Water, broken chain links, and razor-sharp shards of shattered Plexiglass flew outward, surfing on the front edge of an expanding shock wave strong enough to knock the wizards off their feet.

As the wizards rolled in the mud, groaning and muttering curses, a semi-transparent form materialized in the air above them. They barely had time to register that the shape was that of an immense hand before it swept straight down, moving quickly enough to become nearly invisible. The hand's path curved, skimming the ground and scooping about a dozen of them, including Gilbert, Sid, Martin, Gwen, and Phillip into its palm before turning skyward. The hand slowed and tightened into a fist.

Back on the ground, Magnus Rex stood in the center of a circle of bare rock and mud, all vegetation and the remains of the duck blind having been blasted away by the force of the explosion. His fur cloak and robe were wet, but aside from that, he seemed completely unaffected. One hand held his staff, the other was formed into a fist, which he held over his head. The wizards on the ground could look through the giant fist and see their friends, a mass of tangled arms, legs, and staffs trapped in the hollow created by the giant palm and fingers.

Magnus Rex tightened his fist. The giant fist tightened as well, pushing those trapped inside into a cramped ball, squeezed into each other and the fist's palm so forcefully and completely that even their facial features were distorted, as if they were pressed against a sheet of glass.

The wizards left behind on the ground looked up in horror at their friends' plight, except for Gary, who looked at Magnus Rex and shouted, "You missed me!"

Tyler said, "But he got, like, a bunch of us!"

"Yeah," Gary shouted, more at Magnus than to Tyler. "But he missed me! Loser!"

"Gary, is that a new hat?"

"It's Sergio's."

Magnus Rex shook his fist as if preparing to roll dice, then whipped his hand downward at the ground, throwing the people in the phantom hand straight down. The wizards on the ground had just enough time to dive, but not enough to get clear of the landing zone before their friends slammed into them from above.

Magnus Rex said, "I think I got you that time, Gary."

The wizards all lay writhing on the ground, attempting to get their wind back, most of them cursing Gary with what little breath they had, until the giant hand came straight down out of the sky at them.

Martin lay on his back, gasping for air. His last act before the giant palm pressed into him was to turn his head toward Magnus Rex. The pressure of the giant hand pressing on him made movement, speech, or coherent thought impossible. As long as Magnus Rex held them this way, any attempt at fighting back, even by Gilbert and Sid, who still had their magic, was impossible.

Through the ghostly hand, Martin saw Magnus Rex, standing with one hand pressed down into the ground, and the other holding his staff aloft. The staff began to glow. Martin couldn't know what spell Magnus Rex was casting, but he was certain he wouldn't like the result. He was horrified at the idea that whatever Magnus Rex was doing, he was doing it to Gwen. The fact that he would suffer the same fate was secondary to Martin. He also thought of the twins, and how proud and happy he was that they'd proven to be so capable because he feared they might need to fend for themselves, and each other, from now on.

Martin decided that while he had a good idea what was about to happen, he'd rather not see it coming. He began to close his eyes, but then blinked and squinted at Magnus Rex. The forest in the distance behind him seemed to warp oddly, as if there were two dents in the fabric of reality itself that were moving very quickly, warping their environment as they went. He had nearly decided the lack of oxygen was causing him to hallucinate when he saw things extending out of the areas of distortion, like antennae, but thicker, and bent at ninety-degree angles. As his vision began to dim, he could have sworn that one of the distortions resolved into the form of a person in a top hat.

31.

Minutes earlier, in the sky above the flattened ruin of London, Phillip asked Jeff where the Magnuses were hiding and received the answer: "We don't know."

As the wizards bickered about whether or not that was an adequate reply, watched silently while Roy got a cough drop, then engaged in a stunning and out of character display of midair unity, Mattie and Brewster hovered nearby, still cloaked in Sid and Gilbert's invisibility spell, watching the proceedings through their periscopes.

Mattie whispered, "Brewster, Jeff knows where they are, and is trying not to tip his hand. The Magnuses must be close. Come on, wherever they're going, we have to go with them."

She heard no reply, turned her periscope to where Brewster had been floating beside her and didn't see the tip of his periscope. She blinked in confusion for a moment but was jolted out of her mental gridlock when someone directly in front of her hissed. She turned her scope forward. She saw her parents, Gilbert, Sid, and many others all grouped together, but her view was distorted, and she saw the tip of Brewster's periscope.

"What are you waiting for?" Brewster asked. "You coming or what?"

The two of them flew as fast as they could toward the flying clutch of wizards, all making a show of comforting Jeff while grasping each other's arms or shoulders. Mattie gripped Gary's arm, close enough to where Roy was holding it that it probably felt like one hand to Gary. She reached her hand out far enough behind her that it extended out of the invisibility field. Brewster's hand extended out of his own invisibility field and grasped hers.

The group teleported as one.

They materialized a small distance away, directly over the duck blind, and felt a very hard shove to one side. Mattie's fingers immediately lost contact with Gary's arm as he and all of the wizards fell away. Mattie panned her periscope downward and saw them all, tumbling and screaming, still clinging to each other. Sid and Gilbert fell slower than the others, still attempting to fly, but the weight of all the wizards dragged them down to the ground as well.

The wizards flew apart and hit the muddy ground in a cluster, like shotgun pellets hitting wet clay. They all struggled to their feet, swiveling their heads and swinging their hands and staffs around as if they intended to perform either magic or karate at the first thing they saw.

Mattie felt Brewster let go of her hand. She turned toward his floating distortion and said, "None of them knows we're here."

Magnus Rex unzipped and stepped out of his camouflaged tent, smiling and waving. The wizards below them attempted to attack but didn't seem to be capable of flight or any offensive spells.

Magnus Rex said, "Did you think I wouldn't be prepared?"

The twins watched their mother and father as Magnus Rex explained the no-magic zone. They desperately wanted to see some indication that would let them know that their parents were in control of the situation and everything was going according to plan.

Instead, they saw genuine fear on Gwen and Martin's faces as they scrambled to get out of the way of the limp body of Magnus Galka landing at their feet. The expressions of fear did not subside when many tons worth of stone from the surrounding fields lifted into the air and swirled around Magnus Rex.

Brewster said, "They really don't have any magic."

"No," Mattie agreed. "But we do."

"Yeah, and that means that Gilbert and Sid do, too, and Magnus doesn't know it. That gives them a huge advantage, as long as they don't let on."

Sid said, "Pardon me, dear fellow."

Mattie and Brewster both groaned.

Sid continued, "Just to clarify, am I to understand that your macro, as you call it, prevents the castigation . . . is that the word, Gilbert? Castigation? I'm looking for the past tense of the act of casting a spell."

"Casting," Brewster said. "The proper word would be *casting*."

"Or *use*!" Mattie said. "Why not just say *use*?"

Below them, Gilbert said, "Wouldn't it just be *casting*?"

"No, there's got to be a term more baroque than that, but *castigation* doesn't sound right."

Brewster said, "Utilization."

Gilbert said, "Castration?"

Mattie snorted, contemptuously. "We're gonna have to help them. I don't think they can help themselves. Come on, Brewster. Maybe we can sneak around behind him."

Mattie flew around to her left, Magnus Rex's right, taking care not to put herself between him and the powerless adult wizards.

Brewster followed. "Yeah. Let the grown-ups be a diversion. I'm sure we can, I dunno, hit him with a rabbit from behind or something."

Gilbert launched a rabbit that flew straight at Magnus Rex and clamped on to his arm, then hung there, writhing uselessly.

Magnus Rex let the rabbit dangle for a moment, demonstrating the attack's impotence. When he seemed certain his point was made, he sent all of the boulders swirling in his orbit flying directly at Gilbert, Sid, and the wizards surrounding them.

This delighted Brewster and Mattie, as neither of them had liked the idea of trying to make their way through the vortex of boulders like a giant 3D game of *Frogger* with their peripheral vision and depth perception completely blocked by their periscopes. Now that the boulders were out of their way, they floated down and landed softly on the ground behind Magnus Rex.

Across the field, the last of the boulders smashed itself to rubble against the invisible shield Gilbert and Sid had erected.

The magicians counterattacked, wrapping Magnus Rex in chains and sealing him in a tank full of water.

Brewster whispered, "Aren't those designed to be escaped from?"

Mattie said, "Yeah, but I doubt he knows how."

The tank exploded.

"I stand corrected," Mattie said. "We gotta move."

Magnus Rex stooped over and swept his hand in a broad scooping motion along the ground. Across the way, Gilbert, Sid, Martin, Gwen, Phillip, and many others lifted off the ground in the grip of an immense, ghostly hand. Magnus Rex tightened his fist. The ghostly fist tightened as well. Magnus Rex shook his fist and whipped it straight down, slamming the twins' parents and their friends into the ground.

Magnus Rex knelt down and pressed his hand into the ground as if he were trying to push the earth away from himself. The wizards flattened to the ground, pressed under a huge, semi-transparent palm. With his other hand, Magnus held his staff aloft, beginning to cast a spell.

Mattie said, "We need to stop this."

Brewster asked, "But how? What do we do?"

Mattie removed the invisibility spell and reached into her hat. "We do exactly what they told us to do if there's trouble. We teleport away."

Brewster removed his invisibility spell as well, and they both ran toward Magnus's back. Mattie selected a target location as they ran, and the instant she and Brewster made physical contact with Magnus, she initiated the teleportation.

Out in the mud, the giant hands vanished, releasing the pressure on the wizards. As they sat up and looked around, they saw Brewster and Mattie materializing in their midst with their hands on the shoulders of a very confused looking Magnus Rex.

Magnus Rex lurched away from the twins, blinking and emitting random vowel sounds. He spun around no less than three times, coming to grips with the fact that he was standing outside of the area where his magic would work, surrounded by the very people he was just using his magic to mash into the mud. Then, he seemed to get a hold of himself and said, "Everybody, wait right here!"

He took off, running as fast as he could across the muddy ground and wet grass to his duck blind, where he would be able to use his magic again.

Gwen followed, slowing after several steps to spin around to look at the other wizards with a mixture of confusion and disappointment on her face.

Phillip saw what she was irritated about and shouted, "After him!"

The wizards stampeded around Mattie and Brewster, running as fast as they could wearing full-length robes in the soupy conditions, not to mention the fact that none of them was in peak physical condition in the first place.

Gilbert and Sid remained behind, looking at Brewster and Mattie with big smiles on their faces and wet mud on their tuxedos.

The twins looked at the wizards jogging and slipping and cursing their way across the marsh, Magnus Rex well out in front. Brewster turned to the two magicians. "Aren't you going to use your magic to stop him?"

Gilbert shook his head. "No, *you're* going to use *our* magic to stop him."

Sid said, "Indeed. You've already gone ninety percent of the way toward total day-savery. It'd be damned unsportsmanlike for us to swoop in at the last second and claim all the glory. Besides, this is a fine chance for you two to try out a couple of your non-rabbit-based attack options, if we might be so bold as to make a recommendation."

Mattie and Brewster flew over the struggling, mud-caked wizards, their satin capes fluttering in the wind, top hats sitting on their heads with a rakish tilt.

Gwen shouted, "Be careful!"

Martin said, "Go get him!"

"Carefully," Gwen added.

Magnus Rex had only twenty or so muddy yards left to go when he heard Martin and Gwen talking to their children. He made the mistake of twisting around and looking at the twins coming, costing himself valuable speed.

Brewster asked, "Shall we?"

"After you," Mattie said.

Brewster removed his hat, reached in, and made a selection.

The air around Magnus Rex seemed to burst with live doves, flapping and fluttering and flying in circles around him, wrapping him in thick, white cotton cords that tied themselves off in large round knots.

Magnus hopped in place, his legs bound together and his arms pinned to his sides.

Mattie reached into her own hat to choose her attack spell.

A line of three giant metal cups, each the size of a porta-potty, appeared in the sky, their open ends pointing down. They slammed down to the ground, the middle cup covering Magnus Rex. The cups shuffled themselves, sliding around each other in graceful curves, carving muddy gouges in the turf. After ten full seconds of constant, bewildering motion, the cups stopped.

Phillip said, "Good work, both of you."

Mattie and Brewster thanked him.

Phillip asked, "So, uh, which one is he under?"

Mattie said, "You have to guess."

32.

Less than a half hour after Mattie and Brewster delivered Magnus Rex into the welcoming arms and eager fists of his would-be victims, all of the wizards of Europe had reconvened at the former site of the golden castle of Camelot.

The city no longer existed. In its place, a vast plane of hard, compacted rubble stretched for acres in every direction, flanking both sides of the Thames, which flowed gray with residual stone dust washing away from its banks.

Where there had been hills, there were flattened mounds. Where there had been mounds, there were bumps. The sharp-edged crater left behind when the castle exploded was now a deep depression with indistinct, eroded sides and a sparkling yellow sheen from the flecks of pulverized gold mixed in with the gravel.

At the bottom of the glittering pit, the wizards stood in a circle, surrounding the accused. Magnus Galka and Magnus Rex were both chained, spread-eagled, on big, round, slowly spinning theatrical knife-throwing targets. Gilbert and Sid had provided the targets, and they stood in the circle of wizards alongside Mattie, Brewster, Brit the Elder, and Brit the Younger.

The citizens of London looked down from the rim of the crater. Thanks to the giant faces in the clouds and the amplified conversations during the battle, every person in the city knew exactly who had tried to kill them, and who had saved them. Some pointed out that both of those groups could be described simply as "wizards, again," but the overwhelming majority understood that the tally had been two wizards trying to kill versus more than twenty trying to save, which was encouraging, even if the fact that the more than twenty had nearly failed was not.

Phillip turned his head to look beyond several wizards, toward the Brits.

Martin muttered, "Don't you think you should skip the unpleasant preliminaries and get on with it?"

Phillip said, "I will. I just want to say hi to the Brits first."

Gwen said, "You saying hi to Brit the Younger is the unpleasant preliminary Martin's trying to get you to skip."

Phillip frowned at Gwen, then cleared his throat, forced an oversized smile onto his face, and said, "Brit . . . Brits, it's lovely of you, both of you, to attend."

Brit the Younger stared straight ahead. Brit the Elder glanced back at him with a bare hint of a smile, and said, "These two idiots you're about to punish tried to kill my godchildren and the rest of you. My godchildren defeated them and saved the rest of you. It felt like I should be here to celebrate Mattie and Brewster's triumph, and your embarrassment."

Phillip worked hard to keep his smile from fading. "I see. Thanks for coming, in any case. And Brit the Younger. It's especially good to see you."

Brit the Younger looked at Phillip just long enough for him to see the bags under her eyes and the anger in them. "I'm the same person as her, Phillip. I'm here for the same reason, and that isn't to talk to you. Frankly, if I'd known she was coming, I probably wouldn't have. It was necessary for me to be here for the twins, but I don't think I needed to be here twice. That's more times than anyone else is attending."

Brit the Elder said, "Oh hush, Brit. Don't look at it like we're attending twice. Think of it as one of us being here for Brewster, and the other for Mattie."

"Great," Brit the Younger said. "So now we're playing favorites? We've each picked a twin as ours to root for? I don't like that at all."

"Oh, nonsense. We aren't playing favorites. We're not really *we*. We're *I*. And if I am playing favorites I'm doing it twice, in equal measure, so it evens out."

"Yeah, I get it, because I'm just an extension of you. Do you not understand how belittling that is? You've made me the least important character in my own life story."

"That's silly. You are not the least important character. You're the most important character: me!"

Brit the Younger growled. "I'm leaving. Sorry, kids."

Phillip said, "No, no, please don't. I'll start the meeting. It'll only take a minute."

"In fact," Martin said, "it would already be done if Phillip hadn't postponed it to talk to the two of you."

Phillip stepped forward, muttered "*Ĉi tiu iras al la dek unu,*" then cleared his throat to make sure the voice amplification spell had triggered properly. Then, he rapped his staff on the compacted stone.

"People of London, the city formerly called Camelot. Again, we wizards must apologize. Two of our number have made a great many grievous errors, and as has happened before, you have suffered for it. I give you my word, as newly reelected chairman of the wizards, that we will rebuild the city—every road, alley, and building—better than it was before, except for one. The golden castle will not be rebuilt. That land will be returned to the people, to do with what you wish. Now, we wizards will confer with the accused. I will let you know when we are ready to pronounce our judgment and describe their punishment."

Phillip deactivated the amplification spell and walked up to the Magnuses, still slowly spinning on their knife-throwing targets.

"You two have anything to say for yourselves?"

"Yeah," Magnus Rex said. "Come closer, so I can whisper it to you."

"Or so you can try to throw up on me."

"Hey, you're the one who made us spin. Which is just mean, man."

Phillip said, "True."

"Are you gonna stop the spinning, then?"

"No."

Magnus Galka said, "I'd suggest that you consider punishing us separately. I mean, yeah, I froze a bunch of you, but he—"

"And you unleashed ten plagues on us."

"Well, I called them plagues, but they were more like jokes, really."

"Head lice. You gave us all head lice. There's nothing funny about head lice."

"Yeah, but I wasn't serious."

"You had a title ready! *The Ten Plagues of Magnus!* People don't give titles to things they aren't serious about. People don't just pop out to the corner store and decide to name their trip *A Date with Destiny and Doritos.*"

Magnus Galka laughed. "That's really funny, Phillip. You always have been funny. And wise. Hey, maybe as my punishment, I could work as your assistant. You could give me menial tasks and insult me all the time."

"No, you'll both be interested to hear that we've actually already decided on your punishment. You're to be banished."

Magnus Rex said, "What a surprise. Punishing us the same way you punish everyone, every time you punish anybody. Never saw that coming."

Phillip said, "Actually, we have added some new wrinkles, and I think you'll be pleased. You'll be sent back to your original time: the late nineties, roughly. You're only a couple of years removed from each other, so we split the difference. And you'll have your magnetic fields amplified so that you can never again use any device that involves an integrated circuit, preventing you from using a computer to find the file and ever return here. The difference is in *where* we're sending you. We banished Jimmy to life as a foreign vagrant in South America, and it only made him more determined to return. We sent Todd straight to prison for life. He found a way back, too, and was quite miffed. With you two, we're going to try sending you somewhere that isn't actually all that bad. You're losing all of your magic, your invulnerability, and your wealth. That's punishment in and of itself. The idea is to send you somewhere unpleasant, but not so much so that it makes you psychotic."

"Where?" Magnus Rex asked.

"You two settled in Norway by choice, right? So I assume you like the cold. Weather with some teeth. *The land of the ice and snow*, and all that."

Magnus Galka said, "Yeah."

"Good. Magnus. Other Magnus. I hereby sentence you to live out your lives in the greater Miami metroplex. Not Miami proper— your magnetic fields will make living in any densely populated area impossible. No, we've set you up with a trailer on the outskirts of town. It's a nice trailer. I believe it's what they call a double-wide. How American does that sound? We've given you a car, one old enough to still function for you. And we've even purchased a business for the two of you to operate: running airboat tours for cruise-ship patrons."

"Airboats?" Magnus Rex asked. "Those flat ones with the big fans on the back? Those are pretty cool. I could have a lot of fun driving those around."

"You could," Phillip said. "But you won't. They have electronic ignitions and CB radios, which won't work if you're anywhere near them. You'll have to hire some kids to do the piloting while you two work the stall. Take people's information, hand out life vests. Scrape barnacles off the hulls. Heck, you can even take the payments, as long as they pay cash, or you take their credit card with one of those metal slidey things."

Magnus Galka said, "So you're sending us somewhere hot and shark infested to do crap work and watch other people have fun."

"Yes. But look at the bright side. You wanted to be in charge, and now you will be! In charge of Magic Carpet Airboat Tours in fabulous Shark Valley, Florida."

"Shark Valley?" Magnus Galka asked.

"Yes," Phillip said. "But the name's a bit misleading. It isn't really much of a valley. More of a big, flat swamp."

One week later, from Brewster and Mattie's point of view, class let out for the day. Students flooded the halls, talking about what they intended to do with their weekend, or what they had just done with their week.

The sixth-period drama class spilled out of the auditorium, spread out, and mixed into the general hallway traffic. Among them, Brewster Banks and a petite blonde girl walked a bit slower than the traffic, concentrating more on their conversation than on getting anywhere.

"Your audition piece was great, Brewster," the blonde girl said. "I didn't know you could sing."

"Thanks, Abby. I didn't either. I just figured I had nothing to lose by giving it a shot."

"They should make you the lead."

"I doubt it. If I'm lucky, maybe I'll get to play one of the dads, but it's not a big deal if I don't. I mean, the class is putting on the play, so we're all going to get to do something, even if we're not on stage."

"Yeah. There aren't many parts to go around. It's such a weird little musical. *The Fantasticks*." Abby slowed as they reached an intersection.

She nodded down the hall to their left. "You wanna go hang out at the gym?"

Brewster said, "Ugh, nah," and kept walking, motioning for Abby to come along, which she did. "The play's super old-fashioned, I agree. But I think it's kinda cool. I like the lesson they teach the daughter."

"That men lie and manipulate girls?"

"No. Most girls know that. I think the real lesson they teach her is that if you focus on things you think you want but don't have, you might not notice how amazing what's right in front of you is."

Brewster smiled at Abby, who blushed and looked at the floor.

Mattie sat in her chair, drumming her fingers and looking pleased with herself.

Mrs. Hackett sat behind her desk, drumming her fingers and looking displeased with Mattie.

"Mathison, would you mind explaining what happened with today's weekly exam?"

"I prefer to be called Mattie."

"Mathison. Explain yourself."

Mattie widened her eyes in a manner that made her look as if she wanted to appear innocent but knew she couldn't quite pull it off. "What do you mean, Mrs. Hackett? I thought I did well on the quiz."

"You didn't do well on the quiz. You aced it. You got every question right. You even spelled Hermann Göring correctly. You're the only one in the class. Everyone else forgot an *n* or added an *e*, and most did both. You even placed the umlaut correctly."

"I did well. That's good, isn't it? I should think that as my teacher, you'd be pleased."

"I am pleased. I've always known you're smart. But I'm also deeply suspicious because I know that you are immature and devious. Last week you were willfully choosing to flunk my class. This week you're suddenly my best student. I want to know why. What changed? What's your game?"

"Maybe I was inspired by your pep talk last week."

Mrs. Hackett stared at her.

Mattie said, "I thought about it, and I realized that getting into a fight with you was pointless."

"Because there was no way for you to win."

Mattie laughed, then stopped herself. "Sorry, that was rude. I can see why you'd think that. But no, it's not whether or not I knew I could win that put me off. I realized that I'm going to be out of this class in just a few months. After that, odds are I won't be in one of your classes again, and even if I am, I'll leave this school in a couple of years. By the time I'm twenty, I'll barely remember this conversation. When I'm thirty I may not even remember your name. I'm probably going to have some real problems during my life, but frankly, you aren't one of them. It's not that I don't think I can beat you, Mrs. Hackett. I've just decided you're not worth the effort."

Mrs. Hackett stared at Mattie for several seconds. Mattie stared back without blinking.

Mrs. Hackett said, "I should be angry at you for insulting me, but I'm not. Knowing to fight the really important battles and let the petty stuff slide is an important lesson, and you've figured it out a lot younger than most."

Mattie said, "I guess it's a testament to your teaching methods."

That evening, Gwen called out, "Dinner!"

Mattie walked down the hall from her bedroom, while Brewster came up the stairs from the rec room. Both stepped into the kitchen and stopped short, seeing the table set as usual, but with no sign of any food present. Gwen was already seated at the table, in front of an empty plate.

Mattie asked, "Where's . . ."

"Dinner?" Martin asked from the kitchen. He pulled an almost empty two-liter bottle of Dr Pepper from the refrigerator and closed the door. The dim lighting, clean appliances, and total lack of any aromas suggested that no food had been prepared in the kitchen anytime in the recent past. "See, that's the thing. For the last few days we've been living life the way we always have, mostly out of habit, and for stability's sake." Martin walked to the dining room table. "But, tonight, your mother said something very wise. What was it you said again, Gwen?"

"This is stupid."

"Exactly." Martin began pouring Dr Pepper into Gwen's empty glass. Despite the fact that there had been only an inch of fluid in the bottom of the bottle, a healthy stream poured out, filling the glass. When Martin tipped the bottle upright again, the same tired-looking inch of brown fluid puddled in its base. "And it *was* stupid. We were doing all this crap to hide our use of magic, when there's nobody to hide it from anymore."

The twins sat quietly for a moment, thinking. Brewster pointed at the bottle. "Why's it almost empty?"

Martin swung the bottle around gently. "It's a lot lighter this way."

Gwen smiled. "Also, we knew that if the bottle was full, you might try to use it, and then you could discover that it's bottomless. If we made it practically empty, though, you'd never touch it. Nobody wants a third of a glass of pop, but nobody wants to waste it by throwing it out either."

Martin sat down next to Gwen. "Now that you two know what's what, we can just conjure up dinner with magic."

"Instead of cooking," Brewster said.

Martin shook his head. "Instead of pretending to cook as a cover for using magic."

Gwen said, "*Falsa kuijero.*"

Every light in the kitchen came on, sounds of sizzling and bubbling came from the stove, and the air filled with the smell of baking bread and browning meat.

Gwen said, "*Falsa kuijero* stop."

The kitchen lights all switched off, as did the sounds and smells.

"And because we don't have to pretend to cook," Martin said, "that means we can each have whatever we want." Martin produced his sequined wizard hat as casually as if he'd simply picked it up off the table. He reached in and pulled out a burrito. "I lived off of these when Phillip was training me. Would you like one, Gwen?"

"No, thanks. I know how often you wash your hat." She produced her own hat and pulled out a piece of grilled salmon and a salad arranged artfully on a white plate.

"You just pull food out of your hats?" Mattie asked.

"Yeah. That's how most wizards do it. How did you get food when you were at Gilbert and Sid's?"

Brewster said, "Gilbert cooked for us."

Martin and Gwen both looked mildly surprised.

Martin said, "Huh. To each his own. Still, I bet if you look in your top hats, they have a few dishes programmed in for when he doesn't feel like going to the trouble."

Mattie and Brewster both performed the showy little flourish that summoned their hats, along with their capes, canes, and gloves. They poked around inside the hats, peering in at the text interface for some time before Mattie said, "Found it. It's a submenu, under 'Other,' then, 'Biological necessities.'"

Gwen muttered, "I can understand why you didn't look there before."

Brewster said, "I see it. Huh. Toad in the hole, Eton mess, bubble and squeak? Rumbledethumps? Spotted dick? What is all this stuff?"

"British food," Gwen said.

"Yeah," Martin said, through a bite of his burrito. "The English put more effort into naming their dishes than they do into cooking them."

"What kind of thing did Gilbert cook for you?"

Mattie pulled a plate of fish and chips out of her hat. "Mostly big piles of fried meat."

Gwen said, "You know, I bet that was really good."

Martin said, "Yeah. They probably call it a *hedge heap*, or something like that. Why can't they name things sensibly like we Americans do?"

Gwen said, "I don't know. Hey, would anybody else like a glass of Dr Pepper?"

Brewster followed his sister's lead and went with the fish and chips until he could spend some time researching what the other listed dishes actually were.

The four of them ate in relative silence for a while. Then, as the plates grew empty, conversation resumed.

"So," Martin asked. "What do you want to do tonight? It's Friday. None of us needs to be up early tomorrow, and we have all of human history at our disposal. What say we go see *Star Wars*, in the theater, the night it premiered?"

Brewster said, "I don't know. I think instead of just watching a movie, I'd rather see an actual historic event."

Martin's voice became low and serious. "The premier of *Star Wars* was a historic event."

Gwen put her hand on Martin's and said, "How about we go watch the Apollo moon launch?"

Brewster said, "Yeah! That sounds good."

Mattie smiled. "I think I'd rather go watch the Apollo moon landing."

Martin pointed at Mattie, excitedly snapping his fingers. "Yes! That! We do that! Yeah. Airtight forcefield, pressurized and temperature controlled. There's no reason we can't."

Gwen said, "No reason except that the astronauts would see us. There's no place to hide on the moon. We'd stick out like a sore thumb."

Mattie and Brewster looked at each other. Brewster asked, "Think Gilbert and Sid would mind?"

"Probably not, if we invite them along."

"What are you talking about?" Gwen asked.

Brewster said, "We know a spell that would be able to keep us hidden from the astronauts, but I'll have to check with the guys before we show you."

"While he does that that," Mattie said, "I'll teach you about a useful device called a *periscope*."

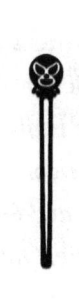

ALSO BY SCOTT MEYER

Basic Instructions Collections:
Help Is on the Way
Made with 90% Recycled Art
The Curse of the Masking Tape Mummy
Dignified Hedonism

Magic 2.0:
Off to Be the Wizard
Spell or High Water
An Unwelcome Quest
Fight and Flight
Out of Spite, Out of Mind

Master of Formalities

The Authorities

Run Program

ACKNOWLEDGEMENTS

You have just read the sixth book in the Magic 2.0 series, unless you're reading the end matter first, in which case I congratulate you on your bold, unconventional approach to recreational reading.

I've been asked more than once if this will be the last book in the series. The truth is, I don't know. I hope it's not. I have a few half-baked ideas for further Magic books, but I don't know when or if I'll get around to fully baking them, or whether I'll get other ideas I like more. It's just hard to say.

I will say this: the six books that do exist wouldn't without the support of the people who read and listened to them. I am grateful to all of you. Thank you.

I'd also like to thank the usual suspects: Matt Sugarman, Eddie Schneider, Joshua Bilmes, Luke Daniels, Eric Constantino, Steven Carlson, Rodney Sherwood, Ric Schrader, and of course, Missy Meyer. I'd like to thank my friends Anne-Marie Cooke and Sophie Nissim for talking me through what an average citizen of the UK would consider "breakfast."

I'd especially like to thank Steve Feldberg and everyone else at Audible, without whom books five and six almost certainly would have happened much later than they did, and might not have happened at all.

ABOUT THE AUTHOR

After an unsuccessful career as a radio DJ, and a so-so career as a stand-up comic, Scott Meyer found himself middle-aged, working as a ride operator at Walt Disney World, and in his spare time producing the web comic *Basic Instructions*. He slowly built a following, which allowed him to self-publish his first novel, *Off to Be the Wizard*. The book's success brought him a publishing deal.

Scott lives in Arizona with his wife, their cats, and his most important possession: a functioning air conditioner.